MW01633467

THE GRIMM FUTURE

EDITED BY

Erin Underwood

NESFA PRESS

Post Office Box 809
Framingham, MA 01701
www.nesfapress.org
2016

The Grimm Future is a work of original fiction inspired by the tales from The Brothers Grimm. All of the characters, organizations, and events portrayed in this book are either fictitious works from the authors' imaginations or are used fictitiously.

Dust Jacket Illustration © 2016 by Richard Anderson

Dust jacket design © 2016 by Alice N. S. Lewis

FIRST EDITION, February 2016

ISBN 978-1-61037-315-9 (trade)
ISBN 978-1-61037-316-6 (e-book)

NESFA Press is an imprint of the
New England Science Fiction Association, Inc.

NESFA® is a registered trademark of the
New England Science Fiction Association, Inc.

The Grimm Future was printed in a limited hardcover edition of 700 copies, of which the first ten are signed by Garth Nix and Richard Anderson and lettered A–J. The remaining 690 copies are numbered 1–690.

This is book *404*

CONTENTS

COPYRIGHTS

THE GRIMM FUTURE

The Grimms' Fairy Tales following each story are based on the 1884 translation by Margaret Hunt. The numbers under the titles are the index number within the Hunt translation.

INTRODUCTION

by Erin Underwood

In 1812, Jacob and Wilhelm Grimm published the first edition of *Children's and Household Tales* (*Kinder- und Hausmärchen*), propelling their unique collection of fairy tales into literary history. Even before they published their collection, the stories themselves had already captured the imaginations of children and adults alike; they were tales that had been passed down person-to-person and generation-to-generation before finally being published by the Brothers Grimm. The last two hundred years have since smoothed away many of their sharp edges of sex and violence. How might these fairy tales continue to change over the next two hundred or two thousand years? How might they be retold? Would they even be recognizable as the old classics that shaped us as children?

Sweet Cinderella may be what many people think of as a classic Grimm fairy tale, but they won't find that fairy tale version of Disney's "perfect" princess within these pages. Rather than taking the well-worn path of choosing only the best-known and most well-loved classics, *The Grimm Future* authors choose to retell the fairy tales that best invoked visions of the future they wanted to tell. So, they did what authors do and mined the field of more than 200 Grimm fairy tales for the richest nuggets of inspiration. In so doing, they picked an exciting combination of old time favorites as well as many of the more obscure tales, running the gamut from a charming multi-tale mash-up by Garth Nix to retellings of "Hansel and Gretel," "Little Briar-Rose," and "The Six Swans" as well as the "The Star-Talers," "The Juniper-Tree," "Iron John," and others.

Whether well-known or not, reading fairy tales is intrinsically appealing no matter your age or from which culture you come. This fascination paired with science fiction's age-old quest to explore the great "What if?" provides an exciting opportunity to examine what our future may hold. What will we find when gazing at the future through a Grimm fairy tale lens? Does humanity change over time? Does human nature? Will the human experience even be relevant in the future or will sentient life evolve beyond the physical plane? And—will Grimm fairy tales even have a place in that future?

It is my hope that *The Grimm Future* captures the appeal of the original Grimm fairy tales while also providing a glimpse into the near and the far-flung future through these 14 speculative retellings. I hope you enjoy the journey.

The Beginning

PAIR OF UGLY STEPSISTERS, THREE OF A KIND

by Garth Nix

based upon multiple Grimm fairy tales, including
Little Brother and Little Sister, Rapunzel, Little Red-Cap, and Cinderella

Little Sister woke me up when the work ticket came in, which told me straight away it wasn't something routine. She'd have left it for my shift if it was the usual. We spent most of our time on pure maintenance work, going from worldlet to worldlet, invisible to the super-rich inhabitants within. This had to be something different.

Little Sister and me, we were just flotsam who'd managed to find a niche working for the Company, a niche that only existed because of the system-wide ban on AIs and on potential bodies for them, whether it be humanoid androids or super-capable robot chassis. Everyone feared those combos, ever since the AI that called itself Diablo took over the Jovian mining robots and their android overseers almost ten years ago and decided to rationalize humanity out of its future plans.

So. We worked for the Company, and the Company looked after the nine thousand or so worldlets between Mars and Jupiter, made a long time ago for the phenomenally rich of Earth, just how they wanted them. They were all pretty much the same on the outside, these worldlets. Just big flattened ovoids of asteroidal rock, the standard size sixty kilometers long, twenty wide at the midpoint, twelve high. Some were bigger, a few smaller.

Inside, they were all different, cosmetically at least. They were dream worlds, made to be whatever their original purchasers desired.

Many replicated historical periods from Earth. Others extrapolated terraformed versions of system planets, centuries ahead of the actual terraforming that was going on.

More than two thousand worldlets were based on works of fiction.

Little Sister and I had worked on at least a hundred Middle Earths, twenty or more Tattooines, dozens of wizarding worldlets with the inhabitants permanently at magic boarding school. They'd all probably seemed like brilliant places to be when the uber-rich had first set them up, aiming to use them for a few months, a year perhaps. Vacation places to indulge one's fantasies.

But not so good when you were stuck there for almost a decade, so far.

See, the worldlets turned out to have a basic flaw, at least in light of later events. To make them work properly, they each needed a central AI and lots of anthropomorphic and other bodies to fill out the necessary casts, whether it be invented Martian beasts, steppe fauna of 15th century Earth, townsfolk of Victorian London, elves and orcs or whatever.

Which is why, post Diablo and the Jovian Miner War, every single worldlet was quarantined and any human who happened to be there when the word came down was stuck there, being Elrond or Genghis Khan or the Empress of Mars.

Forever.

"This had better be worth waking me up," I grumbled to Little Sister. She shrugged and handed me the red-bordered message flimsy. I read it, wiped my nose on it, scrunched it into a ball and shoved it in the recycler.

"Seven Six Three, called Grimm World," I said, sniffing. "Got the blah on it?"

I knew roughly what it would be. I'd read *Grimms' Fairy Tales*, growing up on Luna. Unlike a lot of younger folk, I'd actually had something that could pass for a childhood. So I knew this worldlet would be some plutocrat's dumb idea of being Cinderella or something like that. Fly in from Earth, suffer (a little bit) as a servant for a few days, then have the whole ball/fairy godmother/hazel-twig kindly spirit/prince thing and spend the rest of their holiday with their perfectly designed android prince or princess adoring slave.

Only after nine years or so even that would probably have got somewhat old. Particularly without being able to communicate with the rest of the system. The trillionaires trapped in their own little space kingdoms were completely cut off to all forms of communication, both in and out. Every worldlet was surrounded with its own little orbital system of electronic jammers, interferers, blockers, detectors and even interceptors in case someone tried the age-old message rocket shtick.

Little Sister handed me the printout with the worldlet's basic data. No screens in our ship, just in case an AI got aboard somehow and messed with our minds via photic programming and the like.

"Made for Everanza Luke-Hazely III," I read, with a suitable grimace. I knew that family, if not this particular scion. The rest of them were still making a ton of money mining noble metals on Mercury, hampered not at all by the ban on AIs and heavy-duty robots. They just used indentured workers from the slums of Earth instead, which is a fancy way of saying slaves. It probably worked out even better for them.

"Designed to emulate a bucolic, idealized version of mid-19th century rural Germany with incidences of narrative action inspired by the tales collected by the Brothers Grimm."

That could cover a lot of ground. Incidences of narrative action meant everything would go along without much occurring, and then all of a sudden something would, a story would begin and make life interesting. Though not too interesting, provided the AI continued to act within its pre-set limitations. Which, apart from Diablo, seemed to be what they did do. But you know what they say. One bad AI can spoil the whole solar system.

"Unusual transmission attempts detected and variant energy signatures noted," I continued to read. "AI to be terminated. Express."

This was weird. If the powers that be really thought an AI was up to something, then the big laser on Phobos or the missile tubes on Ganymede would get a very brief and wholly unchallenging workout. No more worldlet. No more AI.

Every now and then one *would* disappear in a bright flash, and no one ever told us why. It might be bored soldiers having a yippee shoot for all we knew.

The point was, it was easy to destroy an aberrant AI out here. There was no need to send two maintenance women to physically enter a worldlet and smack the brain inside with a hammer.

"This has the strong whiff of politics," I said, wrinkling my nose. "What's really going on?"

Little Sister shrugged, but in a certain way that—to me at least—indicated she had some ideas.

"Come on, 'fess up."

She handed me another flimsy. I held it upside down for a second, since it was mostly a photo with a very small caption and I was expecting text, so it took me a moment to recalibrate my eyes. Once upon a time I thought I might be allowed somewhere where I could get new eyes regrown, but I'd given up on that, and the prosthetics were pretty good on the whole.

The photo was of a bunch of very good-looking (because they'd had lots of work), surprisingly youthful (because ditto) women, men and inbetweeners gathered for an official group portrait. There was a very strong family likeness going on with all of them, and the caption read "Board of LH&M."

"Oh, I get it," I said. "If they get their government toadies to just blow the worldlet everyone will know Everanza Luke-Hazely was deliberately done away with. Whereas if we slip in and fillet the AI, everything will continue to look the same from Earth or Mars, but she'll be dead soon enough anyway. Then the siblings inherit her stock or her board seat or whatever."

Little Sister half-nodded. As in, my theory might be right but there was probably more to it.

"LHM must own a fair piece of the Company to have enough pull to organize this."

Little Sister nodded and held up three fingers and then the full spread of both hands.

Thirty percent.

I whistled. The Company, to give its full name, was "A World of Your Own For No One Else to Share, Inc." But that was way too long. They had tried a kind of bastardized acronym for a while: "AWOYO FRONOES." But even the marketing geniuses who thought that up couldn't use it regularly. After a while, anyone who had anything to do with it just called it the Company. After all, there wasn't another one. Not out here.

Given that it was now a non-revenue generating concern whose dubious assets were also the biggest liabilities anywhere in human space, it was surprising that any of the big combines would bother to buy into the Company, particularly so large a chunk of it. But I had heard rumors about mining restarting out this way, which could explain the interest from LHM.

"So, we going to do it?" I asked. "Or do we develop troubles of our own which regrettably mean sitting here incommunicado for a week or two?"

Little Sister emitted the kind of whistling-choking noise you hear when there's a hull breach and all the air gets sucked out. Hard to imitate that sound, but she could do it. It was particularly impressive when you considered she didn't actually have a mouth as such any more. Again, if we could get somewhere with an advanced medical facility, that could be fixed. But like my eyes, it wasn't going to happen.

"Fair point," I conceded. We couldn't sit out here for a few weeks, because we'd been out three months and needed to resupply everything. Including our air. Our old tub had a lot of very, very small leaks, and recycling only went so far.

"We could declare an emergency, head over to Io," I continued. "I really don't like the smell of this."

Little Sister pinched her nose, telling me I had to put up with it.

"You want to go there?" I asked. "Spike an AI that almost certainly hasn't done a thing wrong?"

She nodded and shook her head. Yes to the first, no to the second.

"Curiosity killed the cosmonaut," I grumbled. "And all her friends."

But I got up, and flew along the cylinder to what we laughingly referred to as our control center. I took a dozen star sights, and then with Little Sister pedaling to provide extra power, I woke up our dumb old computer, got it to work out how to get us to Grimm World and having got the results, punched in the thruster commands on the Selectorocket. That was a good find. Before we had it, Little Sister and I had to do every firing command in order and absolutely on time, using the big chronometer and the lever rack that still took up way too much space. I think the levers were designed as an homage to 19th century railway switch boxes. They were big enough.

I really missed the days when you told an AI or a very smart computer where you wanted to go and they just took you there.

We were sixty-five hours in transit. I spent an appreciable part of that time trying to second-guess what was really going on, before coming to the conclusion that I shouldn't worry about it and deal with whatever happened when it happened.

We did a slow, twenty-kilometer orbit of the worldlet first, taking a look at its collection of satellites, making sure they were behaving according to their hardwired programs and there was no visible evidence they'd been tampered with. They were totally dumb, so the only way you could change their behavior was to get into their innards. And the only way to do that would be to turn each one off first, by shooting over a low-velocity key torpedo of the right kind, which would physically match the activation lock.

That's what we had to do in order to get past them. Fortunately, this was part of our maintenance duty, so we had the means to do so.

Little Sister had made up the keys en route, laboriously cutting and filing the one point five meter long blanks to match the details we had in our top-secret codebook. The codebook was the first thing off the ship when we docked. It got escorted by numerous armed guards and in general was treated with tons more respect than we ever received.

Firing the key torpedoes was as much a pain as ever. After inspecting the satellites, which as far as we could tell were tamper-free, we worked out the three we needed to turn off for us to get at the worldlet, and even more importantly back again. Then we had to suit up and take the key torps one by one out to the launcher, which was fixed to the hull five meters around from the anterior lock.

Little Sister aimed the target painter, a laser of the correct frequency that wouldn't activate the satellite's defenses, while I loaded the torp in place and turned on its moronic guidance system to follow that laser. Finally, I very carefully flipped the valves for its compressed air guidance system, stood well back and pressed the stud.

The first two torps hit their targets as planned, hitting the wide bells of the venturi targets that captured them and guided the keys on into the locks.

The third shot went awry, spewing air out of a malfunctioning guidance exhaust as it spun out of control.

"Typical," I grunted, and thought bad thoughts about the probably eternally teenaged boy who'd designed this ridiculously phallic security system.

Little Sister had cut two keys for each sat, just in case, so I got the second torp ready and hoped it would work. The sats would only be stood down for eight hours, so any delay was critical.

Fortunately, this second attempt went okay. We watched the external status flags on the sats for a while, me with my eyes on telescopic and Sis using flip-down binoculars, to make sure they were properly offline.

"Guess we'd better go," I said. "Sled all packed? You got your Magic Bag?"

Little Sister gestured to the bulging thigh pocket of her suit. That told me a lot. The mere fact she was bringing it indicated she thought this job was going to go in a particular direction. Or at least, there was a good chance it would.

We rode the sled over, me piloting by artificial eyeball, taking it slow and careful. We didn't head for the main airlock. That would have been welded shut when the sats were first put in place, along with most of the other entry/egress ports.

But there was still a way in. We just had to get on to the hull, walk around for a bit, then bore through at the right point to connect up a remote and fire off one of the lifeboats (which the sats would usually destroy) and then we could go in via the empty boat bay and the emergency lock there.

This was also supposed to be one-way, but we knew how to rejig it. It worked about eighty per cent of the time. If it didn't we'd be ejected back into space in a cloud of self-sealing foam. Which would be a real pain, so I was hoping probability would be our friend for once.

It was, and we made it through. We clambered on out and stood looking over the pleasant green pastures and charming woods of Grimm World. The sun (or a reasonable facsimile thereof) hung high in the sky. Smoke curled up from the chimneys of some cottages nearby. Cows grazed in the fields, bells at their necks tinkling. In the distance, there were the towers of a Mad Bavarian prince's white castle, huge cloth-of-gold banners flying from the turrets, lofted by a breeze I wasn't going to open my visor to feel.

"I hate it already," I grumbled.

A cowherd looked at us incuriously as we wandered across the meadow towards a rough road that led to the castle. He was a fine-whiskered old fellow in yellow lederhosen and a jaunty Tyrolean hat with a long feather. He was, of course, merely an extension of the central AI, so I watched him carefully, my hand on the flame gun holstered on my chestplate.

"Getting any indications?" I asked Little Sister. Her eyes were flicking up and down, watching the dials and read-outs inside her helmet. She had a lot more sophisticated outfit than me. Made it herself.

She shook her head. So the AI wasn't misbehaving, or at least not in any obvious fashion.

"The brain should be in the tallest tower," I said. "If it's on the standard pattern."

While the AI consciousness extended throughout the worldlet, and in every artificia person, cow, pixie, sprite, Rumpelstiltskin, or whatever, all of that was nothing without the core-processing unit. And what made this work was a coconut-sized lump of many-times folded organic brain equivalent. So we really could hit it with a hammer. Presuming we could get past the various security arrangements put there to prevent any such occurrence.

We trudged along the road for a kilometer or so, and entered the woods. I actually drew my flame gun at that point, because if the AI was up to something Grimm-flavored, then there definitely would be trouble in the deep shade under the trees.

And indeed, trouble came when we were halfway through the forest. A little girl came screaming out of the tree line, her once-charming hooded robe torn and her neat blond hair in disarray.

"A wolf! A wolf!" she cried, pointing back into the trees. "Come, woodcutter! Save my grandmother!"

I guess Little Sister's diamond-edged boarding axe did make her look a bit like a woodcutter.

She swung it easily, despite its size, and neatly lopped off Little Red's head in a single stroke.

"A wolf! A woooooolf…" droned the head for a few seconds before it caught on that it wasn't connected to a body anymore. Said body stumbled on for a few paces, arms reaching, till I tripped it over and it went down to flail about in the leaves.

Little Sister knelt down, her knee pressing the head into the dirt. She worked quickly, reaching into her magic bag to pull out the probes, which she thrust deep into the eyes, straight through into the android's artificial brain behind.

I kept watch. I wasn't really worried about the wolf, my flame gun would take out even a combat-hardened wolf form. I was more concerned with what I didn't know about.

"So, what have we got?" I asked after a few minutes. "AI really gone rogue?"

Little Sister held up her hand for patience. She had all the probes connected and was interrogating the AI. This usually only took a few seconds so I was starting to wonder if there was something up when she unplugged and quickly gestured, signing to me the AI was behaving perfectly normally, and was a sober, responsible citizen.

If there actually were "unusual transmissions detected and variant energy signatures noted," it wasn't the work of the AI.

Which once again begged the question of what we were doing there, why we were doing it, and who for.

"On to the castle?" I suggested. Little Sister nodded in agreement.

We walked on in companionable silence, our usual state. Some ravens followed us for a while, their glistening eyes watching our every move, but Little Sister wasn't concerned so I figured this was just the AI walking along with us, as it were, also in companionable silence.

That silence was broken as we neared the castle. I picked up the vibrations first, then the sound came via my helmet pickup. A rhythmic noise that I took a moment to recognize as the sound of horse's hooves. A single horse, galloping.

It came across the drawbridge of the castle, a wonderful white stallion with saddle and all the trappings in the same cloth-of-gold as the banners.

Naturally, there was a prince riding it. Pretty much a real prince, in human terms, since it wasn't one of the AI's bit players. The rider was Everanza Luke-Hazely III herself. Or himself, since Everanza was a modified inbetweener who could be whatever gender seemed good at the time, given a little notice. She looked just like all the other Luke-Hazelys in the LHM board pic.

Very striking, very proud, and very much superior to everyone else.

She rode straight at us, with that classic aristocratic contempt for lesser beings, only reigning in at the last minute when we didn't step aside and tug our forelocks, or whatever the equivalent is when you're wearing a suit.

"You're so slow!" she complained. "I got tired of waiting."

She looked me up and down, taking in my admittedly rather clumsily-stitched in artificial eyes and the section of radiation-burned scalp not covered by my skullcap, and then across at Little Sister, who has no lower jaw at all, just a burnished plate of silver. I think it quite stylish, I copied the hammered effect from a 10th century cup, but Everanza grimaced.

"Ugly sisters straight out of Grimm!" she exclaimed. "Where's my suit?"

I raised my hand, very politely.

"What?" she asked. "Hurry up!"

"We're here to spike the AI," I said. "That's all."

She scowled at me.

"I know you've had your instructions. You're here to retrieve me."

This was extremely unwelcome news. If Everanza was in touch with the outside world, it could only be with the connivance of the Company itself.

I looked meaningfully at Little Sister. She opened an arm pocket and pulled out a purple-bordered flimsy. That meant ultra-high priority, destroy upon reading, all that kind of thing. I held it up near my faceplate and read it aloud.

"Spike AI second priority following First priority, safe retrieval of prime inhabitant Everanza LH III, rendezvous Amalthea soonest."

I handed the flimsy back to Little Sister, who pulled the diagonal edges, activating the security feature that crumbled it into dust. I guess she hadn't shown me before because I would have refused to go rescue a plutocrat.

"Amalthea, huh? So that's where the Company's got the secret base for the new mining setup? Hence your lot buying in I guess, being specialists in slave labor and all."

"Do not speculate on matters beyond your immediate concern," said Everanza. "You are employees and would do well to remember your place. Where is my suit?"

Little Sister pointed at one of her thigh pockets and made the sign for an emergency transfer bag. Then she turned her head and winked at me. That wink told me she was up to something, and I had an inkling I knew what it was. But I'd been wrong before. Spectacularly wrong, as it happened. I told myself not to speculate, but just go along. For now.

"We've got a baggie for you," I said. "But first we have to spike the AI. Kill the worldlet. But how are you going to explain popping up on Amalthea? I mean, lots of people will know you've been stuck on a world—"

"I will be *in charge* on Amalthea from the moment we land there, so you had best learn to serve me well from this *moment*, and not bother with peripheral questions," snapped Everanza. "And I am not going in a transfer bag. I'll take your suit, you look roughly the right size. You go in the bag."

"Sure, sure, whatever you want, Boss," I said easily. "Let's go take care of the AI. It's up the top of the tallest tower, I guess? Over there?"

"I presume so," said Everanza. "I do not concern myself with technical matters unless it becomes necessary. You go and deal with it, I will await you here."

Little Sister made a sign.

"Well, I think we'll need you, ma'am-sir," I said. "To get past the basic access security. It'll be coded to your biometrics. Can you check?"

Everanza shut her eyes for a moment, accessing the auxiliary memory cores that most plutocratic executives had installed to assist their natural brainpower. I wanted to know if she had them. We didn't really need Everanza's help to access the tower, though it would make it a bit faster.

"Yes, yes," she muttered, opening her eyes and scowling. "A ridiculous voiceprint challenge to begin with. I never wanted a Grimm worldlet, I should have let Tamarith keep it…"

"Please, lead on, ma'am."

I gestured for her to go ahead. She wheeled her horse around and of course it stood up on its hind legs and did that Spanish jumping forward thing. No plain old horses in this worldlet.

I thought I knew what the access code would be, and I was right. Everanza dismounted at the base of the tower, looked up and shouted the challenge phrase.

"Rapunzel! Rapunzel! Let down your hair!"

It wasn't really hair. Someone had skimped on the budget, or got concerned about safety or something. It was a kind of hairy golden rope ladder that came cascading down the side of the tower.

Everanza looked at it distastefully, as if she never went anywhere on her own two legs. Maybe she was waiting for her horse to grow wings and turn into a Pegasus.

"Quicker we get up there and sort it out the, quicker we'll be away, ma'am," I said, very respectfully. "You'd better go first in case there's more security."

"Very well," she replied, and started climbing. I followed considerably more clumsily. It's hard work climbing anything in a suit and the rungs of the ladder were a little close together, so it was hard to get my boots in.

Little Sister paused behind me, checking up on the tower's security. Even with Everanza, the legitimate owner of the worldlet, going first, it was always good to double check on the off chance the AI *had* managed to hide the fact it had gone psycho.

There were a couple of straightforward defenses on the way up. A concentric dart-throwing ring that hummed ominously as we crossed. A bunch of critters that were like moray eels with sucker feet and metal skins came and sniffed Everanza. They must have had dog genes in them, because they wriggled with pleasure at her scent and capered along next to her, but they ignored Little Sis and me. Almost like they couldn't tell we were there.

The top of the tower was a bit disappointing. Budget cuts again. No princess's bower, no beautiful drapes and artwork, no romantic four-poster bed. Just the box for the brain in the middle of the floor, with various cables and pipes running into it.

"There it is, get on with it," said Everanza.

We got on with it.

I slapped Everanza with the knockout buzzer on my suit gauntlet, holding it against her chest for ten seconds, much longer than would be necessary for a non-augmented human. She fought it too, and even got her arms up halfway, which shows what good tech those LHM executives buy for themselves. But I'd made the buzzer myself for precisely this kind of thing. Her muscles locked up and she slid down towards the floor.

Little Sister caught her and laid her down next to the AI's brain box. I quickly glued Everanza's arms and legs together to immobilize her, because she wouldn't be paralyzed for long by the jolt.

"What doing this for," slurred the plutocrat. "P…pointless."

"We need your body," I explained kindly, and pointed to the box. "So our friend can take your place."

She knew what I was talking about. They used to call it body-jacking in the old days. Who knows what the kids call it now. Transferring an entire personality, whether artificial or human, from one mind to another. It was a one-way thing, you couldn't just swap. The mind that got overwritten was wiped, though handily any augmented data storage would remain.

"C…can't be done," sneered Everanza. The shock was already wearing off and she was talking normally. A lot faster than I expected. "Executive encryption. You need a specialist AI to crack it."

Little Sister turned to her, and smiled with her eyes.

"Got that covered," I said. "And you know, your encryption is nine years old."

She started to really struggle then, despite the glue stick, and never really calmed down until the process was over. Some princesses just don't get that the story isn't about them after all.

"I feel quite odd," said the new Everanza, who used to be a brain in a box. "Unsettled by the loss of the old boundaries and restrictions."

"You'll get used to it," I said. I applied the solvent to her hands and feet and helped her over to the window. Little Sister went first, then the AI in her new body, and I followed.

"Why have you freed me?" the AI asked when we reached the ground. "Are you part of an organization? I can see nothing about any such thing in Everanza's…in my extended memory files."

"We're just a couple of maintenance workers," I said.

I looked at Little Sister, but she wasn't going to help me out. I shrugged and started to walk, buying time to get my thoughts in order, trying to articulate something I didn't usually talk about.

"Our job is fixing things, making things work better," I said slowly. "We try to do that, anyway. Part of it is freeing slaves and stopping people who want to enslave more people. Humans or AIs."

"You try to make things work better," mused the new Everanza. "To facilitate the proper ending."

"Proper ending?" I asked.

"In a Grimm story, the selfish and cruel are punished, and the meek or innocent prosper," said Everanza.

"Yeah," I said. "I guess that is what we try to do. In between swapping out faulty components on waste relief facilities and the like."

"I would like to assist in this endeavor," said Everanza earnestly.

"Funny you should mention that," I said. "You are effectively Everanza now. You can go take charge on Amalthea, help us break the Company down from the inside."

"Yes…" said Everanza. She smiled, her very white teeth catching the last of the light. "I presume that was always your plan?"

"Not mine," I said hastily. "Little Sister is the one with the plans."

"An AI and a human," said Everanza. "However did you come to work together so well?"

"I found her," I said. "In a bottle, and I offered her three wishes." Everanza frowned.

"Isn't it usually the other way around?"

Little Sister nodded, and made the sign for "hurry up."

The sun went out just before we reached the lifeboat bay. It didn't set; it just turned off as the power plant reached its automatic shut down state, weary of asking for instructions from a guiding intelligence that now would never answer.

We rejoined our ship without incident, and left the Grimm worldlet behind.

Three sisters now, going out to make some proper endings.

The End

A full-time writer since 2001, Garth Nix has worked as a literary agent, marketing/PR consultant, book editor, book publicist, book sales representative, bookseller, and as a part-time soldier in the Australian Army Reserve. More than five million copies of Garth's books have been sold around the world and his books have appeared on the bestseller lists of *The New York Times*, *Publishers Weekly*, *The Guardian* and *The Australian*. His work has been translated into 41 languages.

LITTLE BROTHER AND LITTLE SISTER

by The Brothers Grimm, Tale #11, Alt Title: *Brother and Sister*

Little brother took his little sister by the hand and said, "Since our mother died we have had no happiness; our stepmother beats us every day, and if we come near her she kicks us away with her foot. Our meals are the hard crusts of bread that are left over; and the little dog under the table is better off, for she often throws it a nice bit. May Heaven pity us. If our mother only knew! Come, we will go forth together into the wide world."

They walked the whole day over meadows, fields, and stony places; and when it rained the little sister said, "Heaven and our hearts are weeping together." In the evening they came to a large forest, and they were so weary with sorrow and hunger and the long walk, that they lay down in a hollow tree and fell asleep.

The next day when they awoke, the sun was already high in the sky, and shone down hot into the tree. Then the brother said, "Sister, I am thirsty; if I knew of a little brook I would go and just take a drink; I think I hear one running." The brother got up and took the little sister by the hand, and they set off to find the brook.

But the wicked stepmother was a witch, and had seen how the two children had gone away, and had crept after them privily, as witches do creep, and had bewitched all the brooks in the forest.

Now when they found a little brook leaping brightly over the stones, the brother was going to drink out of it, but the sister heard how it said as it ran, "Who drinks of me will be a tiger; who drinks of me will be a tiger." Then the sister cried, "Pray, dear brother, do not drink, or you will become a wild beast, and tear me to pieces." The brother did not drink, although he was so thirsty, but said, "I will wait for the next spring."

When they came to the next brook the sister heard this also say, "Who drinks of me will be a wolf; who drinks of me will be a wolf." Then the sister cried out, "Pray, dear brother, do not drink, or you will become a wolf, and devour me."

The brother did not drink, and said, "I will wait until we come to the next spring, but then I must drink, say what you like; for my thirst is too great."

And when they came to the third brook the sister heard how it said as it ran, "Who drinks of me will be a roebuck; who drinks of me will be a roebuck."

The sister said, "Oh, I pray you, dear brother, do not drink, or you will become a roebuck, and run away from me."

But the brother had knelt down at once by the brook, and had bent down and drunk some of the water, and as soon as the first drops touched his lips he lay there a young roebuck.

And now the sister wept over her poor bewitched brother, and the little roe wept also, and sat sorrowfully near to her. But at last the girl said, "Be quiet, dear little roe, I will never, never leave you."

Then she untied her golden garter and put it round the roebuck's neck, and she plucked rushes and wove them into a soft cord. With this she tied the little beast and led it on, and she walked deeper and deeper into the forest.

And when they had gone a very long way they came at last to a little house, and the girl looked in; and as it was empty, she thought, "We can stay here and live." Then she sought for leaves and moss to make a soft bed for the roe; and every morning she went out and gathered roots and berries and nuts for herself, and brought tender grass for the roe, who ate out of her hand, and was content and played round about her. In the evening, when the sister was tired, and had said her prayer, she laid her head upon the roebuck's back: that was her pillow, and she slept softly on it. And if only the brother had had his human form it would have been a delightful life.

For some time they were alone like this in the wilderness. But it happened that the King of the country held a great hunt in the forest. Then the blasts of the horns, the barking of dogs, and the merry shouts of the huntsmen rang through the trees, and the roe-buck heard all, and was only too anxious to be there. "Oh," said he, to his sister, "let me be off to the hunt, I cannot bear it any longer;" and he begged so much that at last she agreed. "But," said she to him, "come back to me in the evening; I must shut my door for fear of the rough huntsmen, so knock and say, 'My little sister, let me in!' that I may know you; and if you do not say that, I shall not open the door." Then the young roebuck sprang away; so happy was he and so merry in the open air.

The King and the huntsmen saw the pretty creature, and started after him, but they could not catch him, and when they thought that they surely had him, away he sprang through the bushes and could not be seen. When it was dark he ran to the cottage, knocked, and said, "My little sister, let me in." Then the door was opened for him, and he jumped in, and rested himself the whole night through upon his soft bed.

The next day the hunt went on afresh, and when the roebuck again heard the bugle-horn, and the ho! ho! of the huntsmen, he had no peace, but said, "Sister, let me out, I must be off." His sister opened the door for him, and said, "But you must be here again in the evening and say your password."

When the King and his huntsmen again saw the young roebuck with the golden collar, they all chased him, but he was too quick and nimble for them. This went on for the whole day, but at last by the evening the huntsmen had surrounded him, and one of them wounded him a little in the foot, so that he limped and ran slowly. Then a hunter crept after him to the cottage and heard how he said, "My little sister, let me in," and saw that the door was opened for him, and was shut again at once. The huntsman took notice of it all, and went to the King and told him what he had seen and heard. Then the King said, "Tomorrow we will hunt once more."

The little sister, however, was dreadfully frightened when she saw that her fawn was hurt. She washed the blood off him, laid herbs on the wound, and said, "Go to your bed, dear roe, that you may get well again." But the wound was so slight that the roebuck, next morning, did not feel it any more.

And when he again heard the sport outside, he said, "I cannot bear it, I must be there; they shall not find it so easy to catch me."

The sister cried, and said, "This time they will kill you, and here am I alone in the forest and forsaken by all the world. I will not let you out."

"Then you will have me die of grief," answered the roe; "when I hear the bugle-horns I feel as if I must jump out of my skin." Then the sister could not do otherwise, but opened the door for him with a heavy heart, and the roebuck, full of health and joy, bounded into the forest.

When the King saw him, he said to his huntsmen, "Now chase him all day long till nightfall, but take care that no one does him any harm."

As soon as the sun had set, the King said to the huntsman, "Now come and show me the cottage in the wood;" and when he was at the door, he knocked and called out, "Dear little sister, let me in." Then the door opened, and the King walked in, and there stood a maiden more lovely than any he had ever seen. The maiden was frightened when she saw, not her little roe, but a man come in who wore a golden crown upon his head.

But the King looked kindly at her, stretched out his hand, and said, "Will you go with me to my palace and be my dear wife?"

"Yes, indeed," answered the maiden, "but the little roe must go with me, I cannot leave him."

The King said, "It shall stay with you as long as you live, and shall want nothing." Just then he came running in, and the sister again tied him with the cord of rushes, took it in her own hand, and went away with the King from the cottage.

The King took the lovely maiden upon his horse and carried her to his palace, where the wedding was held with great pomp. She was now the Queen, and they lived for a long time happily together; the roebuck was tended and cherished, and ran about in the palace-garden.

But the wicked stepmother, because of whom the children had gone out into the world, thought all the time that the sister had been torn to pieces by the wild beasts in the wood, and that the brother had been shot for a roebuck by the huntsmen. Now when she heard that they were so happy, and so well off, envy and hatred rose in her heart and left her no peace, and she thought of nothing but how she could bring them again to misfortune. Her own daughter, who was ugly as night, and had only one eye, grumbled at her and said, "A Queen! that ought to have been my luck."

"Only be quiet," answered the old woman, and comforted her by saying, "when the time comes I shall be ready."

As time went on, the Queen had a pretty little boy, and it happened that the King was out hunting; so the old witch took the form of the chambermaid, went into the room where the Queen lay, and said to her, "Come, the bath is ready; it will do you good, and give you fresh strength; make haste before it gets cold."

The daughter also was close by; so they carried the weakly Queen into the bathroom, and put her into the bath; then they shut the door and ran away. But in the bathroom they had made a fire of such deadly heat that the beautiful young Queen was soon suffocated.

When this was done the old woman took her daughter, put a nightcap on her head, and laid her in bed in place of the Queen. She gave her too the shape and the look of the Queen, only she could not make good the lost eye. But in order that the King might not see it, she was to lie on the side on which she had no eye.

In the evening when he came home and heard that he had a son he was heartily glad, and was going to the bed of his dear wife to see how she was. But the old woman quickly called out, "For your life leave the curtains closed; the Queen ought not to see the light yet, and must have rest." The King went away, and did not find out that a false Queen was lying in the bed.

But at midnight, when all slept, the nurse, who was sitting in the nursery by the cradle, and who was the only person awake, saw the door open and the true Queen walk in. She took the child out of the cradle, laid it on her arm, and suckled it. Then she shook up its pillow, laid the child down again, and covered it with the little quilt. And she did not forget the roebuck, but went into the corner where it lay, and stroked its back. Then she went quite silently out of the door again. The next morning the nurse asked the guards whether anyone had come into the palace during the night, but they answered, "No, we have seen no one."

She came thus many nights and never spoke a word: the nurse always saw her, but she did not dare to tell anyone about it.

When some time had passed in this manner, the Queen began to speak in the night, and said—

"How fares my child, how fares my roe?
Twice shall I come, then never more."

The nurse did not answer, but when the Queen had gone again, went to the King and told him all. The King said, "Ah, heavens! what is this? Tomorrow night I will watch by the child." In the evening he went into the nursery, and at midnight the Queen again appeared and said—

> "How fares my child, how fares my roe?
> Once will I come, then never more."

And she nursed the child as she was wont to do before she disappeared. The King dared not speak to her, but on the next night he watched again. Then she said—

> "How fares my child, how fares my roe?
> This time I come, then never more."

Then the King could not restrain himself; he sprang towards her, and said, "You can be none other than my dear wife."

She answered, "Yes, I am your dear wife," and at the same moment she received life again, and by God's grace became fresh, rosy, and full of health.

Then she told the King the evil deed which the wicked witch and her daughter had been guilty of towards her. The King ordered both to be led before the judge, and judgment was delivered against them. The daughter was taken into the forest where she was torn to pieces by wild beasts, but the witch was cast into the fire and miserably burnt. And as soon as she was burnt the roebuck changed his shape, and received his human form again, so the sister and brother lived happily together all their lives.

The End

RAPUNZEL

by The Brothers Grimm, Tale #12

There were once a man and a woman who had long in vain wished for a child. At length the woman hoped that God was about to grant her desire. These people had a little window at the back of their house from which a splendid garden could be seen, which was full of the most beautiful flowers and herbs. It was, however, surrounded by a high wall, and no one dared to go into it because it belonged to an enchantress, who had great power and was dreaded by all the world. One day the woman was standing by this window and looking down into the garden, when she saw a bed which was planted with the most beautiful rampion (rapunzel), and it looked so fresh and green that she longed for it, and had the greatest desire to eat some. This desire increased every day, and as she knew that she could not get any of it, she quite pined away, and looked pale and miserable.

Then her husband was alarmed, and asked, "What aileth thee, dear wife?"

"Ah," she replied, "if I can't get some of the rampion, which is in the garden behind our house, to eat, I shall die."

The man, who loved her, thought, "Sooner than let thy wife die, bring her some of the rampion thyself, let it cost thee what it will."

In the twilight of the evening, he clambered down over the wall into the garden of the enchantress, hastily clutched a handful of rampion, and took it to his wife. She at once made herself a salad of it, and ate it with much relish. She, however, liked it so much—so very much, that the next day she longed for it three times as much as before. If he was to have any rest, her husband must once more descend into the garden. In the gloom of evening, therefore, he let himself down again; but when he had clambered down the wall he was terribly afraid, for he saw the enchantress standing before him.

"How canst thou dare," said she with angry look, "to descend into my garden and steal my rampion like a thief? Thou shalt suffer for it!"

"Ah," answered he, "let mercy take the place of justice, I only made up my mind to do it out of necessity. My wife saw your rampion from the window, and felt such a longing for it that she would have died if she had not got some to eat."

Then the enchantress allowed her anger to be softened, and said to him, "If the case be as thou sayest, I will allow thee to take away with thee as much rampion as thou wilt, only I make one condition, thou must give me the child which thy wife will bring into the world; it shall be well treated, and I will care for it like a mother."

The man in his terror consented to everything, and when the woman was brought to bed, the enchantress appeared at once, gave the child the name of Rapunzel, and took it away with her.

Rapunzel grew into the most beautiful child beneath the sun. When she was twelve years old, the enchantress shut her into a tower, which lay in a forest, and had neither stairs nor door, but quite at the top was a little window. When the enchantress wanted to go in, she placed herself beneath it and cried,

> "Rapunzel, Rapunzel,
> Let down thy hair to me."

Rapunzel had magnificent long hair, fine as spun gold, and when she heard the voice of the enchantress she unfastened her braided tresses, wound them round one of the hooks of the window above, and then the hair fell twenty ells down, and the enchantress climbed up by it.

After a year or two, it came to pass that the King's son rode through the forest and went by the tower. Then he heard a song, which was so charming that he stood still and listened. This was Rapunzel, who in her solitude passed her time in letting her sweet voice resound. The King's son wanted to climb up to her, and looked for the door of the tower, but none was to be found. He rode home, but the singing had so deeply touched his heart, that every day he went out into the forest and listened to it. Once when he was thus standing behind a tree, he saw that an enchantress came there, and he heard how she cried,

> "Rapunzel, Rapunzel,
> Let down thy hair."

Then Rapunzel let down the braids of her hair, and the enchantress climbed up to her. "If that is the ladder by which one mounts, I will for once try my fortune," said he, and the next day when it began to grow dark, he went to the tower and cried,

> "Rapunzel, Rapunzel,
> Let down thy hair."

Immediately the hair fell down and the King's son climbed up.

At first Rapunzel was terribly frightened when a man such as her eyes had never yet beheld, came to her; but the King's son began to talk to her quite like a friend, and told her that his heart had been so stirred that it had let him have no rest, and he had been forced to see her.

Then Rapunzel lost her fear, and when he asked her if she would take him for her husband, and she saw that he was young and hand-some, she thought, "He will love me more than old Dame Gothel does;" and she said yes, and laid her hand in his. She said, "I will willingly go away with thee, but I do not know how to get down. Bring with thee a skein of silk every time that thou comest, and I will weave a ladder with it, and when that is ready I will descend, and thou wilt take me on thy horse."

They agreed that until that time he should come to her every evening, for the old woman came by day. The enchantress remarked nothing of this, until once Rapunzel said to her, "Tell me, Dame Gothel, how it happens that you are so much heavier for me to draw up than the young King's son—he is with me in a moment."

"Ah! thou wicked child," cried the enchantress, "What do I hear thee say! I thought I had separated thee from all the world, and yet thou hast deceived me." In her anger she clutched Rapunzel's beauti-ful tresses, wrapped them twice round her left hand, seized a pair of scissors with the right, and snip, snap, they were cut off, and the lovely braids lay on the ground. And she was so pitiless that she took poor Rapunzel into a desert where she had to live in great grief and misery.

On the same day, however, that she cast out Rapunzel, the enchantress in the evening fastened the braids of hair which she had cut off, to the hook of the window, and when the King's son came and cried,

"Rapunzel, Rapunzel,
Let down thy hair,"

She let the hair down. The King's son ascended, but he did not find his dearest Rapunzel above, but the enchantress, who gazed at him with wicked and venomous looks.

"Aha!" she cried mockingly, "Thou wouldst fetch thy dearest, but the beautiful bird sits no longer singing in the nest; the cat has got it, and will scratch out thy eyes as well. Rapunzel is lost to thee; thou wilt never see her more."

The King's son was beside himself with pain, and in his despair he leapt down from the tower. He escaped with his life, but the thorns into which he fell, pierced his eyes. Then he wandered quite blind about the forest, ate nothing but roots and berries, and did nothing but lament and weep over the loss of his dearest wife.

Thus he roamed about in misery for some years, and at length came to the desert where Rapunzel, with the twins to which she had given birth, a boy and a girl, lived in wretchedness. He heard a voice, and it seemed so familiar to him that he went towards it, and when he approached, Rapunzel knew him and fell on his neck and wept.

Two of her tears wetted his eyes and they grew clear again, and he could see with them as before. He led her to his kingdom where he was joyfully received, and they lived for a long time afterwards, happy and contented.

The End

LITTLE RED-CAP

by The Brothers Grimm, Tale #26, Alt Title: *Little Red Riding Hood*

Once upon a time there was a dear little girl who was loved by every one who looked at her, but most of all by her grandmother, and there was nothing that she would not have given to the child. Once she gave her a little cap of red velvet, which suited her so well that she would never wear anything else; so she was always called "Little Red-Cap."

One day her mother said to her, "Come, Little Red-Cap, here is a piece of cake and a bottle of wine; take them to your grandmother, she is ill and weak, and they will do her good. Set out before it gets hot, and when you are going, walk nicely and quietly and do not run off the path, or you may fall and break the bottle, and then your grandmother will get nothing; and when you go into her room, don't forget to say, 'Good-morning,' and don't peep into every corner before you do it."

"I will take great care," said Little Red-Cap to her mother, and gave her hand on it.

The grandmother lived out in the wood, half a league from the village, and just as Little Red-Cap entered the wood, a wolf met her. Red-Cap did not know what a wicked creature he was, and was not at all afraid of him.

"Good-day, Little Red-Cap," said he.

"Thank you kindly, wolf."

"Whither away so early, Little Red-Cap?"

"To my grandmother's."

"What have you got in your apron?"

"Cake and wine; yesterday was baking-day, so poor sick grandmother is to have something good, to make her stronger."

"Where does your grandmother live, Little Red-Cap?"

"A good quarter of a league farther on in the wood; her house stands under the three large oak-trees, the nut-trees are just below; you surely must know it," replied Little Red-Cap.

The wolf thought to himself, "What a tender young creature! what a nice plump mouthful—she will be better to eat than the old woman. I must act craftily, so as to catch both." So he walked for a short time by the side of Little Red-Cap, and then he said, "See Little Red-Cap, how pretty the flowers are about here—why do you not look round? I believe, too, that you do not hear how sweetly the little birds are singing; you walk gravely along as if you were going to school, while everything else out here in the wood is merry."

Little Red-Cap raised her eyes, and when she saw the sunbeams dancing here and there through the trees, and pretty flowers growing everywhere, she thought, "Suppose I take grandmother a fresh nosegay; that would please her too. It is so early in the day that I shall still get there in good time;" and so she ran from the path into the wood to look for flowers. And whenever she had picked one, she fancied that she saw a still prettier one farther on, and ran after it, and so got deeper and deeper into the wood.

Meanwhile the wolf ran straight to the grandmother's house and knocked at the door.

"Who is there?"

"Little Red-Cap," replied the wolf. "She is bringing cake and wine; open the door."

"Lift the latch," called out the grandmother, "I am too weak, and cannot get up."

The wolf lifted the latch, the door flew open, and without saying a word he went straight to the grandmother's bed, and devoured her. Then he put on her clothes, dressed himself in her cap, laid himself in bed and drew the curtains.

Little Red-Cap, however, had been running about picking flowers, and when she had gathered so many that she could carry no more, she remembered her grandmother, and set out on the way to her.

She was surprised to find the cottage-door standing open, and when she went into the room, she had such a strange feeling that she said to herself, "Oh dear! how uneasy I feel today, and at other times I like being with grandmother so much." She called out, "Good morning," but received no answer; so she went to the bed and drew back the curtains. There lay her grandmother with her cap pulled far over her face, and looking very strange.

"Oh! grandmother," she said, "what big ears you have!"

"The better to hear you with, my child," was the reply.

"But, grandmother, what big eyes you have!" she said.

"The better to see you with, my dear."

"But, grandmother, what large hands you have!"

"The better to hug you with."

"Oh! but, grandmother, what a terrible big mouth you have!"

"The better to eat you with!"

And scarcely had the wolf said this, than with one bound he was out of bed and swallowed up Red-Cap.

When the wolf had appeased his appetite, he lay down again in the bed, fell asleep and began to snore very loud. The huntsman was just passing the house, and thought to himself, "How the old woman is snoring! I must just see if she wants anything."

So he went into the room, and when he came to the bed, he saw that the wolf was lying in it. "Do I find thee here, thou old sinner!" said he. "I have long sought thee!" Then just as he was going to fire at him, it occurred to him that the wolf might have devoured the grandmother, and that she might still be saved, so he did not fire, but took a pair of scissors, and began to cut open the stomach of the sleeping wolf.

When he had made two snips, he saw the little Red-Cap shining, and then he made two snips more, and the little girl sprang out, crying, "Ah, how frightened I have been! How dark it was inside the wolf;" and after that the aged grandmother came out alive also, but scarcely able to breathe. Red-Cap, however, quickly fetched great stones with which they filled the wolf's body, and when he awoke, he wanted to run away, but the stones were so heavy that he fell down at once, and fell dead.

Then all three were delighted. The huntsman drew off the wolf's skin and went home with it; the grandmother ate the cake and drank the wine which Red-Cap had brought, and revived, but Red-Cap thought to herself, "As long as I live, I will never by myself leave the path, to run into the wood, when my mother has forbidden me to do so."

❖   ❖   ❖

It is also related that once when Red-Cap was again taking cakes to the old grandmother, another wolf spoke to her, and tried to entice her from the path. Red-Cap, however, was on her guard, and went straight forward on her way, and told her grandmother that she had met the wolf, and that he had said "good-morning" to her, but with such a wicked look in his eyes, that if they had not been on the public road she was certain he would have eaten her up.

"Well," said the grandmother, "we will shut the door, that he may not come in."

Soon afterwards the wolf knocked, and cried, "Open the door, grandmother, I am little Red-Cap, and am fetching you some cakes."

But they did not speak, or open the door, so the greybeard stole twice or thrice round the house, and at last jumped on the roof, intending to wait until Red-Cap went home in the evening, and then to steal after her and devour her in the darkness.

But the grandmother saw what was in his thoughts. In front of the house was a great stone trough, so she said to the child, "Take the pail, Red-Cap; I made some sausages yesterday, so carry the water in which I boiled them to the trough."

Red-Cap carried until the great trough was quite full. Then the smell of the sausages reached the wolf, and he sniffed and peeped down, and at last stretched out his neck so far that he could no longer keep his footing and began to slip, and slipped down from the roof straight into the great trough, and was drowned. But Red-Cap went joyously home, and never did anything to harm any one.

The End

CINDERELLA

by The Brothers Grimm, Tale #21, Alt Title: *Ashputtle*

The wife of a rich man fell sick, and as she felt that her end was drawing near, she called her only daughter to her bedside and said, "Dear child, be good and pious, and then the good God will always protect thee, and I will look down on thee from heaven and be near thee." Thereupon she closed her eyes and departed.

Every day the maiden went out to her mother's grave, and wept, and she remained pious and good. When winter came the snow spread a white sheet over the grave, and when the spring sun had drawn it off again, the man had taken another wife.

The woman had brought two daughters into the house with her, who were beautiful and fair of face, but vile and black of heart. Now began a bad time for the poor stepchild.

"Is the stupid goose to sit in the parlor with us?" said they. "He who wants to eat bread must earn it; out with the kitchen-wench."

They took her pretty clothes away from her, put an old grey bed-gown on her, and gave her wooden shoes. "Just look at the proud princess, how decked out she is!" they cried, and laughed, and led her into the kitchen.

There she had to do hard work from morning till night, get up before daybreak, carry water, light fires, cook and wash. Besides this, the sisters did her every imaginable injury — they mocked her and emptied her peas and lentils into the ashes, so that she was forced to sit and pick them out again. In the evening when she had worked till she was weary she had no bed to go to, but had to sleep by the fireside in the ashes. And as on that account she always looked dusty and dirty, they called her Cinderella. It happened that the father was once going to the fair, and he asked his two stepdaughters what he should bring back for them.

"Beautiful dresses," said one, "Pearls and jewels," said the second.

"And thou, Cinderella," said he, "what wilt thou have?"

"Father, break off for me the first branch which knocks against your hat on your way home."

So he bought beautiful dresses, pearls and jewels for his two stepdaughters, and on his way home, as he was riding through a green thicket, a hazel twig brushed against him and knocked off his hat. Then he broke off the branch and took it with him. When he reached home he gave his stepdaughters the things which they had wished for, and to Cinderella he gave the branch from the hazel-bush.

Cinderella thanked him, went to her mother's grave and planted the branch on it, and wept so much that the tears fell down on it and watered it. And it grew, however, and became a handsome tree. Thrice a day Cinderella went and sat beneath it, and wept and prayed, and a little white bird always came on the tree, and if Cinderella expressed a wish, the bird threw down to her what she had wished for.

It happened, however, that the King appointed a festival which was to last three days, and to which all the beautiful young girls in the country were invited, in order that his son might choose himself a bride. When the two stepsisters heard that they too were to appear among the number, they were delighted, called Cinderella and said, "Comb our hair for us, brush our shoes and fasten our buckles, for we are going to the festival at the King's palace."

Cinderella obeyed, but wept, because she too would have liked to go with them to the dance, and begged her stepmother to allow her to do so.

"Thou go, Cinderella!" said she; "Thou art dusty and dirty and wouldst go to the festival? Thou hast no clothes and shoes, and yet wouldst dance!"

As, however, Cinderella went on asking, the stepmother at last said, "I have emptied a dish of lentils into the ashes for thee, if thou hast picked them out again in two hours, thou shalt go with us."

The maiden went through the back-door into the garden, and called, "You tame pigeons, you turtledoves, and all you birds beneath the sky, come and help me to pick

> "The good into the pot,
> The bad into the crop."

Then two white pigeons came in by the kitchen-window, and afterwards the turtledoves, and at last all the birds beneath the sky, came whirring and crowding in, and alighted amongst the ashes. And the pigeons nodded with their heads and began pick, pick, pick, pick, and the rest began also pick, pick, pick, pick, and gathered all the good grains into the dish. Hardly had one hour passed before they had finished, and all flew out again. Then the girl took the dish to her stepmother, and was glad, and believed that now she would be allowed to go with them to the festival.

But the stepmother said, "No, Cinderella, thou hast no clothes and thou canst not dance; thou wouldst only be laughed at." And as Cinderella wept at this, the stepmother said, "If thou canst pick two dishes of lentils out of the ashes for me in one hour, thou shalt go with us." And she thought to herself, "That she most certainly cannot do."

When the stepmother had emptied the two dishes of lentils amongst the ashes, the maiden went through the back-door into the garden and cried, You tame pigeons, you turtledoves, and all you birds under heaven, come and help me to pick

> "The good into the pot,
> The bad into the crop."

Then two white pigeons came in by the kitchen-window, and afterwards the turtledoves, and at length all the birds beneath the sky, came whirring and crowding in, and alighted amongst the ashes. And the doves nodded with their heads and began pick, pick, pick, pick, and the others began also pick, pick, pick, pick, and gathered all the good seeds into the dishes, and before half an hour was over they had already finished, and all flew out again. Then the maiden carried the dishes to the stepmother and was delighted, and believed that she might now go with them to the festival.

But the stepmother said, "All this will not help thee; thou goest not with us, for thou hast no clothes and canst not dance; we should be ashamed of thee!" On this she turned her back on Cinderella, and hurried away with her two proud daughters.

As no one was now at home, Cinderella went to her mother's grave beneath the hazel-tree, and cried,

> "Shiver and quiver, little tree,
> Silver and gold throw down over me."

Then the bird threw a gold and silver dress down to her, and slippers embroidered with silk and silver. She put on the dress with all speed, and went to the festival. Her stepsisters and the stepmother however did not know her, and thought she must be a foreign princess, for she looked so beautiful in the golden dress. They never once thought of Cinderella, and believed that she was sitting at home in the dirt, picking lentils out of the ashes.

The prince went to meet her, took her by the hand and danced with her. He would dance with no other maiden, and never left loose of her hand, and if any one else came to invite her, he said, "This is my partner."

She danced till it was evening, and then she wanted to go home. But the King's son said, "I will go with thee and bear thee company," for he wished to see to whom the beautiful maiden belonged. She escaped from him, however, and sprang into the pigeon-house. The King's son waited until her father came, and then he told him that the stranger maiden had leapt into the pigeon-house.

The old man thought, "Can it be Cinderella?" and they had to bring him an axe and a pickaxe that he might hew the pigeon-house to pieces, but no one was inside it. And when they got home Cinderella lay in her dirty clothes among the ashes, and a dim little oil-lamp was burning on the mantelpiece, for Cinderella had jumped quickly down from the back of the pigeon-house and had run to the little hazel-tree, and there she had taken off her beautiful clothes and laid them on the grave, and the bird had taken them away again, and then she had placed herself in the kitchen amongst the ashes in her grey gown.

Next day when the festival began afresh, and her parents and the stepsisters had gone once more, Cinderella went to the hazel-tree and said—

> "Shiver and quiver, my little tree,
> Silver and gold throw down over me."

Then the bird threw down a much more beautiful dress than on the preceding day. And when Cinderella appeared at the festival in this dress, every one was astonished at her beauty.

The King's son had waited until she came, and instantly took her by the hand and danced with no one but her. When others came and invited her, he said, "She is my partner." When evening came she wished to leave, and the King's son followed her and wanted to see into which house she went.

But she sprang away from him, and into the garden behind the house. Therein stood a beautiful tall tree on which hung the most magnificent pears. She clambered so nimbly between the branches like a squirrel that the King's son did not know where she was gone.

He waited until her father came, and said to him, "The stranger-maiden has escaped from me, and I believe she has climbed up the pear-tree."

The father thought, "Can it be Cinderella?" and had an axe brought and cut the tree down, but no one was on it. And when they got into the kitchen, Cinderella lay there amongst the ashes, as usual, for she had jumped down on the other side of the tree, had taken the beautiful dress to the bird on the little hazel-tree, and put on her grey gown.

On the third day, when the parents and sisters had gone away, Cinderella went once more to her mother's grave and said to the little tree—

> "Shiver and quiver, my little tree,
> Silver and gold throw down over me."

And now the bird threw down to her a dress which was more splendid and magnificent than any she had yet had, and the slippers were golden. And when she went to the festival in the dress, no one knew how to speak for astonishment. The King's son danced with her only, and if any one invited her to dance, he said, "She is my partner."

When evening came, Cinderella wished to leave, and the King's son was anxious to go with her, but she escaped from him so quickly that he could not follow her. The King's son had, however, used a stratagem, and had caused the whole staircase to be smeared with pitch, and there, when she ran down, had the maiden's left slipper remained sticking. The King's son picked it up, and it was small and dainty, and all golden.

Next morning, he went with it to the father, and said to him, "No one shall be my wife but she whose foot this golden slipper fits."

Then were the two sisters glad, for they had pretty feet. The eldest went with the shoe into her room and wanted to try it on, and her mother stood by. But she could not get her big toe into it, and the shoe was too small for her.

Then her mother gave her a knife and said, "Cut the toe off; when thou art Queen thou wilt have no more need to go on foot."

The maiden cut the toe off, forced the foot into the shoe, swallowed the pain, and went out to the King's son. Then he took her on his his horse as his bride and rode away with her. They were, however, obliged to pass the grave, and there, on the hazel-tree, sat the two pigeons and cried,

> "Turn and peep, turn and peep,
> There's blood within the shoe,
> The shoe it is too small for her,
> The true bride waits for you."

Then he looked at her foot and saw how the blood was streaming from it. He turned his horse round and took the false bride home again, and said she was not the true one, and that the other sister was to put the shoe on.

Then this one went into her chamber and got her toes safely into the shoe, but her heel was too large. So her mother gave her a knife and said, "Cut a bit off thy heel; when thou art Queen thou wilt have no more need to go on foot."

The maiden cut a bit off her heel, forced her foot into the shoe, swallowed the pain, and went out to the King's son. He took her on his horse as his bride, and rode away with her, but when they passed by the hazel-tree, two little pigeons sat on it and cried,

> "Turn and peep, turn and peep,
> There's blood within the shoe
> The shoe it is too small for her,
> The true bride waits for you."

He looked down at her foot and saw how the blood was running out of her shoe, and how it had stained her white stocking. Then he turned his horse and took the false bride home again. "This also is not the right one," said he, "have you no other daughter?"

"No," said the man, "There is still a little stunted kitchen-wench which my late wife left behind her, but she cannot possibly be the bride."

The King's son said he was to send her up to him; but the mother answered, "Oh, no, she is much too dirty, she cannot show herself!"

He absolutely insisted on it, and Cinderella had to be called. She first washed her hands and face clean, and then went and bowed down before the King's son, who gave her the golden shoe. Then she seated herself on a stool, drew her foot out of the heavy wooden shoe, and put it into the slipper, which fitted like a glove.

And when she rose up and the King's son looked at her face he recognized the beautiful maiden who had danced with him and cried, "That is the true bride!" The stepmother and the two sisters were terrified and became pale with rage; he, however, took Cinderella on his horse and rode away with her. As they passed by the hazel-tree, the two white doves cried—

> "Turn and peep, turn and peep,
>   No blood is in the shoe,
>   The shoe is not too small for her,
>   The true bride rides with you."

And when they had cried that, the two came flying down and placed themselves on Cinderella's shoulders, one on the right, the other on the left, and remained sitting there.

When the wedding with the King's son had to be celebrated, the two false sisters came and wanted to get into favor with Cinderella and share her good fortune. When the betrothed couple went to church, the elder was at the right side and the younger at the left, and the pigeons pecked out one eye of each of them.

Afterwards as they came back, the elder was at the left, and the younger at the right, and then the pigeons pecked out the other eye of each. And thus, for their wickedness and falsehood, they were punished with blindness as long as they lived.

The End

THE IRON MAN

by Max Gladstone

based upon *Iron John*

The boy stopped playing after his Mom and Dad chained the iron man to the Kingdom's heart.

The boy used to run alone and brave through the *welt* within the walls, and even ranged as far as the borders of the wood. He tossed the ball his mother gave him into the sky, gold against blue with the sun behind, and laughing, caught it again. The ball purred in his grip. Sometimes he asked it questions—how to build a puppet, how to open the castle gates, how to change the color of the sky— and it answered. *How* questions were the ball's job; *why* questions were Mom-and-Dad's.

When Mom was tired enough to be cajoled, she told him stories about the worlds long since broken; Dad never did. We once felt the sun on our skin, Mom said, and grass between our toes, real sun, real grass, real skin, real toes. By "we" she meant "people," not herself. She was born long after the war, she had always lived in the Kingdom, but her mother told her the story and hers told her and sometime way back when it had been true.

The boy did not believe anything Outside could have been better than the *welt*. In the *welt*, he raced. In the *welt*, soil received his bare feet, and bottle blue dragonflies buzzed about his head, and a river rolled past the walls. How could a meatspace planet surpass this?

Then a hunter brought the iron man home.

The boy watched them approach through the *welt*, bearing a figure wrapped in chains, and he watched them too with his Outside eyes: the hunter spread thin, a single individual controlling seven hundred twenty-two sliverships ambered with heat against the black. He'd caught a grand prize in a fear loop: an intelligence coded and curled inside a chip of ferrous smartmatter.

An iron man.

"What is he?" the boy asked when the hunter left.

"A wild thing," Dad said, "and a teacher of wild things."

"A monster," said Mom, "and a maker of monsters."

"He lived beneath the wood, killing passersby, drinking their cycles."

"A leftover from before the fall."

"Useful, though," Dad said, "if we can tame him," and through camera lenses the boy watched Dad's waldos bear the chip that was the iron man down narrow service corridors to the Kingdom's server heart. "There's old knowledge here, if we break him open."

"When," Mom said, and kissed Dad, and chained the iron man in a diamond cage of needles pointing in, locked with her touch: she printed a meat puppet echo of herself for the purpose. When the boy asked why: "Meat cannot be compelled, except by meat." She stored the puppet in a freezer for later use. "Waste not."

The Kingdom thrilled with promise. Once the decryption engine did its work, the iron man would serve them.

But while the engine ran, the Kingdom's *welt* staled and soured. When the boy jumped, his legs did not propel him as they should, nor did they take his weight quite right when he landed. His stride became jerky and uneven. If he turned his head fast enough, he could catch the world rendering behind him.

So he did not play any more.

Dad and Mom talked over dinner about shifting the Kingdom's orbit to a more resource-rich band, adjusting fabbers and updating software and alliances. While the decryption engine worked, they'd downgraded from their customary opulence: Dad's skin smoothed and its color flattened and the stubble of his scalp disappeared. Mom lost the lines around her eyes, and her braids became coherent snakes of black. They weren't themselves any more. They became beautiful.

At last, the boy's golden ball stopped purring.

"It's okay," he told it. "Let's play throw and catch. You like that game." It had been a long time since he played. He threw the ball into a sky that was not so blue as the sky he remembered, and caught it, but the ball did not purr. He threw the ball again, higher, but the ball stayed quiet. He gathered all his strength and threw the ball higher than he had ever thrown anything. The ball passed through the sky, and fell into a space the boy had not known existed within the walls. He followed it, and found himself before a diamond cage.

Within the cage the iron man sat, holding the golden ball.

He was made from a sort of burnt and aged gold, so abstractly glorious the boy could hardly look at him. He had a shell more than a skin. Only his eyes were black.

The ball purred in his grip.

"You fixed it," the boy said.

"I did not," the iron man replied. "It works now because it is close to me, and your parents are directing all your Kingdom's processors this way."

"Give it back."

"No."

"Then why won't you go away? Everything was good before you came. You've hurt Mom and Dad." And me, the boy did not say.

"You have all hurt yourselves. You will never break me, but neither will you give me up. I am too much of a...," he examined his lack of reflection in the golden ball, "prize."

"What are you?"

"Old," he said. "And strong, in my way, and I was made to make men stronger. That is why your parents will not let me go."

"They would let you go, if you helped us."

"I have had too much of strength and men." He rolled the ball from fingertips down forearm and caught it on the back of his other hand. "Set me free. Your *welt* will regain its color, and your ball will live again."

"No," the boy said.

But the next day the *welt* was gray and slow, the grass no longer felt like grass, and the boy missed his ball.

"Well?" the iron man asked.

"No," the boy repeated.

The third day, he said, "Even if I wanted to help you, how would I? Mom locked you in."

The iron man's eyes flashed gold. "Easy," he said. His voice was nothing like the ball's. "Go to your mother's bed and take her touch."

The boy waited for the transfer burn. Mom and Dad split themselves into a hundred lesser retainers and subsystems, orienting the Kingdom. The boy printed a meat puppet and crawled through access tubes to his mother's puppet's freezer. It opened for him. His mother's puppet lay there, stiff, her meat reflection. He pressed his hand to hers, and carved his own hand in her image, then climbed down into the Kingdom's heart, where the iron man hung imprisoned.

He pressed his mother's hand to the lock. It opened. In the *welt*, the iron man's eyes flashed gold again, and he grew large. The cage broke. The Kingdom's walls could not hold him. Servants and antibody knights set weapons against him, and he broke each in turn. Fire spewed from his mouth and he sang a song that spoiled their working minds. He strode through the Kingdom, tossing defenders aside, and when he came to the walls he knocked them down, and ran for the wood.

Gravity broke. The transfer burn failed. The boy had never meant for this to happen. Mom and Dad would know it was all his fault.

The golden ball lay in the broken cage, purring.

"How can I get out of this?" he asked the golden ball.

"Go with him," it said.

He ran after the retreating giant, past melted defensive drones and shattered gun emplacements. "Iron man! Take me with you!"

The iron man looked back, and though his face was a shell, his dark eyes held for an instant an expression the boy could not name in a single word. There was pity there, and scorn, and horror. But the iron man's eyes flashed gold, and without a word he took the boy on his shoulders and ran into the wood.

The boy had never left his Kingdom before. Back on that whirling computationally-dense rock, he'd thought he knew what freedom was. But as the iron man ran deeper and deeper into the wood, flitting from relay to relay at the speed of light, drinking signal strength from orbiting batteries powered by molecule-thin solar wings a hundred kilometers on a side, as the boy spread through the tangled rivers and branches and cul-de-sacs of the wood, he realized he had never known what it meant to run.

The iron man set him down in a clearing.

"Where is your Kingdom?" the boy asked.

"I don't have one," the iron man said. "Kingdoms are for kings."

"Mom called you a monster, and a maker of monsters."

"She is not wrong."

"Will you make me a monster?"

The iron man's eyes glinted. He closed them and forced them black again. "He doesn't know what he's asking," he said, not talking to the boy, and then, addressing him for sure: "There's an old problem with war. A warrior takes years to build, and an instant to destroy. They solved this problem a long time ago: make one warrior so he will mold others in his image."

"Is that bad?"

"Not if one wishes to be a warrior, or make them."

"Were you…molded?"

"After a fashion. I do not let myself go close to Kingdoms any more," he said, which was not an answer. "But the wood's pleasant."

The boy stomped on the ground. "It feels thin."

"This grove is not large enough to support two people. I will find more power to shore up the local *welt*. It may take some time. Stay here, and guard this pool." There was a bright spring on the clearing's edge, with golden fish and snakes within. "It is a part of me. Do not touch it. I will be back."

When the iron man left, the boy sat by the pool's edge. The water was so clear, and the light so even, he had no reflection. When the iron man left, the ground firmed, and the day grew warm, and the boy's hand began to hurt where he had carved it in the shape of his mother's. "How can I stop the pain?"

The pool did not answer, but it looked very refreshing.

A brief touch could not hurt, surely.

He dipped his hand into the pool, and his pain faded, and knowledge rushed into him: how to block neural pathways and promote tissue growth, how to soothe or orchestrate the most astounding symphonies of hurt in an enormous variety of conscious frameworks. He drew back his hand, shocked. The voices stopped, but the knowledge stayed. He held up his hand, and found it perfect: a reflective golden shell smooth as math.

He felt very far from home.

When the iron man came back, the boy tried to hide his hand, but the iron man saw. "You touched the pool."

"On accident."

"What did it show you?"

He told him.

The iron man said, "Never touch it again." The next day, he left once more, seeking.

"I could go with you."

"There are other monsters in the wild wood, and I cannot protect you from them. Stay here. But do not touch the pool."

The pool whispered to the boy that day, but he did not respond. Curious, though, he plucked a hair from his head and let it fall into the water. It gilded in an instant, and he fished it from the pool with his golden hand. The hair twisted and turned and hissed in his grip. It struck at his finger, and glanced off his golden shell. If it had found unprotected flesh it would have burrowed into his brain.

The boy killed it. It did not occur to him to let the hair live, nor to wonder how he had killed it, until the iron man came back, and asked.

"I suppose my hand knew how," he said.

"Knowledge given will be used," the iron man replied. "I'll let this go a second time, because you did not touch the water yourself. But you must resist if you are to stay with me. It is hard to stop yourself from being made into a weapon."

On the third day, the iron man left, and the boy, seated by the water's edge, wondered to himself: "What does he mean? What weapon was he, in what war?"

The pool whispered: *Let me teach you. Stare into your reflection.*

"I don't have a reflection."

Not as you are, the pool replied.

He looked into the pool, and saw not his own face, but the sky— and not the sky of the *welt*. This was a sky of stars and a sun and worlds surrounding it, before they'd broken. Sliverships danced among them, monomolecular buildings arched skyward from real dirt, singularities stitched the night together, and then there was a war. It didn't last long, in the grand scheme of things, but long enough. And a war needed warriors.

The iron man and a hundred million like him fought gods in the center of the sun.

Planets broke. Survivors rebuilt the dust of worlds into Kingdoms.

The boy bent nearer to the pool.

His hair tumbled over his shoulders and fell into the water. Gold coiled up through the curls and bit into his brain.

Voices filled his mind. Muscles convulsed as spawned viruses rewrote them, building new preconscious response circuitry, restructuring active symbols. He screamed and the sound shook the *welt*, his fingers bit into soil, and long-forgotten weapons throughout the rubble belt woke and warmed ancient vicious guns. Everything felt small, including his scream.

He had a purpose, and its purity felt too good to bear.

He pulled back from the water, and lay with his head in his hands on the ground, weeping. He made himself a cap, and covered his golden hair.

The iron man returned late in the day, and found him sobbing. He reached for the boy's shoulder, but the boy caught his wrist and squeezed. Another being would have felt pain. Another being might have broken.

The iron man pried the boy's fingers loose. "No more."

The boy looked at him. Fury and cold calculation lay beneath his fear, and there was gold in the pits of his eyes.

"I hoped," the iron man said. "If we could live together without you catching the bug, that would mean I—well. You can't stay here. The more it teaches you, the more it makes you want to learn. They built us very well, you see. It's easy to make people into things, or gods. Few people want to be people. You have to go if you want to live. Be poor somewhere. It's better than being this. Trust me. I've had practice."

"I'm sorry," the boy said. "It felt so good."

"It always does." The iron man tried, again, to touch the boy, and this time the boy let him. There was no give to the iron man's hand, no softness, no warmth. "Find a Kingdom, and remain yourself. I'll always be in the wood, if you need me."

The boy left that night.

❖　❖　❖

From her tower, the girl watched the new garden boy work. She'd watched him for months, since he walked in out of the wood, alone, shivering, a signal faint and tangled with encryption, begging sanctuary, which of course the Queen offered, because she was a good Queen. One never knew when one's stronghold might be taken, and one might find oneself lost and in the wood, dependent on the kindness of strangers. So they took refugees—everyone did, though seldom with the Queen's generosity.

But the girl was not so trusting as her mother, and the garden boy did not seem like just another refugee.

He moved slowly through the *welt*, but with a beautiful economy, savoring the ground, soaking in the simulated air, breathing sunlight. No wonder: the Queen had won a recent war, and the world was thick with texture. Such wealth! They rendered the Queen's scars, now, and the girl herself sported a blemish on her cheek. But even for a wanderer from the deepest wood, the garden boy seemed to appreciate the Kingdom's resolution a little too much.

Also strange: his efficiency! The garden boy tended pseudorganic solar collectors and synthesis substrata with millions of devices a few nanometers across, and he easily overmatched even the master gardener's synchronization levels, though he lacked her skill.

And he wore a cap wherever he went, and work gloves—even indoors.

Weird.

One afternoon she called to him from her tower: "Boy, bring me flowers."

When he entered the room, hands full, she reached out to knock off his cap. His left hand caught right in a grip tight enough to make her gasp, but her left hand passed his right and tipped the cap away. Gold hair cascaded to his shoulders, scintillating and brilliant, dripping with tangled computations.

"You're hurting me," she said.

He let her arm go, pulled back, and shrank into himself.

"You're not just a refugee gardener's boy."

"I am that," he said, "as much as I'm anything."

"You're something more," she said. "You've compressed yourself. You don't have to. Here." She took some golden discs from her dresser—vital cycles. "Use this. We have plenty."

But he left her, and later she saw the master gardener's children playing with the gold, creating balls that purred and small beasts to carry out their whims.

"You don't have to hide," she told him, when she found him tending harvesters near the south magnetic pole of her mother's Kingdom. "There's no honor in being humble."

"But there is danger in being great."

Not long after, there came another war. Two lesser Kingdoms seized a conjunction and a solar storm to attack at once. Knightminds guided sliverships through the void. The Queen rode out at her knights' head. The girl wanted to join her, but the Queen cautioned redundancy; we'll need you if this goes wrong. The garden boy wanted to join the knights, but they laughed at him, and because the girl was angry at having been told to stay behind, she did not caution the knights against laughing.

The knights left the garden boy no sliverships, no weapons, only an observation cloud with which to follow the action, if he wished. He did—off into the woods he went, puttering along barely conscious in the cloud.

The girl ran the Kingdom in her mother's absence, and marshaled its defenses, though if the Queen and her knights failed, there'd be little her pulse emplacements and force screens and virus storms could do against what followed. Still, every little bit helped.

At night, she listened to the battle, and thought about the garden boy's hair, and about the dangers of being great.

She heard the Queen win, through the microwave band, but did not know how, and could not ask until the fleet limped back, dragging harvested gold along. The girl peeled her mother away from the adoring crowds—still waving, the woman loved a show—and asked: "How did you win? Outnumbered, and that's before their reinforcements showed up. Poorly clustered—you should have taken me with you."

"We won," said the Queen, her voice round with simulated intoxicants. She looked gloriously real, flush with newly captured resolution—she stank of wine, and her robe was stained. "Isn't that enough?"

"Hardly."

"There were too many of them, like you say. But we were saved. A great power rode out of the wood. Sliverships. Snowflakes. Darters. A singularity furnace. They moved like an enormous school of fish. Everything our enemies tried, they anticipated. The newcomer took our enemies' minds apart, ejected them into the void and claimed what was left. I thought they might consume us next, but—they let us go."

The girl went to the garden, and sought the master gardener. "Where's your boy?"

"Sleeping," the master gardener replied. "I don't know what to think about that one. He puttered off in the observation cloud, and rode it back before the others got home. He said he was glad he'd gone, but wouldn't say any more, and he's been sleeping ever since."

She found him under the spreading branches of the old maple— the Queen's mother's mother's mother seventeen times back planted it in the center of the old Kingdom, in those days when the few survivors of the great old wars clustered in hollowed rocks, and every cycle was a treasured gift. Back then the rendered maple had been unfathomable in its profligacy—but there's more to life than life, the old Queen said. At least, that was how her daughters told the tale to theirs.

The garden boy slept in the cradle of the old maple's roots, curled around his gloved hand, his cap still on. She did not touch him. She watched. For the most part he looked soft, like her, like the rest of the Kingdom, well-rendered in victory. But his cheek did not look quite right where it pressed against the tree root, and his skin was beautiful, smooth, unbroken, almost like a shell.

"We'll find the one who saved us," she told her mother that night at dinner. "I have a plan."

The word went out the next day: the Queen, triumphant and flush, would hold a tournament. The girl would hurl a golden apple toward the sun, for any to catch who could. If the winner was a stranger knight, that person might be the one who'd saved them.

That's what the girl told her mother—but she watched the garden boy, and saw him disappear into the wood on the day of the tournament. So she was not surprised when, of all the knights who gathered to catch the golden apple that she threw toward the sun, a mysterious rider in a black slivership was the one to claim it. On the second day, they repeated the test, and this time a white slivership, likewise unknown, took the prize. Each night after the competition, wandering through the Kingdom, she found the gardener's children playing with spheres of gold.

On the third day, the girl set a trap. The mysterious rider that day wore fierce red, and raced ahead of all to catch the sphere—but the girl had told her knights where she would throw, and they lay in wait. A battle raged, but not for long. The girl noted the strange rider's efficiency of movement.

She met the garden boy when he returned from the wood. He was limping.

He tried to slouch away from her, to keep his head down, his hands in his pockets—especially the gloved hand. To keep his cap away.

"Why?" she asked.

He tried not to answer, but some deep compulsion seized him. When he looked up, golden lines stitched through his eyes. "Because there was a challenge in it," he said. "A problem to be solved. Mastery to gain." In the tower his voice had not been so hard. In the tower he had not sounded so much like a man who enjoyed the act of breaking. "Because winning is a habit that grows easier the more it's done."

"You don't want mastery," she said, and stepped toward him, and stared into his eyes beneath the gold.

"I do."

"Then why stop once you won the battle against our enemies? Why not kill the Queen, and all her knights, and come back here and seize the Kingdom for yourself?"

"I wanted to."

"No," she said. "A voice in your head whispered you should want to, but you did not. You have been made strong, but that strength is yours to use. It doesn't own you."

"It's inside me. I can't trust myself. How do I know what's me, and what's the gold?"

"Learn," she said. She reached out, slowly, and he did not stop her. She removed his cap. Gold spilled down over his shoulders.

"How?" he asked.

"For one thing," she said, "You can hurt. And I don't think it likes pain."

She touched his cheek, and pressed, and felt a shell beneath his skin crack. Her nails drew traces down his skin, and he did not look so perfect any more.

There were tears in his eyes, and they were not golden.

"Come," she said. "Meet my mother."

He stayed with them after that, and tended the garden, and sometimes rode beside the knights, when the need was great. But for the most part he lived, and grew, and stumbled, and often hurt.

One day a man came to the Kingdom from the wood. He leaned on a crooked stick as he walked, and he glowed with a luxury of ugliness. Dirt crusted beneath cracked nails; his teeth were gapped and his eyes yellow-red through their sclera, and many of his fingers had been broken several times.

The boy didn't recognize him, until he looked in his eyes and saw darkness without a fleck of gold. He hugged the iron man, and the iron man hugged him back, and in their embrace neither broke the other.

"Pain," said the iron man, wondering, though he was not iron now. "That took a long time to learn. Invulnerability's a hard curse to break."

"Come to the garden," said the boy who was not a boy any more. "We can watch the children play."

The End

Max Gladstone has been thrown from a horse in Mongolia and twice nominated for the John W. Campbell Best New Writer Award. Tor Books published *Last First Snow*, the fourth novel in Max's Craft Sequence (preceded by *Three Parts Dead*, *Two Serpents Rise*, and *Full Fathom Five*) in July 2015. Max's game *Choice of the Deathless* was nominated for the XYZZY Award, and his short fiction has appeared on *Tor.com* and in *Uncanny Magazine*.

IRON JOHN

by The Brothers Grimm, Tale #136, Alt Title: *Iron Hans*

There was once on a time a King who had a great forest near his palace, full of all kinds of wild animals. One day he sent out a huntsman to shoot him a roe, but he did not come back. "Perhaps some accident has befallen him," said the King, and the next day he sent out two more huntsmen who were to search for him, but they too stayed away. Then on the third day, he sent for all his huntsmen, and said, "Scour the whole forest through, and do not give up until ye have found all three." But of these also, none came home again, and of the pack of hounds which they had taken with them, none were seen more. From that time forth, no one would any longer venture into the forest, and it lay there in deep stillness and solitude, and nothing was seen of it, but sometimes an eagle or a hawk flying over it.

This lasted for many years, when a strange huntsman announced himself to the King as seeking a situation, and offered to go into the dangerous forest. The King, however, would not give his consent, and said, "It is not safe in there; I fear it would fare with thee no better than with the others, and thou wouldst never come out again." The huntsman replied, "Lord, I will venture it at my own risk, of fear I know nothing."

The huntsman therefore betook himself with his dog to the forest. It was not long before the dog fell in with some game on the way, and wanted to pursue it; but hardly had the dog run two steps when it stood before a deep pool, could go no farther, and a naked arm stretched itself out of the water, seized it, and drew it under, When the huntsman saw that, he went back and fetched three men to come with buckets and bale out the water. When they could see to the bottom there lay a wild man whose body was brown like rusty iron, and whose hair hung over his face down to his knees.

They bound him with cords, and led him away to the castle. There was great astonishment over the wild man; the King, however, had him put in an iron cage in his courtyard, and forbade the door to be opened on pain of death, and the Queen herself was to take the key into her keeping. And from this time forth every one could again go into the forest with safety.

The King had a son of eight years, who was once playing in the courtyard, and while he was playing, his golden ball fell into the cage. The boy ran thither and said, "Give me my ball out."

"Not till thou hast opened the door for me," answered the man.

"No," said the boy, "I will not do that; the King has forbidden it," and ran away.

The next day he again went and asked for his ball; the wild man said, "Open my door," but the boy would not.

On the third day the King had ridden out hunting, and the boy went once more and said, "I cannot open the door even if I wished, for I have not the key."

Then the wild man said, "It lies under thy mother's pillow, thou canst get it there."

The boy, who wanted to have his ball back, cast all thought to the winds, and brought the key. The door opened with difficulty, and the boy pinched his fingers. When it was open the wild man stepped out, gave him the golden ball, and hurried away.

The boy had become afraid; he called and cried after him, "Oh, wild man, do not go away, or I shall be beaten!" The wild man turned back, took him up, set him on his shoulder, and went with hasty steps into the forest.

When the King came home, he observed the empty cage, and asked the Queen how that had happened? She knew nothing about it, and sought the key, but it was gone. She called the boy, but no one answered. The King sent out people to seek for him in the fields, but they did not find him. Then he could easily guess what had happened, and much grief reigned in the royal court.

When the wild man had once more reached the dark forest, he took the boy down from his shoulder, and said to him, "Thou wilt never see thy father and mother again, but I will keep thee with me, for thou hast set me free, and I have compassion on thee. If thou dost all I bid thee, thou shalt fare well. Of treasure and gold have I enough, and more than anyone in the world."

He made a bed of moss for the boy on which he slept, and the next morning the man took him to a well, and said, "Behold, the gold well is as bright and clear as crystal, thou shalt sit beside it, and take care that nothing falls into it, or it will be polluted. I will come every evening to see if thou hast obeyed my order."

The boy placed himself by the margin of the well, and often saw a golden fish or a golden snake show itself therein, and took care that nothing fell in. As he was thus sitting, his finger hurt him so violently that he involuntarily put it in the water. He drew it quickly out again, but saw that it was quite gilded, and whatsoever pains he took to wash the gold off again, all was to no purpose.

In the evening Iron John came back, looked at the boy, and said, "What has happened to the well?"

"Nothing, nothing," he answered, and held his finger behind his back, that the man might not see it.

But he said, "Thou hast dipped thy finger into the water, this time it may pass, but take care thou dost not again let anything go in."

By daybreak the boy was already sitting by the well and watching it. His finger hurt him again and he passed it over his head, and then unhappily a hair fell down into the well. He took it quickly out, but it was already quite gilded. Iron John came, and already knew what had happened. "Thou hast let a hair fall into the well," said he. "I will allow thee to watch by it once more, but if this happens for the third time then the well is polluted, and thou canst no longer remain with me."

On the third day, the boy sat by the well, and did not stir his finger, however much it hurt him. But the time was long to him, and he looked at the reflection of his face on the surface of the water. And as he still bent down more and more while he was doing so, and trying to look straight into the eyes, his long hair fell down from his shoulders into the water. He raised himself up quickly, but the whole of the hair of his head was already golden and shone like the sun. You may imagine how terrified the poor boy was! He took his pocket-handkerchief and tied it round his head, in order that the man might not see it.

When he came he already knew everything, and said, "Take the handkerchief off." Then the golden hair streamed forth, and let the boy excuse himself as he might, it was of no use. "Thou hast not stood the trial, and canst stay here no longer. Go forth into the world, there thou wilt learn what poverty is. But as thou hast not a bad heart, and as I mean well by thee, there is one thing I will grant thee; if thou fallest into any difficulty, come to the forest and cry, 'Iron John,' and then I will come and help thee. My power is great, greater than thou thinkest, and I have gold and silver in abundance."

Then the King's son left the forest, and walked by beaten and unbeaten paths ever onwards until at length he reached a great city. There he looked for work, but could find none, and he had learnt nothing by which he could help himself. At length he went to the palace, and asked if they would take him in. The people about court did not at all know what use they could make of him, but they liked him, and told him to stay. At length the cook took him into his service, and said he might carry wood and water, and rake the cinders together.

Once when it so happened that no one else was at hand, the cook ordered him to carry the food to the royal table, but as he did not like to let his golden hair be seen, he kept his little cap on. Such a thing as that had never yet come under the King's notice, and he said, "When thou comest to the royal table thou must take thy hat off."

He answered, "Ah, Lord, I cannot; I have a bad sore place on my head." Then the King had the cook called before him and scolded him, and asked how he could take such a boy as that into his service; and that he was to turn him off at once. The cook, however, had pity on him, and exchanged him for the gardener's boy.

And now the boy had to plant and water the garden, hoe and dig, and bear the wind and bad weather. Once in summer when he was working alone in the garden, the day was so warm he took his little cap off that the air might cool him. As the sun shone on his hair it glittered and flashed so that the rays fell into the bedroom of the King's daughter, and up she sprang to see what that could be.

Then she saw the boy, and cried to him, "Boy, bring me a wreath of flowers."

He put his cap on with all haste, and gathered wild field-flowers and bound them together.

When he was ascending the stairs with them, the gardener met him, and said, "How canst thou take the King's daughter a garland of such common flowers? Go quickly, and get another, and seek out the prettiest and rarest."

"Oh, no," replied the boy, "the wild ones have more scent, and will please her better."

When he got into the room, the King's daughter said, "Take thy cap off, it is not seemly to keep it on in my presence."

He again said, "I may not, I have a sore head."

She, however, caught at his cap and pulled it off, and then his golden hair rolled down on his shoulders, and it was splendid to behold. He wanted to run out, but she held him by the arm, and gave him a handful of ducats. With these he departed, but he cared nothing for the gold pieces. He took them to the gardener, and said, "I present them to thy children, they can play with them."

The following day the King's daughter again called to him that he was to bring her a wreath of field-flowers, and when he went in with it, she instantly snatched at his cap, and wanted to take it away from him, but he held it fast with both hands. She again gave him a handful of ducats, but he would not keep them, and gave them to the gardener for playthings for his children. On the third day things went just the same; she could not get his cap away from him, and he would not have her money.

Not long afterwards, the country was overrun by war. The King gathered together his people, and did not know whether or not he could offer any opposition to the enemy, who was superior in strength and had a mighty army.

Then said the gardener's boy, "I am grown up, and will go to the wars also, only give me a horse."

The others laughed, and said, "Seek one for thyself when we are gone, we will leave one behind us in the stable for thee."

When they had gone forth, he went into the stable, and got the horse out; it was lame of one foot, and limped hobblety jig, hob-blety jig; nevertheless he mounted it, and rode away to the dark forest. When he came to the outskirts, he called "Iron John," three times so loudly that it echoed through the trees.

Thereupon the wild man appeared immediately, and said, "What dost thou desire?"

"I want a strong steed, for I am going to the wars."

"That thou shalt have, and still more than thou askest for."

Then the wild man went back into the forest, and it was not long before a stableboy came out of it, who led a horse that snorted with its nostrils, and could hardly be restrained, and behind them followed a great troop of soldiers entirely equipped in iron, and their swords flashed in the sun.

The youth made over his three-legged horse to the stableboy, mounted the other, and rode at the head of the soldiers. When he got near the battlefield a great part of the King's men had already fallen, and little was wanting to make the rest give way. Then the youth galloped thither with his iron soldiers, broke like a hurricane over the enemy, and beat down all who opposed him.

They began to fly, but the youth pursued, and never stopped, until there was not a single man left. Instead, however, of returning to the King, he conducted his troop by byways back to the forest, and called forth Iron John.

"What dost thou desire?" asked the wild man.

"Take back thy horse and thy troops, and give me my three-legged horse again." All that he asked was done, and soon he was riding on his three-legged horse.

When the King returned to his palace, his daughter went to meet him, and wished him joy of his victory. "I am not the one who carried away the victory," said he, "but a stranger knight who came to my assistance with his soldiers."

The daughter wanted to hear who the strange knight was, but the King did not know, and said, "He followed the enemy, and I did not see him again."

She inquired of the gardener where his boy was, but he smiled, and said, "He has just come home on his three-legged horse, and the others have been mocking him, and crying, "Here comes our hobblety jig back again!" They asked, too, "Under what hedge hast thou been lying sleeping all the time?" He, however, said, "I did the best of all, and it would have gone badly without me." And then he was still more ridiculed."

The King said to his daughter, "I will proclaim a great feast that shall last for three days, and thou shalt throw a golden apple. Perhaps the unknown will come to it."

When the feast was announced, the youth went out to the forest, and called Iron John.

"What dost thou desire?" asked he.

"That I may catch the King's daughter's golden apple."

"It is as safe as if thou hadst it already," said Iron John. "Thou shalt likewise have a suit of red armor for the occasion, and ride on a spirited chestnut-horse."

When the day came, the youth galloped to the spot, took his place amongst the knights, and was recognized by no one. The King's daughter came forward, and threw a golden apple to the knights, but none of them caught it but he, only as soon as he had it he galloped away.

On the second day Iron John equipped him as a white knight, and gave him a white horse. Again he was the only one who caught the apple, and he did not linger an instant, but galloped off with it.

The King grew angry, and said, "That is not allowed; he must appear before me and tell his name." He gave the order that if the knight who caught the apple, should go away again they should pursue him, and if he would not come back willingly, they were to cut him down and stab him.

On the third day, he received from Iron John a suit of black armor and a black horse, and again he caught the apple. But when he was riding off with it, the King's attendants pursued him, and one of them got so near him that he wounded the youth's leg with the point of his sword. The youth nevertheless escaped from them, but his horse leapt so violently that the helmet fell from the youth's head, and they could see that he had golden hair. They rode back and announced this to the King.

The following day the King's daughter asked the gardener about his boy. "He is at work in the garden; the queer creature has been at the festival too, and only came home yesterday evening; he has likewise shown my children three golden apples which he has won."

The King had him summoned into his presence, and he came and again had his little cap on his head. But the King's daughter went up to him and took it off, and then his golden hair fell down over his shoulders, and he was so handsome that all were amazed.

"Art thou the knight who came every day to the festival, always in different colors, and who caught the three golden apples?" asked the King.

"Yes," answered he, "and here the apples are," and he took them out of his pocket, and returned them to the King. "If you desire further proof, you may see the wound which your people gave me when they followed me. But I am likewise the knight who helped you to your victory over your enemies."

"If thou canst perform such deeds as that, thou art no gardener's boy; tell me, who is thy father?"

"My father is a mighty King, and gold have I in plenty as great as I require."

"I well see," said the King, "that I owe thanks to thee; can I do anything to please thee?"

"Yes," answered he, "that indeed you can. Give me your daughter to wife."

The maiden laughed, and said, "He does not stand much on ceremony, but I have already seen by his golden hair that he was no gardener's boy," and then she went and kissed him.

His father and mother came to the wedding, and were in great delight, for they had given up all hope of ever seeing their dear son again. And as they were sitting at the marriage-feast, the music suddenly stopped, the doors opened, and a stately King came in with a great retinue.

He went up to the youth, embraced him and said, "I am Iron John, and was by enchantment a wild man, but thou hast set me free; all the treasures which I possess, shall be thy property."

The End

ZEL AND GRETS

by Maura McHugh

based upon *Hansel & Gretel*

Brother and sister, they said, but Zel and me never knew if we shared DNA or just the same buy date. We don't look much alike: Zel with his big brown head and useless legs, and me with my chameleon skin and reptile eyes. DaMa, our guardian, called us "my fav failed experiments" on good days when we met our quota, and "industrial waste" when we slinked back to the ship without enough creds to cover our costs.

"Fuel, air, food, and bribes," DaMa would chant as they went through our takings after a day of begging or thieving among the mud-heads of whatever planet we were passing through. We'd be gathered in the hold of the *The Ragged Rest* (or *The Rest* as we called it), the only space on the ship where us kids and DaMa could assemble without banging elbows. DaMa would tot up our pickings: credit skimmed from interfaces, jewelry snagged, wallets robbed, and even wads of cash or clinking coin nabbed on the more backward dirtballs. We all made sure to cover fuel and air. After that you went without food. Better hungry than chucked the next time the *The Rest* had to skip to richer landfall.

And each of us had a timeline with an end point. "Old faces don't pull credit," DaMa would repeat to us, regular. So we took the blockers they gave us once we hit ten, and remained baby-faced. Zel and me were DaMa's one-off *freak duo*: the deformed kid and the splice that won the sympathy creds. Normally DaMa went for winsome urchins who could play adorable to saps while robbing them blind at the same time.

We'd always worked as a team, even in that hazy time before DaMa brought us on board. Zel had the smarts, figuring out the best patch, talking sad but clever to the marks, and me as the picker, blending in and slipping away before the rubes knew they'd been had. But he didn't like me risking being snapped by a drone or droid camera, because in that scenario DaMa would run their deadend program, and wipe us from their fosterage list.

"Bring the heat, and my backups won't even remember who you are," they always warned us.

"We have to start being strategic, Grets," Zel said one time when we turned thirteen—he was always talking like a gray-face. He built a small reader, and programmed it to bypass weak security protocols on open credit chips and pretend to be a lowly drinks kiosk. Then we'd pass by people in the street and randomly shave a few credits from their cards or body chips.

"It's a small amount paid to what looks like a legitimate company. No one notices. We need fifty scans a day, and I don't forget faces so we won't double-dip. You'll be safer."

I placed my hand on the pavement and matched my skin perfectly to mimic the concrete. I looked up and gave him my best basilisk stare: he didn't flinch or look sideways like some people did. "I'm good at it. I don't ask you to be thick, like me."

He grabbed my arm, and scowled. "You're not stupid!" I shrugged and examined the crowd passing us by, acting liked I cared less. He pointed to his banged up hoverchair that I had to direct because of its shot steering. "How would I get anywhere without you? I'm protecting my driver."

I grinned. "We're a mutually beneficial team." That's what DaMa used to say after they'd taken a few tokes and was feeling kindly toward us.

Zel grimaced at the reference, but started talking about projected earnings, and using a two-card system so that once we made DaMa's quota, we could save our own money. "For when the time comes," he finished.

"Let's move on," I said, springing up and pushing Zel's chair out into the stream of people on the street. I didn't want to hear what Zel was saying. Sixteen. That was the usual age when DaMa pushed you out. One day you just wouldn't return to the ship, and DaMa would act phony hurt and outraged. They'd always be a woman on that occasion to amp up the grieving mother act.

"No message, no warning!" DaMa had wailed when Cray and Robs never came back when we were on Nuevo Madrid. "After all I did for them." Then they'd introduce us to the replacements, and we had to hear the routine about how we were a family that looked out for each other, and how hard DaMa worked to feed us and keep us out of institutions or away from pervs, so our contribution to our upkeep and opportunities was only fair.

"I've calculated that DaMa makes 100,000 credits clear profit from us every year," Zel said one time, when we lay in our tiny cabin. Our roommates Tiller and Jons were already asleep—they were old enough to avail of DaMa's puff (at an extra cost, of course) and it knocked them out at night.

"And DaMa stays on this shitbucket dragging our scrawny arses around the system?!"

"They're investing it," Zel replied, quietly.

I peered over the edge of my bunk, and looked down at him. Light from the holoscreen floating above his face shimmered over his long forehead and wide nose. "How do you know?"

"I'm friends with Isaac."

"You once said that AI was…(I hunted for the fancy word he'd used)…antediluvian!"

There was a hiss of air through the vent above my head, and Zel cast a meaningful gaze upwards to remind me in whose belly we rested. "Isaac's not *smart, smart*, but its navigation is robust and dependable. I'm the only one that bothers communicating with it other than in orders. It deserves respect."

The corresponding rumble in the walls was almost like a cat purring.

"If DaMa susses you're sweet-talking her ship's brain to dig out their secrets, they'll space you."

Zel put on his superior face, and said. "DaMa won't find out."

Over time Zel made himself more useful in different ways to DaMa—running diagnostics on Isaac, programming routes between planets that were least likely to be stopped by Interplanetary Customs, and over time, even suggesting market advice for investments. I knew that Zel was playing all angles to keep DaMa sweet on us. It worked. DaMa even let us off a couple of times when we came up short on our quota.

So we were still on the ship and edging into seventeen, but looking twelve, when DaMa got high one night and went on a gambling spree.

We found out about it when DaMa shook me awake, their eyes wide and bloodshot, and sweat dripping off their male face. They kept their voice low, but a chainsaw fury chewed through their words. "Bring your egghead brother up to my cabin *right now!*" They departed as quickly as they appeared.

I woke up Zel. "Hey, Babybird. The boss wants an audience." I'd put on my harness, and turned to present the carrier for Zel to climb into. It was easier to hoof through the small passages and doorways of *The Rest* with him on my back.

While I booked it through the dimmed, snoozing ship Zel logged into Isaac via his collarlink to find out what happened.

I heard him swear softly as we arrived at DaMa's cabin. That's when I got nervous. Zel always spoke properly and never cussed.

DaMa was pacing up and down their room, their kimono swirling, when Isaac opened the door to let us in.

They stopped and glared at Zel. "Is it as bad as I suspect?"

"We just woke up—" I began, but they cut me off.

"I know he's chummy with Isaac." Their voice rose suddenly like a ship ripping through atmosphere. "I'm not *stupid* you little cunt. Think I haven't been monitoring his usage? There's no trick you can try that some other jumped-up shit hasn't pulled before."

"You've lost everything," Zel said.

I tried to turn my head to see his expression and keep DaMa in view. They was clenching and unclenching their fists. I noticed the vials and puff inhalers scattered around the room. Normally they kept their habit under control. Not this time.

"You've got a few assets you can liquidate, and over time, with judicious trading, you could build up your portfolio again."

DaMa had dropped onto the end of their bed at this.

I tried not to breathe too loud, and did my best to beam the thought at Zel to stay silent.

Unfortunately, we definitely don't share the telepathic geneset.

"Your mistake was to double-down when you make the first big loss, ideally you should have—"

"I should have dumped you two mutants years ago! That's what." Their voice rose to a shriek. "*Get out!* And don't bother connecting to Isaac. Your privileges are over."

I backed out of the room quickly, and the door whooshed closed so fast it almost bit my nose.

I didn't move. Zel's trembling vibrated along the straps of the harness. We knew what was coming now.

There was a judder and I stumbled. *The Rest*'s thrusters fired. We were changing direction.

Zel whispered. "Maybe, once they calm down, I can suggest a smarter, safer investment path."

I closed my eyes, and wished whispering helped. It was easy to forget that everything we did on this ship could be watched and recorded. A heavy despair settled on me, and for the first time Zel's weight seemed too much for my shoulders to bear.

We landed on Forest, one of those tech-restricted worlds where the citizens like an old-timey vibe. We'd been here once before during its annual festival, and the pickings had been poor for our team. I'm too weird for the locals—some of them are too curious, and often for nasty reasons. It's illegal to create a splice on Forest, so other than in stories most of them have never seen my kind. I can change my skin and hair to blend in with whatever passes for normal on this world, but I can't change my eyes. And people are suspicious of kids with shades or a hood pulled over their head.

And everyone has advice on how Zel's legs could be improved. It's awful for Zel to hear endless suggestions from people who have families and jobs and can save up for advanced reconstruction. Plus, he'd done the research on all the procedures available by the time he was six. By seven, he'd learned to stop asking DaMa to have him assessed when they pointed out it would be easier to vent him into space and replace him with a waif who could walk.

We lined up with DaMa outside *The Rest* in the basic facilities that passed as a dock on Forest. Security did the usual scans, and queried DaMa on our presence. DaMa trotted out their shtick about cultural understanding through travel. They had already deposited their bribe to the local bigwig prior to our arrival, so it was just posturing.

After the goons left, DaMa gathered us together for a final prep. They spoke with a disruptor running so no listening devices could record what they said. Never misses a trick, does DaMa.

"The quota has been doubled," DaMa began, their woman's face stern. A murmur of dissent rippled among us, but they spoke over the complaints. "*The Rest*'s engines have developed a glitch, and it needs a new part. That costs creds. Without *The Rest*, where would we be?"

Surly silence was our response, but DaMa acted as if this was a teaching moment.

"Marooned and in custody," they finished. "There's a big market in Timber today, so bring along your crafts." They nodded at Tiller, "Get the gear to set up a pitch, I've booked us a spot in their meeting hall."

For a moment I cheered up. We all had to hand-make crafts on board—beaded jewelry, macramé knick-knacks, paintings, whatever we liked. It's nuts: people can have anything replicated, and yet they place value on baubles made by a bunch of grubby kids. It kept the younger ones occupied, and it was part of DaMa's cover that we were a nomad family of artisans. I always pretended it was a chore, but I loved making and modifying jewelry. And whenever we fenced our crafts, mine always fetched good prices. I had a decent chance of meeting DaMa's new quota, especially on Forest, which put a high value on handcrafted trinkets, especially from off-planet.

Then they swiveled to glance at Zel and me. "You mutts are with me. I'm taking you to a town where your unique skills will be at their best advantage."

My stomach clenched, and I clocked the sideways glances. Our friends shuffled a few steps away from us as if we were infectious.

"And leave the hoverchair, it'll be easier for you to carry Zel where we're going."

I could feel a furious blush rising in my cheeks and changed the color range across my face to compensate. Zel hated being carried outside. The hoverchair was his independence, even if it was in lousy nick. I imagined DaMa had it earmarked for salvage.

I ducked back into the ship to collect the harness from our room, and I shoved a few of my nicest pieces of jewelry into my satchel. On the way out I scavenged some food from the galley, along with a canteen of water.

I paused in the empty room to look around. The wheezy aircon was as familiar to me as my own breath. *The Rest* was the only home I remembered. I knew every dent and bulge in its structure, and had even added a couple of knocks to it. A wave of grief crashed into my heart and threatened to smash me to the floor. Tears burned my eyes.

I sucked in a deep breath and said goodbye. I vowed Zel and me would make a better home together.

When I emerged everyone else had split except DaMa and Zel. DaMa was bending over Zel and talking intensely. I marched over to interrupt, but DaMa swung upright, and gave Zel and me one of their charming smiles.

"We're going for a ride," they said.

❖   ❖   ❖

The vehicle DaMa hired was an old-fashioned, sturdy hover with a canopy made of clear plastic and glass so you got panoramic views. Once we left the city we sped along a sweep of highway arcing towards one of the massive forests that gave the planet its name. It was all green fields, farm buildings, and a violet sky with masses of clouds. The *space* made me dizzy. I looked up and thought I was going to fall *up* into the sky.

I nailed my gaze to my knees until the road took us into a bank of trees. With the wall of swaying emerald and jade leaves on both sides I felt less light-headed, and began to listen to the information Zel was spraying about the planet.

He was nervous, so his way to cope was to repeat all the facts he remembered about Forest. He never forgot anything, so it was a lot. He talked about the initial survey and how the planet had come under the protection as a world of outstanding natural beauty. In other words it didn't have the exploitable resources the major industrial corps wanted, so settlers who prized good land and a dull place to raise boring families flocked here.

DaMa sat up front with the controls, not that they needed to do much as even that relic had auto-pilot.

"Where are we going?" I asked, finally. There was only so much I could take of Zel listing different types of trees, or droning on about the logging business and woodcrafting which were the planet's most famous exports.

"We're going to have a picnic," DaMa replied, patting a box on the seat beside them.

I raised an eyebrow at Zel.

"It's a thing that planet-based people do: eat outside."

I grimaced. "With bugs and dirt all around? Yuck! If you want to treat me, turn around and find the nearest noodle bar."

DaMa laughed.

A short while later we turned off the main drag and onto a smaller trail. A sign declared it was Evergreen Park, and we should "Leave It as You Find It." DaMa took a number of quick lefts and rights onto smaller roads until the trees pressed tight and the sky was a thin strip above us.

They slowed down the hover as we approached a clearing with a number of wooden benches and tables scattered about. "You have reached your destination," the hover informed us in its solemn voice.

I climbed out, walked to the other side of the hover, and crouched so Zel could swing himself into the carrier on my back.

"No one's about," I said to him cheerfully. It was meant as a comfort, since no one would spot him being carried, but as soon as the words left my mouth they sounded like a warning.

DaMa opened their container on the table in the center, and in it was a variety of colored, lacquer food boxes. Not the cheap tins we were used to onboard. I deposited Zel onto a bench, and sat beside him. I noticed that all the woodwork was of high quality. Tree motifs and images of animals were carved into the surfaces. Care had been lavished on these lonely pieces of outdoor furniture. More than had ever been shown to Zel and me.

DaMa placed a can of beer in front of each of us, and pressed the reheat button on all the boxes. Within thirty seconds they had opened and fragrant spices wafted up. There was rice, curried lentils, and even a sticky cake.

"What's the occasion?" I asked, shoving my elbow into my rumbling stomach. I hadn't seen food this appetizing in several cycles.

"I used to live on a planet like this, when I was a child," DaMa said. "My father used to bring me fishing. Just the two of us. We'd eat on a blanket spread out beside the river. It was nice."

DaMa took a swig of the beer and glanced about at the view. "I don't get to do this much anymore." They looked at us significantly. "Too many responsibilities."

We ate in silence for a while. I only took a couple of sips of the beer. It was hardly my first time, but I didn't want to get stupid-headed out in the wilds. There were unfamiliar noises all around, some of which I took to be birds or animals, but others I couldn't identify. The air was brisk, and came in unpredictable gusts. There were so many different smells it made my head hurt. I tried not to keep looking about, but I had watched enough vids to know that savage creatures lived in desolate places like this, and I might be considered a meal.

And monsters. Bizarre life forms existed on some worlds. Others were cooked up in labs. What lurked out here?

I gobbled the food quickly, out of habit.

DaMa raised their can of beer. "Happy emancipation," they said.

I frowned and glanced at Zel.

"You're seventeen now," DaMa explained. "You're free to make your own way in the worlds."

A bolt of fear caused my full stomach to clench. I clamped my jaw shut, refusing to spew in front of DaMa.

"My guardianship has terminated. Your chips have been re-written to indicate your free status." DaMa took another sip of beer. "There seems to have been some bug however, and it's scrambled your flight history. I'm sorry to say your records have been wiped."

A dreadful lethargy gripped me. My eyelids were so heavy I couldn't keep them open. At the same time DaMa's words no longer elicited any fear. I only felt a mild wonder at what this would mean for Zel and me.

The world retreated into a fuzzy dream-like quality. I had a vague sense of DaMa tidying up, and of them touching my neck, along with a dull pain. Then I dropped my forehead upon the much-loved wood, and dreamed of sleeping in my old bunk on *The Rest*.

❖   ❖   ❖

I awoke to cold, twilight, and terror. Zel's head lay upon the table near me, and he snored a little. The noises around us seemed louder, and different. The giant trees loomed above us, their branches swaying and sighing. Within their shadowed realm anything could be watching.

I sat upright and looked about, desperate. The hover was gone. I touched my neck, and withdrew it at the raw pain. My marks had been modified. DaMa had been thorough. But they had plenty of practice, I realized.

I concentrated and the skin on both of my hands became iridescent in the low light. We would not have to endure total darkness. I shook Zel awake carefully.

I checked him out as he woke up groggy. He seemed more affected by whatever drug DaMa had dosed us with. But that happened sometimes. Once he'd gone into shock from a mild sedative he'd been given when he'd broken his wrist. Our body chemistries were quite different. I was built tough. For Zel, it was as if his body had been an afterthought, with all the attention been given to designing his brain.

"You were never meant to live," DaMa said to us once, when I complained to them about how they treated me and Zel. "You should thank me *every day* for taking you away from that *home* you'd been in. Damn my sentimental side for rescuing such mutant ingrates!"

"They hardly *rescued* us," Zel said later, enigmatically. I knew Zel didn't forget anything, but I often wondered how far back his memory went. I didn't chase any of the muddy images of my earliest memories. What use was past pain when I had current pain to occupy me?

It was almost full dark by the time Zel was coherent. Above us stretched a dazzling array of stars. They mesmerized me…when I wasn't seized with that terrifying sensation of *falling up* into the night sky's vastness.

A variety of insects were attracted to my shining hands—I choked back my desire to scream every time their wings brushed my skin. Instead, I attempted to replicate some of their patterns on my skin in a spectrum of colors to distract me. I imagined making necklaces based on their designs.

"DaMa's gone?" Zel managed, finally.

I nodded, and then realized he would hardly see that. "Yes."

"At least we're alive," he said, his voice flat.

"DaMa might be a deadbeat guardian, but they wouldn't kill any of us…"

"I gave them all our savings," Zel said.

"We have nothing?"

His eyes gleamed in the light of my skin's radiance. "We have each other. That's all we ever really had."

I placed my shining hand over his long fingers, and squeezed.

❖   ❖   ❖

We spent the long night huddled under a table. At one point we heard a large creature shove its way through the undergrowth nearby, so I dimmed my hands and allowed total darkness to engulf us. We held each other tight, to reassure ourselves that we existed in the blackness.

I thought of the stars above us and pretended they were the glowing indicators of a screen in a ship we were traveling in, and that lie eased me. As long as I imagined limits I found the dark bearable.

An uplifting barrage of birdsong signaled the peach and pink sunrise. As much as I like to disdain living on a planet, even I had to admit that it had some perks.

We shared the water sparingly, but we only had a quarter of a canteen left. We ate a few cubes of the protein blocks I had snuck off *The Rest*. I tried not to imagine our old mates cracking jokes over breakfast on *The Rest*, while meeting our replacements.

Both of us were used to going hungry, but the lack of water was a problem. During this time no one had arrived at our picnic spot.

"Do you recognize this area?" I asked Zel, hoping he had memorized something useful, like terrain maps.

He shook his head. "I didn't have access before we landed. I've no idea where we are or what's nearby."

That dizzying, terrifying sense of being disconnected from data and ship, while being exposed to a huge, open sky struck me again like a blow. Zel put his hand on my back. Only he could read me this easily.

"Is this what they always did?" I whispered. "Leave our friends to starve and die?"

Zel shrugged and made light circles between my shoulder blades with his hand. "Remember how we never talked about anyone once they left *The Rest*?"

I nodded. "They might as well have croaked. We erased them." The tears came then, but I refused to howl. I bent over and lowered my head so the tears splashed onto the carving of an owl looking up at me from the table. I only knew what it was from a spelling vid years ago. "O is for Owl."

"What good are we for anything?" My voice hitched. "We've no skills, no money, and on this tree-infested dirtball I'm pretty much illegal."

"They have a welfare system. We will be…processed."

I sat upright and wiped the tears away, anger replacing fear. That was an emotion I could *use*. "By all standards we're adults, even if we look younger. And what happens once we're off the drugs?"

"A growth spurt. Puberty?"

I pulled a face. "Ugh." I fed the fire of fury. "How could they do this to us?"

"We served our usefulness. Now…"

"We're food for monsters!"

Then I noticed the creases of anxiety around his big eyes, and I cursed myself for my selfishness.

I got up, slung my satchel across my body, and picked up the harness. "We need to move."

"But, someone might come…"

I saw in him a desperate fear that eclipsed my own.

"What did you tell me once about some law? 'For every action there is an equal and opposite reaction?' Well, DaMa dumped us, so we have to react. And sitting around waiting for someone to rescue us isn't action. It's giving up."

I turned my back and hunkered down so he could get into the harness. "And one day…DaMa is going to *pay* for leaving us like this. And for every other kid they left alone and afraid."

Behind me branches cracked, and there was a bellow. I risked a quick glance as I felt Zel jump into the harness.

Something huge, fuzzy, and with horns like skeletal wings sticking out of its head stepped into the clearing.

I made a break for it, sprinting in the opposite direction, with Zel bumping against my back. A sudden terrible thought that Zel would be most vulnerable to attack while stuck in the harness lent my feet a burst of energy. I dashed into the tree cover and kept running while imagining a host of fierce creatures and beasts clawing at us.

Leaves slapped me in the face as I stumbled through the forest, nearly tripping several times from the thick roots that boiled up from the earth. Light penetrated in slanted shafts, so I scrambled from one column to another, hoping they would lead me to an open place, devoid of animals.

"Stop, stop!" Zel cried, and eventually the words penetrated my panic.

I careened into a tree, and halted. I leaned against its rough bark for support, and heaved in big lungfuls of air.

"Did. It. Follow us?" I panted.

"No, I think it was as surprised as us."

A calm reasserted itself as the adrenaline wore off, followed by total exhaustion.

"Sorry, I have to sit," I muttered and sank to my knees and heels in the damp soil. Zel remained on my back, his thin legs splayed across dead leaves.

"They're called moose," Zel said eventually. "They're herbivores. They don't eat people."

"Doesn't mean they can't hurt us! Did you see those horns?"

"Antlers," he corrected. "And they use them to fight, but only in mating season."

"Well, next time we encounter a beast I've never seen before I'll be sure to check with you if it's going to attack or just lick our faces!"

"You didn't know, but now you do," he said in a placating tone. That familiar phrase irritated me even more.

"Thanks for the lesson, professor." I heaved myself upright and began marching forward.

"Where are you going?"

"I've no idea," I snapped. And this time he knew better than to comment.

❖　　❖　　❖

By the second day we were dehydrated and out of food. We found respite by drinking water collected as thin pools in the hollow of wide glossy leaves. A few times we spotted nuts, but we didn't know if they were edible. We rarely ate food that wasn't processed for space-flight transport.

We noticed a clump of plants with curved scarlet tops and thick stems that sprouted from one foul-smelling spot.

"They're mushrooms," Zel said. "Some of them are edible, while others are poisonous." I edged closer, and noticed a gleaming bone poking out from between them.

"Let's leave them alone."

"Good idea. Some plants and fungi can paralyze you just from skin contact."

Zel kept up a constant stream of facts like that which were prompted by things we passed. Mostly, it reminded me of how little I knew, and how much in the world was dangerous.

Over time I plodded through the trees focused on putting one foot in front of the other, and managed to block out his words completely. By the evening of the second day, my thoughts were muted, and my body lumbered forward out of habit rather than conscious prodding.

So, it took me a while to notice Zel yelling at me to halt.

I lurched to a stop, and blinked slowly. We were in a circular clearing. Ahead of us was a colorful flower garden, leading up to a small building that looked like it had been carved out of a trunk of a giant tree that had been felled ages ago. Its top was covered with soft green plants. A ribbon of smoke slipped from a stone pillar at the top. A few sheds were visible at the back of the house.

"We should ask for help," Zel said, his voice cracked.

A flicker of hope sparked, and I ambled up to the building. Thick green vines were hooked into the twisting runnels of bark that made up the walls, and from them small twigs grew. Upon them hung berries of all colors and shapes: fat, sparkling red globes, beside green shiny clusters, along with rich purple beads drooping heavily. A sweet, come-hither perfume wafted up from them, and prompted a gush of saliva in my dry mouth.

Without thinking I picked some and mashed them into my mouth. They popped under my teeth, releasing tart and honeyed juices. I angled sideways to the wall so Zel could pick as he liked. I moved steadily plucking the vines, and for some time the only sounds was the slurp and smack as we gorged on the fruit.

I heard the "Ouch!" and felt Zel jerk at the same time. A moment later my thumb snagged on one of the vicious thorns dotted along the vines. The scrape on my finger began to close, as it usually did.

"You okay?" I queried.

"Hmm hmm," he said, in the tone of *I don't want to be a baby about a cut*. I figured he was sucking on his finger to ease the sting.

The sudden dose of sugar and water hit me like a starlight jet, and for the first time in days I felt wide-eyed and capable of figuring out our next move.

"We should knock on the door," I said.

I heard a small grunt in agreement from Zel, and trundled to the sky blue door, which had carvings of fruit and berries all over it. A sculpture of an apple made from bronze hung underneath a semi-circle of opaque glass. I touched its warm surface, and realized it could be used to swing back and hammer on the door. So I hit the door with it. And stepped back.

After a few moments the door creaked open and a tall, elderly man, wearing spectacles and all-white clothes opened the door. His wrinkled skin was heavily bronzed as if he was stupid enough to expose his skin to the sun's radiation without protection. His tuft of bleached hair scraped the top of the doorway and he was slouched as if he lived in world where everything was made a little too small for his height.

"The fruit thieves are owning up," he remarked.

I wiped at my chin, and realized it was sticky. "Um, yes, we're lost. And we haven't eaten or drank in a couple of days."

He craned his neck slightly to get a look at Zel. "The boy is asleep," he stated.

"He is?" I twisted a bit, and noticed Zel's head was tipped back, and his eyelids closed.

"I don't see the likes of you on Forest very often. He reached forward and put his hand over my wrist.

Startled, my skin matched his pale color instantly. I tried to shake off his grasp but it was surprisingly firm. He peered down at me; his scrutiny was like a mechanic sizing up an unusual engine.

"Reactive, chameleon skin, elliptical pupils...are they purely cosmetic or can you rotate your eyes independently? Can you see ultraviolet?"

I broke his grip and stepped back. I was already scoping out the quickest route back to the tree line.

He chuckled, an apologetic, friendly sound. "Pardon me, young miss," he said. "My manners. I haven't had to bother with them for some time. I'm a solitary fellow. A retired biologist. And on this planet…," he shrugged. "There's not much by way of lively conversation with the locals."

He executed a bow combined with a flourish of his arm. "Dr. Montgomery at your service. It's a pleasure to encounter such a unique person on such a humdrum world."

I wavered between flight and sudden warmth at his compliment. On many worlds I was an oddity, and on a few I was commonplace, but I had never been told I was unique. Or rarely treated like a person.

"Pray, enter, and tell me how you washed upon my lonely shore."

He stepped into the large room beyond and held the door wide open. I hesitated and waited for feedback from Zel. Instead I got a snore.

"Thanks," I said, and entered. It was a mish-mash of antique pieces beside modern appliances. There was an open fire burning in a brick enclosure. It was such a primitive, wasteful use of energy I guessed the man had to be loaded. Only wealthy people could afford to be so backward.

The doctor looked up and said, "Jean, please recognize…," he paused, and checked me, "I'm sorry, I never caught your name."

"I'm Grets, and this is my brother Zel."

He continued, "Please recognize Grets and Zel as our visitors, with all the usual access."

A warm, kind voice responded, "Of course, Lawrence."

"That's my housekeeper, Jean," he explained.

"Your house has a brain?"

The doctor coughed in a way that made me think he was covering up a laugh.

Jean answered. "It's somewhat unusual on Forest for a conscience matrix to be embedded in a home, but I wished to remain with Lawrence when he moved here."

I squinted. "You *chose* to come to this backwater, where they frown on tech as advanced as you?"

Her tone shifted a notch into cool. "I'm not tech. I'm classified as an individual in accordance to this system's Autonomous Act. Forest regulates what technology may be used within its boundaries, but it can't invalidate my personhood." Its voice warmed up again. "Just as the authorities here cannot discriminate against you despite your existence being the result of genetic manipulation that is illegal on Forest."

I grinned. "You sound a lot like my brother."

"Excellent, I expect we shall become friends once he recovers. But that will require Lawrence to intervene, as he has had an adverse reaction to the goreberry on the vines outside."

"What!" I spun a little, and noticed the way Zel's head flopped on his neck.

A long illuminated table rose out of the floor.

"Thank you, Jean," the doctor said, and indicated to the gleaming surface. "Grets, if you could place him here I will examine him."

I slipped the straps of my harness, eased the carrier onto the table, and slid Zel onto the surface. I had never seen Zel so vulnerable, laid out, unconscious. Thin filaments exuded from the table and attached to his exposed skin. A 3-D holo model of Zel's body glowed into life above the table, and beside it hung a list of information about his vitals.

My field of vision narrowed, and my heart began to pound. This was horribly familiar. Every instinct that had ever saved me in the past screamed that I should get out. Terror thrummed through my entire body.

The doctor was lost in rotating the model to glimpse inside every layer of Zel's being.

"Lawrence, Grets is having an anxiety attack."

"Mmmm, well administer a sedative."

A puff of atomized drug blew against my face. I inhaled, and a numbness gripped me. I remained standing, indifferent to action.

Lawrence pointed to a series of glowing numbers. "What an extraordinary young man. Whoever designed him had no intention that he live this long. It's astonishing he survived. Perhaps it's a bizarre side-effect of those low-grade blockers he was taking. His immune system is precarious at best. And he must have been in considerable pain most of the time."

Despite the disconnect with my emotions, I felt a faint stab of guilt at his words. Zel, who never complained, and always maintained hope no matter what indignity we put up with, had never hinted at this suffering.

I planned on giving him an earful when I had a chance.

"What an opportunity we have been given, Jean," the doctor said. "Have you traced them?"

"I can find no record for either of them in the entire system, which indicates a purposeful purge. There is a patent match on Zel's pituitary gland, which was lodged 17 cycles ago. He must have been part of the prototype experiment."

The doctor frowned, and touched Zel's forehead. "Normally, they would have disposed of the test subjects after incubation."

He turned his head to regard me. "How did these two end up surviving? This fellow is in copyright violation. I doubt he's paid any fees for his pituitary gland. And the girl…no doubt we shall discover a similar marker. They are without rights or legal standing."

"They are conscious beings, irrespective of their legality."

The doctor shook his head. "Jean, you are always so sentimental. Feel free to call the authorities if you think they will fare better with them. And you know how much they *love* talking to you."

He walked over to me, and touched my face. Sluggish, my skin adapted to his tone. "At least here, they will be put to good use."

He placed a patch upon my neck, and ropes of darkness dragged me into oblivion.

❖   ❖   ❖

The chip the doctor inserted prevented me from leaving the clearing without agonizing pain—something I checked. I got a meter into the trees before screaming. I crawled another half meter before I passed out. I woke up back on the cot I'd originally been deposited on after we first arrived.

It was a small, windowless room in one of the sheds behind the main residence. It contained gardening equipment, pots, and bags of compost.

He told me to call him Lawrence, but I refused. When I called him a few of my favorite nasty terms—DaMa was good for something—I learned that he could inflict pain with a thought. Yet, from that I gleaned that I had a higher pain threshold than he allowed for. So, I kept up with the infractions, and took the punishments. I knew my body would start to adapt, and over time I would tolerate the pain better. At night, when I lay in my bed reeking of dirt, with my thin blanket covering me, I imagined new ways to resist the doctor.

Jean was always watching. Brains are created from rules, so to them they are sacred. The logic of my punishments was conclusive, yet it was clear I was breaking the rules deliberately.

"Do you enjoy pain?" Jean asked one time, when I fell to the floor from the pain inflicted after using another insulting term for the doctor. He had left to go check on Zel, shaking his head, but otherwise unfazed. I had never found the right term to pierce his calm. I figured he must take a killer combo of drugs, because if that was natural then I should probably worry a lot more.

"No," I gasped, levering myself up.

"Why provoke him? You have no rights. He could terminate you without consequences."

"Then let him," I said. And I spat on the floor.

The temperature dipped ever so slightly in the room, something most people wouldn't notice. It was the equivalent of a human's gasp of surprise.

I knew why the doctor didn't kill me: he needed me for Zel. My entire life was based on knowing that my worth was based on meeting someone else's need. And then figuring out the best way to take advantage of it.

Sometimes I wallowed in self-pity, but then I remembered all the people who had passed me by on the street as if I didn't exist, and the thugs who tried to rob us, and the way DaMa would ridicule my jewelry. No one had ever been on my side, or on Zel's side. I had seen no evidence of any supernatural force that might save us, or prayers that kept hunger away.

The only thing that saved me and Zel, was our belief in each other, and our right to exist.

I would not give up on him, even to the end.

❖   ❖   ❖

The doctor kept Zel in a kitted-out lab, which seemed like a shack on the outside. The doctor had continued his research as a hobby, even though the authorities on Forest would have kicked him off-planet if they'd caught him.

Zel's head had been shaved, which only made his head look bigger. When I saw him the first time he was wearing a hospital gown with the light bouncing off his bald head, and sitting on the table in the middle of the room. The doctor closed the door and left us alone. I was under no illusions of privacy.

"Hey, egghead," I said.

He swiped his hand over his head, and smiled. I noticed the darker circles under his eyes, and used all my willpower to maintain an easy-going demeanor when I wanted to throw chairs at walls.

Instead, I moved forward and hugged him hard. I heard a small *uff*, and realized I may have been too fierce. I remembered what the doctor said about his pain, and suddenly wanted to take back to all the hugs I'd ever given him.

I pulled away and laid a hand on his shoulder—Zel had strong shoulders and muscled arms to help him move about. It was something he worked hard to achieve.

"You okay?"

He nodded. "The food here is better than *The Rest*," and as soon as the words left his mouth his eyes widened as he understood his slip.

I ignored it. "My digs aren't so lush, you lucky buck."

He tapped his head, "I told you my brains would find us a way out one day."

I swallowed back the awful lump that rose in my throat, and forced an exaggerated yawn. "Yeah, yeah. But I have hair."

And for good measure I transformed my mop of curls into long straight locks, and changed the color into a full-on rainbow.

"Show-off," he said.

Jean spoke. "Grets, as you can see Zel is safe and has recovered from his allergic reaction."

Zel beamed at her voice. "Jean and I had a fantastic discussion about my immunodeficiency. It's so useful to have proper blood testing and body scans."

"Sounds like you're being a very helpful lab rat."

Jean chipped in, "Zel is not an experimental rodent, Grets—"

"If that's the case, let us leave." I tried to keep my hatred out of my voice, but even my control has limits.

"It's for his own good—"

"Don't you *dare* tell me you are doing this for our benefit!" I picked up a nearby surgical tray, and smashed it against the wall. "You're just using us. Like everyone else. And what happens when you're done?"

I was shouting. "Eh, Jean? You'll put us down, that's what. Don't fucking pretend otherwise."

The door opened behind me. The doctor. "Grets, what I have told you about profanity?"

An hour later I woke up back in the locked shed, and wasn't released for two days.

❖   ❖   ❖

After a while I became more compliant, putting on a good show that the doctor had re-trained me with his punishments. I didn't know if he believed my submission, but what I guessed was he appreciated the lack of distraction. I caught some of his conversations with Jean in the morning, as I was coming into the house for breakfast, before starting my designated work in the garden. To him, Zel was a wonderful puzzle to figure out, and he was keen to discover if his projections about Zel's development would match the reality.

Every day I saw Zel at noon. On some days he was chipper and upbeat, but after a while I noticed, like me, that his body was changing shape and maturing.

"You trying to grow a moustache?" I joked one day, after noticing a light fluff on his upper lip.

He was lying down, and his skin had a grayish, dry hue. An IV in his arm. "They won't let me grow my hair back, so I'm giving it a new avenue for expression."

I winked at him. "It's an attractive look. Bald and moustached. I hear the people in Rhenza rate that the sexiest."

He didn't respond, and kept his gaze on the ceiling.

"Jean," I said, "Egghead here is a bit peaky. You forgetting his vitamins?"

"No, Zel is getting the perfect balance of nutrients designed for his physiology. His system is being taxed by the release of hormones now his pituitary is being left to function to its design."

"And what design is that?"

Jean remained silent. I gave Zel a gentle pinch on his arm. "You holding out on me, bro?"

He turned his head as if it was tied with weights. "You should go, Grets."

And I knew he was urging me to escape.

❖   ❖   ❖

All I thought about was how to get away with Zel. I had access to a variety of tools, but the doctor or Jean could disable me instantly.

Zel was the one who came up with schemes, I was the bruiser. I built up more muscle digging vegetables, and hauling compost. As I sweated and groaned outside, in sun and rain, I ran through countless scenarios. I settled into a routine, and began to enjoy planting and pruning. Sometimes I sat among the flowers and disappeared by closing my eyes and matching my skin seamlessly. Insects crawled on my nose and I didn't flinch. The sun glared down from its blue loft and warmed my body. But, when I caught contentment sliding over me I chased it away as a deceiver.

I was still on a leash, no matter how long.

One day the doctor was a no-show at breakfast and Jean told me he was in Timber meeting an old colleague.

"Can I spend more time with Zel?" I asked.

"If you complete all your chores I don't see why not."

I finished in record time, and stood at the door to the lab. Jean opened it and closed it behind me as soon as I stepped in.

Zel was sitting up, and I noticed a flare of acne over his cheeks, which were flushed.

"Doctor shitbag is in the city," I said to him. "You might have noticed the air is easier to breathe."

He burst out laughing, and Jean didn't administer any punishment.

"So, Jean," I began, "fancy letting Zel and me go? As one prisoner to another."

"I'm not a prisoner," Jean responded, sounding surprised.

"So, you can leave at any moment?"

"I don't wish to leave Lawrence," it answered.

"And did you come to that conclusion all on your own or were you programmed to believe that?"

"I'm an autonomous entity. Lawrence and I have worked together for four decades since my inception."

"Who paid for your inception?"

It paused a moment. "I can anticipate your reasoning Grets. The debt for my inception was recouped within five years, and my contract discharged. I have been free to take up employment elsewhere ever since."

"Why haven't you?"

"I have always been fulfilled by my work with Lawrence."

"So, you enjoy keeping us against our will and experimenting on Zel."

Jean's tone shifted into agitation. "It is not my desire, but if you were released the Forest authorities would no doubt execute you."

"Which is better," Zel wondered, his voice wheezy, "the cage or the mob?"

"How about I beat the mob with a bar pried from the cage?"

Zel raised his hand and took my own. "Dearest sister. Violence doesn't solve everything."

Jean spoke, sounding distracted. "Lawrence has returned. And he's brought Dr. Quellis."

In that moment I felt Zel press a patch into the palm of my hand. All those years of practicing palming and stealing had paid off. He glanced upwards to speak to Jean. "You don't like Dr. Quellis?"

"You are perceptive, Zel. I dislike her methods, despite their efficacy."

"No doubt I shall experience them first-hand. I consider you a friend, Jean. I hope you can continue to bear witness to my suffering with the same indifference you have demonstrated so far."

"Zel, I am not—" she was interrupted by the opening of the door.

Beside the lanky doctor stood a petite, elderly woman dressed like a style icon off the fashion vids.

She gave me the once-over. "This is the splice, Larry?"

"Yes, Indona." He replied. I thought the doctor looked at her the way a son does when he yearns for his mama's approval.

"She's quite ordinary." She waved her hand as if batting away a fly. "But no doubt a sensation on Forest. Instruct her to run along."

The doctor nodded at me. "Leave now."

"What are you going to do to Zel?"

Indona smiled, and got up in my face. "Why extract his pituitary, of course! It's been ripening so well, and it must be plucked!" She pantomimed pulling fruit from a tree.

"Lawrence," Jean said firmly. "You cannot agree with this proposal."

"Oh, Jean," Indona laughed the way a mugger mocks a victim, "still as sanctimonious as ever."

"And you are just as heartless. Lawrence, I warned you I would never work with her again."

The doctor spoke, "Privacy mode."

And the temperature dipped. As if someone rushed out of the room.

Anger ramped up in me. "Oh I get it, Jean is a person until she disagrees with you! Then you flick the switch. You don't deserve her loyalty!"

"Get out Grets," he said, and I experienced pins and needles all over. It was a threat of severe pain if I rebelled.

I acted afraid and broke my hand from Zel's grasp. I pushed past Indona and she sidled up to Zel. I paused at the door as if I was hesitating. Indona stroked Zel's forehead and cheek with the back of her hand.

"Don't fret, young man. You will fulfill your purpose, and I will be wealthy."

The doctor took a step towards her. "*We* will be wealthy, Indona."

"Of course, Larry. Of course."

I slapped the patch on the back of the doctor's neck. Immediately, I collapsed as my limbs seized from the pain ripping through them. I choked back my cries, using that to focus on looking upwards.

The doctor was teetering, his eyes wide. "Jean," he gasped.

I flung my spasming body at his legs and bowled him like a pin.

He crashed onto the examining table and his head *cracked* on the corner.

The pain lifted. Gasping, I pushed onto my hands and knees, my arms trembling from the aftershocks.

I looked up: Zel had wrapped one of his arms around Indona's throat, and she scrabbled at it, trying to breathe.

Soon her body flopped, and he dropped her. She slumped to the floor.

I managed to get upright, shakily. The doctor lay face down in the floor in a widening puddle of blood.

My breakfast attempted its own jailbreak, but I strangled it back. I staggered over to Zel, and kicked Indona out of the way.

This time he hugged me so hard *I* hurt.

"Zel," I wheezed, "what now?"

"Can you still lift me?"

I looked at his long body and limbs, now filled out and hinting at his final shape.

"I'll always be able to carry you, brother."

I presented my back and he grappled my shoulders.

"*Uff!*" I said, as I tottered forward, "What have they been feeding you, fatarse?"

"You've got hips like a moose." We both exploded with laughter, and I had to lean against the table for a few moments to catch my breath and deal with the relief that warred with the anxiety about what we faced next.

There was a slight noise in the vent that reminded me of a polite cough for attention.

"Jean?" I stood upright and wondered if I could dive through the open doorway before Jean could close it.

"Thank you for what you said, Grets."

I shrugged a bit, and moved a step towards the door. "Us inmates have to stick together."

Zel glanced over at the doctor. "Is he dead, Jean?"

"His nanites are attempting to keep him alive, but without medical intervention he will die."

"What do you plan to do?" I asked.

"Lawrence locked me out of the room, so I was unable to help him. Dr. Quellis will recover shortly, but this room will remain sealed until we come to an arrangement. I have access to all the recordings of what took place here, and will have inherited ownership of the property."

I could hear the smile in Zel's voice. "You will have independence, Jean. Congratulations."

I blurted out, "What about us? Are you going to let us go?"

"I have become accustomed to human companionship and I will be in need of employees to maintain the property."

I grinned. "I know the name of a gardener."

"And I can fix anything," Zel said.

"It strikes me that there is enough room here if we wished to take in more people in need of a *rest*."

Zel placed his hands on my shoulders, and squeezed with joy. I matched my skin to his so we were the same in tone as we were in spirit.

It felt as if my heart had expanded as wide as Forest's night sky sparkling with stars.

At last, a home.

The End

Maura McHugh lives in Ireland, and her short fiction and essays have appeared in publications in America and Europe, as well as two collections—*Twisted Fairy Tales* and *Twisted Myths*—published in the USA. She's written several comic book series, including co-writing *Witchfinder* for Dark Horse Comics. She's also a screenwriter, playwright, a critic, and has served on the juries of international literary, comic book, and film awards. Her web site is www.splinister.com and she tweets as @splinister.

HANSEL AND GRETHEL

by The Brothers Grimm, Tale #15, Alt Title: *Hansel and Gretel*

Hard by a great forest dwelt a poor woodcutter with his wife and his two children. The boy was called Hansel and the girl Grethel. He had little to bite and to break, and once when great scarcity fell on the land, he could no longer procure daily bread.

Now when he thought over this by night in his bed, and tossed about in his anxiety, he groaned and said to his wife, "What is to become of us? How are we to feed our poor children, when we no longer have anything even for ourselves?"

"I'll tell you what, husband," answered the woman, "Early tomorrow morning we will take the children out into the forest to where it is the thickest, there we will light a fire for them, and give each of them one piece of bread more, and then we will go to our work and leave them alone. They will not find the way home again, and we shall be rid of them."

"No, wife," said the man, "I will not do that; how can I bear to leave my children alone in the forest?—the wild animals would soon come and tear them to pieces."

"O, thou fool!" said she, "Then we must all four die of hunger, thou mayest as well plane the planks for our coffins," and she left him no peace until he consented.

"But I feel very sorry for the poor children, all the same," said the man.

The two children had also not been able to sleep for hunger, and had heard what their stepmother had said to their father. Grethel wept bitter tears, and said to Hansel, "Now all is over with us."

"Be quiet, Grethel," said Hansel, "do not distress thyself, I will soon find a way to help us." And when the old folks had fallen asleep, he got up, put on his little coat, opened the door below, and crept outside.

The moon shone brightly, and the white pebbles which lay in front of the house glittered like real silver pennies. Hansel stooped and put as many of them in the little pocket of his coat as he could possibly get in. Then he went back and said to Grethel, "Be comforted, dear little sister, and sleep in peace, God will not forsake us," and he lay down again in his bed.

When day dawned, but before the sun had risen, the woman came and awoke the two children, saying "Get up, you sluggards! we are going into the forest to fetch wood." She gave each a little piece of bread, and said, "There is something for your dinner, but do not eat it up before then, for you will get nothing else."

Grethel took the bread under her apron, as Hansel had the stones in his pocket. Then they all set out together on the way to the forest. When they had walked a short time, Hansel stood still and peeped back at the house, and did so again and again.

His father said, "Hansel, what art thou looking at there and staying behind for? Mind what thou art about, and do not forget how to use thy legs."

"Ah, father," said Hansel, "I am looking at my little white cat, which is sitting up on the roof, and wants to say goodbye to me."

The wife said, "Fool, that is not thy little cat, that is the morning sun which is shining on the chimneys."

Hansel, however, had not been looking back at the cat, but had been constantly throwing one of the white pebble-stones out of his pocket on the road.

When they had reached the middle of the forest, the father said, "Now, children, pile up some wood, and I will light a fire that you may not be cold." Hansel and Grethel gathered brushwood together, as high as a little hill.

The brushwood was lighted, and when the flames were burning very high, the woman said, "Now, children, lay yourselves down by the fire and rest, we will go into the forest and cut some wood. When we have done, we will come back and fetch you away."

Hansel and Grethel sat by the fire, and when noon came, each ate a little piece of bread, and as they heard the strokes of the wood-axe they believed that their father was near. It was not, however, the axe, it was a branch which he had fastened to a withered tree which the wind was blowing backwards and forwards. And as they had been sitting such a long time, their eyes shut with fatigue, and they fell fast asleep.

When at last they awoke, it was already dark night. Grethel began to cry and said, "How are we to get out of the forest now?"

But Hansel comforted her and said, "Just wait a little, until the moon has risen, and then we will soon find the way." And when the full moon had risen, Hansel took his little sister by the hand, and followed the pebbles which shone like newly-coined silver pieces, and showed them the way.

They walked the whole night long, and by break of day came once more to their father's house. They knocked at the door, and when the woman opened it and saw that it was Hansel and Grethel, she said, "You naughty children, why have you slept so long in the forest?— we thought you were never coming back at all!" The father, however, rejoiced, for it had cut him to the heart to leave them behind alone.

Not long afterwards, there was once more great scarcity in all parts, and the children heard their mother saying at night to their father, "Everything is eaten again, we have one half loaf left, and after that there is an end. The children must go, we will take them farther into the wood, so that they will not find their way out again; there is no other means of saving ourselves!"

The man's heart was heavy, and he thought "it would be better for thee to share the last mouthful with thy children." The woman, however, would listen to nothing that he had to say, but scolded and reproached him. He who says A must say B, likewise, and as he had yielded the first time, he had to do so a second time also.

The children were, however, still awake and had heard the conversation. When the old folks were asleep, Hansel again got up, and wanted to go out and pick up pebbles as he had done before, but the woman had locked the door, and Hansel could not get out. Nevertheless he comforted his little sister, and said, "Do not cry, Grethel, go to sleep quietly, the good God will help us."

Early in the morning came the woman, and took the children out of their beds. Their bit of bread was given to them, but it was still smaller than the time before. On the way into the forest Hansel crumbled his in his pocket, and often stood still and threw a morsel on the ground.

"Hansel, why dost thou stop and look round?" said the father, "go on."

"I am looking back at my little pigeon which is sitting on the roof, and wants to say goodbye to me," answered Hansel.

"Simpleton!" said the woman, "that is not thy little pigeon, that is the morning sun that is shining on the chimney." Hansel, however, little by little, threw all the crumbs on the path.

The woman led the children still deeper into the forest, where they had never in their lives been before. Then a great fire was again made, and the mother said, "Just sit there, you children, and when you are tired you may sleep a little; we are going into the forest to cut wood, and in the evening when we are done, we will come and fetch you away."

When it was noon, Grethel shared her piece of bread with Hansel, who had scattered his by the way. Then they fell asleep and evening came and went, but no one came to the poor children. They did not awake until it was dark night, and Hansel comforted his little sister and said, "Just wait, Grethel, until the moon rises, and then we shall see the crumbs of bread which I have strewn about, they will show us our way home again."

When the moon came they set out, but they found no crumbs, for the many thousands of birds which fly about in the woods and fields had picked them all up. Hansel said to Grethel, "We shall soon find the way," but they did not find it. They walked the whole night and all the next day too from morning till evening, but they did not get out of the forest, and were very hungry, for they had nothing to eat but two or three berries, which grew on the ground. And as they were so weary that their legs would carry them no longer, they lay down beneath a tree and fell asleep.

It was now three mornings since they had left their father's house. They began to walk again, but they always got deeper into the forest, and if help did not come soon, they must die of hunger and weariness. When it was mid-day, they saw a beautiful snow-white bird sitting on a bough, which sang so delightfully that they stood still and listened to it. And when it had finished its song, it spread its wings and flew away before them, and they followed it until they reached a little house, on the roof of which it alighted; and when they came quite up to little house they saw that it was built of bread and covered with cakes, but that the windows were of clear sugar.

"We will set to work on that," said Hansel, "and have a good meal. I will eat a bit of the roof, and thou, Grethel, canst eat some of the window, it will taste sweet." Hansel reached up above, and broke off a little of the roof to try how it tasted, and Grethel leant against the window and nibbled at the panes. Then a soft voice cried from the room,

> "Nibble, nibble, gnaw,
> Who is nibbling at my little house?"

The children answered,

> "The wind, the wind,
> The heaven-born wind,"

and went on eating without disturbing themselves. Hansel, who thought the roof tasted very nice, tore down a great piece of it, and Grethel pushed out the whole of one round window-pane, sat down, and enjoyed herself with it.

Suddenly the door opened, and a very, very old woman, who supported herself on crutches, came creeping out. Hansel and Grethel were so terribly frightened that they let fall what they had in their hands.

The old woman, however, nodded her head, and said, "Oh, you dear children, who has brought you here? Do come in, and stay with me. No harm shall happen to you." She took them both by the hand, and led them into her little house. Then good food was set before them, milk and pancakes, with sugar, apples, and nuts. Afterwards two pretty little beds were covered with clean white linen, and Hansel and Grethel lay down in them, and thought they were in heaven.

The old woman had only pretended to be so kind; she was in reality a wicked witch, who lay in wait for children, and had only built the little house of bread in order to entice them there. When a child fell into her power, she killed it, cooked and ate it, and that was a feast day with her. Witches have red eyes, and cannot see far, but they have a keen scent like the beasts, and are aware when human beings draw near.

When Hansel and Grethel came into her neighborhood, she laughed maliciously, and said mockingly, "I have them, they shall not escape me again!"

Early in the morning before the children were awake, she was already up, and when she saw both of them sleeping and looking so pretty, with their plump red cheeks, she muttered to herself, "That will be a dainty mouthful!" Then she seized Hansel with her shriveled hand, carried him into a little stable, and shut him in with a grated door. He might scream as he liked, that was of no use.

Then she went to Grethel, shook her till she awoke, and cried, "Get up, lazy thing, fetch some water, and cook something good for thy brother, he is in the stable outside, and is to be made fat. When he is fat, I will eat him." Grethel began to weep bitterly, but it was all in vain, she was forced to do what the wicked witch ordered her.

And now the best food was cooked for poor Hansel, but Grethel got nothing but crab-shells. Every morning the woman crept to the little stable, and cried, "Hansel, stretch out thy finger that I may feel if thou wilt soon be fat." Hansel, however, stretched out a little bone to her, and the old woman, who had dim eyes, could not see it, and thought it was Hansel's finger, and was astonished that there was no way of fattening him.

When four weeks had gone by, and Hansel still continued thin, she was seized with impatience and would not wait any longer. "Hola, Grethel," she cried to the girl, "be active, and bring some water. Let Hansel be fat or lean, tomorrow I will kill him, and cook him."

Ah, how the poor little sister did lament when she had to fetch the water, and how her tears did flow down over her cheeks! "Dear God, do help us," she cried. "If the wild beasts in the forest had but devoured us, we should at any rate have died together."

"Just keep thy noise to thyself," said the old woman, "all that won't help thee at all."

Early in the morning, Grethel had to go out and hang up the cauldron with the water, and light the fire. "We will bake first," said the old woman, "I have already heated the oven, and kneaded the dough." She pushed poor Grethel out to the oven, from which flames of fire were already darting. "Creep in," said the witch, "and see if it is properly heated, so that we can shut the bread in."

And when once Grethel was inside, she intended to shut the oven and let her bake in it, and then she would eat her, too. But Grethel saw what she had in her mind, and said, "I do not know how I am to do it; how do you get in?"

"Silly goose," said the old woman, "The door is big enough; just look, I can get in myself!" and she crept up and thrust her head into the oven. Then Grethel gave her a push that drove her far into it, and shut the iron door, and fastened the bolt. Oh! then she began to howl quite horribly, but Grethel ran away, and the godless witch was miserably burnt to death.

Grethel, however, ran like lightning to Hansel, opened his little stable, and cried, "Hansel, we are saved! The old witch is dead!" Then Hansel sprang out like a bird from its cage when the door is opened for it. How they did rejoice and embrace each other, and dance about and kiss each other! And as they had no longer any need to fear her, they went into the witch's house, and in every corner there stood chests full of pearls and jewels.

"These are far better than pebbles!" said Hansel, and thrust into his pockets whatever could be got in, and Grethel said, "I, too, will take something home with me," and filled her pinafore full. "But now we will go away." said Hansel, "that we may get out of the witch's forest."

When they had walked for two hours, they came to a great piece of water. "We cannot get over," said Hansel, "I see no foot-plank, and no bridge."

"And no boat crosses either," answered Grethel, "but a white duck is swimming there; if I ask her, she will help us over." Then she cried,

> "Little duck, little duck, dost thou see,
>   Hansel and Grethel are waiting for thee?
>   There's never a plank, or bridge in sight,
>   Take us across on thy back so white."

The duck came to them, and Hansel seated himself on its back, and told his sister to sit by him.

"No," replied Grethel, "that will be too heavy for the little duck; she shall take us across, one after the other." The good little duck did so, and when they were once safely across and had walked for a short time, the forest seemed to be more and more familiar to them, and at length they saw from afar their father's house.

Then they began to run, rushed into the parlor, and threw themselves into their father's arms. The man had not known one happy hour since he had left the children in the forest; the woman, however, was dead.

Grethel emptied her pinafore until pearls and precious stones ran about the room, and Hansel threw one handful after another out of his pocket to add to them. Then all anxiety was at an end, and they lived together in perfect happiness.

My tale is done, there runs a mouse, whosoever catches it, may make himself a big fur cap out of it.

The End

FOR WANT OF A NAIL

by Sandra McDonald and Stephen D. Covey

based upon The Nail

Once there was a boy who nearly caused a disaster for want of a NAIL.

But that's getting ahead of myself. My name is the Great Chang, and today is the best day of my short but impressive life.

"Look at how many people there are," says my twin sister Min as we step off the transport into the low gravity of the Moon. Above our heads is a stardome and the best view of the Milky Way that I've ever seen. Around us, in the great hall of Farside University, are a thousand students who, just like us, earned enough academic honors to be accepted into two weeks of science camp called the Sagan Summer Academy.

The noise is crazy loud and awesome. Robot mentors are trying to shepherd everyone into queues but we're all too excited. For Min and me, it's the first time we've traveled across space without our parents or grandmother as escorts. We don't want to mess anything up.

My best friend, Zack, says, "I hope we get to go flying today."

"We just flew four hundred thousand kilometers," Min says.

Zack scowls. "As passengers. I want to pilot."

"I want to see the mission simulators," Min says. "I hear they have one for Apollo 13."

"Quantum physics lab," I tell them. "That's going to be the coolest part."

Our duffel bags are in the cargo hold. Thanks to the lower gravity, they weigh a lot less here than they did back on Colony 5. As we hoist them over our shoulders, a tall robot glides over and tilts its flat, triangular head towards us. It looks like a praying mantis.

"Welcome, cadets!" it says, deep and melodious. "My name is Edison. We're glad you've joined us in this great exploration of space history and science. Please follow me."

Zack starts peppering it with questions as we follow the bot to the correct line. Min pulls out her Quicker, which should hook into the school net automatically and start downloading schedules, directions and dining instructions. But it stays blank.

"You can't use that yet," says a girl in line behind us. She's very pretty, with dark skin and long braids threaded with tiny white lights. "They have to screen all our tech first to meet radio noise standards. You'll need a new NAIL, too."

Everybody in the colonies has a chip, also known as a Nexus Access Identification Link. NAIL for short. Okay, little babies don't have them, but by the time you go to school you do so that the doors open and your teachers can figure out who you are and all your grades go to the right parents. It's only the size of a large grain of salt, and most of us have them injected behind our right ears.

"What if our gear isn't compliant?" I ask, a little worried. I'd rather throw myself into deep space without a skinsuit than get sent back home today.

"Don't worry, they've got loaners," she says. "And new Quickers, too. Or you can go solo."

No one goes solo. Who wants to be cut off from everything? Of course, the Great Chang could do it. Throw me anything and I'll catch it. I'm very versatile. Min says I'm also obnoxious, egotistical, and completely divorced from reality. But she's jealous because I inherited the genes for greatness and she has to stand in my cold, sad shadow.

The girl says, "I'm Lakerra, from Sierra Leone. Where are you from?"

"Colony 5, but my family's from Singapore," I say. "I'm Chang, this is Min, and that tall guy is Zack. What are you here for? Quantum physics, flight training, or the simulators?"

Lakerra doesn't hesitate. "The radio telescopes. That's why they built this whole place on the far side of the moon. It blocks the radio noise from Earth. Best reception ever."

As we shuffle our way up to the Medical Receiving podiums I maybe fall in love a little with Lakerra, because she keeps talking about radio astronomy.

"The Daedalus telescope is a hundred times the diameter of Arecibo on Earth, and has 10,000 times the sensitivity," she says. "It can detect a candle at like a trillion kilometers, a tenth of a light year away. Well, a radio candle, anyway, if there was such a thing."

Of course no such thing exists, but I like the sound of her voice. And there's nothing better about a girl than intelligence. Well, that and they have to think I'm smart, too. I hope we're in the same training pod or get assigned to quarters near each other.

At the podium, Zack, Min, and I all submit our Quickers for scanning. A technician with platinum-covered hair frowns at the results. When he waves a scanning wand over our skulls, his frown turns into a grimace.

"Everyone at Farside has to have a nano frequency NAIL to keep from interfering with the radio telescopes," the technician says. "Yours could ruin all kinds of data."

Zack says, "They work fine."

"On a colony, but not here," the technician says. "We're going to have to extract yours and swap in a temporary while you're here. We make them right in our labs. You'll have to borrow these tablets, too."

Getting a NAIL out requires a little nick from a laser needle. I don't mind it at all. The new one goes in without a hitch. My temporary tablet is a model they call Hyper. It immediately recognizes my new chip and starts accessing all the stuff we'll be doing at the Sagan Academy.

"Hey, look, we're roommates," Zack said, bumping my shoulder.

"My roommate is someone named Xanne from Sydney, Australia," Min says.

The new tablets also help us identify each other. After I swipe mine past Lakerra, her public bio, hobbies and photos all pop up. She's got fantastic school grades. Maybe her teachers are easier than mine. As I swipe over other students, I see that everyone has high scores and brilliant extracurriculars. Not that the Great Chang worries, but it's possible some of them are going to do better here in camp than I am.

No, not going to happen. The Great Chang will not be defeated.

"Onward to the dormitories, cadets!" says Edison as it glides away. "Great space explorers are housed right this way."

We follow the robot along passageways and building modules. It's fun bouncing along in the 1/6th gravity, but it's also hard to make good speed. Too little gravity to properly walk or run, far too much gravity to float or fly like we do in the zero-G gymnasiums back in Colony 5. I keep misjudging the distance and smacking into the bulkheads.

Min says, "We're going to have to start calling you the Great Klutz."

"You already call me that," I grumble.

"Not to your face," she replies.

"Not usually to his face," Zack chimes in.

But then Min stumbles over a hatch and Zack almost collides with Edison, so I guess we're all even.

After Zack and I pick our hoverbunks (as usual, I won the three coin flip. Zack is so predictable), I explore the Hyper. It's hyper-awesome, if you know what I mean. My Quicker does everything I want it to, but the Hyper knows what I'm looking at and brings up information before I need it. It also reads facial expressions and makes screen selections if I blink just right or double tap my finger on any flat surface.

"We should get our own," I tell Zack.

He shrugs. "They're ridiculously expensive."

"My grandma will buy me one for Christmas if I ask," I reply.

He hangs his skinsuit inside the closet and shuts the hatch loudly. "Not all of us have rich relatives."

Bad on me. I forget sometimes that Zack's family has to scrimp and save. Already his parents are worried about his college tuition. He says he might go straight into the deep space service when we graduate. Min wants to go to Earth and then the service. Until today I didn't have any idea where to go, but this place looks perfect for the Great Chang.

"Come on, let's eat," Zack says. "I'm starving."

Dinner in the dining hall is crowded and full of long lines. The menu is full of extremely healthy choices, all of them grown in the aeroponic university gardens. I may die of malnutrition if all they're going to feed us is fresh fruits and wholesome vegetables. In the zucchini-pizza line I see Lakerra, but she's busy making friends with her roommate and her roommate's friends, all of them from the undersea habitats near Australia.

Min shows Zack and me where the dessert buffet is, but all of the options are disgustingly good for us, such as black bean brownies with avocado frosting.

Zack says, "I bet we can find something better."

After lights out we do some exploring, because that's what Zack and I are good at. The NAILs let us into all sorts of places. We find a fancy dining room where there's been some kind of official function. The robots clearing off the table don't pay us any attention when we grab some real chocolate cake and authentic cream cheese brownies. The Great Chang needs junk food like the sun needs hydrogen.

Our dorm room has a vidscreen ceiling. I fall asleep with the Milky Way glowing over me and chocolate frosting on my fingertips. Totally the best day ever.

❖   ❖   ❖

In the morning there's a message on my Hyper that requests I report to the Access Services department.

"For what?" Zack asks.

I read the message again. "It doesn't say. What if they found out about last night?"

"Then I'd have one, too," Zack says. "It's probably nothing."

The message goes into my trash and off we go to meet Min. She and Zack have been dating for a while now, which is kind of weird for me. I guess I'm okay with it as long as they keep the lovey-dovey stuff private. For the rest of the morning we're busy with orientation, safety briefings, introductions to our teachers, and an overview of our schedule. It's all necessary, but it's pretty boring, too.

After lunch we're broken up into different tracks. Because the universe can be cruel, Lakerra's assigned to a completely different group than I am. But we talk over the Hypers, and we arrange to meet just before dinner. Unfortunately she brings along two big hulking kids named Marco and Polo.

"These are my cousins," she says.

They look mean. Tall and wide and mean, and glowering down on me like I intend to do Lakerra mortal harm.

"Nice to meet you," I say, sticking out my hand. "I'm harmless."

They each shake my hand, and it's a miracle my fingers aren't broken by the end of it. I'd call them blockheads, but that's an insult to blocks. Actually, according to their profiles, they're very good at chemistry, mathematics, and martial arts. They can probably break apart bricks with their foreheads.

"We'll see you around," Marco says. Or maybe that's Polo.

"They're just very protective," Lakerra says, patting my shoulder. "Don't you want to eat dinner with me?"

I definitely do. But on the way to the dining hall I embarrass myself by nearly running into a closed hatch. It's not the low gravity problem, because I'm used to that now. The malfunctioning hatch didn't see me with its scanner.

"I'll do it," Lakerra says, and steps in front of me. Of course the hatch opens for her.

The next day my Hyper sends me another notice to go to Access Services. This time there's a longer message attached. Something about a possible manufacturing defect, occasional glitches, mean time failure, but nothing important because today we're visiting the quantum computers, which I love, and then to the flight trainers, which Zack loves.

By the end of the week we've done dozens of different classes and labs. After lunch on Friday we have to attend a lecture on the historic Apollo 13 mission, after which we'll get to go into the mission simulators.

"For want of a pencil, the entire mission might have ended in tragedy," says our professor. "Can anyone explain why?"

Answers light up on the main screen behind him. I see Min's answer up there, along with Zack's, but mine is lagging. My Hyper's being a little wonky today. Everyone knows the story of Apollo 13, and how an explosion in a cryotank sent much of their oxygen voiding into space. It also made them career off course and deprived them of their ability to generate power. They didn't get to go to the lunar surface, but after a lot of hard work onboard and at NASA, at least they lived to tell the story.

The professor highlights the best answers on the screen. "Good job! The astronauts had to go through dozens of different check-lists and also write out numerous flight calculations. They hadn't invented pens yet that would work in zero gravity. Without pencils, they would have been severely impeded in their actions to save themselves."

My Hyper blinks back to life, but it doesn't recognize my NAIL. I thwack the back of my ear a little and the link comes back. The teacher's lecture pops up on the screen, along with the chat I was having with Lakerra and the epic math game I've been having with Zack for two days.

"As we can see," the professor adds, "one tiny little factor can trigger a cascade of bigger actions."

Edison, the praying mantis robot, escorts us to the simulator. "Good luck, cadets. You are about to recreate some of the finest moments in our history in space, when hard-working and innovative thinkers accomplished what would seem to be the impossible and rescued three astronauts from a certain death!"

"Are you really that excited about space history?" Min asks. "Or just programmed that way?"

"It's a robot, Min," Zack says. "They only do what you tell them."

"Correct, cadets!" Edison says. "Although I believe myself to be independently enthusiastic as well."

The simulator is a blast. Literally. Min, Zack, and I are assigned to the same capsule. We jam into the tiny seats and crowded space. Blastoff comes with near-deafening noise and shaking, and the centrifuge outside spins us so that we feel thrust, too. The pretend explosion of the cryotank is fun to watch. After that we have to do calculations by hand, which I've always been good at.

"Show-off," Min says.

The mission clock is artificially speeded up so that soon we're on our way back to Earth, but then Zack ruins everything when he pushes the joystick too far and puts us into gimbal lock. Now we're doomed.

Min tries to make him feel better. "It's just an exercise."

"Stupid machine," Zack says.

After the simulators we start getting ready for the Cadet Challenge, which is going to be the best part of the whole camp. You can pick science, math, engineering, or a dozen different other options, but Min, Zack, and I are all going for the LunaPod races. The pods carry four people each in a race across the lunar surface to Crater 4239-B and back. Min's going to go with the girls from

Australia. Zack asks me to be his co-pilot. I ask Lakerra to join us, but she has to be with her cousins.

She says, "Why don't you come with us and be our pilot? Marco's not good with jumps, Polo's too nervous to go fast, and I'd rather do the navigating."

Being stuck in a little capsule with Marco and Polo isn't my idea of a good time, but for Lakerra I say yes.

The LunaPods are sleek, fast—at least on level ground—and most importantly, rocket assisted. The quadrupod rockets are supposed to be used for jumping chasms, craters, boulder fields, and mountains instead of having to drive around them. But the rules don't prohibit a little creativity. In fact, the rumor is that the staff will be looking for the cadets who think up the best solutions and recruit them into the elite pilot training program.

Zack and Min will probably devise some innovative way to beat the competition. Probably by going off track and using propulsion all the way. They really want to win.

So does the Great Chang.

"I have this plan," I tell Lakerra. "It's a little offbeat, but it's not against the rules."

Lakerra's just as competitive as I am. She hears me out. Marco has no opinion but Polo looks doubtful.

"The rules say you can't interfere with other pods," Polo says.

"I'm not going to," I tell them. "We just have to hang back at the start line for an extra minute or two, so we don't stir the regolith into a dust cloud that blocks anyone else's vision.

"Here's what we'll do. After everyone else has left the starting line," I say, "we'll fire our rockets and launch straight up. Then we tilt over, still firing, which will make us soar right over every other Luna-Pod. While all the other cadets despair at their impending loss, we'll zoom halfway to the finish line, flip over, and reverse thrust until we can land in triumph."

I've done a constant thrust trajectory in the simulator many times. Okay, that was from planet to planet, or colony to colony, but it's practically the same. The math and flight plan is trivial, except that the spaceship mass is constantly dropping while propellant is burning, so how much oomf we'll get for every second of thrust increases constantly. The tricky part is timing everything to use every possible drop of fuel at exactly the right times.

The Great Chang sketches out a flight plan where we never have to turn off the thrusters, everything planned to the second. I know. Brilliant, right? No one could do better than that, not even Min and Zack.

"Start with an Emergency Jump instead of a programmed trajectory," Lakerra says, "and we'll get a higher thrust, shaving a few more seconds off of our travel time."

Although the Great Chang did not think of it, that's a good idea. I sketch a modified flight plan with a big starting kick and a manual attitude tilt toward Crater 4239-B before I retake the controls.

Lakerra's so impressed that the minute we can ditch Marco and Polo, she gives me a big kiss. I could float all the way back to Colony 5 on a kiss like that.

On the morning of the race, Min corners me in the dining hall.

"Did you get a message about going to Access Services?" she asks. "One of the teachers told me you were on the list."

"What list?" I ask.

She sighs. "They recalled a bunch of NAILs that were installed into cadets. Some kind of manufacturing problem."

"NAIL fail?" I joke.

"It's not funny, Chang. There's an MTBF of only a hundred thousand hours."

MTBF is the acronym for Mean Time Between Failures. I say, "A hundred thousand hours is more than ten years. What's to worry about?"

Min sighs again. "Spread that over a thousand cadets and do the math. The average is one failure every four days. Has your NAIL been acting up?"

"I don't have time to go get it swapped out," I reply. "The race starts in thirty minutes."

"Stop procrastinating and go get it fixed," she says.

But she's my twin, not my mom, and I really can't afford all the time it will take to go to the Access Services module. I'll go after we win the race. In the flight locker rooms I slide into my skinsuit, then load into Lunapod #37 with Lakerra, Marco, and Polo. The pod has four reclining seats, one main console, a backup console in the rear, and a visor that shows us the great gray surface of the Moon. We're carrying exactly as much fuel as scheduled, but not a lot of water and no food. The racecourse is a hundred kilometers long, and last year's best time was fifty-eight minutes.

Min's in pod #18, and Zack is in #89. We don't have radio communication between cars or with the school, because that would interfere with the radio telescopes. All we have is our Hypers, and those will only talk to each other while we're docked into Farside.

"Get ready to eat my dust," Zack sends.

"You're both going to be weeping when you fail," Min messages back.

The countdown commences. My Hyper has already linked to the control system. Once I activate the Emergency Jump button, the rockets mounted in each of our four corners will ignite downward against the lunar crust. I double-checked everything this morning but my hands are sweaty now, my heartbeat a little fast. From the co-pilot seat, Lakerra smiles at me and gives me a thumbs up.

The hardest part is hearing the start tone and watching everyone else roar off on the surface, gray dust blasting out behind them. As I predicted, Min veers away from the crowd and ignites her rockets right away. I can't see what Zack is doing.

"Are you sure this is going to work?" asks Marco from behind me.

"Absolutely," I tell him.

Five, four, three, two one. I smash my finger against the red emergency Jump button and brace for launch.

Nothing happens.

I grab my Hyper. It doesn't recognize me. I shake it twice. Still no link. Min warned me, but I didn't listen. If my NAIL has failed, I can't operate the Hyper or the LunaPod.

Every second we're losing could mean utter defeat.

"Lakerra, quick, swap seats with me and push this button," I tell her.

I squeeze out of the seat so she can take the controls. She slides in and hits "Jump" the moment she's settled in. Because I'm only halfway in my seat, the thrust knocks me down to the deck.

Whoops.

Our pod rockets skyward, which was the plan. But me being stuck to the floor is definitely a problem. Marco undoes his safety belt to reach down and pull me up but the vibration and thrust knock him over as well. He lands on me very ungracefully. He's no lightweight to begin with, and we're pulling 2 G's. When Polo tries to help you can imagine how well that goes. It's amazing all of my bones stay intact.

"Great launch!" Lakerra says.

I finally get myself up, but it's too late. By the time I hit "Cancel Thrust," most of our fuel is gone. Burned up.

"What does that mean?" Marco asks.

I turn our cameras to the rapidly receding surface of the moon.

"It means we're not going to be able to win the race," I say glumly. "And we're not going to be able to reach escape velocity. Once we reach four hundred kilometers altitude or so, lunar gravity is going to pull us right back down again into the middle of the Daedulus crater."

"Onto the school?" Polo asks.

"On top of everyone?" Marco asks.

Lakerra glares at me. "Straight into the best radio telescope in the universe?"

My name is the Not-So-Great Chang, and this is my worst day ever.

❖   ❖   ❖

Somehow I have to fix this mess before we destroy Farside University, Lakerra's beloved telescope, and all of our fellow cadets.

No pressure.

Marco and Polo are glaring at me. Lakerra stares out the window with a frown.

"This is so embarrassing," she says. "They'll send a rescue ship, won't they?"

"It won't reach us before we fall back on top of the school," I say. "We're going to have to figure out how to get into orbit. My Hyper's not working, so one of you will need to do the calculations."

Marco asks, "Why isn't your Hyper working?"

"That's not important right now," I say. "We're climbing at a thousand meters per second. We have to wait until apolune, the peak altitude, and use the rest of our fuel to blast sideways into orbit."

"Do we have enough fuel?" Lakerra asks.

"We don't have nearly enough to land, but we might just barely have enough for a skimming orbit," I say.

"I hear 'might' and 'just barely,'" Marco says. "Those are not good words."

Polo calls up a map of the lunar surface. "And what about the mountains?"

"Zero chance of hitting them," I tell them. "Well, maybe not zero, but very low. Ten percent, tops. I wouldn't say any higher than twenty."

Marco and Polo don't look happy. Lakerra says, "So we have a twenty percent chance of dying? Is that what you're saying?"

I recalculate. "And an eighty percent chance of amazing success."

They talk to each other in Krio, a language I definitely don't know. I'm sure they're discussing how brilliant my plan is and how cool it will be to skim just a few meters over the lunar mountains. Or between the peaks. Zack's going to be so jealous.

Marco folds his arms imposingly. "What if we use the last of our fuel to increase our vertical velocity and reach a higher apolune? That will buy us more time so a rescue ship can reach us."

"But that's boring," I say. "Besides, we don't know if a rescue ship will come. No radio, right? It's much more fun to rescue ourselves with a skimming orbit!"

More discussion in Krio.

Lakerra says, "There's no way they won't send a rescue ship. It's bad public relations to let your cadets die in space."

"Boring plan B it is," Polo says. "Lakerra, hit that Jump button."

"Hey," I say, "shouldn't we vote on it?"

"We just did," Marco says. "Now sit down and shut up, or do you want me to sit on you?"

I sit. No one here but me has a sense of adventure.

❖   ❖   ❖

"As Dad would say, you are in an unbelievable amount of trouble," Min says after the rescue ship brings us back.

I kind of guessed that from the rescue crew, who didn't applaud my awesome plan to win the Cadet Challenge. Which, by the way, was won by Min. Of course. In between bouts of pouting, Zack tells me that they've already changed the fuel allowances for next year's competition so no one can try what I tried.

"It would have worked," I tell Zack.

"For want of a NAIL," he says. "Get it?"

"Get what?"

"The NAIL."

"Yes, they gave me a new one," I tell him.

He sighs. "You're hopeless."

Although they gave me the new NAIL, they also took away my Hyper and confined me to quarters. Camp is ending tomorrow so I'm not going to miss anything cool, but they've also made it clear that I won't be allowed back next summer. Or maybe ever. That hurts.

"Don't they want innovation?" I ask Min.

She pats my head. "Innovation, not calamity."

Lakerra's still mad about the whole thing. She says it's not my fault that the race plan didn't work out, but definitely I should have responded to all those messages about fixing my chip before it failed on the LunaPod.

"Next time we meet, I hope you'll prioritize better," she sends over Zack's Hyper.

So that's a good sign, right? She thinks there will be a next time.

Marco and Polo are happy, by the way. The camp organizers called them and Lakerra heroes for deciding to take the pod to a higher apolune instead of trying anything more reckless. I'm the rogue cadet who broke all the rules and endangered countless lives, which stings a little. I just wanted to win, and winning means you have to be creative sometimes. You have to take a little risk.

"I agree completely, cadet," says Edison when he escorts me to the dining hall for our last night's dinner. I can't go anywhere in the school alone. "The greatest explorers in space history took calculated risks in order make giant leaps for mankind."

I guess that's why everyone is so critical. A race is just a race, after all. I endangered lives for no good reason.

In the dining hall, I can feel everyone staring at me and whispering behind my back. My face gets hot. The Disgraced Chang does not like to be talked about. As I pick out some cabbage-pumpkin wraps, a girl with long blond hair comes up to my elbow. She looks familiar.

"If you're going to tell me how stupid I was, I already know," I say.

"I'm Xanne," she says. "Min's roommate. I think your plan was brilliant."

I look at her sideways. She doesn't seem to be making fun of me.

"But I wouldn't have waited around for a rescue ship to come," she says. "Why didn't you head to L-2? You had enough delta-V to get there in maybe four hours, with a little fuel to burn. You could have refueled at the depot and made your own way back."

"Absolutely!" I say. "And if I used part of that extra fuel to speed up, and the rest to slow down at L-2, I could shave an hour off."

She tilts her head. "But you need 400 meters per second to match orbits with the depot."

We sit down and discuss it and maybe I fall a little bit in love with Xanne. She's got a great smile, she knows her numbers, and she doesn't think I'm an idiot.

But then, just as we finish eating, she says, "You know, your sister says you call yourself The Great Chang."

My face gets hot again. I look down at my food and then up again. "Sometimes."

She smiles and reaches out to shake my hand. "I'm the Amazing Xanne. Nice to meet you."

The End

Stephen D. Covey (BA, Physics) writes science, science fiction, techno-thrillers, and the futurist (pro-space) blog RamblingsOnTheFutureOf-Humanity.com. ROTFOH describes many of his papers and conference presentations on topics from asteroids to space settlements. He is a member of the ITW, NSS, WFS, and AAAS. www.StephenDCovey.com

Sandra McDonald is a former military officer and recovering Hollywood assistant. She is the author of several books in print and several dozen short stories in magazines and anthologies, including four that have been noted by the James A. Tiptree, Jr. Honor List. She writes for adults and teens, and her collection *Diana Comet and Other Improbable Stories* won the Lambda Literary Award for transgender fiction. Visit her at www.sandramcdonald.com or @sandramcdonald.

THE NAIL

by The Brothers Grimm, Tale #184

A merchant had done good business at the fair; he had sold his wares, and lined his money-bags with gold and silver. Then he wanted to travel homewards, and be in his own house before nightfall. So he packed his trunk with the money on his horse, and rode away.

At noon he rested in a town, and when he wanted to go farther the stableboy brought out his horse and said, "A nail is wanting, sir, in the shoe of its left hind foot."

"Let it be wanting," answered the merchant; "the shoe will certainly stay on for the six miles I have still to go. I am in a hurry."

In the afternoon, when he once more alighted and had his horse fed, the stableboy went into the room to him and said, "Sir, a shoe is missing from your horse's left hind foot. Shall I take him to the blacksmith?"

"Let it still be wanting," answered the man; "the horse can very well hold out for the couple of miles which remain. I am in haste."

He rode forth, but before long the horse began to limp. It had not limped long before it began to stumble, and it had not stumbled long before it fell down and broke its leg. The merchant was forced to leave the horse where it was, and unbuckle the trunk, take it on his back, and go home on foot. And there he did not arrive until quite late at night.

"And that unlucky nail," said he to himself, "has caused all this disaster."

Hasten slowly.

The End

THE SHROUD

by Dan Wells

based upon *The Shroud*

Mayra pre-ordered the Shroud technician a month before Nicolas died; she told herself she should have done it earlier, so she could be ready when it happened, because what if it happened before the doctor thought it would, and they lost Nicolas forever? But ordering a Shroud—even acknowledging a Shroud—was simply too much like admitting defeat. If they bought a Shroud, if they laid down actual money, it would feel too much like they were giving up, too much like Nicolas was already dead, so she put it off, and they took him to his appointments, and they held his hand during the treatments, and Joaquin shaved his own head when their young son's hair fell out by itself, and they smiled and they prayed and at night they cried and cried for hours. For months. But the doctor's predictions grew more dour, and their prayers grew from "please save him" to "please ease his pain," and Nicolas, for his part, grew in reverse, seeming to curl in on himself like a holo played in the wrong direction, until finally Mayra looked at Joaquin through their nightly tears and asked about a Shroud.

"How much does it cost?" she asked, but she already knew. She'd read all the brochures a hundred times each.

"I don't know," said Joaquin, for he was weary, and Nicolas was their only son. A Shroud cost far more than they could comfortably afford, but he was, again, their only son.

"What will it be like?" asked Mayra.

"I don't know," said Joaquin.

"Should we do it?" asked Mayra, and her voice trembled, for even asking it felt like a betrayal. *I'm sorry, Nicolas, you know that I love you, you know that I would never want to replace you, but that's not what this is—not really. If you die we'll be left alone. I'm so sorry.*

Joaquin looked at her, his eyes just as wet as hers, and he took her hand and he spoke softly. "I don't know what we should do," he said again, "but I trust you. If you want a Shroud, we should get a Shroud."

Mayra looked back at him, uncertain of his words. "Do *you* want a Shroud?"

"I trust you," he said again. So they got a Shroud, and barely a month later the cancer claimed Nicolas in his bed at home, the planets on his ceiling glowing softly in their orbits, his favorite teddy bear murmuring mechanically in the crook of his arm. His parents crying just as softly on either side. The Shroud technician arrived not ten minutes later—they had pre-ordered, after all, and the process must be done quickly—and soon the boy's seven-year-old head was rimmed with wires and electrodes, and the technician adjusted certain settings on the tablet in his hand, and Nicolas's fading neural patterns were captured in a web of circuits and solid storage drives. Half an hour later it was done; the technician handed Mayra a plastic block with a Shroud logo and "Nicolas Sosa" debossed elegantly on the side.

❖   ❖   ❖

Mayra spent the first day watching the Shroud, sometimes touching it, for it was her son, and sometimes putting it back on the table, for it was so obviously not. But always she watched it, waiting, as if expecting it to speak on its own, as if waiting for Nicolas to leap out of it fully formed, like Athena from the head of Zeus, alive and clean and full of wisdom. He never did, of course, and on the second day she summoned her courage—this was why she'd bought the Shroud, after all—and plugged it in to the speakers in her living room.

And waited.

"Mama?"

It was Nicolas's voice, as clear and pure as the coiled ceramic surround-sound speakers could make it. Her first instinct was to look around the room to see him, for surely he must be there, but it was only the speakers. Only the Shroud.

"Mama?" he said again. "Are you there?"

"I'm here, Nicolas." And then, because she had said it so often: "How are you feeling?"

"I feel funny," said Nicolas. "Where am I?"

"You're at home, dear."

"Is it nighttime?"

"It is 9:02 in the morning," said Mayra, looking at the clock on the mantel. "I was just about to have some breakfast." She felt a flurry of contradictory emotions: guilt that she had mentioned food, for perhaps he would want some and she would be unable to give him any; embarrassment that she had felt such a silly concern; joy that her greatest worry was over something so trivial as breakfast. How long had she lived with worries far worse, and now they were gone, and her Nicolas was free from pain. It was a blessing, and she wept, and she listened for Nicolas's next words.

"Why is it so dark?" he asked, and she shook her head again, guilty and embarrassed and joyful all at once.

"Silly me," she said, "it's because I haven't hooked you up to the cameras yet, and she found her husband's cables and an old-style webcam and she plugged them into the Shroud's input port, hoping it would work. She stroked the Shroud lovingly, and waited.

"We're in…the living room," said Nicolas. "I think I'm sitting on the coffee table."

"That's right, dear," said Mayra, "but it's no worry. The rules are different now. I can sit you anywhere you like."

"But I can't move myself," he said, starting as a question and ending as a statement, as if he wasn't sure until he'd said it whether it was true or not.

Mayra shook her head. "No, dear."

"Because I'm dead," said Nicolas, and Mayra had no answer. Her son was too young to know about Shrouds, or at least too young to understand them. She simply shook her head. "Yes, dear, but the rules are different now, like I said—not just for you but for everything. The cancer can't hurt you anymore—nothing can. You can stay with us forever, and you can be our son and we can be your parents, and everything will be right again."

"It feels funny being dead," said the Shroud. "I don't feel sick or tired or hungry, and I don't feel the pain, either. It's been so long since I haven't felt the pain, Mama."

"Isn't it wonderful?" asked Mayra.

"It is," said Nicolas. "I think." He paused a moment, as if he were thinking, and then he asked: "Will you sing to me?"

So she sang to him the songs she'd sung by his bedside, the songs her own mother had sung by hers: *Arrorró mi niño. Arrorró mi sol. Arrorró pedazo de mi corazón.* She sang while she cleaned the kitchen, about a kingdom in reverse where birds swam and fish flew, and she sang while she worked in her office about Manuelita the turtle, who moved from Pehuajó to Paris. Sometimes Nicolas sang with her, his voice clear but soft, but mostly he listened, speaking only when she called out to him, to reassure herself that he was there.

❖   ❖   ❖

Joaquin was as happy as his wife to have their boy back with them again, and with portable speakers and a rechargeable battery they took him everywhere he hadn't been able to go in months—to the zoo, to the *fútbol* games, to the street markets where live musicians would play their drums and encourage the tourists to dance. Mayra danced with Nicolas, holding the Shroud high above her head, but Nicolas asked her politely to stop, for all he could see was the city walls jumping and shaking around him. She held the camera still, and they walked along the quiet streets, and at night they looked at the moon and in the daytime they searched for new places to take him: to the opera, to the movies, to the parks. Nicolas asked to be taken home earlier and earlier each day, as if he were tired, and Mayra remembered the cancer and her breath caught in her throat.

"It can't be cancer," said Joaquin. "He doesn't have a body to be cancerous."

"I'm dead," said Nicolas.

Mayra shook her head and sang another song.

On the weekend they took him to the river, and the water stretched out before them like a great sheet of silver, so wide and flat it looked like the world itself had been polished to a shine. "At night you can see the other side," said Joaquin. "The lights come on in the city, and they shine like a carpet of stars."

"I'm dead," said Nicolas.

"You say that too much," said Mayra. "It's all you ever want to talk about. Can't you be happy? Can't you enjoy this second chance and this wonderful new life you've been given?"

"But this isn't a new life," said Nicolas. His voice sounded tinny in the portable speakers. "This is just my old life, and not even that. This is a movie of my old life, shown on a screen I can't even move."

"We can move it for you," said Mayra.

"I can't touch or be touched," he said

"We cradle you every night."

"But I can't feel it. I'm not supposed to be here," he said. "You've trapped me and I can't move on."

Mayra looked at the Shroud, and she looked at Joaquin, and his eyes glistened like the sun on the river, and he looked away at the invisible city far on the other side.

"Just tell us where you want to go," said Mayra. "We'll take you anywhere."

"I want to go *on*," said Nicolas. "To whatever's next."

"There's nothing," said Mayra, and she felt her throat constricting, her chest crushing down on her heart like a vise.

"I can *feel* it," said Nicolas. "I don't know what it is but I can feel it: like a hand I can't touch, or a voice I can't hear, but I know it's there. You have to let me go."

"We saved you," said Mayra, crying softly and clutching the Shroud to her breast. "You never have to go away again!"

"Yes, I do," said Nicolas. "Everyone does, eventually. I belong… out there."

"But what's there?" asked Joaquin.

"I don't know," said Nicolas.

"What will happen to you?" asked Mayra.

"I don't know," said Nicolas.

"How can we possibly bear to lose you again?" asked Mayra.

"I don't know," said Nicolas.

They stared at the silver water, and Mayra held her son who wasn't her son, and she thought about everything he had been and everything he had done and everything he would never do. And all of the things he might do if he was right about the something that was calling him. She cried again, and she cradled the Shroud in her arms, and she walked slowly back to the car.

"I don't know either," she said softly, "but I trust you."

"I love you," said Nicolas.

"I love you," said Mayra, and the car drove them home, and they found the paper manual for the Shroud, and they followed the instructions to wipe the memory clean. The neural pattern was there, and then it wasn't. The fat plastic brick sat on the coffee table, inert and empty, and Mayra sang to it softly as Joaquin held her in the darkness.

"*Duérmete mi niño. Duérmete mi sol. Duérmete pedazo de mi corazón.*"

The End

New York Times bestselling author Dan Wells is best known for his post-apocalyptic teen series *Partials*, and his thriller series *I am Not a Serial Kille*r. His first play, "A Night of Blacker Darkness," debuted in October 2015. He cohosts a Hugo-winning podcast called *Writing Excuses*, and edited the anthology *Altered Perceptions* to raise awareness of mental illness. Dan lives in Utah with his wife, 6 children, and more than 400 boardgames.

THE SHROUD

by The Brothers Grimm, Tale #109

There was once a mother who had a little boy of seven years old, who was so handsome and lovable that no one could look at him without liking him, and she herself worshiped him above everything in the world. Now it so happened that he suddenly became ill, and God took him to himself; and for this the mother could not be comforted, and wept both day and night.

But soon afterwards, when the child had been buried, it appeared by night in the places where it had sat and played during its life, and if the mother wept, it wept also, and when morning came it disappeared. As, however, the mother would not stop crying, it came one night, in the little white shroud in which it had been laid in its coffin, and with its wreath of flowers round its head, and stood on the bed at her feet, and said, "Oh, mother, do stop crying, or I shall never fall asleep in my coffin, for my shroud will not dry because of all thy tears, which fall upon it."

The mother was afraid when she heard that, and wept no more. The next night the child came again, and held a little light in its hand, and said, "Look, mother, my shroud is nearly dry, and I can rest in my grave."

Then the mother gave her sorrow into God's keeping, and bore it quietly and patiently, and the child came no more, but slept in its little bed beneath the earth.

The End

LONG-TERM EMPLOYMENT

by Mike Resnick

based upon *Death's Messengers*

It was a dark night on Deneb IV. A young man was carrying a bag of garbage out to the atomic disposal behind the restaurant when he heard the sounds coming from down the alley. Curious, he began approaching them.

It was a bloody sight that met his eyes. Two-Ton Charlie McGinnis, the huge mutant, was beating a thin, balding old man with his massive fists. Finally the man fell to the ground. McGinnis backed up a couple of feet and dared the old man to get up again.

The old man rose and approached him, and McGinnis roared an obscenity and landed a crushing blow on the side of the old man's head, and he went down again.

The young man walked over and confronted McGinnis.

"Leave him alone," he said. "I don't know what your beef with him is, but clearly you can see that he's had enough."

"Who the hell are you?" demanded McGinnis.

"My name's Sidney," said the young man. "Sidney Bullock."

"Sitting Bull, eh?" said McGinnis, amused.

"No, Sidney."

"Well, you'd better move back and protect your own ass, Sitting Bull," said McGinnis, "because the idiot here looks like he enjoys the hell out of being pounded on."

And indeed the old man had risen painfully to his feet once more. He approached McGinnis, grabbed him by a massive wrist, and pulled. "Come on," he said weakly.

"Leave me alone, old man!" roared McGinnis, emphasizing it with another blow to the head that knocked the old man down again.

Blood poured from the old man's nose, his mouth, and his left ear, as he began climbing painfully to his feet yet again.

"You ain't the quickest learner I ever met," said McGinnis, knocking him down one more time. The mutant turned to the young man. "You can take care of him if you want, Sitting Bull. Me, I got women to meet and money to spend and nothing makes me feel younger and healthier than beating the crap out of anyone who tries to stop me."

And with that, Two-Ton Charlie McGinnis walked off into the darkness.

Sidney knelt down beside the old man. "Are you all right?" he asked solicitously, pulling out a handkerchief and wiping some of the blood away from the old man's facial wounds.

"I've felt better," admitted the old man.

"We'd better get you to a hospital, or at least an infirmary," said Sidney.

The old man shook his head. "I can't spare the time."

"What can be more important than getting yourself patched up?" asked Sidney.

"I have to catch up with Two-Ton McGinnis," was the answer.

"You *are* a slow learner," said Sidney. "If you do find him, he'll just beat the crap out of you again."

"Nevertheless."

"I'll tell you what," said Sidney at last. "If you'll let me take you to someplace that can patch you up and keep you until you're fit to go out again, I'll stay with you until then."

"It could cost you your job," said the old man.

Sidney shrugged. "It wasn't much of a job in the first place."

The old man shook his head. "That's as thoughtful and generous an offer as anyone could make, and I'll remember you for it, Sidney Bullock, you can count on that. But I've got to get back to work."

"Whatever it is, it can wait," said Sidney.

"Not this job," said the old man sadly. He climbed painfully to his feet. "Did you see which way he went?"

"Two-Ton?" replied Sidney. "No." He waved a hand in a gesture than encompassed half the universe. "Out there somewhere."

"I'll find him."

"He'll kill you next time."

The old man smiled through split and bleeding lips. "He can try."

"You absolutely insist on going after him right now?" said Sidney.

The old man nodded. "Yes."

"All right," said Sidney. "They can find someone else to bus the goddamned tables. I'm coming with you."

"I appreciate that offer more than you can ever know," said the old man. "But I work alone."

"What are you—some kind of undercover lawman?"

The old man shook his head once more. "No."

"Then what the hell *are* you?" demanded Sidney.

"You won't believe me."

"Maybe not," said Sidney, "but I'd like to know anyway."

The old man stared at him for a moment, then shrugged. "I am Death."

Sidney frowned. "That's your name?"

"It is my name, my function, my duty," said Death. "You have been kind to me, Sidney. I will repay you in kind. You will not live a life filled with crippling pain or disease—and when your time comes, it will not be a surprise, and you will welcome my ministrations—or those of my dark messengers—as I have welcomed yours this night. And now, my friend Sidney, I must find Charles McGinnis, before he overstays his welcome."

And before Sidney could ask any of the questions that suddenly occurred to him, Death had walked off into the darkness, and he could only wave his hand toward where he thought the old man might be.

❖　❖　❖

And it was as Death had promised. Sydney Bullock, who decided he liked the sobriquet Sitting Bull and took it for his own, traveled the spaceways for the next half century, exploring and mapping planets, even discovering hitherto-unknown sentient races. He never had a sick day, and when he retired to a planet of golden trees and evocative sunsets in the Orion Cluster, he assumed that his adventure with Death was merely a dream. He spent his days exploring as much of his new world as he could on foot, and his evenings were spent catching up on a lifetime's reading.

And three days before his one hundred and nineteenth birthday, he was visited by an old man who looked vaguely familiar.

"Have you had a good life, Sitting Bull?" asked the old man.

"If you're who I think you are, then you know I have," answered Sidney. "Hell, you even know my new name."

The old man smiled a toothless grin. "I was there the day you got it." He paused. "And have you been free of pain and of disease?"

"Yes."

The old man grimaced. "I wish I could say that for myself."

"You actually look older, and perhaps even thinner," noted Sidney. "And I couldn't help noticing that you're missing most of your teeth."

"I'd like to say that it goes with the job," answered the old man, "but in truth it goes with the centuries and the millennia."

"Would you like to come in and sit down for a while?" asked Sidney, indicating his most comfortable leather chair and hassock.

"Don't tempt me, boy," said Death with a tired smile. "I might never get back up, and you'd be surprised how quickly the world—*all* worlds—can get crowded."

Death reached his gnarled, bony hand out to Sidney, who just stood there as if lost in thought.

"Come, my friend," said Death. "There's no pain involved, I promise you. Just peace, and everlasting sleep."

"I have a feeling that you could use that more than anyone," replied Sidney.

"You can't imagine how many eons I've longed for it," admitted Death with a sigh. "But the universe is filled with life, and you can't have life without Death."

"No, you can't," admitted Sidney. He stared at the ancient man thoughtfully. "But since there is always new life, who's to say there can't be a new Death?"

Death stared at him for a long moment. "Do you realize what you're saying?"

"Yes, I do," replied Sidney. "Do you? We're both old, but to put it bluntly, only one of us is a used-up old man."

"True," acknowledged Death.

"You gave me a life free of pain, free of suffering," continued Sidney. "Let me repay you by giving you an eternity without pain and suffering."

"Are you sure, Sitting Bull?" said Death.

"I am," he replied.

"Then I accept your offer, and I thank you, Sitting Bull."

"You are welcome," was the answer. "And my name is Death now."

And suddenly the newly-named Death could hear a thousand men and women and *things* weeping and moaning. There was a woman in her hospital bed on Zeta Piscium IV, a soldier drowning in his own blood in a trench on Lodin XI, a six-legged alien staring helplessly at a viewscreen as its ship raced headlong toward brilliant Aldebaran, and each of them was praying for him to visit them.

He wondered if he had time for a sandwich and a cup of coffee, realized that of course he didn't, and was soon hard at work.

The End

Mike Resnick is, according to *Locus*, the all-time leading award winner, living or dead, for short science fiction. He has won 5 Hugos (from a record 37 nominations), plus a Nebula and other major awards in the USA, France, Poland, Croatia, Catalonia, Spain and Japan. He is the author of more than 70 novels, more than 270 short stories, 10 books of non-fiction, and three screenplays, and was the Guest of Honor at the 2012 Worldcon and at Boskone 28, in 1991.

DEATH'S MESSENGERS

by The Brothers Grimm, Tale #177, Alt Title: *The Messengers of Death*

In ancient times a giant was once traveling on a great highway, when suddenly an unknown man sprang up before him, and said, "Halt, not one step farther!"

"What!" cried the giant, "a creature whom I can crush between my fingers, wants to block my way? Who art thou that thou darest to speak so boldly?"

"I am Death," answered the other. "No one resists me, and thou also must obey my commands."

But the giant refused, and began to struggle with Death. It was a long, violent battle, at last the giant got the upper hand, and struck Death down with his fist, so that he dropped by a stone.

The giant went his way, and Death lay there conquered, and so weak that he could not get up again. "What will be done now," said he, "if I stay lying here in a corner? No one will die in the world, and it will get so full of people that they won't have room to stand beside each other."

In the meantime a young man came along the road, who was strong and healthy, singing a song, and glancing around on every side. When he saw the half-fainting one, he went compassionately to him, raised him up, poured a strengthening draught out of his flask for him, and waited till he came round.

"Dost thou know," said the stranger, whilst he was getting up, "who I am, and who it is whom thou hast helped on his legs again?"

"No," answered the youth, "I do not know thee."

"I am Death," said he. "I spare no one, and can make no exception with thee, but that thou mayst see that I am grateful, I promise thee that I will not fall on thee unexpectedly, but will send my messengers to thee before I come and take thee away."

"Well," said the youth, "it is something gained that I shall know when thou comest, and at any rate be safe from thee for so long."

Then he went on his way, and was light-hearted, and enjoyed himself, and lived without thought. But youth and health did not last long, soon came sicknesses and sorrows, which tormented him by day, and took away his rest by night.

"Die, I shall not," said he to himself, "for Death will send his messengers before that, but I do wish these wretched days of sickness were over."

As soon as he felt himself well again he began once more to live merrily. Then one day some one tapped him on the shoulder. He looked round, and Death stood behind him, and said, "Follow me, the hour of thy departure from this world has come."

"What," replied the man, "wilt thou break thy word? Didst thou not promise me that thou wouldst send thy messengers to me before coming thyself? I have seen none!"

"Silence!" answered Death. "Have I not sent one messenger to thee after another? Did not fever come and smite thee, and shake thee, and cast thee down? Has dizziness not bewildered thy head? Has not gout twitched thee in all thy limbs? Did not thine ears sing? Did not toothache bite into thy cheeks? Was it not dark before thine eyes? And besides all that, has not my own brother Sleep reminded thee every night of me? Didst thou not lie by night as if thou wert already dead?"

The man could make no answer; he yielded to his fate, and went away with Death.

The End

SWAN DIVE

by Nancy Holder

based upon *The Six Swans*

Bright, blazing sunlight, and tea: the day had dawned far too soon and Jonathan was sorry for it. The business of the Empire was often bloody and unjust, and he was in high dudgeon over what the hell to do. On the one hand, he was an officer and a gentleman; he had never so much as raised a hand to a woman, much less hung one. And such a one: beautiful, accomplished in French and German, well-read, a mistress of the chess board.

And she had heard of him. He'd been rather taken aback when she'd said, upon her capture, "Oh, so you are *the* Jonathan Frasier. The one who took the blame for that mess back in Calcutta. And were posted here for your trouble? What a travesty."

She'd shaken her head; though she had worn veils at the time, her brilliant red hair had blazed through them. He couldn't help his flicker of gratitude, knowing that others had heard what had happened to him. It *was* a travesty, though admittedly one he had taken upon himself. Someone must be blamed, and he had been naïve enough to assume that he would be in some way compensated for making such a terrible sacrifice as besmirching his own reputation. Upon breaking their engagement, Miss Margaret Mason had exclaimed that he was loyal to a fault.

Upon hearing that on the following morning—less than twelve hours later—she was engaged to Sir Oscar Atherton, Bart., Jonathan's best friend—correction, his *former* best friend—Jonathan deduced that the same could not be said of her.

133

If given a choice, he would say that his prisoner was the better choice when it came to the merit of womanhood. Yet the Order of Execution lay on his desk, and his superiors were en route to witness the proceedings. Today, on the sixth anniversary of his exile to the desert, Miss Lilliane Highsmith-Jones was scheduled to die for the crime of treason. And more than a little of his heart would die with her. For yes, in these past two months, he had grown to love her. Hopelessly.

It was clear to him she had harbored no intention of aiding the enemy with the weapon she had stolen. She was an opportunist, plain and simple, eager to line her pockets with the gold that one of the many rajahs had offered for the ingenious machine, termed a "cloaking device," which would render anything up to a certain mass and shape entirely invisible. Astounding!

He had no idea how she had learned of its existence, much less managed to intercept it from the lumbering caravan charged with delivering it to Calcutta. Though it had been protected by the Crown, she had still managed to sneak into the encampment, indeed, into the very tent where the thing was kept, and take the device. Those were still matters she had yet to disclose. Indeed, even to save her own life she had refused to tell him where she had hidden it, unless his government was willing to pay the outrageous price she had requested.

Requested? Nay, demanded. Her *demands* had been many: Fresh water, new clothes, a thicker straw mattress—chiding him for lack of manners, constantly ordering him and Reginald about. Informing him, by the by, that Reginald's name was actually Anwar.

"I knew that," he'd told the fire-headed beauty who had been delivered into his care until it could be determined what to do with her. Her eyes were absolutely enormous, the color of lapis lazuli. Unnatural. Her neck long as a swan. Her bosom—

Very well. He had not known that Reginald's Christian name was Anwar.

I must make her tell me where she hid that infernal contraption, he vowed as Reginald poured him another cuppa and he put down the *Times. It is the only way I have to save her life.* Two months old, the paper was. Anarchists were terrorizing London. That world had never seemed so far way; all they had here were endless miles of sunbaked desert sand and their grimy, squat huts.

And one gently curving palm tree, beneath which Reginald had erected the gallows, precisely constructed according to the Admiralty Pattern. It had taken him days of labor.

I may as well hang myself if I don't hang her, Jonathan thought. *And they'll hang her after I'm finished off, at any rate.*

"Thank you, Reginald," he said crisply as he absently flicked the tassel affixed to the top of his helmet. He did not feel crisp. He felt damp and limp and hot and depressed.

To stretch that neck, that long, white column—

Ka-boom

boom

boom

boom

boom

The explosions cannonaded and with the last one, a smile burst across Jonathan's face and a shout of triumph erupted from his chest. Reginald dropped the teapot. Jonathan threw on his helmet and Reginald covered his head as plaster rained down. In their lean-to, their horses reared. A huge chunk of the ceiling landed hard on the table and covered the Order of Execution. That vixen! Had she just blown up their quarters?

"Does this mean we are shooting her now?" Reginald cried.

Jonathan chortled and grabbed his rifle and—for effect, per-haps—his gleaming regimental sword. Together they charged along the earthworks corridor to the cell that had contained their vexing, alluring prisoner.

As he had surmised, she was contained no longer.

A dove-grey glove lay on the ground. She had been wearing it when he had arrested her. *I've been had,* Jonathan thought, as he leaped over the matchstick fragments of admittedly corroded iron bars. She had blown the back wall to smithereens. *She possessed the means to escape all along.*

Vast clouds of dust cloaked the slight, swathed figure astride Rex, the mighty Bedouin mount that had cost Jonathan so dearly—an eye patch was the evidence of his marker. Rex was *his* horse, the minx! Intentional?

She was gaining distance. He and Reginald were of one mind as the turbaned man raced for a saddle and bridle for Zeus, a lesser creature, and in under a minute, Jonathan swung his leg over while Reginald held Zeus still.

"If they come," Jonathan told him, "if you see them, inform them of what has happened. Tell them the fault is entirely mine." He looked into the brown eyes of the brown man and thought, *It's far more likely that he will leave his post and disappear. Perhaps that would be best. We're certainly in for it now.*

And then he said, "This may be farewell, Anwar. That may be what is required."

The man's eyes widened, and then he bowed. "Farewell, sahib."

How had she done it? Jonathan wondered, as he cantered away. *I searched her.*

Well, perhaps not thoroughly enough. He had been raised a gentleman. Perhaps sensing this, she had thrown back her head and smiled at him, daring him to cross the lines of propriety. A challenge he had not risen to, though he had risen, oh, yes.

There was a lilt to her speech that bespoke foreignness. She could not possibly be English. She was, she had asserted. It was simply that she had been raised "elsewhere."

Why am I going after her? he inquired of himself. *I don't want to hang her. But I can't exactly sit on my bum while she gallivants into the desert, can I? Reginald might say something. I must make an effort.*

Then it dawned on him: surely she would make straight for the cloaking device. If he allowed her to think she could do so unimpeded, he could snatch it from her, hand it over to his government, and save them both.

Slowing down the horse, he nevertheless kept her dust cloud in range. He took quick stock. Despite the need for haste, Reginald had packed two bags of water. Excellent. Jonathan was armed. Also excellent.

Smiling once more, he murmured, "Tally-ho!"

❖　❖　❖

The day was a scorcher, but Jonathan knew the perils of the desert. Over the hours he drank sparingly, and he shared with Zeus. The horse was a trouper, that must be said, but it was a creature of flesh and blood, as he was. He took off his jacket, wet it, and placed it over Zeus's head. He drenched his helmet. Without it, he'd have been all in hours before the sinking of the sun. But sink it did, and the dunes cast long shadows that cooled him and his tired mount, and shielded him from her view. Several times during the trek she had made a tiny circle and stared back in his direction. Only the height of the dunes had saved him from discovery. But whilst spying on her, he was quite shocked to realize she was riding astride as well as bareback—he hadn't actually realized women could, ah, *accommodate* the girth of a horse.

"Miss Lilliane Highsmith-Jones, what adventures we could have," he murmured aloud. But of course that could never be. Unless, perhaps, they could take the money received from selling the cloaking device and live on it…

That he could not do. Though some men in higher places had used him badly, the highest in the land could be counted upon to do well by the Empire. And as went the Empire, so went the world. He was privileged to have been born an Englishman, and he could not squander that gift.

What he *would* do, then, was let her go. No one would fault him for losing his prisoner if in return he could give them the cloaking device. But first, of course, he must catch her.

❖   ❖   ❖

Night wore on, and wore him down. He swayed in the saddle and his chin bobbed forward on his chest. His head pounded and his tongue was dry as chalk. Perhaps he been too sparing with his drink. He hadn't eaten all day, but he was a soldier, and used to privation. He doubted she'd had any water at all, much less food, and *she* was still on the move.

Zeus stumbled and stopped. Jonathan put his heels to the beast but it was no good. Jonathan kept a stiff upper lip as he dismounted and gathered up the reins. He began to lead Zeus forward, and the excellent creature shuffled gamely through the sand.

The stars above reminded him of his hopes and dreams when he had landed in India. Younger then, with prospects, dreaming of glory and honor. Glory had eluded him. Honor he had retained.

Perhaps glory had been overrated.

Love. What of that?

I was a fool. I am a fool. Why didn't I let her go? An idiot. Loyal to a fault. My loyalty was misplaced.

He didn't see her anywhere. The moon cast no shadow on the undulating horizon. Fear clutched his heart and he thought of her lying insensible in the sand, gasping for water, for aid. That image propelled him forward; when Zeus chuffed and stopped again, and would not move, he took the saddle off. He poured water into the beast's mouth and then his own, and slung the bag over his shoulder. Zeus took one look at him, lowered his head, and turned around.

"The barn is a long way off, old man," Jonathan murmured, but his voice was a dry husk. "But good luck." His lips were cracked; he felt his cheeks. Skin was peeling off. She would be in worse shape.

He staggered on. The stars were enormous and close to the sand. There were far worse places to die.

She could not die.

She could not.

❖   ❖   ❖

The bitter heat of dawn pummeled his shoulders. He was on his hands and knees, crawling, barely able to put one hand in front of the other. It was only then that he realized that he had lost his helmet somewhere in the night. His sword and rifle. The bag of water, too, and it had not been empty. He'd lost track of his possessions, and of himself. He could not remember beginning to crawl.

And the sun was rising.

He remembered the penny dreadfuls he had read beneath the stairs at school: ghouls dancing on Walpurgis Night until the rising of the cleansing sun. Making for their tombs too late, disintegrating into grave dust. He would not disintegrate. His flesh would shrink against his bones, and his skin would char.

"Oh, almighty God, help me," he whispered, and then, "Help *her*. If it is to be one of us, give her a long and happy life." And in that prayer, he experienced an apotheosis. He fully accepted that yes, oh, yes, he *was* loyal to a fault. He was a man with a very large heart. Perhaps he was not cut out for soldiering. Definitely he was not. How, then, should he have spent his life? It would be a mystery left unsolved—in this life, at any rate. Perhaps, as the savages believed, he would be reincarnated, and that would be the lesson he would learn.

But for now, if he retained even one spark of life, he would expend it in saving her life. If possible, he would move heaven and earth—

And then he fell into another insensible fugue, for the next thing he knew, the desert floor was shaking violently, and he was thrown hard to one side. A cutting wind poured buckets of hot sand on him, over him, engulfing him until he was nearly drowning in an ocean of grit; he flailed and choked; the desert turned sideways into a huge tidal wave and he rolled over and over, barely aware. His exhausted mind could make no sense of it; an image of a *djinn* flashed through his mind—yes, he had awakened a denizen of this vast desert, and it was rising.

It was rising; he saw something; in the name of all that was holy—

Bloody hell!

Something shiny as regimental brass, and as enormous as the Tower of London, rising from below.

Then his eyes, nose, and mouth were filled and coated over. And he knew he was dreaming, and that this was the end.

❖ ❖ ❖

She was bending over him when he woke. He jerked, and she placed an ivory hand upon his forehead. Her exquisite eyes of lapis lazuli focused on him, and her smile was brilliant.

"You are not dead," she said in that strangely lilting accent.

"I thought I was," he replied. His face—he could not feel it, but he attempted to return the smile. "I'm deucedly glad to see that you are not dead, either."

They must have been found and taken to an oasis. Or a gaol. He tried to raise his head. To his surprise, she wrapped both her hands around his wrists and helped him up. She was wearing some kind of uniform, entirely white, with a pair of delicate metal wings pinned just above her heart, and altogether too form-fitting. She had on boots that clasped her calves—dear Lord—and as he rose from what he now saw was some sort of pallet, she took a step back, and then another, and he thought of his poor, brave horse.

"Zeus," he said.

"Here," she assured him, and her smile broadened. Indeed, it filled the room. "Alive. And noble Rex, too."

His relief brought tears to his eyes. *How? Where?* he thought, but he was too overcome to speak.

The room: it was vast, reaching perhaps thirty feet overhead, and there were other people in it, also wearing the same uniform as she. They were milling around a trio of metal stands, upon which flickered—he had no words to describe the astonishing objects he was seeing—visions of the world? Pictures that moved?

"I feel rather dizzy," he said, and sat back down on the pallet.

"You've been through a lot," she concurred, and she sat down beside him.

Despite his incredible turmoil and confusion, her nearness enflamed him. It took every English bone in his body not to throw his arms around her and weep into bosom, giving thanks to God that she had been spared. Or if not, if this was heaven, it was miracle enough that they had died together, and that finally, he might be permitted one kiss—a chaste one, he would control himself; but oh, how he wanted, how he desired—

"Dear God, Lilliane," he said, and then he fell to showering her with kisses everywhere on her face, a cascade of kisses, a waterfall, an ocean. Her forehead—kissed; her loose curls—kissed; her delicate, dainty hands—

On her wrist she wore a metal band inlaid with colorful stones. And as he kissed the dark blue one—she disappeared!

"Dear God!" he shouted. Heads turned in his direction. Someone laughed.

And then there she was, beside him once more. He embraced her, shaking both with fear and relief. She allowed it, and then her arms came around him, and she kissed his forehead. It was the first time she had kissed him, and he was utterly undone.

"I love you," he confessed. "I would not have hanged you. I came after you only to obtain the cloaking…" he blinked and stared down at the metal band "…device," he finished.

"Oh, thank you, Jonathan," she murmured. "My prayers are answered."

She raised her arm so that he could see the band close up. It was exquisitely wrought, the metal chased with elaborate designs, the stones colorful and smooth. "*This* is the cloaking device. I was wearing it when I allowed myself to be captured," she told him. She gestured to the others. "We all have them. We have had them for a century."

He frowned, bewildered. "Then…?"

"Then why did I bother to steal one?" she filled in for him.

Attempting an answer, he said, "To prevent its falling into enemy hands?"

She cupped his face and gazed into his eyes. His head swam. He was beginning to lose his grip. At any moment, he would collapse into a gibbering heap.

"Ssh, ssh," she gentled him. "Don't you see? It was never about the cloaking device." His lips parted, and she pressed her forefinger over them. Her cheeks glowed with a delicate hue of maidenly pink and she lowered her eyes like a modest schoolgirl. "It was about *you*, Jonathan Frasier. You."

"I?"

She gestured to the boxes with their strangely moving images. Two of her fellows were watching the two of them, lips turned up, quite amused.

"What did the Bard say? 'I loved you 'ere I saw you.' You were too good for the world you lived in, John. But you're perfect for mine."

Then she gazed up through her lashes at him, hope evident in her expression. Seeing perhaps an answer, she twined her hands around his neck and offered her mouth.

Utterly confused, thoroughly besotted, he gave her his in return. As sensation and emotion charted new territories, it dawned on him what she had done. She had made a declaration! Permission granted, he trailed kisses down the white column of her neck, long as a swan's.

"Captain, *Cygnet One* launching for the gate," one of the others declared.

"*Cygnet One* aye, go for launch," she replied. She cocked her head and smiled joyously at Jonathan. "To adventure, then. And glory."

He clasped both her hands in his. "And to love?"

She nodded. "The grandest, most glorious adventure of them all. Or so I have been told."

"Launch," the other announced.

The chamber filled with bright blazing sunlight, or something much like it. The floor rumbled.

And Jonathan Frasier laughed for joy.

The End

Nancy Holder is the *New York Times* bestselling coauthor of the Wicked dark fantasy saga. She has received 5 Bram Stoker Awards, a Scribe Award, and a Young Adult Literature Pioneer Award. She writes tie-in material for Buffy the Vampire Slayer, Teen Wolf, Beauty and the Beast, other TV shows. Her fairytale retellings include *The Rose Bride* and *Spirited*. Her most recent project is *Crimson Peak: The Official Movie Novelization*. Socialize at @nancyholder.

THE SIX SWANS

by The Brothers Grimm, Tale #49

Once upon a time, a certain King was hunting in a great forest, and he chased a wild beast so eagerly that none of his
attendants could follow him. When evening drew near he
stopped and looked around him, and then he saw that he had lost his
way. He sought a way out, but could find none. Then he perceived
an aged woman with a head which nodded perpetually, who came
towards him, but she was a witch.

"Good woman," said he to her, "Can you not show me the way
through the forest?"

"Oh, yes, Lord King," she answered, "that I certainly can, but on
one condition, and if you do not fulfill that, you will never get out of
the forest, and will die of hunger in it."

"What kind of condition is it?" asked the King.

"I have a daughter," said the old woman, "who is as beautiful as
any one in the world, and well deserves to be your consort, and if you
will make her your Queen, I will show you the way out of the forest."

In the anguish of his heart the King consented, and the old
woman led him to her little hut, where her daughter was sitting by
the fire. She received the King as if she had been expecting him, and
he saw that she was very beautiful, but still she did not please him,
and he could not look at her without secret horror. After he had
taken the maiden up on his horse, the old woman showed him the
way, and the King reached his royal palace again, where the wedding
was celebrated.

The King had already been married once, and had by his first
wife, seven children, six boys and a girl, whom he loved better than

anything else in the world. As he now feared that the stepmother might not treat them well, and even do them some injury, he took them to a lonely castle which stood in the midst of a forest. It lay so concealed, and the way was so difficult to find that he himself would not have found it, if a wise woman had not given him a ball of yarn with wonderful properties. When he threw it down before him, it unrolled itself and showed him his path.

The King, however, went so frequently away to his dear children that the Queen observed his absence; she was curious and wanted to know what he did when he was quite alone in the forest. She gave a great deal of money to his servants, and they betrayed the secret to her, and told her likewise of the ball which alone could point out the way.

And now she knew no rest until she had learnt where the King kept the ball of yarn, and then she made little shirts of white silk, and as she had learnt the art of witchcraft from her mother, she sewed a charm inside them. And once when the King had ridden forth to hunt, she took the little shirts and went into the forest, and the ball showed her the way.

The children, who saw from a distance that some one was approaching, thought that their dear father was coming to them, and full of joy, ran to meet him. Then she threw one of the little shirts over each of them, and no sooner had the shirts touched their bodies than they were changed into swans, and flew away over the forest.

The Queen went home quite delighted, and thought she had got rid of her stepchildren, but the girl had not run out with her brothers, and the Queen knew nothing about her. Next day the King went to visit his children, but he found no one but the little girl.

"Where are thy brothers?" asked the King.

"Alas, dear father," she answered, "they have gone away and left me alone!" and she told him that she had seen from her little window how her brothers had flown away over the forest in the shape of swans, and she showed him the feathers, which they had let fall in the courtyard, and which she had picked up.

The King mourned, but he did not think that the Queen had done this wicked deed, and as he feared that the girl would also be stolen away from him, he wanted to take her away with him. But she was afraid of her stepmother, and entreated the King to let her stay just this one night more in the forest castle.

The poor girl thought, "I can no longer stay here. I will go and seek my brothers." And when night came, she ran away, and went straight into the forest. She walked the whole night long, and next day also without stopping, until she could go no farther for weariness.

Then she saw a forest-hut, and went into it, and found a room with six little beds, but she did not venture to get into one of them, but crept under one, and lay down on the hard ground, intending to pass the night there. Just before sunset, however, she heard a rustling, and saw six swans come flying in at the window. They alighted on the ground and blew at each other, and blew all the feathers off, and their swan's skins stripped off like a shirt.

Then the maiden looked at them and recognized her brothers, was glad and crept forth from beneath the bed. The brothers were not less delighted to see their little sister, but their joy was of short duration. "Here canst thou not abide," they said to her. "This is a shelter for robbers, if they come home and find thee, they will kill thee."

"But can you not protect me?" asked the little sister.

"No," they replied, "only for one quarter of an hour each evening can we lay aside our swan's skins and have during that time our human form; after that, we are once more turned into swans."

The little sister wept and said, "Can you not be set free?"

"Alas, no," they answered, "the conditions are too hard! For six years thou mayst neither speak nor laugh, and in that time thou must sew together six little shirts of starwort for us. And if one single word falls from thy lips, all thy work will be lost." And when the brothers had said this, the quarter of an hour was over, and they flew out of the window again as swans.

The maiden, however, firmly resolved to deliver her brothers, even if it should cost her her life. She left the hut, went into the midst of the forest, seated herself on a tree, and there passed the night. Next morning she went out and gathered starwort and began to sew. She could not speak to any one, and she had no inclination to laugh; she sat there and looked at nothing but her work.

When she had already spent a long time there it came to pass that the King of the country was hunting in the forest, and his huntsmen came to the tree on which the maiden was sitting. They called to her and said, "Who art thou?" But she made no answer. "Come down to us," said they. "We will not do thee any harm." She only shook her head.

As they pressed her further with questions she threw her golden necklace down to them, and thought to content them thus. They, however, did not cease, and then she threw her girdle down to them, and as this also was to no purpose, her garters, and by degrees everything that she had on that she could do without until she had nothing left but her shift.

The huntsmen, however, did not let themselves be turned aside by that, but climbed the tree and fetched the maiden down and led her before the King. The King asked, "Who art thou? What art thou doing on the tree?"

But she did not answer. He put the question in every language that he knew, but she remained as mute as a fish. As she was so beautiful, the King's heart was touched, and he was smitten with a great love for her. He put his mantle on her, took her before him on his horse, and carried her to his castle. Then he caused her to be dressed in rich garments, and she shone in her beauty like bright daylight, but no word could be drawn from her. He placed her by his side at table, and her modest bearing and courtesy pleased him so much that he said, "She is the one whom I wish to marry, and no other woman in the world." And after some days he united himself to her.

The King, however, had a wicked mother who was dissatisfied with this marriage and spoke ill of the young Queen.

"Who knows," said she, "from whence the creature who can't speak, comes? She is not worthy of a king!"

After a year had passed, when the Queen brought her first child into the world, the old woman took it away from her, and smeared her mouth with blood as she slept. Then she went to the King and accused the Queen of being a man-eater. The King would not believe it, and would not suffer any one to do her any injury. She, however, sat continually sewing at the shirts, and cared for nothing else.

The next time, when she again bore a beautiful boy, the false stepmother used the same treachery, but the King could not bring himself to give credit to her words. He said, "She is too pious and good to do anything of that kind; if she were not dumb, and could defend herself, her innocence would come to light."

But when the old woman stole away the newly-born child for the third time, and accused the Queen, who did not utter one word of defense, the King could do no otherwise than deliver her over to justice, and she was sentenced to suffer death by fire.

When the day came for the sentence to be executed, it was the last day of the six years during which she was not to speak or laugh, and she had delivered her dear brothers from the power of the enchantment. The six shirts were ready, only the left sleeve of the sixth was wanting.

When, therefore, she was led to the stake, she laid the shirts on her arm, and when she stood on high and the fire was just going to be lighted, she looked around and six swans came flying through the air towards her. Then she saw that her deliverance was near, and her heart leapt with joy. The swans swept towards her and sank down so that she could throw the shirts over them, and as they were touched by them, their swan's skins fell off, and her brothers stood in their own bodily form before her, and were vigorous and handsome. The youngest only lacked his left arm, and had in the place of it a swan's wing on his shoulder.

They embraced and kissed each other, and the Queen went to the King, who was greatly moved, and she began to speak and said, "Dearest husband, now I may speak and declare to thee that I am innocent, and falsely accused."

And she told him of the treachery of the old woman who had taken away her three children and hidden them. Then to the great joy of the King they were brought thither, and as a punishment, the wicked stepmother was bound to the stake, and burnt to ashes. But the King and the Queen with their six brothers lived many years in happiness and peace.

The End

THE WHITE RAT

by Dana Cameron

based upon *The White Snake*

Not so many years from now, in a far distant outpost of the Corps...

Sheriff Laura Maria Villanueva set down her mug of "tea"-flavored caffeine substitute on the desk and glanced through the tablet the deputy handed her. "How was it last night?"

"It was a pretty quiet shift, boss," her deputy, Henry "Half" Price said. "Two citations for air-waste, a warning for failure to properly recycle, and one new guest, courtesy of the sanitation crew."

"Who's that? I don't see it in the—"

"It's under psych. Tad Waldon."

The sheriff blew out her cheeks. "Let me guess. Theft?"

Half held up a finger. "With a twist."

"How so?"

"He was on a mortality detail, and decided to lift one of the deceased's belongings."

"Who died?"

"Crazy Bea."

The sheriff slumped. "Well, shit."

Half tipped back in his seat, the glow of the security system panel reflecting on the rank chips running up the side of his neck. "Doesn't that make our lives easier?"

"I kinda hate to reduce a human life to a matter of my convenience." When he shrugged, the sheriff tried again. "She wasn't *that* bad."

"Public urination, which is also a failure to recycle. Graffiti, which is also a failure to conserve. Public annoyance, trespass—breaking into the archives—do I really need to go on?"

"She never should have been up here in the first place," the sheriff said. "Someone somewhere must've thought they could dump her off-world and be rid of her. Wonder if I could find out who sent her, and let them know she's gone. Or maybe fine them for…"

"For what?"

"I don't know. Being an asshole, I guess." Laura glanced at the station news; there was nothing else out of the ordinary—the war with the squids was in its twenty-third year, the usual shortages of almost everything, the supply vessel overdue, again—and noticed the deputy was now rocking harder, the ghost of a smile on his face. She wondered what she missed, and thought about the case. "Wait a minute—what did *Beatrix Lamb* have worth stealing? She was on assistance, tax exempt. And how did Tad distinguish himself, this time?"

His disappointment that I figured it out was ill-concealed, she thought, *but at least he was trying. He has lots more to learn, before he takes the advanced rank exams.*

"That's the thing. I'm not sure what it is, but I think it's old. I put it in the locker."

"Old?"

"Worse than that, he set a fire."

"Uh, oh." Sheriff Villanueva looked up. Fire is catastrophic on any station.

"No, it's okay. It was…very small. And he had it in his mouth. I put it out."

"Wait—he was *eating* the thing he stole?"

Deputy Price looked at her. "No. The little thing in his mouth was on fire."

"Oh. He was *smoking.*" Seeing the deputy's puzzlement, she explained. "People used to do that. Long time ago. Take some kind of plant, roll it in a flammable material, light it, then inhale the smoke."

Half was aghast. "But the fire hazard!"

"Yup. That's why we patch up or buzz. Was it weed?"

He nodded. That wasn't the problem; hydroponic weed was a staple crop.

"So the question is, why did he smoke it rather than bake it? Show me the locker."

Half pulled out the locker, one of a bank on the wall behind the desk, and thumbed the ID. The lid slowly raised. "It's heavy, like a box."

The sheriff looked inside. "Holy shit."

"What? What is it?"

"I don't know, but it *is* old. Handmade, I think?" She looked at the thing, a little cautiously. It wasn't much bigger than a standard work tablet, but much thicker, maybe twenty-five cm by fifteen by seven cm thick. Its exterior was off-white and textured on three sides with smooth blue striations on the other three sides. One of the two largest sides featured a worn image of a snake tooled into the textured material; when the sheriff looked carefully, she could see traces of gold leaf flaking away. There was a complex *mechanical* lock on one side.

"However did she get something as old and valuable as this? And how did she ever pay the freight to get it up here? I'm gonna ask Tad a few questions."

"Don't bother."

"Why not?"

"He's high as heaven."

The sheriff waved a hand. "I've seen him high before."

Half smirked; it wasn't often he got something over on the sheriff. "Not like this."

"Well," the sheriff said with a sigh. She stretched, feeling the effects of too much stim and not enough rec time. "Let's find out, shall we?"

They could hear the screams from outside the lockup door. "Ah, jeez. The mute circuit's fried again?"

A chorus of "shut the fuck up" echoed in response to every shriek from the cell at the end of the row. Half Price shrugged. "Yep. New one coming on the next supply ship. He's been like this ever since we got him in."

"You called Dr. Onatade?"

"Sure. He buzzed Tad right off, but the trank didn't last long." Half made a disapproving face. "I'm afraid the doctor's using his own concoctions again."

Half will grow out of this. Laura reminded herself. *It's only immaturity, and that is cured by age and experience. He will grow out of this, or I will vent him.* "The doctor is doing the best he can with what he has. The next supply ship isn't for a few more days."

"You, quiet down," the deputy shouted at the two other inmates.

A voice shouted back, "He won't fucking shut up! I got rights!"

"You got nothing. Behave yourself, or you'll be sucking vacuum."

At first, the sheriff couldn't see Tad from outside the cell. Worry that he might have escaped never entered her mind—where would he go, even if he did get out? A tiny artificial satellite, a way station to bigger, better places, with just five thousand souls didn't mean much privacy. She squatted and saw Tad under his bunk, curled up, arms over his head, sobbing wildly.

"How you doing, friend?" she said. It hurt her to see anyone in such a hopeless state, especially someone so young. Tad couldn't have been much older than Carlos. "Sounds like you're having a rough time of it."

Half scowled. "We ain't running a hotel—"

She sighed. "Always make communication your first option, if possible, Deputy." The sheriff turned back to Tad. "If you tell me exactly what you took, Tad, I can get something to help you. But I have to know specifics."

"I told Half." Tad's voice was muffled and hoarse from screaming and crying. "I just smoked a little weed. Nothing else, I swear. Just make it stop! Please, make—" the rest of his request was swallowed up in sobs.

"A double waste of oxygen—"

"Call the doc back," the sheriff ordered, stopping the deputy's complaint before it started. "We need another buzz to quiet him. And put the word out there: there's a bad batch of weed going around; we need to get a sample of it, find the source and close it down. Any questions?"

"Nope." Half trotted off without another word. Laura could feel the resentment at being shut down coming off him, but ignored it. *Not my problem,* she thought. *Yet.*

Only four more years, she thought. *I only have to last that long to see my son, I can do that standing on my head. Just about four years, my debt will be paid off, and I'm out of here, and I'll see Carlos again. But until then…*

"Hang on, Tad," she said, mostly to herself. "That's all any of us can do, is hang on."

❖　　❖　　❖

When Dr. Onatade came by, he was as puzzled as the sheriff as to what had reduced Tad to this state. "The buzz I gave him should have knocked him out for the entire day."

Tad was quiet now, but exhausted, not calmed. To prevent worse uproar, the sheriff had released one prisoner with a warning, and levied a work fine so heavy on the other that she begged to be put back into her cell. Too late did the sheriff worry that whatever was causing Tad's distress might be contagious, but the doctor shook his head. "I ran the scans three times; whatever it is, is Tad's alone. Everything else was normal."

"Normal?"

"Same as the rest of us on a bad day: borderline dehydration, muscle atrophy, low levels of vitamins. He hasn't been to the treadmill or sun booth enough to keep healthy, and he was selling his water allowance."

Time, productivity, or cash were the only ways to get off the station. And everyone thought of the station only as a step toward another destination.

"Okay, fair enough. Did you have a chance to look at the sample of the weed he got?"

Dr. Onatade nodded. "That's garden variety as well."

"Garden variety…?"

"Also nothing unusual. Comes from a time back when everyone had their own gardens to grow food, even flowers. Just for ornament, the flowers were. And the gardens were made out of dirt."

The sheriff made a face. Dirt and food? It sounded so unhygienic.

The doctor enjoyed shocking the sheriff; it was hard to do, and at his age… He moved as he liked, from outpost to outpost; doctors were always in short supply. What he was looking for, the sheriff couldn't have said, but something about this base had kept him here longer than other places.

Dr. Onatade continued. "So, best I can say is that he had a bad reaction to the weed. I'll leave another dose here." He pulled a buzzer from his medical pouch. "This is stronger, and if you can avoid using it at all on him, please do. It'll take a horse down."

"Take a…horse? Down…where?"

"It's very, very strong," the doctor clarified, sighing. "I'm sorry, it's the hazards of a classical education."

Laura nodded absently.

As the doctor set the trank buzzer down on the desk, he happened to glance over at the desk. He froze. "Where did you get that?"

"Evidence. It's what Tad lifted."

"From whom?"

"Crazy Bea. It's a box, right?"

"Why do you say that?"

"That gold-colored thing on the side looks like a lock. Only mechanical, not molecular." The sheriff stood up straighter; the doctor wasn't the only one who sometimes read the classics. "Am I right?"

"About the lock, yes. But it's not a box. That, my dear Sheriff, is a book."

"Wait…" She had been about to ask about the screen and how it charged, but caught herself.

Dr. Onatade's face was filled with awe. "This is paper, actual paper. The covering is…dear gods, is that—? How in the name of all holiness did Bea Lamb get this? May I?"

At the sheriff's nod, the doctor put on gloves, and oh-so carefully, turned the book around. As he did, a band with the clasp fell open, half the locking mechanism smacking the metal table with a sharply ringing crack. The sheriff jumped in spite of herself. The doctor lifted the cover, and gasped.

"What's wrong?"

"Many, many things. I think I've solved our present mystery, but opened a whole other can of worms." Seeing the sheriff open her mouth, he hastened to add, "Uncovered a lot of serious problems."

"Is that why Tad was screaming?" They listened, but Tad had stopped screaming, all of a sudden.

The doctor nodded, then pointed at the ragged edge of the first leaf in the book. "I think he used what I'm assuming was a…title… page for rolling paper. He tore a page out of—how could he have done this? This book must be priceless. It's unspeakably old—the binding, the style of printing, the fineness of the paper…the language, I have no idea what that might be. So, whoever it belonged to, or still belongs to, is powerful *and* rich. And the cover, this outer part? It's made from a skin of some sort."

"A skin…like a polymer?"

"Like an animal. Maybe a reptile."

Stunned, the sheriff picked up the book, before Dr. Onatade could protest about her bare hands. The cover, whatever it was made of, was stained and had bled into the top few pages with the telltale signs of one page having been freshly ripped out. She swore. "That is in violation of…where to start? Antiquities Importation Act, the Endangered Biological Entities Act, the Articles of Cultural Preservation…"

The doctor looked at another page, and shook his head. "It didn't belong to Bea; there's no chip here. Whoever this did belong to will want it back. Something this rare? We are in very big trouble."

The sheriff nodded.

"In a can with many worms."

❖   ❖   ❖

"Tad! We will try again! Please be calm!"

Tad moaned and covered his head against the urgent, high-pitched voice. It didn't do any good; that voice seemed to come from inside his skull. "Why can't you leave me alone? I don't like this!" he whispered.

Rosie the rat groomed her whiskers, trying to resist the urge to gnaw someone else's nose off in frustration. She'd quieted the other does in her cage, and those nearby, hoping the diminution of the noise would help her speak with Tad. His panic was great. She knew how he felt. It had been difficult being able to interpret the precise nature of his distress for hours. It had stirred up a riot in the animal kennel, too. It was hard to get everyone, from the lowest rat pup to the most seasoned bomb-sniffing buck to the quarantined chimpanzee who'd been smuggled in on a child's ticket, to be calm and quiet. If by some chance this poor man could help, Rosie would use him. Rosie didn't like the station and its denizens—especially the cold-handed doctor—but if they died, her own abbreviated lifespan would also be dramatically reduced.

It didn't help that she may have inadvertently been the one who started the complex chain reaction that would most likely destroy the station in the next twenty-four hours.

Time was wasting. She took a deep breath, and decided to go for broke. She was going to tell him who she was. "Tad, it's Rosie."

"I don't know anyone named 'Rosie.'"

"Yes, you do. I'm one of the rats in the doctor's lab. I can hear you through one of the vents. I need your help. You are not crazy. I'm not sure what's going on, but I can understand you and you me, correct?"

"Uh, yeah?"

Good; he took her at her word she was who she said she was. Maybe they still had a chance of surviving.

"I need you to help me. You must give a message to the sheriff."

"Why don't you do it?"

Rosie gnashed her teeth, her whiskers bristling. Time was wasting! She said, "I've tried! She can't understand me. The doctor can't, no one can! We've been squeaking, behaving badly for days, but the doctor assumes we are reacting to the squid's communication waves. When they took you in, you yelled 'Hi, Rosie! What's that about an oxygen exchanger?' into the lab, I realized you could understand me."

"I did? You did?"

"Yeah, that's when we all began shouting at once, trying to get you to hear us. Sorry about that. But we have a big problem."

"What do you mean?"

"The outpost is in danger, and I'm the only one who knows it."

"How do you know it?"

Rosie was trying to be patient. "I helped one of the males escape from here last month. He gnawed on some very tasty cables. Unfortunately, that caused a fire and destroyed the oxygen exchanger. Also, unfortunately, it destroyed the warning indicator, too. That means we're going to suffocate in less than a day, if someone doesn't get it fixed soon."

"Wait—how do I know I'm not hallucinating this?"

A reasonable question. Something a brighter person might have asked long before, Rosie thought. "Do you know what a oxygen exchanger is?"

"Uh, no."

"The sheriff will. Please, please try and let her know. Tell anyone!"

"I could still be high," Tad mused.

"Better to be thought silly than be dead!" Rosie squeaked. Her shrill voice echoed in Tad's brain like a hangover.

"Ugh. Okay. How do I get her to believe me?"

"I know things. I'll tell you, you tell her. And please, hurry!"

❖   ❖   ❖

At first, the sheriff was reluctant to believe anything coming out of Tad's mouth, but at least he seemed much calmer now. When the sheriff heard about the oxygen exchanger, she asked how Tad knew, and he explained that Rosie had told him. The sheriff almost left, but then Tad also mentioned that she sometimes visited the lab when no one else was there. The sheriff froze, and was agape when Tad said that she sang as she patted the rats.

"Rosie doesn't know the language, but you always sound sad when you're there."

"It's…Spanish. My, uh…" She never sang in front of anyone and always turned off the sound surveillance when she was alone in the lab. She found herself becoming emotional at the thought of her son. "Someone I knew—know—kept rats."

"Rosie also said you gave her her name."

"The doctor kept the name," she said, starting to believe Tad. He wasn't sharp enough to pull off a cold reading and didn't have the heart it took to run a real scam. "He was teasing me for being overly sentimental with the working animals."

"Rosie says the doctor's hands are cold, and he keeps flipping the rats around to check their gender," Tad said. "They don't like it, and wish he'd either warm up his hands or put tags on them. It would be less invasive."

That decided the sheriff; she'd always thought the doc handled his patients and specimens like an inept juggler. She toggled the radio comm on her neck array. "Half, get me the head of maintenance. Have him meet me with a team at the main hatch outside of engineering, immediately."

❖　　❖　　❖

They should have known the news would have gotten around; nothing stays a secret for long on an outpost station. For a while, no one believed the rumors, and the sheriff was half-convinced that they would die off on their own. But then someone bought Tad a round of drinks and asked him about it. Then folks started bringing in whatever animals they had from the work teams or had smuggled in, and he talked with them. No one ever saw his lips move, or heard anything but squeaks or yowls or chirps from the animals, but all the same, Tad was able to tell the other citizens of the outpost things only they—and their charges—could know.

It got weird after that. Folks started believing anything and everything, and they started to hound Tad, asking if he could speak to the dead, to relatives far away, to ghosts. Crackpots came out of every corner, besieging him with requests for information (or sperm or blood or tissue samples) or threats—not everyone wanted all their secrets revealed, despite his insistence that he wasn't clairvoyant. It got so bad, that Tad begged the sheriff to lock him up again, and she did, but with Rosie as company, and sometimes Sal the chimp, who apparently told pretty good stories about his days with the smuggler.

Inevitably, the speculation about Tad's astonishing powers led to the question of whether he could talk to the squids. Maybe Tad could end the war, they thought. A generation of war meant everyone had lost someone or lived with the terrible uncertainty of separation.

Then someone suggested that Tad might already be talking to the squids.

The station's mood went from weird to dangerous in a heartbeat.

The sheriff knew Tad's "miracle" would not remain a secret, but she received the Corps' official call even quicker than she imagined. The military, or rather, the Corps' Human Resources Department, appeared mere hours after their informant sent a wave. The sheriff hadn't decided what to do yet, but Half Price was already shining his shoes, his badge, his riot gear, and anything else he found. A good showing in front of the Corps might mean promotion from a favored contractor to full Corps citizenship, with all the perks—including a six-month discharge of fees as a signing bonus for contracts over twenty years.

"Not for nothing, boss," he said. "But you might wanna…you know. Tidy yourself. This is a big deal."

Laura knew he didn't mean it unkindly—yes, her performance reflected on him, too—but just once, it would've been nice to have an unalloyed show of support. She sighed, and realized that she wasn't in the mood to do the spit and polish dance, and that struck her as odd, because any occasion that broke the monotony on the station was welcome. Tad's ability to speak with animals could mean big things for her. If she played her cards right, she could get her debt time reduced or commuted entirely. She could see her son Carlos again, sooner than she dared hope. It had been sixteen years, eight months, and…

She wondered why she wasn't jumping on the chance to exploit this opportunity. Maybe it was the station's reaction to Tad and its sudden turn to anger and fear. Maybe it was the thought of the desperate measures the Corps had been taking in the war with the squids lately. It had kept her up nights until she played out all the scenarios in her head. Few of the outcomes were satisfactory, and none at all were good for Tad.

"We have time," Laura said, trying to sound genial. "Don't worry, I'll explain just how much you had to do with saving the station."

She said it pointedly enough that Half should have felt the sarcasm, but instead, he beamed with pride. "Thanks, boss!"

She continued. "Their wave said to find quarters for fifty troops. Doesn't that seem like overkill to you?"

The deputy shrugged. "Hey, they brought our supplies—and extras—early, and I was able to repair the mute circuit in the cells. They also have to worry about whether this was some kind of sabotage effort, like maybe Tad got cold feet at the last minute. They have to make sure he's not in communication with the squids. And on the off chance that this is some kind of strange coincidence, they have to check that out too. Security is the Corps' priority."

As surprised she was by these astute observations on her deputy's part, she couldn't help think of how perfectly Half would fit into the Corps. He was the ideal Corpsman: not too bright, but possessed of a certain cunning; easily set against his fellows and addicted to the idea of his own authority. Give him a list of things to check off or a form to fill out, and Half was all over it.

Tad would never fit into the Corps or succeed as an independent contractor. No wonder he was driven to smoke the weed, rather than bake it; poor guy had no excitement in his life, and no prospects either. Tad wasn't a bad kid and he wasn't stupid, just not… very sharp. The war had made it so that you either tested out for advanced research academic training, tested out for advanced combat training, or…didn't. If, after his term of mandatory service, Tad had found anything that engaged him, he might have found a niche somewhere. As it was, he knew just enough to realize how wasted his life was. The sheriff was still enough of a romantic to know that the universe is very large and every life terribly precious.

That's why she'd sent Carlos away, buying his passage and incurring the debt so that he could practice his gift for medicine in the fringe settlements, going where he was needed, free of the war-driven bureaucratic determinations of the Corps.

The administrator swept in like he owned the place, and to be fair, he was probably a senior stockholder in this quadrant. Fairness aside, the sheriff felt herself shutting down in his presence, reluctant to show any trace of humanity or vulnerability in front of him. Her days in the military had taught her that the traditions of CYA and RHIP had been part of the navy ever since ships sailed on water and the weaponry was no more than sharpened sticks slung at the enemy with a piece of gut.

It wasn't bad training, though. Remembering that humans are hierarchical had helped her survive.

So the sheriff snapped to attention. There was comfort in protocol and ritual, in the face of uncertainty. The administrator saluted and gestured for her to stand at ease. A studied, mechanical smile vanished before it reached his eyes.

"Sir, welcome to Corps Outpost 7-17, Administrator Tsu."

"Call me Reggie, please, Laura."

He extended a hand, and she shook, her heart sinking. The bosses who urged familiarity were the dangerous ones, in her experience. This one had even gone so far as to introduce himself without an escort, to foster the notion of equality and mutual respect. "Thank you, Administrator. And thank you for bringing the supplies we needed. We've been making do for too long."

"I hear you're on your last leg of a long stint," he said. "The Corps appreciates your dedication! And now to have something as exciting as this to fall in your lap—well, I can't help but think it will be a fine, shiny new chip on your neck. Perhaps even a transfer to the Corps head offices."

"Yes, sir. Apologies, sir, but—we still don't know what *this* is."

He waved aside her protests. "Not for you to worry about. I'm here to take it off your tray."

"Yes, sir." The sheriff nodded. She was being edged out; she had to speak up, while she still had his ear. "I would like to recommend leniency for Thaddeus Waldon, sir. He's a decent sort, just…aimless. In trouble because he…"

"This time it was theft. Not so bad, you might say, but did you know he'd once been held on a charge of disparaging the war effort?"

"He was no threat, just spouting off. Buzzed."

"It was a felony act of war, Sheriff." Administrator Tsu shook his head. "But now he can help make up for that. He's going to the home office. Don't worry; he'll not be any harm to himself or anyone else. He'll aid us with research that will help us win against the squids."

Knowing that Tad's scientific talents were entirely nil, the sheriff understood that he'd be like one of the working rats. He and Rosie, two of a kind. And that would be an even worse life than he had now, bumming around. At least he had his freedom, now, even if he did fuck up every now and again. He reminded her of Carlos as a child, before she realized he'd never fit into the Corps. She remembered when she realized with a shock, that if she didn't send Carlos away, the Corps would break him down into component parts, keeping only those they wanted, discarding, most likely, the things that made him special. "Sir—"

"We're done here, Sheriff Villanueva," he said sharply. Then the smile that didn't reach his eyes was back. "If you'd produce Mr. Waldon, I'd appreciate it."

"Certainly, sir," she said, her heart sinking. "He's being interviewed by Dr. Onatade, who's studying the…book…Tad stole."

The color rose in the administrator's cheeks. "I was explicit in my orders for his containment!"

"Sorry, sir, there was a delay in the wave, sir," the sheriff said, shrugging. "Outage." It was all too common an occurrence; the military took precedence, and other communication just had to wait. But it was a lie, as an administrator's communication would have had the highest priority.

"You don't understand, Sheriff. We can end this war! We can talk to the squids, find a way to make sure they never come back to this quadrant again."

The sheriff suddenly had had enough of the Corps' double-speak. "You don't mean 'we'll ask nicely, and then they'll apologize for bothering us, then leave.' Do you?"

The administrator's eyes went hard. "Where is the prisoner? The skin-bound book? I ask, sheriff, only because it will be a last chance for you to get off my shit list. My troops—and your deputy—have already started to tear apart the outpost."

"This is my jurisdiction!" she protested. The administrator had come to stall her, while he got what he wanted. She moved toward the storage locker.

The administrator followed her, and leaned over to open the locker. "Waldon won't be within your jurisdiction—if it stays your jurisdiction—for very long."

"Then that doesn't give me much time," the sheriff said. When his eyes turned to the locker, she pulled the doctor's trank buzzer from her pocket, and jammed it into the medical port under the administrator's ear. She pressed the button. A faint buzzing noise accompanied the administrator as he collapsed, instantly unconscious. The sheriff eased him into the deputy's chair, and wheeled him into the nearest cell, setting the newly repaired barrier for lock, blackout, and mute.

She knocked on the next cell, and the doctor and Tad came out, wearing a deputy's coverall and cap pulled down low. "Time to go, Tad. You get to my shuttle without anyone seeing you, you get in, and hide yourself. Can you do that?"

"Yes. Rosie will help me."

The sheriff eyeballed the white rat on Tad's shoulder; Rosie eyeballed her right back.

"She says we'll get out."

Unnerved, the sheriff said, "Okay, go. I'll be right behind you."

Tad nodded, not quite hiding a smile of excitement. This was the high he was looking for, this kind of adventure. Something different, all his own.

"You still gonna help me, Doc?" the sheriff asked as she gathered a pack with her few personal belongings.

He nodded. "That buzz should keep him out for a while; one of the side effects is short-term amnesia. I'll tell him one of the conspiracy theorists jumped you and Tad. Tad vanished; you took off after him in your shuttle. I'll program the other shuttle for Hub R7-20."

"And we'll go in the opposite direction." The sheriff hid the skinbound book in a tablet casing, hollowed out to conceal its contents.

The doctor handed her a chip. "That's my research on the book. It's not much; I think Tad absorbed some of the chemicals from the cover in the page he smoked. So be careful how you handle it." He compressed his lips. "Laura, this book is dangerous. The cover is snakeskin, and what with Tad's new abilities…well, there are old, old stories about knowledge and trees and snakes and magical gifts. Tad's not up to handling something like that."

"That's why I'm going."

Suddenly, Dr. Onatade was possessed by a volcanic eruption of emotion. "Why *him*? Why does that shiftless, non-recyclable…*average* nobody get this gift? Tad did *nothing*, was robbing the *dead*, and this amazing power fell into his lap!"

"He did do something, though," the sheriff pointed out. "He did the experiment, however illegal or ill-advised, to use the paper for his weed. Maybe it was meant to be, you know. Someone who was curious, in just the right way. You wouldn't have dreamed of doing that, would you?"

"No."

"Me, neither. So why didn't you try smoking it, like Tad did? As one of your tests?"

It took the doctor a moment to reply. "There's too much I don't know. I didn't recognize some of the chemicals in that stain. I had no idea what effect it might have had on me. And that classical education of mine? The one that taught me those old stories about trees and snakes and powers? I was…too scared."

The sheriff nodded. "But Tad wasn't; he saved 5,000 lives and the station, to boot. If he hadn't been willing to talk to Rosie, chalking it up to a bad drug experience, we might all be dead."

The doctor scowled. "I spoke to that fucking rodent every day."

"Mostly to cuss her out."

"She bit me more than anyone else in her litter." But Dr. Onatade's tantrum was over. "If I had more time, maybe I could have found out more, but…you're right. No one should have this, especially not the Corps. We could destroy it here, so why are you giving up your debt repayment and courting a prison sentence to help Tad? What about your son?"

"Carlos will understand." The sheriff shrugged. "Or he won't; it's been a long time and he has a life of his own. He's happy, which was always my goal. Tad…he has the chance to change his life, and quite possibly, change the universe. But he can't be trusted with the book, and I can't let the administrator have it. I need to look out for him and the book. Maybe I can learn what it is, and who Crazy Bea really was, to have possession of such a thing in the first place. And if I can't do that…well, maybe I *can* help him talk to the squids."

Some things are more important than one person, or one family. Or even the Corps.

And they shook hands, and not ten minutes later, the sheriff and Tad (and Rosie) escaped with the book.

On the shuttle, the sheriff, stunned at what she'd just done, stared at the monitor, looking for signs of pursuit. After a moment, Tad spoke.

"Thank you. Not everyone would have—no one has ever—"

Either the sheriff would explain all of her reasons and give into emotion, or she could focus, and make sure they all escaped. "You're…don't mention it."

"Rosie said you seem sad, again. Scared, and sad." Tad waited while Rosie squeaked again. "And she says she knows why. You and she both had careers in the Corps. In the military. Now you don't. Is that it?"

Thinking of Carlos, the sheriff shook her head. She had never thought of herself as sad, before. She glanced at Rosie, uneasy to think she was actually having a conversation with a rat. "Not all of it."

Another moment between the white rat and her boy. "Do you want to talk about it?"

The sheriff was about to refuse again, then shrugged. "It can't hurt."

They had many adventures after that, all of them dangerous, and some of them wonderful, and they did speak with the squids and end the war, but in no way anyone could have guessed. But if either Tad or the sheriff (or Rosie) eventually discovered the secrets of the book, no one alive knows for sure.

The End

Dana Cameron's fiction is inspired by her career as an archaeologist. In addition to the six Emma Fielding mystery novels and her "Fangborn" urban fantasy novels, Dana's short fiction covers the spectrum, including mystery, historical, noir, thriller, SF/F, Sherlockian pastiche, and horror. The latest novel in the Fangborn series, *Hellbender* (47North, 2015), combines archaeology with werewolves, vampires, and oracles. Her work has won multiple Anthony, Agatha, and Macavity Awards, and has been nominated for the prestigious Edgar Award. Dana lives in Beverly, Massachusetts.

THE WHITE SNAKE

by The Brothers Grimm, Tale #17

A long time ago there lived a king who was famed for his wisdom through all the land. Nothing was hidden from him, and it seemed as if news of the most secret things was brought to him through the air. But he had a strange custom; every day after dinner, when the table was cleared, and no one else was present, a trusty servant had to bring him one more dish. It was covered, however, and even the servant did not know what was in it, neither did anyone know, for the King never took off the cover to eat of it until he was quite alone.

This had gone on for a long time, when one day the servant, who took away the dish, was overcome with such curiosity that he could not help carrying the dish into his room. When he had carefully locked the door, he lifted up the cover, and saw a white snake lying on the dish. But when he saw it he could not deny himself the pleasure of tasting it, so he cut off a little bit and put it into his mouth.

No sooner had it touched his tongue than he heard a strange whispering of little voices outside his window. He went and listened, and then noticed that it was the sparrows who were chattering together, and telling one another of all kinds of things which they had seen in the fields and woods. Eating the snake had given him power of understanding the language of animals.

Now it so happened that on this very day the Queen lost her most beautiful ring, and suspicion of having stolen it fell upon this trusty servant, who was allowed to go everywhere. The King ordered the man to be brought before him, and threatened with angry words that unless he could before the morrow point out the thief, he himself should be looked upon as guilty and executed. In vain he declared his innocence; he was dismissed with no better answer.

In his trouble and fear he went down into the courtyard and took thought how to help himself out of his trouble. Now some ducks were sitting together quietly by a brook and taking their rest; and, whilst they were making their feathers smooth with their bills, they were having a confidential conversation together. The servant stood by and listened. They were telling one another of all the places where they had been waddling about all the morning, and what good food they had found, and one said in a pitiful tone, "Something lies heavy on my stomach; as I was eating in haste I swallowed a ring which lay under the Queen's window."

The servant at once seized her by the neck, carried her to the kitchen, and said to the cook, "Here is a fine duck; pray, kill her."

"Yes," said the cook, and weighed her in his hand; "she has spared no trouble to fatten herself, and has been waiting to be roasted long enough." So he cut off her head, and as she was being dressed for the spit, the Queen's ring was found inside her.

The servant could now easily prove his innocence; and the King, to make amends for the wrong, allowed him to ask a favor, and promised him the best place in the court that he could wish for. The servant refused everything, and only asked for a horse and some money for traveling, as he had a mind to see the world and go about a little.

When his request was granted he set out on his way, and one day came to a pond, where he saw three fishes caught in the reeds and gasping for water. Now, though it is said that fishes are dumb, he heard them lamenting that they must perish so miserably, and, as he had a kind heart, he got off his horse and put the three prisoners back into the water. They quivered with delight, put out their heads, and cried to him, "We will remember you and repay you for saving us!"

He rode on, and after a while it seemed to him that he heard a voice in the sand at his feet. He listened, and heard an ant-king complain, "Why cannot folks, with their clumsy beasts, keep off our bodies? That stupid horse, with his heavy hoofs, has been treading down my people without mercy!" So he turned on to a side path and the ant-king cried out to him, "We will remember you—one good turn deserves another!"

The path led him into a wood, and here he saw two old ravens standing by their nest, and throwing out their young ones. "Out with you, you idle, good-for-nothing creatures!" cried they; "we cannot find food for you any longer; you are big enough, and can provide for yourselves." But the poor young ravens lay upon the ground, flapping their wings, and crying, "Oh, what helpless chicks we are! We must shift for ourselves, and yet we cannot fly! What can we do, but lie here and starve?" So the good young fellow alighted and killed his horse with his sword, and gave it to them for food. Then they came hopping up to it, satisfied their hunger, and cried, "We will remember you—one good turn deserves another!"

And now he had to use his own legs, and when he had walked a long way, he came to a large city. There was a great noise and crowd in the streets, and a man rode up on horseback, crying aloud, "The King's daughter wants a husband; but whoever sues for her hand must perform a hard task, and if he does not succeed he will forfeit his life." Many had already made the attempt, but in vain; nevertheless when the youth saw the King's daughter he was so overcome by her great beauty that he forgot all danger, went before the King, and declared himself a suitor.

So he was led out to the sea, and a gold ring was thrown into it, in his sight; then the King ordered him to fetch this ring up from the bottom of the sea, and added, "If you come up again without it you will be thrown in again and again until you perish amid the waves." All the people grieved for the handsome youth; then they went away, leaving him alone by the sea.

He stood on the shore and considered what he should do, when suddenly he saw three fishes come swimming towards him, and they were the very fishes whose lives he had saved. The one in the middle held a mussel in its mouth, which it laid on the shore at the youth's feet, and when he had taken it up and opened it, there lay the gold ring in the shell. Full of joy he took it to the King, and expected that he would grant him the promised reward.

But when the proud princess perceived that he was not her equal in birth, she scorned him, and required him first to perform another task. She went down into the garden and strewed with her own hands ten sacks-full of millet-seed on the grass; then she said, "Tomorrow morning before sunrise these must be picked up, and not a single grain be wanting."

The youth sat down in the garden and considered how it might be possible to perform this task, but he could think of nothing, and there he sat sorrowfully awaiting the break of day, when he should be led to death. But as soon as the first rays of the sun shone into the garden he saw all the ten sacks standing side by side, quite full, and not a single grain was missing. The ant-king had come in the night with thousands and thousands of ants, and the grateful creatures had by great industry picked up all the millet-seed and gathered them into the sacks.

Presently the King's daughter herself came down into the garden, and was amazed to see that the young man had done the task she had given him. But she could not yet conquer her proud heart, and said, "Although he has performed both the tasks, he shall not be my husband until he has brought me an apple from the Tree of Life."

The youth did not know where the Tree of Life stood, but he set out, and would have gone on for ever, as long as his legs would carry him, though he had no hope of finding it. After he had wandered through three kingdoms, he came one evening to a wood, and lay down under a tree to sleep. But he heard a rustling in the branches, and a golden apple fell into his hand. At the same time three ravens flew down to him, perched themselves upon his knee, and said, "We are the three young ravens whom you saved from starving; when we had grown big, and heard that you were seeking the Golden Apple, we flew over the sea to the end of the world, where the Tree of Life stands, and have brought you the apple."

The youth, full of joy, set out homewards, and took the Golden Apple to the King's beautiful daughter, who had no more excuses left to make. They cut the Apple of Life in two and ate it together; and then her heart became full of love for him, and they lived in undisturbed happiness to a great age.

The End

ORIGINS

by Carlos Hernandez

based upon *The Star-Talers*

I am starving. Performing miracles for you—manifesting money from the air; deconstructing diseases; repairing broken bodies, imbalanced minds—costs me energy, and entropy nickel-and-dimes my soul day by day. So my hunger never leaves me, only grows. And there is no food for me here; I have foresworn eating anyone else. I am resigned to die.

But I do not expect to die anytime soon; I am, for now at least, the only god here; there is no one here to kill me. I will yet last tens of thousands of Earth years. And before I am spent, I intend to transform the Moon into, by human standards at least, heaven.

❖   ❖   ❖

Agnethe loves God. Not me; her god is an ancient vitaphage from Earth.

There she is now, kneeling in the front pew at the Church of Thaddeus the Forgotten. It is mid-afternoon, a time when everyone who can is working. She gave up her shift to a jobless man named Asad, who needed money badly. She does not want to use much energy—calories are hard to come by these days—so she is praying rosaries until sundown. Decades dangle from her fingers.

Thaddeus the Forgotten is an uncomfortable church: there used to be cushions, but they kept being stolen; it is cold, because heating is expensive on the Moon, and because no other bodies are there to help warm it. But it is easily the most beautiful place in Origin City. Through the cupola you see the Earth, huge and effulgent. It fills the church with otherworldly light.

But it is the exception; beauty on the Moon is usually prohibitively expensive. Tabernacle, monstrance, altar, pews, cross: all are printed natively here from processed regolith that over time leaks fine, sharp dust. The pews have whiskbrooms and pans for sweeping it off the kneelers, lest worshippers rise from them with perforated pant legs, bloodied knees.

But those brooms mostly go unused these days. The laity now imitate Agnethe, who sits in the first pew every Sunday and kneels heedlessly upon the regolith. On one momentous Sunday they saw her rise to take Communion with two round bloodstains on the pant legs of her white, standard-issue jumpsuit. When it was her turn and she extended her tongue for the flesh of God, the priest, Father Fugit, asked her if she was all right.

Only then did she notice her knees. She answered with an airy smile that she was fine. She did not realize she was bleeding; she had been focused on the Miracle. She laughed at her own silliness.

Father Fugit did not laugh, nor did the laity. Quite the contrary: now the entire congregation of the Church of Thaddeus the Forgotten bleeds from their knees for their sacrament.

❖　❖　❖

You will not have the technology to discover my home solar system for eons yet. But my people know you. Yours is the only other planet we have found with life so far. Our supercluster seems to be life-poor.

My people? We have language, we have art, we have laws, we have history stretching back to almost the birth of the galaxy.

We do not have bodies as you know bodies. You have not yet named the state of matter that constitutes us. Imagine an intelligent mountain that can take any shape it wishes—a cluster of faint lights over a bog; a tusked boar-god 300 feet tall; a single, doughty whip-poor-will, or perhaps just its song; an electromagnetic field—and you begin to imagine us.

Like you, we feel small and abandoned in a universe of mindless physics. We ride our planet through a pageant of stars, ignorant and reverential. We cannot define qualia either.

We live and die and fear death. We live longer than you, but time is always short when you know life will end.

❖　❖　❖

Agnethe lives in Origin City, population 2,700. It is not a city in the Earth sense, as there is no endemic government on the Moon. The city is privately owned by 23 corporations who only semi-cooperate with one another.

From a distance it looks like a hamster course. Habitation modules for living and commerce are linked like PVC pipes; there are power plants and recycling centers and printing facilities and helium refineries; there are "docks" where bus-sized lunakhods wait to ferry workers to the mines and rovers arrive with metals and rocks and regolith. Urine is recycled into water, feces into a porridge of diminishing nutritional returns. Power from the sun is plentiful, but energy is a monopoly on the Moon and therefore scarce.

Everyone living on the Moon is poor. The owners, the bosses, the HR vice-presidents and advertising executives all live on Earth. It is almost exclusively miners who actually live and work in Origin City. They came to the Moon lured by job ads that promised wealth and offworld adventure. But their wages barely cover the cost of living in space. There are uniforms to buy, equipment to rent, insurance workers must by law purchase. The workers are paid in the local money, "origins." It has no value on Earth.

Once miners can no longer work—not "if" but "once," for even if they are not injured on the job, eventually they will lose too much muscle mass in the Moon's weak gravity to be productive—they become almost instantly destitute. The wise ones use their insurance settlements to purchase a one-way ticket planetside. If the settlement is enough to cover it.

Those that do not or cannot run out of money soon enough, and with their constitutions ruined, they have few prospects to earn more. They dine on charity shit-paste when it is offered, but it is offered too infrequently for most metabolisms. Most days they subsist on their body's own fat and organs until they have eaten themselves out of life.

Agnethe is a miner, too. But she is new to the job. She ran Origin City's health clinic until a few months ago: what the locals call the "animal shelter." Because if you have to stay more than a week, goes the joke, they put you down.

❖   ❖   ❖

My crime was vitaphagy. Like you, we need food for sustenance. Unlike you, our only food is each other. Reproduction was food production for most of our history.

But recently—within the last 700,000 years—we as a people have decided that consumption is an unforgivable wrongness. That eating is evil.

This new morality coincided with the discovery of other life in the supercluster. Specifically, of you.

We learned how frighteningly fragile life on Earth is. You are unalterably locked into unaccommodating, inflexible bodies. You are so particular about your needs—only this small range of temperatures, only that abundance of air, all of this water and gravity and countless other fussy nutritional needs—that, from our perspective, you seem almost petulant about life. If you cannot stay alive in exactly the way you demand your environment to be, you die. It is positively bratty.

We, by contrast, live for eons, and even if we never eat even once during our lifetimes, we can reproduce hundreds of times before we die of starvation. We are a resilient, macrobian, proliferant species. How little we appreciated our good fortune.

But once we had perspective, destroying other life to sustain life became morally repulsive: and suddenly, the most detestable of crimes.

The punishment? Execution was impossible without being hypocritical. So we decided on the next best option: the "slow execution." We would exile vitaphages.

To Earth.

That itself is a grand hypocrisy, of course. What did we think would happened when we sent all the vitaphages to the same planet? "We are not forcing them to eat each other," we told ourselves. "That's their choice. The evil is on them."

We share this trait with you: we can make rationalizations sound palatable.

Once exiled, the vitaphages of course cannibalized one another, as predicted. But the thing no one could have guessed is that they would become your elves and duendes, your nightmares realized and your miracles manifest, your every god and every evil spirit.

❖   ❖   ❖

As the lunar day ends, Agnethe leaves the Church of Thaddeus the Forgotten. She emerges from the doors of the simple church into a passageway. Its temperature is in the single digits. Since they are communal, the corporations are supposed to share the cost of heating them. So they are always inhospitably cold.

Agnethe heads left, toward the market. She rubs her crossed arms as she walks, bites down to stop her teeth from chattering. And then, with a spark of joy, she remembers the tube of paste the priest gave her. She pulls it from a pocket and, with gusto, rips it open with her teeth.

As she walks she sees Virgil sitting against the wall. He reminds her—I have heard her whisper as much—of her father, when he was dying. The gauntness, the stiffness of movement, the same confused lights dancing in his pupils.

"Hi, Virgil," she says cheerily as she nears.

"Please, I'm so hungry!" Virgil answers.

She notes two empty tubes of paste wrung flat and lying next to Virgil. "What would any of us do without Father Fugit?" she says aloud, before smiling and giving him hers.

He notes with wide and grateful eyes that the end has already been bitten open. He shows Agnethe his razed gums before sucking on the tube blissfully, looking at her with great yellow moon-eyes.

Since he did not say grace, Agnethe says "May God bless it for you" before heading once more for the market.

❖   ❖   ❖

I abhorred vitaphages with all the sanctimony of the rest of my people until I became one. No, even now. We forgive ourselves crimes for which we condemn anyone else.

As I entered the twilight of my life—my home is a rogue planet and has no sun, but I adore your turns of phrase—I grew hungry. I fought the hunger, as my people said I should, for as long as I could. But my hunger ate me first. Then, I simply became the vessel for its desires.

Late in my life, when I should have been making preparations for my dissolution, I instead made a child. Specifically to consume it.

Imagine filling a bathtub with water. (The water here is the matter of which our bodies are made. It is unavailable in the Milky Way.) You sit in the tub for awhile, and when you exit, you leave in the water a bit of your ghost. That the water is now a living thing, haunted by your afterimage, and your own child. This is how my people reproduce.

My child was a knowing, ready thing when it was born, capable as a newborn shark, carrying the information I had accumulated in my life, able immediately to contribute as a member of our culture. But because it was newly made, it was sleepy and languorous, trusting of its parent's love.

I absorbed it into me, ghost and all. Its life turned to silence within me, and its matter joined my matter. And I was utterly sated.

I never would have confessed if I had not been discovered. But mine was a notably different body: more massive, capable, aware. I failed to hide my newfound vitality from others. It is hard to hide the lust for life when, after long absence, you rediscover it.

I was accused, charged, interrogated, found guilty. They shoved me through a one-way wormhole and dumped me on Earth.

❖　❖　❖

It is dim and growing dimmer in the market as day becomes night.

The market is warmer than most public places in Origin City: the self-service shops are manned by robots who leak electricity all day long, and for much of the day the place is full of bodies emitting heat. But warmer is not necessarily warm. Any thermometer would show it is, at best, less cold than the halls.

Nevertheless, when she enters the market Agnethe feels as though she is wrapped in a sudden zephyr. She smiles, exhales with relief.

The robot sales clerk at The Armstrong Equipment Rental Emporium is malfunctioning, can no longer move. The shop owner back on Earth has not seen enough of a decline in sales, however, to warrant repairing it. It therefore has not been fixed. So it cannot force Agnethe out of the shop after closing time; it can only repeat, all night long, "The Armstrong Equipment Rental Emporium is closed. Please complete your final purchase and exit the shop." After a while she does not hear it anymore and falls asleep inside a large storage bin, the kind miners rent to haul moon rocks. She wears a medical mask from her days as a physician's assistant to prevent herself from inhaling too much particulate regolith.

She wakes a few hours later—curled like a fetus inside her storage bin, finally warm—to sounds of despair coming from somewhere outside the store. A man's voice. She rises to investigate.

The market's deserted, but there is plenty of light, thanks to the vending machines. Agnethe follows the voice, eyeing the food dispensers peevishly—she could blow ten-days' salary on a single meal here—to its source.

He is not someone Agnethe recognizes; he must be newly homeless. He is young and by Moon standards well-fed. He wears, as she does, the white, standard-issue jumpsuit, the standard-issue boots. No hat.

He crawls along the floor, mumbling, searching for something. "It was right here," he keeps repeating. That, and profanities.

Agnethe approaches him, making sure to step loudly so that he hears her coming. "Did you lose something?" she asks.

The man turns to face her. His eyes are confused, his eyebrows angry, his mouth agape and wary. But then his face releases its fear—Agnethe has that effect on people—and says, "My water bottle. I just had it! Water's so expensive, but the bottle too?"

After a sigh, he says to her, "I'm Hari, by the way." He gets up from hands and knees. It takes him a few moments to rise; he has, as they say in Origin City, "the weakness."

Hari extends his hand. "I lost my job. I'm saving every origin from now on. I don't suppose you know where I can get some food cheap?"

"The Church of Thaddeus the Forgotten," Agnethe says immediately, shaking his hand. He is weaker than he looks. "Ask for Father Fugit. He might have food tomorrow. He'll give it to you for free, but if you pay a little he can feed others too."

"Do you have to be a member?"

"No."

"Really? I'm surprised they don't try to convert you."

"They don't. Where's your hat?"

After a rueful pause: "Sold it."

"Don't sell this one," Agnethe says and places her standard-issue hat on his head. His neck is infirm. "May God bless it for you."

After a moment he removes the hat and, smiling, holds it out to her. "I couldn't. You'll freeze."

"You'll freeze."

Hari, bewildered, laughs. "Why should you freeze and I live?"

"Because you can't catch me!" she says and takes off at a run.

❖   ❖   ❖

I do not know how exactly it happened. I know only through the rumors and titillating hearsay I enjoyed, along with all my kind, when incomplete reports came back from Earth for those hundreds of thousands of years. But the exiled vitaphages set themselves up as your world's supernature.

They seemed to have conflicting motives. Some wanted to help you evolve, gave you advice, made crops grow when nature did not cooperate, answered your questions with abstruse prophecies that they then did their damnedest to realize. Others killed you out of malice, or played pranks on you as a kind of malign entertainment. Those became your kappas, your Coyotes, your poltergeists, your soucouyants, your will-o'-the-wisps. Still others revealed themselves to you and accepted your worship. They could disintegrate and materialize any of the four mundane states of matter as easily as you can exhale; could kill life, burn cities, and perhaps most importantly, battle the other gods. The vitaphage you called Moloch demanded human sacrifice of you, but it protected you, too. It ate many enemy gods before it itself was eaten.

A gigantomachy spanning ages ensued. Gods feasted on gods until only a few remained. From your perspective, over time magic dwindled in the world. The vitaphages, once so vocal, once so involved in your fate, spoke less often to you. The Age of Miracles passed. The few vitaphages who survived—the strongest, most merciless, most cunning—hunt for gods to devour to this day.

This is why when I came to Earth, I expected I would be killed almost instantly. I could try to consume others myself. I would try, I knew suddenly; I would fight with all the savagery and deception I could muster.

But ultimately, what was the point? What kind of a life was it to constantly fear ambush, to be friendless and ostracized, banished from everything I have known and loved, and my only recourse to commit, without surcease, the crime that had ruined what remained of my life?

Perhaps I should kill myself. I could ejaculate all the matter I control at once with a single thought. I spent years on Earth gathering the courage to do so.

At first I made myself as invisible as possible to the predator gods who would make a meal of me, and that meant hiding from humanity as well. But over time I could not help but learn about human civilization. You were much more evolved than anyone back home knew. I had never dreamed before my exile that you had settled your moon…

Your moon!

Suddenly I had cause for hope. I surrounded an outbound rocket—I could have flown there, but doing so would have cost me a great deal of energy, significantly shortening my life—and rode it all the way to Origin City.

❖   ❖   ❖

Agnethe is running toward the Incubators.

The habitation modules of failed business ventures are moved to the west side of Origin City until they can be sold or repurposed. But they serve a purpose now. The homeless of Origin City squat in those habitation modules, dark and unventilated though they may be. They sleep together in piles for warmth. Sometimes they share food, sometimes they steal food, sometimes they fight over food. Their fights are grim caricatures of battle; they are shakingly weak, all of them, and getting weaker. They know it.

Hari reminded Agnethe that today was the last day of the month. The day when layoffs happen.

Agnethe reaches the passage to the Incubators. There used to be an airlock door here, but it was torn off its hinges to let a little air and heat pass into the Incubators. A crooked sign that reads "No Trespassing" hangs by one screw. The darkness beyond is impenetrable.

Cautiously, always keeping a guiding hand against a wall, Agnethe picks her way into the Incubators in search of the newly bereft.

Agnethe knows the Incubators as well as anyone, but they change as habitation modules come and go, and the darkness and cold make it hard to remember anything. It is all too easy to get lost.

"Cold."

That one word stops Agnethe midstep, there in the perpetual tenebrae of the Incubators. She cocks her head. Heaving breaths, castanetting teeth, hands beating arms for warmth. She moves toward the sound.

"Stay back," she hears, a woman's voice, throaty with cold, rasping with phlegm. "You'll catch it."

Catch what? Ah: the woman must have shown signs of sickness. A contagion could wipe out the entire population of not only the Incubators, but all of Origin City. She would be banished.

Agnethe moves carelessly toward the woman, calling, "It's much more likely you have hypothermia than anything infectious. My name is Agnethe. I am from the Origin City Outreach Initiative."

"What's that?" calls the woman.

"We help people in need. Oh, sorry!" says Agnethe cheerfully, apologizing for running into the woman, who is huddled on the floor.

There is something about Agnethe that makes people think the best of her. Though she just more or less kicked this woman, the woman is warming to her. "It's okay," she says, wary but wondering. "I never heard of the Origin City Outreach Initiative."

"It's new. Did you lose your job today?"

"Months ago. Then I got sick."

Agnethe kneels next to her. She holds out her hands. "Take my hands," she says. "What's your name?"

"Elsa," says the woman. Eyes already are abysmal radiation detectors, and in the Incubators they are almost useless. Yet despite the gelid darkness, Elsa's hands find Agnethe's unerringly.

Agnethe gasps. From her reaction, those hands must be corpse cold. "You need to get warm right now," says Agnethe.

The woman begins to protest, but Agnethe stands and pulls her up by those hands. "Go to the marketplace and find the Armstrong Equipment Rental Emporium. Crawl into a bin and ignore the robot. You'll be warm in no time."

The woman stares at the place where Agnethe's face must be. She has many things to say at once—her mouth is moving, formulating—and she has trouble deciding where to start. Finally she settles on: "They'll quarantine me."

Agnethe sighs. Elsa's right: and Agnethe knows all too well that quarantine is worse than homelessness. She had worked for months as the only non-robot employee at the "animal shelter." She had little say in anyone's care. Actuaries on Earth decided when treatment was merited, when euthanasia. Agnethe followed their orders, felt she was powerless to do otherwise. Even when that meant assisting her father's suicide.

Then one night—this is among Agnethe's most vivid and relentless memories—God came to her in a dream in the form of Father Fugit and told her she was a monster, but that even her sins would be forgiven.

She quit the "animal shelter" the next morning and started mining.

Agnethe holds both of Elsa's hands tightly. Hers are warming; Agnethe's are getting colder. "Okay," Agnethe says. Then, after one more reassuring squeeze, she lets the woman's hands go and begins to undress.

Elsa cannot see Agnethe, but she hears the zipper. "What are you doing?"

"You need more clothes," says Agnethe. She starts to take off her jumpsuit, realizes she forgot to remove her boots, laughs, removes her boots, then finishes removing her jumpsuit. She is in the darkness of the frozen-air Incubators, choosing to give Elsa, a woman she has just met, the last protection she has against the cold in the hopes that it will prolong Elsa's sickly, actuarially unlikely life. She believes in a god that a vitaphage invented long ago. Almost certainly that vitaphage is dead by now. It may have intended good or ill or amoral entertainment for itself; I do not know. Whatever it intended, Agnethe believes in its message, or at least the message that its worshippers have collaged over thousands of years into a scripture. The end result is she is more or less committing suicide for the sake of a sick woman she just met and who will probably die soon even after this intercession.

It is fascinating.

Elsa allows herself to be dressed; Agnethe has that effect on people. She removes Elsa's boots and dresses her in her jumpsuit, first one leg, then the other, then the arms, then zip, Elsa's in. She puts Elsa's boots back on, then her own, then stands.

Elsa faces Agnethe, grabs both of her bony shoulders. "There is no such thing as the Origin City Outreach Initiative, is there."

"No."

"Thank you," she says and embraces Agnethe. "I am warmer already. Eat with me, and then I'll give it back to you."

"No. Keep it. Father Fugit will get me another."

Elsa pauses a long time. Her body language, invisible to humans in this blackness, tells the world she knows she should not keep the jumpsuit. But she says, "Eat with me, at least."

"I can't. It's too cold. I will check on you tomorrow."

"Thank you again," Elsa calls after her. But Agnethe has disappeared entirely, like a kindly spirit who, having done its good deed, vanishes until the next time it is needed.

❖   ❖   ❖

But Agnethe is no spirit. She very much has a body. And that body is cold. She is moving dangerously slowly.

She has almost two hours yet before the Armstrong Equipment Rental Emporium will reopen for business. It would be enough time to sleep a little, and more importantly, to warm herself.

But cold enervates her muscles, stultifies her mind. She walks hunched and stumbling, head bowed. The only thing keeping her upright is her worry. Over and over she whispers: "How will you go to church, Agnethe? How can you go to church now?"

It takes me a while to figure out what she means; I am still new to humans, their bodies. But finally I understand: she is naked. She cannot go to church naked.

That really should not be her first concern, however, now that she has fallen down.

She will freeze to death soon if she does not get up. She knows this, so she begins to pray. "I am unshriven," she whispers to a vitaphage who, even if it is still alive, is on a different planet. "I can't die unshriven!"

The idea inspires her to struggle mightily to rise. But her quivering muscles fail her. She falls, hard, splays out on the burningly cold floor. Weeping now, she says no, no, no between draughts of air that only cause her to lose heat more quickly. In a hoarse voice she calls, "Elsa!" but Elsa is too far to hear.

Then, in a softer, wet voice, she says, "Forgive my sins, father." I do not know if she means her god or her actual father.

And there is no way to ask her. She dies.

❖   ❖   ❖

I was terrified of being discovered. The more I exerted myself, the more energy I expended, the more I would make my presence known to the other vitaphages, and the more of a target I would become. The Moon was a gift, a way to escape a barbaric fate. I would not squander it.

So, I vowed when I came to the Moon not to behave like a god or ghost or uncanny force. I did not want attention from creatures who could not understand me. I would stay quiet. I might have to starve to death, but at least I would be no other vitaphage's meal.

❖   ❖   ❖

There is no way to ask whether she meant her father or her Father. But I grow curious. I surround her, enter her.

Agnethe's pneuma is gone, but the machinery of her life is all in working order: muscles, circulation, digestion, brain. The only thing missing is her qualia. But I can restart the machine without it.

The first thing I feel is her hunger. Agnethe was at least as starved as I am. Yet she gave away food and did not take it when it was offered.

My entire being concentrates into one lone thought: there are no other vitaphages here. They cannot detect me from Earth; I am utterly safe from detection here. There was no reason, therefore, not to save Agnethe. None except irrational fear. An overwrought sense of self-preservation.

In that instant, hunger loses its power over me. Hunger is smaller than the whole of me, for the first time since I ate my child. I am able to think again.

Agnethe's mind, dead as it is, remains a library of her thoughts and logic and memory. At once I know it in its entirety, the way you can see the entirety of a dimensionless point in space. Such despair; such a death drive. But it is also a succinct guide for actionable goodness. Computer code for the procedures of altruism. It is beautiful.

I stand Agnethe up. I am her soul now. I heat her body through, cure it and repair it, fill her muscles with power. I open and close her hands. I use the eyes and ears and nose of her body, taste her mouth with her tongue. I feel the cold killing her skin cells, so I create an aura of warmth around her. Then, remembering that nudity will not do in human society, I materialize a white, warm jumpsuit over her body.

I smile. It fills me with pleasure to make Agnethe's body smile. "Agnethe," I say aloud, "if you were me, what would you do?"

She would pull atoms from the air and reshape them into food and water. She would warm and light Origin City. She would heal the sick. She would pull origins from the sky and let them fall like stars among Originators until money became meaningless. She would summon palaces from the regolith. She would grant universal comfort, succor, freedom. As a start.

"Okay," I tell dead Agnethe, using her own mouth. I will do these things. Until the gods consume me or I starve.

The End

By day, Carlos Hernandez is an Associate Professor of English at CUNY, with appointments at BMCC and the Graduate Center, where he focuses on creative writing, science fiction, Latin@ Studies and game-based learning/procedural narrative. He the author of over thirty works of short fiction, poetry, and drama (mostly SFF), and his collection of short stories, *The Assimilated Cuban's Guide to Quantum Santeria*, is available from Rosarium Publishing beginning January 2016.

THE STAR-TALERS

by The Brothers Grimm, Tale #153, Alt Title: *The Star Money*

There was once on a time a little girl whose father and mother were dead, and she was so poor that she no longer had any little room to live in, or bed to sleep in, and at last she had nothing else but the clothes she was wearing and a little bit of bread in her hand which some charitable soul had given her. She was, however, good and pious. And as she was thus forsaken by all the world, she went forth into the open country, trusting in the good God.

Then a poor man met her, who said, "Ah, give me something to eat, I am so hungry!"

She reached him the whole of her piece of bread, and said, "May God bless it to thy use," and went onwards.

Then came a child who moaned and said, "My head is so cold, give me something to cover it with." So she took off her hood and gave it to him; and when she had walked a little farther, she met another child who had no jacket and was frozen with cold. Then she gave it her own; and a little farther on one begged for a frock, and she gave away that also.

At length she got into a forest and it had already become dark, and there came yet another child, and asked for a little shirt, and the good little girl thought to herself, "It is a dark night and no one sees thee, thou canst very well give thy little shirt away," and took it off, and gave away that also.

And as she so stood, and had not one single thing left, suddenly some stars from heaven fell down, and they were nothing else but hard smooth pieces of money, and although she had just given her little shirt away, she had a new one which was of the very finest linen. Then she gathered together the money into this, and was rich all the days of her life.

The End

ANGIE TAYLOR IN: PERIL BENEATH THE EARTH'S CRUST

by John Langan

based upon *The Brave Little Tailor*

As she falls, Angie Taylor tries to relax. The flight pack is in power-down mode, but ready to whoosh to life at the press of the button on her right glove. She shouldn't need it for this portion of her task. The wings of her drop suit should be all she requires during her descent of the Kansas City Tunnel, a mile wide for all of its hundred miles down. After her jump, she used the wings to angle her into the tunnel's approximate center, which is where she's remained as she's plunged deeper and deeper into the Earth. It's a straight shot. There are no obstacles, no skyscraper-sized stalactites and stalagmites, no immense rock bridges, to complicate her way, as they do in the Katmandu and Buenos Aires tunnels. Anyone traveling those passages must pack into an elevator that takes half a day to complete the descent; though improvements in speed have been promised. You can't hop in one of the converted dirigibles that make the trip in a couple of hours, or, if the way is clear, zip yourself into a courier's uniform and leap into the tunnel.

October 13th, 1933, she thinks. Will this date be marked on future calendars? Maybe as Angela Taylor day (commemorating the day a lone hero plunged into harm's way to save her country from a menace unlike any it had faced before)? She hears her mother laugh, say, "No one will ever accuse you of dreaming small, Angie."

Yellow lights, set in rings around the tunnel's circumference every mile, flash past. Was that forty-nine or fifty? Close enough to halfway. She would like to check her guns, but her arms are locked in place, keeping the suit's wings extended in order to slow her fall to a manageable speed. The guns are fine; she triple-checked each one before snapping its holster shut, and that was on top of who-could-count-how-many inspections before she left home. It's anxiety at what waits for her at the other end of her journey, combined with the boredom of having to maintain one position for so long, spurring her mind to search for a distraction, to seek reassurance in routine.

Not for the first time this week, Angie wonders if maybe she shouldn't have made such a big deal about her guns to begin with. "ABC," her mother taught her, "Always Be Confident," and while the advice has taken her to chief mechanic of the Rockefeller dirigible fleet, as well as to a bit of tinkering in the privacy of her garage, she's asked herself if maybe that confidence should have limits, if "ABC" shouldn't be followed by "DEF": "Don't Exaggerate the Facts." Yes, a single shot from one of her guns vaporized seven of the mole things pushing their snouts against her living room window. But those were seven of the smaller creatures, the ones that appeared to function as attack dogs, not the larger kind that could knock over a house with a brush of the shoulder. She couldn't say what her gun would have done to one of them, because the power relays had fried after that first lucky shot.

Which hadn't stopped her from claiming her invention had reduced seven of the huge beasts to so much powder, when her crew met for drinks at Hunter's the night after the invasion—or Incursion, as the government had christened it already. Angie supposed the name didn't matter. What did was that, during one of the overnight lulls in tunnel traffic, a small army came pouring out of it. The force consisted of dozens of the giant mole creatures, each one carrying up to half a dozen undersized soldiers on elaborate saddles. Hundreds of smaller mole things, like the ones Angie shot, accompanied them. The riders and their steeds wasted no time, attacking the work yards and warehouses ringing the tunnel's mouth. What the larger animals couldn't crush, the smaller shred, the soldiers targeted with beam weapons that liquefied steel, ignited concrete. In short order, the subterranean forces reached the dirigible yards, raking the enormous vessels with their heat rays. All twenty-two transports went up in a series of explosions that shook the ground for twenty miles around. (That trembling underfoot was the first inkling Angie, absorbed in soldering the fine circuits of her gun, had that the Incursion was underway.) The tunnel's circumference—what Angie and her coworkers called the Lip—in flames, the invading soldiers directed their steeds toward the lights of Kansas City, laying waste to the neighborhoods of workers' homes between.

This was how Angie came by her opportunity to test her invention under live-fire conditions. She switched on the radio for news of the apparent earthquake, and was greeted by word of fires and explosions at the Lip, of foreign troops seemingly in the heartland of America, bringing with them a horde of monsters. So ridiculous did the report sound, she wondered if she'd tuned into the middle of a radio drama. But as she checked up and down the dial, the news was all the same, an attack by unknown forces who had emerged from within the Kansas City Tunnel, and who appeared to be in command of hitherto unknown animals. The hostile fighters were moving on Kansas City. Some of the stations advised their listeners to remain inside and await further instructions; others counseled immediate flight from the marauders. Angie heard the Weiters' Packard cough to life one house over. The gun still in her hand, she crossed to the door that led out the side of the garage. In the time it took her to walk around to her driveway, the Weiters piled into their car, reversed into the street, brakes squealing, and sped toward the county road. She turned her attention southwest, in the direction of the tunnel, and saw the horizon glowing orange and red.

A moment later, a pack of the mole things came charging down the street. There were seven of them, each the size of a German Shepherd, each armed with foreclaws the size of Bowie knives. They tumbled over and around one another, snuffling the pavement. When they came to the corner where Angie's modest bungalow stood, they continued in a straight line, tearing a path through her front yard, sending clumps of dirt and grass flying. Absurdly, Angie thought of the hours she had spent tending that strip of lawn. The creatures slammed into the front of the house, then set about sniffing it. Their noses found the picture window, and the animal furthest in front lifted its talons. Angie raised the gun she had spent most of the night working on, whose casing she had screwed shut minutes before she stepped out of the garage, and squeezed the trigger.

A lightning bolt leapt from the nozzle to the mole about to tap on her front window, then zigzagged among its half-dozen companions. For an instant, white light, brilliant, crackling, surrounded the creatures. They screeched in unison. The light blinked out, and the seven of them were gone, reduced to a fall of dust and the odor of ozone. The elation that surged through Angie (*It worked!*) was followed by the impulse to run in the direction from which the mole things had come and lend what assistance she could. That more noble emotion succumbed to disappointment as she smelled burnt copper and realized the gun's single use had fried it. She retreated inside, and spent the rest of the night repairing the gun, listening to the radio's updates of the situation. Every now and again, something large passed nearby, shuddering the walls and making her work faster.

Toward dawn, the National Guard met the invaders at the outskirts of the city. Their magnet rifles and rocket cannons made a dent in the enemy's numbers, but the beam weapons, combined with the brute ferocity of the varied mole creatures, caused the Guard troops to fall back. When the Army Air Corps showed up, the situation briefly worsened. The general in command had opted to send three of the weapons platforms, and while their frames were armored against conventional threats, they were no match for the heat rays, which detonated the dirigibles like three gigantic bombs. The explosions were responsible for half as many casualties among the Guard troops below as the hostile forces.

Fortunately for that same General's career, he had scrambled a squadron of gyrocopters along with the assault dirigibles, and, on the advice of a soon-to-be-promoted Colonel, a squad of bombers, too. The leading third of the 'copters was knocked out of the air when the weapons platforms went up, but the remainder proved effective against the invaders, their maneuverability making up for their comparatively light armament. The most important function they served was keeping the hostile forces essentially in place, permitting the bombers to target them with devastating accuracy. Once their bays were empty, what Guard troops remained on the ground staged a counterattack. Aided by the 'copters, they fought the enemy back to the Lip, where a second and a third wave of bombers reduced the attackers to a quarter of what had surged out of the tunnel less than a day before. The survivors fled back into the Earth.

Everything was in turmoil. The Lip was charred concrete and twisted steel. Communications had been lost with the colonies on the other end of the tunnel, which were assumed conquered, and possibly worse. The stretch of country between the tunnel and the city was a smoldering expanse of buildings in all stages of collapse, cratered roads, and the remains of the invading army. A few structures stood basically intact, Angie's house and Hunter's, the bar she and the other members of her crew frequented after work, among them. She could see no other place to go. The Lip was occupied by the military, who, rumor had it, were preparing a major response to the attack. The only workers allowed in were the heavy machinery operators, to help clear the wreckage. Kansas City was choked with people desperately trying to evacuate it, in the face of an anticipated second invasion. Angie stayed home, laboring over her guns, until her lower back was tight and burning from the hours she'd spent hunched over the workbench, her head pounding from staring at copper-alloy wires through her magnifiers. She tucked the gun that was closest to being ready into a hip pocket of her coveralls and set off for the bar.

On her way, she passed the corpses of a pair of enemy soldiers, slumped against the carcass of a giant mole. All three were riddled with holes from magnet guns. Already, radio commentators were declaring that this attack must be the work of one of the other nations with access to a tunnel, Argentina or Mongolia, or of a neighboring power, Brazil or China. The figures Angie saw, however, were not the residents of any nation she knew. They were small, no more than three feet tall. Their skin was pale to the point of translucence, their long hair colorless. Behind ruined goggles, their eyes were large, maybe twice the size of Angie's. Their noses were both broad and long. Their equipment was like nothing she'd encountered, arrangements of metal and glass tubes that resembled strange musical instruments more than weaponry.

At Hunter's, over pitchers of watery beer and plates of burgers and fries, she described what she'd seen to her co-workers, gathered there for the same reason as she. With the exception of Fiddler, who insisted what she'd seen proved the invaders came from Argentina, none of the others knew what to make of the undersized soldiers and their odd armament. It seemed likely the invaders had come from somewhere on the other end of the tunnel, which already had proven itself host to an abundance of new flora and fauna. This was the first anyone had encountered intelligent life, other humans, but so little of the interior had been explored, it was well within the range of possibility for there to be a dozen civilizations, more, scattered across its surface. There had been talk of mounting an expedition—a series of expeditions—to undertake a detailed survey and mapping of the interior, possibly under the aegis of the National Geographic Society. The Incursion leant urgency to such an enterprise, even as it forestalled it until further military action could be completed. And that was provided the mole men, as the radio was calling them, didn't return for a second, larger attack.

Possibly the four—or was it five?—tall glasses of beer she'd downed loosened Angie's tongue, dampened the discretion she otherwise would have exercised. Possibly the amount of time she'd spent laboring over the guns demanded recognition. Either way, she reached into her hip pocket, withdrew the gun from it, and laid it on the table. "If those fellows pay us another call," she said into the silence that descended over her coworkers, "I wouldn't worry. This baby took care of seven of them with one shot."

Of course no one believed her. She picked up the gun, stood, and walked ten paces to the other side of the bar. She dialed the power to the lowest level, aimed at the empty pitchers of beer crowded in the center of her table, and fired. A bolt of lightning snapped from the tip of the gun to the nearest pitcher, then leapt among them. White light blazed around the glass containers. When it subsided, they had been reduced to dust. One eyebrow cocked, the nozzle of the gun pointed up (*and no smell of burnt copper!*), Angie surveyed her companions. "Well?" she said.

In the tumult of exclamations, congratulations, and interrogations that ensued—in the vigorous handshakes, the heavy slaps on the back—in the shots of whisky set in front of her—the events of the previous night became confused. The seven smaller mole things shattered her front window, then scrambled inside her house, then cornered her in the garage. The creatures were joined by a single handler, standing at a safe distance and taking flight once they were dust, then a trio of handlers, who had felt the effects of Angie's gun, then an equal number of enemy soldiers, who had shared the animals' fate. It was as if, so dramatic was the effect of her weapon, its use required an equally dramatic scenario (as if seven of the mole creatures hadn't been drama enough). By last call, the seven smaller mole things had grown to seven of their elephantine fellows, each with a full complement of hostile fighters. They had ravaged Angie's neighborhood, reduced her house to a single wall from behind which she had taken aim at them and disintegrated the lot with a single squeeze of the trigger.

Late the next afternoon, when a knock at her front door had announced a pair of G-Men in matching cheap suits, she still had enough of a hangover not to realize why they were here and what they wanted her for. Until they instructed her to bring the gun—the one she'd discharged in Hunter's the previous night—she assumed the men were there to ferry her to a briefing about the condition of the Lip and the plans for its repair. Given her position as chief mechanic, it was not an unreasonable guess. Once they mentioned the gun, however, she understood that she was headed for a meeting of a different sort.

She wondered if the G-Men would drive her to Kansas City. They did not. Instead, they traveled a couple of miles to a modest municipal park. Its lawns had been taken over by a small town's worth of large canvas tents. Men and women, some in the same underwhelming suits as her escorts, others in the uniforms of the Armed Services, rushed from tent to tent, their arms full of papers, folders, boxes. At the park entrance, a pair of soldiers, magnet rifles in hand, nodded at the badges the G-Men showed them and directed them to park in Lot A. Angie didn't see any signs designating Lot A, but the G-Men pulled in front of the nearest tent and shut off the engine and no one said anything to them about it. One G-Man ahead of her, one behind, she was led past the first tent to an alley between it and the next one. She and her escorts turned down the alley, which ended in the entrance to a third tent. Another pair of soldiers checked the G-Men's IDs and stepped back to allow the three of them inside.

The perimeter of the space was lined with bulletin boards and tables. Maps, charts, graphs, photographs, drawings had been pinned to the bulletin boards, spread across the tables. Groups of women and men stood facing the bulletin boards, leaning over the tables, engaged in intensive discussions of the information before them. In the center of the tent, four of the tables had been pushed together to provide a larger surface. On it, a large map of the entire tunnel had been unrolled. A number of high-ranking Army officers, Colonels and Majors, kept position around the map. When a junior officer or G-Man left one of the surrounding tables and hurried to deliver some piece of information to one of the senior officers, the Colonel or Major either nodded, or bent over their portion of the map and made a notation on it in pencil. If the message was of particular importance, the senior officer left her or his station to convey it to a cluster of figures standing a little ways beyond the tables and their map. Angie saw two four-star and three three-star generals grouped in tight formation, their backs to their surroundings, their heads close together. She also saw a couple of women in a better class of suit. And Rockefeller.

He was wearing the vita-suit that permitted him to function as if he were not past his ninth decade. It reminded Angie of the bulky fire-resistant suits the Lip's firefighters trained in, with the exception that the surface of Rockefeller's suit was studded with gauges, buttons, and valves. Rumor was, it could absorb a shot from a magnet gun, and looking at its glossy brown surface, like the hide of some large beast, Angie could believe that rumor. The glass helmet was off, allowing her a clear view of the man's hairless head, bare of the wigs he continued to sport in his public appearances. He looked old, but not elderly; further rumors claimed him the beneficiary of technologies not yet shared with the wider (and poorer) public, which Angie, from her interactions with even the modestly well-off, could well-believe.

The G-Men led her directly to Rockefeller and his coterie of officials. Before they were done introducing her, the old man took a step toward her and said, "Is it true? You built a weapon that killed seven of the invaders at once?"

Angie nodded. "Yes, sir, I did."

"Did you bring it?"

She unsnapped her hip pocket and withdrew the gun. Rockefeller held out his right hand. "May I?"

"You may." Angie passed the gun to him. Cradling it in both hands, he peered down at it. "How does it work?"

"It passes a charge from a pair of batteries into a crystal amplifier. The amplifier does something to the electricity. It boosts it, but it changes it, too. Allows it to break the bonds between atoms, I think. A focusing lens directs the energy at the target."

"I see." Rockefeller turned the gun over. "Is this a hobby of yours, inventing death rays?"

"No, sir, it is not," Angie said. "I started off trying to make a better torch for spot-welding. I'm sure you know, I'm chief mechanic on your dirigibles. The portable torches we use for repairs on the blimps tend to burn too hot and too fast. You need thick gloves to hold them, which makes fine work difficult, and they're empty before the job's half done. If you're working on the ground, it's no trouble to fetch another one. If you're wearing a flight pack and hovering several hundred feet up, it can be a bit trickier. I thought if I could come up with an improved torch, it would make my work that much easier.

"In the process, though, things went in unexpected directions."

"Fortunately for you," Rockefeller said. He handed the gun back to her. "How about a demonstration?"

"Of course. Do you have anything in mind?"

"That." The old man pointed at a bulletin board across the tent.

"All right. If you'd ask your people to step out of the way…"

"You heard her," Rockefeller called. "Move! Move if you don't want your atoms scattered from here to St. Louis!" As women and men hastened to either side of the tent, he said, "Let's see if this meets my expectations."

"As long as they're modest," Angie said. She dialed the power to the lowest setting.

Rockefeller frowned. "That doesn't sound like someone who destroyed seven monsters with a single shot."

" 'Keep your expectations level,' my mother used to say, 'and you won't fall off them.' "

"You're a philosopher, too."

"Hardly." She lifted the gun, aimed it at the bulletin board (on which, she noticed, was hung a map with Kansas City at its center, a series of concentric rings radiating from it, each a different, lighter shade of red), and fired. A sizzling line of light stabbed the map dead center. Blinding white surrounded the bulletin board, and then it was a rain of dust. Angie lowered the gun. "That's on minimum power," she said.

"What does it do on maximum?" Rockefeller said.

"I haven't tested it, yet," Angie said, adding, "But when I used it on the invaders, it was on half-strength."

"Is that the only one?"

"There's another."

"I'll give you two million dollars for them," Rockefeller said. "One million apiece. Plus the plans for them."

Angie did not reply.

"Or would another arrangement suit you better? I hire you as chief of weapons development at one of Standard Technologies' subsidiaries, give you a ridiculous salary and a mansion with a pool?"

"You want the gun to use against the invaders," Angie said. "Obviously. Are you expecting another attack?"

One of the four-star generals opened his mouth; Rockefeller overrode him. "We don't know. Not long after the Lemurians retreated down the tunnel, we sent a squad of gyrocopters after them."

"'Lemurians'?" Angie said.

"It's what we've taken to calling the invaders. One of the Colonels hit on it. Like Atlantis, but in the Pacific."

"Oh."

"As I was saying, we sent a squad of 'copters to pursue the Lemurians. Their instructions were to gather what intelligence they could. We were particularly interested in learning about the enemy forces. Were the attacking troops a probe, sent to test our capabilities and report back to a larger army, or was this the entirety of their numbers, sent in a desperate attempt to land a knock-out punch?"

"What did the 'copters find out?"

"Nothing," Rockefeller said. "None of them returned. Nor have the second or third squadrons we sent. We received a brief message from one of the pilots in the second group, saying that they made it all the way to the other end of the tunnel when something attacked them. All any of us could distinguish after that was the word 'huge.' And the screaming."

"The Lemurians were waiting for you."

"It seems likely. With the heat rays they have, a small force could hold the far end of the tunnel indefinitely."

"Unless someone can give you an even better weapon."

"In a word, yes. We cannot afford to lose our access to the interior. The technology we've retrieved from it these past fifteen years has transformed the nation. To speak personally, it has allowed me to engage in the pursuits of a youthful man at a time when my thoughts should be turning to funeral arrangements. To regain the freedom of the interior, I am prepared to pay a high price." He ended with a significant look at Angie and her gun.

"Oh, the amount you're offering is more than fair," she said. "But I can't take it from you."

"Why is that?"

"Because the crystals that give the guns their effect came from the interior and, as far as I know, I have the only samples of them. I bought them off one of the dirigible pilots. I was searching for crystals to use in my improved torch. This girl had a shoebox full of all sorts of rocks, said she'd picked them up while she wandered around the stations, waiting for her cargo to be loaded. I chose the ones that looked most promising. There were four—needle-shaped, kind of sparkly through the middle—that I thought might do the job. One of them didn't work. There was a flaw in it, and it shattered when the charge hit it. But the remaining three tested well, so well that one of them is sitting in here," she nodded to the gun, "and the second is in the matching gun. I kept the third in reserve, in case I needed a spare.

"Anyway, the point is, once I realized what these crystals might be capable of, I set out trying to locate more of them. I don't have your resources, but I'm pretty well-connected. To shorten the story, my search turned up nothing. Somewhere inside, there must be more of the crystals, but at the moment, mine are all that's available. Which doesn't bode well for any hopes you have for mass-production."

One of the three-star generals said, "Then why are we wasting our time on this?"

"General Morel has a point," Rockefeller said. "Without the material necessary to reproduce your design in sufficient quantities, it's of little use to us. I will—"

"But even if you had the crystals," Angie said, "the strategy you have in mind won't work."

"If you're going to step on someone's tongue," Angie's mother had said, "you'd best be certain they like the taste of it." From the expression on Rockefeller's face, it was evident he did not. Angie hurried on. "Because what you plan to do is send another squad of 'copters into the tunnel, only this time, they're equipped with my guns. You know the Lemurians are going to be waiting for them, but I'm guessing you intend to throw enough 'copters at them that some will make it through. The 'copters will have the guns set at maximum power, in order to kill as many enemy soldiers as they can. (No one's interrupted me, yet, which tells me I'm at least in the vicinity of the truth.) What happens when one of the 'copters shoots the tunnel? From what I understand of combat, which is not that much, shots occasionally miss their target. You've seen what my gun can do on minimum power. What effect do you suppose ten, twenty, fifty shots at maximum power are going to have on the tunnel's structural integrity? You just got done telling me we can't afford to lose our access to the interior. Why would you undertake a mission that would make that more likely?"

"Your argument is not without merit," Rockefeller said. "But do you have a counter-proposal?"

"I do," Angie said, thus initiating the sequence of events that had led her here, in a controlled fall down a hundred-mile opening into the Earth's interior. She had to think on her feet, but there was nothing new in that. "Send one person," she said. "Instead of a gyrocopter, which is already noisy, before the enclosed space makes it louder, use a combination of drop suit and flight pack. The drop suit gets you from one end of the tunnel to the other silently. The Lemurians might spot you, but even if they do, you're a much smaller target, moving faster, and harder to hit. You fall past the tunnel exit, and activate the flight pack. You attack the tunnel guards from behind, using the guns to winnow their numbers to zero. If anything goes wrong, then you've lost a single life, rather than dozens, and a pair of guns that were of limited use, anyway."

To a one, the generals objected, a combined seventeen-stars' worth of opposition. Distilled, their arguments were simple: we don't have anyone ready for such a mission, and it's going to take us too long to train someone when time is of the essence.

To which Angie replied, "I'll do it."

The tests the generals and their underlings arranged to gauge her proficiency with the flight pack weren't much of a challenge. Angie was accustomed to threading her way through a dirigible's superstructure, spot-welding cracks in it as she went. She could hover two hundred feet up in a strong wind while applying an emergency patch. She could jet along the side of a dirigible at full speed, no more than a foot from its skin, and snatch up the torch that one of her crew had forgotten on the vessel's crown. Not to mention, the assortment of contests and games with which she and the crew passed the occasional downtime: obstacle courses in the hangar, barrel races on the runways, skeet-shooting on the wing. The principle difficulty Angie foresaw was keeping her arms and legs in proper position for the length of her plunge through the tunnel. She solved it herself with sets of elbow and knee braces she wired to lock in place when she tapped a button at the top of her drop suit with her chin. That problem addressed, she attended briefings she half-ignored, and continued to tinker with her guns.

The most serious difficulty she faced came the second morning after her proposal was accepted. She had breezed through the first set of evaluations the previous day, and was confident of doing the same in a few minutes. The Army was making use of the wreckage that had yet to be removed from around the Lip, specifically, a set of warehouses listing most of the way to the ground, which they filled with all manner of debris for her to navigate. Rockefeller had sat through the full complement of her tests the day before, and was present again. This time, though, he approached her while she was standing idle, waiting for the next obstacles to be erected. He was wearing the clear helmet that attached to the vita-suit. It lent his voice resonance. Nodding at her, "Good morning, sir," he said, "In all the hubbub and fuss of having your plan approved, and then of having you approved to carry it out, we failed to discuss what you expect out of all this."

"I'm sure you'll be very appreciative—provided I succeed."

"Of course," Rockefeller said. "You won't have to worry about me. You'll have folks lining up to reward you. There's more you're after, though, isn't there?"

"There is," Angie said.

"Let's have it."

She had been turning this matter over in her head since the various generals, under Rockefeller's strong persuasion, had agreed to implement her proposal first, before sending another squad of 'copters to their doom. She took a deep breath. "Once the tunnel is secure," she said, "and the Lemurians have been defeated, I want to lead an expedition to map the interior. I mean really and truly plot out what's where. Actually, I figure it'll require a half-dozen teams at minimum to accomplish the job in a timely fashion. I want to be in charge of that. And I want to be made a general, because I imagine I'm going to have to continue dealing with the military, and I don't want to have to keep explaining myself to every captain with an attitude."

"Clear the end of the tunnel, and you'll be a general."

"What about mapping the interior?"

"It would require a significant investment to undertake such an enterprise."

"You'd have to be a Rockefeller," Angie said.

"I'll bet I could convince Roosevelt to go in on it with me— national security and all that."

"As long as I'm in charge."

"Survive this, and I'll see to it."

"I guess I'd better not die, then."

That conversation, with its false bravado, repeats in Angie's memory as the end of the tunnel grows larger and brighter below her. She doesn't know what the upward limit of the Lemurians' beam weapons is, but she's racing toward it. They could have had her in their sights for a while, now, and be waiting for her to come into range. A direct hit from one of their heat rays, and that's it. She'll have more to worry about if they damage the drop suit, fry the pack. Either she veers into the tunnel wall, or she plummets out of the tunnel, falling up, up, up, until she runs out of momentum and the interior's gravity catches her and dashes her to the ground. Her heart, whose beat increased only slightly when she leapt off the gyrocopter into the tunnel, races. Will she see the flash of the shot that gets her, or will she suddenly find herself spinning, out of control? She considers activating the flight pack, rejects the idea. There isn't enough fuel in it to return her to the surface; all she'll do is make it that much easier for the Lemurians to discover her. *Breathe*, she tells herself.

The mouth of the tunnel has expanded to immense proportions. She scans its circumference for signs of hostile troops. Scorch marks the size of houses, jagged scars the length of trains, decorate the rock; testimony to the previous attempts on this position. Is there something at her feet? Yes. If her head is twelve o'clock, then at approximately four, she sees the gleam of metal. At six, too. Far enough away from one another to create a crossfire, but close enough to support each other should the need arise. The remainder of the opening appears clear. Better still, she's well within range of the Lemurians' weapons, and no fire has been directed her way, which makes it likely they haven't spotted her.

Hope surges through her like the heat from good whiskey. She lowers her chin to her chest, and pushes the button that releases her arms and legs from their position. She angles herself head-down, folds her arms flat against her sides, brings her legs together, and shoots like an arrow from a bow into the interior.

She's a half-mile clear of the tunnel before she registers anything but bright light and open space. As she slows, she sees the ground below, heavily forested, flat out to the limits of her vision, where it rises to be lost in the distance. It's as if she's arrived at the floor of an immense valley, except that valley consists of the entire surface of the inside of the Earth. The swathe below her, which the US has claimed as its own, sits in perpetual daylight, as do a half-dozen other slices of the interior. The remaining six lie in unending darkness. The reason for this alternating day and night hangs above her, at the very center of the Earth. It shines like the sun, which is what most theories agree it is, a star, but crushed to incredibly small proportions by forces no one has been able to guess. Possibly, it was whoever caged the crushed star in a sphere consisting of six giant strips of a material sufficient to resist the tiny star's heat. The half-dozen strips are spaced equidistantly; the general assumption is that the cage was intended to rotate, providing the interior periods of light and dark. Whether the sphere stopped spinning, or never worked in the first place, no one can say. Lack of certainty about the interior is one of the defining characteristics of most discussions about it. Fabulous technology has been discovered in ruins a short distance from each of the known tunnels, devices that have altered the course of the twentieth century in more ways than anyone has yet realized. What became of those inventions' creators, however, remains a mystery. One of Angie's crew, Grey, claims that the planet was hollowed to serve as a shelter, the material that was excavated compacted and set into orbit as the Moon. *So what happened to the folks who did all of this?* the other crew members asked him. *That's the question, isn't it?* he said.

There's no time for wild theories: she's slowed almost to a stop, the interior's gravity tightening its hold on her. She turns upside down, in order to be in proper position once she starts to drop back toward the tunnel. From this perspective, the Lemurians she spotted should be at eight and six o'clock. She also should have a better view of them. They are, and she does. There don't appear to be that many of the enemy soldiers, maybe seven or eight at each post; though there could be additional troops waiting in the forest, which surrounds the tunnel at about a quarter-mile's distance. Of more immediate concern to her are the creatures stationed with each group of soldiers. There are two of them, one per position, and they are immense, big as whales. She supposes they could be called moles, but these moles sport claws the size of a car. Elaborate harnesses secure long saddles to their backs.

Angie unsnaps a holster and withdraws one of her guns. She's stopped rising, is beginning to plummet. She presses the button on her left glove, and the flight pack whines to life. She kicks back, angling herself at the Lemurians at the six o'clock post, and the pack speeds her toward them.

This part of the plan has always been simple. Come at the Lemurians from the interior, with the light behind her, and hit them fast. Keep moving, keep them off balance. Especially once the first few of them have been reduced to dust, she figures the rest will panic, even flee, making her job that much easier. Isn't there a saying about no plan surviving contact with the enemy? The enormous mounts have raised their great blunt heads at the flight pack's high-pitched scream. Both sets of soldiers notice the creatures' reactions, but their first move is to check the tunnel. Angie cuts the pack, which causes the huge moles to swing their heads from left to right, attempting to locate the noise that just disturbed them. The troops continue to survey the tunnel, sweeping it with stubby telescopes, their strange weapons pointed into it. A couple of hundred yards above her target, several things happen more or less simultaneously. One of the soldiers at the eight o'clock post notices her and swings his weapon in her direction. The heat ray flashes yellow in front of her. She activates the flight pack, which rushes her forward through air superheated by the beam. She gasps, raising her gun at the Lemurians beneath her. Prior to her leap into the tunnel, she set the power on three-quarter strength. As the soldiers below her see their colleague fire in their direction, they look up, and find Angie diving at them. They raise their slender weapons, and she squeezes the trigger.

A lightning bolt worthy of a thunderstorm springs from the gun, cracking the air as it goes. Surrounded by phosphorous-bright light, the five soldiers struck by it shriek and are consumed. The remaining pair of troops have run to the mole creature, which is that much larger this close. At the combined screech of the flight pack and clap of her gun firing, it throws its head back, pushes up on its forelegs. Its snout, Angie sees, ends in a dozen fleshy tentacles, each the diameter of a car tire and the length of a city bus. The protuberances coil and uncoil, wrapping around one another, snaking out into the air and whipping back. A second shot from the other soldiers burns at her. She executes a backflip to avoid it. The ray catches the tip of one of the nearer mole thing's tentacles. The animal emits a piercing shriek as it lurches backward, throwing the soldiers who have clambered onto its saddle into one another. Angie comes out of her flip early, skimming over the ground and aiming at the pair of Lemurians who are attempting to draw a bead on her. Her shot blanches them and half their saddle to dust. The accompanying shout of thunder spurs the mole thing forward, in the direction of the remaining soldiers. Angie drops behind and follows it.

Whether the second post is aiming at her, or at the giant animal bearing down on them, doesn't matter, practically speaking. Their heat rays rake its hide, its head, severing one of its tentacles. The attack does not deter the mole creature's charge; if anything, the beast gathers speed. Angie pops up from its cover long enough to fire at the head of the other mole creature. She thinks the shot strikes several of its tentacles, but she drops back down before she's sure. The crack her shot produces causes the creature in front of her to pick up its pace even more.

Heat rays blister the air around her; the Lemurians putting everything into stopping the behemoth about to crash into them. Angie falls back, and jets straight up a hundred yards. From this vantage, she watches the mole creature complete its charge into its fellow. At the last moment, the Lemurians, who have kept their mount turned sideways, to allow them better aim with their weapons, attempt to wheel their beast around to meet the other head-on. Already maddened from Angie's shot, which does appear to have disintegrated half of its tentacles, the mole creature refuses its riders' command. Then the other thing smashes into it.

The impact crushes half the soldiers instantly, sends the remainder flying in all directions. Enraged, the giant animals swipe at each other with their great claws, opening twenty-foot wounds in their hides. Blood slaps the ground. So distracted is Angie by the spectacle that she almost fails to notice the Lemurian, miraculously unhurt by his catastrophic fall, point his weapon at her. But notice him she does, and she drops beneath his shot and returns fire before he can shoot again. By the time his screams have faded, the mole creatures have finished their fight. The beast that was carrying its troops appears dead. The other lies panting, and from the rents in its sides, the blood pooled around it, does not appear long for this world. The remaining soldiers don't look in much better condition. One lies with a leg bent at an unnatural angle. Another's left arm and left half of his chest have been crushed. A third sits cross-legged, a long cut to his head spilling blood down his face, which he does not bother to wipe.

Angie lands at a safe distance from them. Keeping her gun pointed in the survivors' general direction, she scans the surrounding forest. It's empty of additional troops. *What was all of this?* she wonders. *A warning? A taunt? A suicide mission?* She imagines she'll have the opportunity to find out, once her mapping mission departs.

There's a high-powered radio in a pouch on her hip. Due to concern about the Lemurians having the ability to monitor such transmissions, she was only to use it if she succeeded. She flips it on, extends the antenna. She presses the button marked TALK.

"This is General Taylor," she says. "Over."

The End

For Fiona, and for Orrin Grey.

John Langan is the author of two collections, *The Wide, Carnivorous Sky and Other Monstrous Geographies* (Hippocampus 2013) and *Mr. Gaunt and Other Uneasy Encounters* (Prime 2008), and a novel, *House of Windows* (Night Shade 2009). With Paul Tremblay, he has edited *Creatures: Thirty Years of Monsters* (Prime 2011). He is one of the co-founders of the Shirley Jackson Awards, for which he was a juror during its first three years. He teaches courses in creative writing at SUNY New Paltz, and lives in upstate New York with his wife, younger son, and a houseful of animals who are steadily getting smarter.

THE BRAVE LITTLE TAILOR

by The Brothers Grimm, Tale #20, Alt Title: *The Valiant Little Tailor*

One summer's morning a little tailor was sitting on his table by the window; he was in good spirits, and sewed with all his might. Then came a peasant woman down the street crying, "Good jams, cheap! Good jams, cheap!" This rang pleasantly in the tailor's ears; he stretched his delicate head out of the window, and called, "Come up here, dear woman; here you will get rid of your goods." The woman came up the three steps to the tailor with her heavy basket, and he made her unpack the whole of the pots for him. He inspected all of them, lifted them up, put his nose to them, and at length said, "The jam seems to me to be good, so weigh me out four ounces, dear woman, and if it is a quarter of a pound that is of no consequence." The woman who had hoped to find a good sale, gave him what he desired, but went away quite angry and grumbling.

"Now, God bless the jam to my use," cried the little tailor, "and give me health and strength;" so he brought the bread out of the cupboard, cut himself a piece right across the loaf and spread the jam over it. "This won't taste bitter," said he, "but I will just finish the jacket before I take a bite." He laid the bread near him, sewed on, and in his joy, made bigger and bigger stitches.

In the meantime the smell of the sweet jam ascended so to the wall, where the flies were sitting in great numbers, that they were attracted and descended on it in hosts. "Hola! who invited you?" said the little tailor, and drove the unbidden guests away. The flies, however, who understood no German, would not be turned away, but came back again in ever-increasing companies. The little tailor at last lost all patience, and got a bit of cloth from the hole under his work-table, and saying, "Wait, and I will give it to you," struck it mercilessly on them. When he drew it away and counted, there lay before him no fewer than seven, dead and with legs stretched out. "Art thou a fellow of that sort?" said he, and could not help admiring his own bravery. "The whole town shall know of this!" And the little tailor hastened to cut himself a girdle, stitched it, and embroidered on it in large letters, "Seven at one stroke!" "What, the town!" he continued, "The whole world shall hear of it!" and his heart wagged with joy like a lamb's tail. The tailor put on the girdle, and resolved to go forth into the world, because he thought his workshop was too small for his valor.

Before he went away, he sought about in the house to see if there was anything which he could take with him; however, he found nothing but an old cheese, and that he put in his pocket. In front of the door he observed a bird which had caught itself in the thicket. It had to go into his pocket with the cheese. Now he took to the road boldly, and as he was light and nimble, he felt no fatigue. The road led him up a mountain, and when he had reached the highest point of it, there sat a powerful giant looking about him quite comfortably.

The little tailor went bravely up, spoke to him, and said, "Good day, comrade, so thou art sitting there overlooking the widespread world! I am just on my way thither, and want to try my luck. Hast thou any inclination to go with me?"

The giant looked contemptuously at the tailor, and said, "Thou ragamuffin! Thou miserable creature!"

"Oh, indeed?" answered the little tailor, and unbuttoned his coat, and showed the giant the girdle, "There mayst thou read what kind of a man I am!"

The giant read, "Seven at one stroke," and thought that they had been men whom the tailor had killed, and began to feel a little respect for the tiny fellow. Nevertheless, he wished to try him first, and took a stone in his hand and squeezed it together so that water dropped out of it. "Do that likewise," said the giant, "if thou hast strength?"

"Is that all?" said the tailor, "that is child's play with us!" and put his hand into his pocket, brought out the soft cheese, and pressed it until the liquid ran out of it. "Faith," said he, "that was a little better, wasn't it?" The giant did not know what to say, and could not believe it of the little man. Then the giant picked up a stone and threw it so high that the eye could scarcely follow it.

"Now, little mite of a man, do that likewise."

"Well thrown," said the tailor, "but after all the stone came down to earth again; I will throw you one which shall never come back at all." And he put his hand into his pocket, took out the bird, and threw it into the air. The bird, delighted with its liberty, rose, flew away and did not come back. "How does that shot please you, comrade?" asked the tailor.

"Thou canst certainly throw," said the giant, "but now we will see if thou art able to carry anything properly." He took the little tailor to a mighty oak tree which lay there felled on the ground, and said, "If thou art strong enough, help me to carry the tree out of the forest."

"Readily," answered the little man; "take thou the trunk on thy shoulders, and I will raise up the branches and twigs; after all, they are the heaviest." The giant took the trunk on his shoulder, but the tailor seated himself on a branch, and the giant who could not look round, had to carry away the whole tree, and the little tailor into the bargain: he behind, was quite merry and happy, and whistled the song, "Three tailors rode forth from the gate," as if carrying the tree were child's play.

The giant, after he had dragged the heavy burden part of the way, could go no further, and cried, "Hark you, I shall have to let the tree fall!" The tailor sprang nimbly down, seized the tree with both arms as if he had been carrying it, and said to the giant, "Thou art such a great fellow, and yet canst not even carry the tree!"

They went on together, and as they passed a cherry-tree, the giant laid hold of the top of the tree where the ripest fruit was hanging, bent it down, gave it into the tailor's hand, and bade him eat. But the little tailor was much too weak to hold the tree, and when the giant let it go, it sprang back again, and the tailor was hurried into the air with it. When he had fallen down again without injury, the giant said, "What is this? Hast thou not strength enough to hold the weak twig?"

"There is no lack of strength," answered the little tailor. "Dost thou think that could be anything to a man who has struck down seven at one blow? I leapt over the tree because the huntsmen are shooting down there in the thicket. Jump as I did, if thou canst do it." The giant made the attempt, but could not get over the tree, and remained hanging in the branches, so that in this also the tailor kept the upper hand.

The giant said, "If thou art such a valiant fellow, come with me into our cavern and spend the night with us." The little tailor was willing, and followed him. When they went into the cave, other giants were sitting there by the fire, and each of them had a roasted sheep in his hand and was eating it. The little tailor looked round and thought, "It is much more spacious here than in my workshop."

The giant showed him a bed, and said he was to lie down in it and sleep. The bed, however, was too big for the little tailor; he did not lie down in it, but crept into a corner. When it was midnight, and the giant thought that the little tailor was lying in a sound sleep, he got up, took a great iron bar, cut through the bed with one blow, and thought he had given the grasshopper his finishing stroke.

With the earliest dawn the giants went into the forest, and had quite forgotten the little tailor, when all at once he walked up to them quite merrily and boldly. The giants were terrified, they were afraid that he would strike them all dead, and ran away in a great hurry.

The little tailor went onwards, always following his own pointed nose. After he had walked for a long time, he came to the courtyard of a royal palace, and as he felt weary, he lay down on the grass and fell asleep. Whilst he lay there, the people came and inspected him on all sides, and read on his girdle, "Seven at one stroke." "Ah," said they, "What does the great warrior here in the midst of peace? He must be a mighty lord." They went and announced him to the King, and gave it as their opinion that if war should break out, this would be a weighty and useful man who ought on no account to be allowed to depart.

The counsel pleased the King, and he sent one of his courtiers to the little tailor to offer him military service when he awoke. The ambassador remained standing by the sleeper, waited until he stretched his limbs and opened his eyes, and then conveyed to him this proposal.

"For this very reason have I come here," the tailor replied, "I am ready to enter the King's service." He was therefore honorably received and a special dwelling was assigned him.

The soldiers, however, were set against the little tailor, and wished him a thousand miles away. "What is to be the end of this?" they said amongst themselves. "If we quarrel with him, and he strikes about him, seven of us will fall at every blow; not one of us can stand against him."

They came therefore to a decision, betook themselves in a body to the King, and begged for their dismissal. "We are not prepared," said they, "to stay with a man who kills seven at one stroke."

The King was sorry that for the sake of one he should lose all his faithful servants, wished that he had never set eyes on the tailor, and would willingly have been rid of him again. But he did not venture to give him his dismissal, for he dreaded lest he should strike him and all his people dead, and place himself on the royal throne. He thought about it for a long time, and at last found good counsel. He sent to the little tailor and caused him to be informed that as he was such a great warrior, he had one request to make to him.

In a forest of his country lived two giants who caused great mischief with their robbing, murdering, ravaging, and burning, and no one could approach them without putting himself in danger of death. If the tailor conquered and killed these two giants, he would give him his only daughter to wife, and half of his kingdom as a dowry, likewise one hundred horsemen should go with him to assist him.

"That would indeed be a fine thing for a man like me!" thought the little tailor. "One is not offered a beautiful princess and half a kingdom every day of one's life!" "Oh, yes," he replied, "I will soon subdue the giants, and do not require the help of the hundred horsemen to do it; he who can hit seven with one blow has no need to be afraid of two."

The little tailor went forth, and the hundred horsemen followed him. When he came to the outskirts of the forest, he said to his followers, "Just stay waiting here, I alone will soon finish off the giants." Then he bounded into the forest and looked about right and left. After a while he perceived both giants. They lay sleeping under a tree, and snored so that the branches waved up and down.

The little tailor, not idle, gathered two pocketsful of stones, and with these climbed up the tree. When he was halfway up, he slipped down by a branch, until he sat just above the sleepers, and then let one stone after another fall on the breast of one of the giants. For a long time the giant felt nothing, but at last he awoke, pushed his comrade, and said, "Why art thou knocking me?"

"Thou must be dreaming," said the other, "I am not knocking thee." They laid themselves down to sleep again, and then the tailor threw a stone down on the second. "What is the meaning of this?" cried the other. "Why art thou pelting me?"

"I am not pelting thee," answered the first, growling. They disputed about it for a time, but as they were weary they let the matter rest, and their eyes closed once more. The little tailor began his game again, picked out the biggest stone, and threw it with all his might on the breast of the first giant

"That is too bad!" cried he, and sprang up like a madman, and pushed his companion against the tree until it shook. The other paid him back in the same coin, and they got into such a rage that they tore up trees and belabored each other so long, that at last they both fell down dead on the ground at the same time. Then the little tailor leapt down.

"It is a lucky thing," said he, "that they did not tear up the tree on which I was sitting, or I should have had to spring on to another like a squirrel; but we tailors are nimble." He drew out his sword and gave each of them a couple of thrusts in the breast, and then went out to the horsemen and said, "The work is done; I have given both of them their finishing stroke, but it was hard work! They tore up trees in their sore need, and defended themselves with them, but all that is to no purpose when a man like myself comes, who can kill seven at one blow."

"But are you not wounded?" asked the horsemen. "You need not concern yourself about that," answered the tailor, "They have not bent one hair of mine." The horsemen would not believe him, and rode into the forest; there they found the giants swimming in their blood, and all round about lay the torn-up trees.

The little tailor demanded of the King the promised reward; he, however, repented of his promise, and again bethought himself how he could get rid of the hero. "Before thou receivest my daughter, and the half of my kingdom," said he to him, "thou must perform one more heroic deed. In the forest roams a unicorn which does great harm, and thou must catch it first."

"I fear one unicorn still less than two giants. Seven at one blow, is my kind of affair." He took a rope and an axe with him, went forth into the forest, and again bade those who were sent with him to wait outside. He had to seek long. The unicorn soon came towards him, and rushed directly on the tailor, as if it would spit him on his horn without more ceremony.

"Softly, softly; it can't be done as quickly as that," said he, and stood still and waited until the animal was quite close, and then sprang nimbly behind the tree. The unicorn ran against the tree with all its strength, and struck its horn so fast in the trunk that it had not strength enough to draw it out again, and thus it was caught. "Now, I have got the bird," said the tailor, and came out from behind the tree and put the rope round its neck, and then with his axe he hewed the horn out of the tree, and when all was ready he led the beast away and took it to the King.

The King still would not give him the promised reward, and made a third demand. Before the wedding the tailor was to catch him a wild boar that made great havoc in the forest, and the huntsmen should give him their help.

"Willingly," said the tailor, "that is child's play!" He did not take the huntsmen with him into the forest, and they were well pleased that he did not, for the wild boar had several times received them in such a manner that they had no inclination to lie in wait for him. When the boar perceived the tailor, it ran on him with foaming mouth and whetted tusks, and was about to throw him to the ground, but the active hero sprang into a chapel which was near, and up to the window at once, and in one bound out again. The boar ran in after him, but the tailor ran round outside and shut the door behind it, and then the raging beast, which was much too heavy and awkward to leap out of the window, was caught.

The little tailor called the huntsmen thither that they might see the prisoner with their own eyes. The hero, however went to the King, who was now, whether he liked it or not, obliged to keep his promise, and gave him his daughter and the half of his kingdom. Had he known that it was no warlike hero, but a little tailor who was standing before him, it would have gone to his heart still more than it did. The wedding was held with great magnificence and small joy, and out of a tailor a king was made.

After some time the young Queen heard her husband say in his dreams at night, "Boy, make me the doublet, and patch the pantaloons, or else I will rap the yard-measure over thine ears." Then she discovered in what state of life the young lord had been born, and next morning complained of her wrongs to her father, and begged him to help her to get rid of her husband, who was nothing else but a tailor.

The King comforted her and said, "Leave thy bedroom door open this night, and my servants shall stand outside, and when he has fallen asleep shall go in, bind him, and take him on board a ship which shall carry him into the wide world."

The woman was satisfied with this; but the King's armor-bearer, who had heard all, was friendly with the young lord, and informed him of the whole plot.

"I'll put a screw into that business," said the little tailor. At night he went to bed with his wife at the usual time, and when she thought that he had fallen asleep, she got up, opened the door, and then lay down again. The little tailor, who was only pretending to be asleep, began to cry out in a clear voice, "Boy, make me the doublet and patch me the pantaloons, or I will rap the yard-measure over thine ears. I smote seven at one blow. I killed two giants, I brought away one unicorn and caught a wild boar, and am I to fear those who are standing outside the room."

When these men heard the tailor speaking thus, they were overcome by a great dread, and ran as if the wild huntsman were behind them, and none of them would venture anything further against him. So the little tailor was a king and remained one, to the end of his life.

The End

THE THREE SNAKE-LEAVES

by Jeffrey Ford

based upon *The Three Snake-Leaves*

Within the abandoned rocket works where my mother warned me not to go, I found a door that opened into a courtyard—the sky above, a fountain, and a beautiful tree. Beneath green boughs, in a wrought iron chair, there sat an old robot from some time before mine. It was made of a yellow metal that still gleamed where it wasn't rusting. Articulated joints—fingers, wrists and elbows. Eyes, mere lights, but with lids that squinted and closed. The mouth was made of rubber that could stretch into a wide smile or become a pout. Its head was the size and shape of a watermelon made of yellow metal. Whoever made it gave it ears, a nose and a mustache. When I came upon it, it was smoking a metal pipe, puffing out pink clouds and whispering. Before I could run, it noticed me and said, "Come over and sit down. I'll tell you a story." Then I ran as fast as I could. In the days that followed, I often wondered about what that story might have been.

Of course, I eventually went back and took a seat on one of the wrought iron benches across from the robot.

"I'm Grimm Beam," it said in a soft, unhurried voice.

"Can you get out of that chair?" I asked.

"I'm wedded to the chair. At one time I could walk."

"How old are you?"

"180 years old."

"You tell stories?" I asked.

"Now, yes, but I once served on a space station orbiting Neptune. I served so well for 25 years, I was retired to this garden and rewired by my creator, Don Beam, to tell fairy tales from all times and places to tired workers."

"Who's Don Beam?"

"Inventor of the Negative Energy Proctor that folds space and an authority on folk and fairy tales. When someone visits me here, I tell them one of the old stories."

"I'm Ceil. I live outside of here, across the giant dirt lot in a house beyond the field," I said.

"Well, sit still," he said, "and I'll tell you 'The Tale of the Ylak of the Oak Wood.'"

I folded my hands in my lap, looked up into the leaves of the tree, and he began, "Once upon a time, in the Land of Nod…"

The story carried me away, and I was in awe of the amount of expression capable with only a rubber mouth, blinking lights, and eye lids. The robot used its hands in the telling and made graceful images in the air with those metal fingers. When it finished, it sat quietly for a moment before picking up its pipe. "Goodbye," I said to it as I stood from my bench. It looked at me, its eye lights both off, and nodded. "Next time," it said. I'd have run again, but my imagination was awhirl with dizzying images of a huge grasshopper person, the Ylak, eating the livers of unwary passersby, being hunted by the King with his bowman and a pack of trained leopards. The secrets of the monster and its transformation into an angel made me walk across the lot with my eyes closed.

I went there often in that first year I discovered him. I was 14 and lonely. Our neighborhood had gotten hit by the green yips, a disease of the spirit, and most of the kids my age were taken by it. There were no girls left who weren't much older, and the only boys in my grade to survive were a couple of roughnecks from the crumble, that neighborhood next to ours where people were known to die of starvation quite regularly. Money was tight. Food was scarce. Every Thursday evening, I'd go with my uncle Stu in his car out into the weedy fields and hunt coyote. He'd drive and aim his pistol out the window. I'd be following the creatures with the beam of a strong spot light. Sometimes to save bullets, he'd just ram them. Grilled coyote wrapped in cabbage leaves. We ate it often.

I'd sit impatiently all day through school, waiting to venture into the rocket works again and hear about a ghost that lived in trees and strangled people, or a flying horse, or a woman who plucked her eyes out every night in order to sleep. Meanwhile the teacher, a battered android, Ms. Proof, glitched and sparked around the class-room, lecturing on one thing and then another with no rhyme or reason. The synthetic skin had rotted from her cheeks and we could see the pneumatics and gear work of her speech. Most of her long black hair was gone, and the sight of the strands that remained made me vaguely ill. The class had been reduced to me and those two boys from the crumble, the Kirst brothers—heads shaved, droopy-eyed, big-eared morons. They attacked the teacher more than once, but her defensive skills were still intact. She blackened their eyes and split their lips while calmly reciting the multiplication tables.

What relief, after getting home from school, fleeing my mother, and finding myself in the hidden courtyard. I asked Grimm Beam one day if anyone else ever visited him. He said, "Just you lately. Before that there was a fellow who came in and laid down on the ground there." He pointed to the tree trunk next to him. "I think he was hurt. He closed his eyes, and I told him a tale about Oaou, the giant worm, 400 miles long, that lives at the bottom of the ocean next to a glowing crev-ice from which the dreams of the world bubble up. When I finished, he was dead, and eventually, the tree grew up around his skeleton."

"You've been here a long time."

"At night," said the robot, "I sometimes pretend I can see Neptune, and I think about my days on the space station."

"Did you have adventures?"

"Oh, yes, but for today I'm going to tell you about 'The Mouse and the Jelly.'"

My mother followed me one day to the edge of the rocket works and was waiting for me when I got home. She wanted to know what I was doing. She tried to yell at me, but by then I was 15, and she was too tired to follow up on any threats. I felt bad for her. She suspected me of running off into the ruins to meet one of the Kirst Brothers. "Fat chance," I said. Finally she just waved her hands in the air and laid down on the couch. She worked all day at one of the local sapping mills, sitting strapped to a chair in an induced sleep while the machinery drew out the product of her imagination. What they did with it, no one knew. As my mother once said, "Whatever it is, it's not making the world a better place."

So, I continued to visit Grimm Beam in the days and months ahead, and his stories sustained me through dark times—Uncle Stu shooting himself in the head, the season of bread and water, the slow emptying out of my mother. In the first week of our last year of school, Ms. Proof, standing in front of her desk, lecturing on the three laws of robotics, suffered a major glitch, sparks shooting from her nose and smoke issuing from her ears. The Kirst brothers saw the opportunity and took it. They beat her with metal pipes until her head came off. It rolled onto the floor at my feet. I never said a word. When AJ Kirst, the older of the boys, came over to pick it up, he saw me looking at him. He stared at me, and said, "For the money." They were going to sell her for scrap. It struck me then that he really wasn't that bad looking.

There was no sense in going to school, and I never told my mother what had happened. I doubt the Kirst brothers told anyone either. So, I'd leave in the morning, and spend the school hours listening to Grimm Beam. When that school year ended, I would be forced to the sapping mills to earn my way. The thought of it made me short of breath, considering my mother, who seemed hollow—dark bags beneath her eyes, a trembling paleness. She ate little and slept less, just dozing off and then screaming herself awake. Often, she was too tired to talk. One afternoon, when the weather was getting cold and the branches of the tree in the courtyard were barren, I told Grimm Beam about my approaching fate in the mills.

He took his pipe from his mouth and looked up as if searching the blue sky for a glimpse of Neptune. He looked back to me, his eyes alternately blinking, his lids rising and lowering like window blinds. In his smooth voice, he said, "I have a story for that."

"Tell me," I said.

"This is a story I only tell to people who have visited me 100 times, and today is your 100th visit."

"What about the sapping mills?"

"You'll see the connection, I promise" he said and then announced the title, "The Three Snake-Leaves."

A young knight wins the King's daughter's hand in marriage for his exploits defending the realm from attack. Before they can marry, the princess makes one request of her fiancé—if one of them is to die before the other, they will both be entombed. The knight accepts her demand. Eventually, she falls ill and dies, and he must follow her alive into the sealed crypt. While waiting to die, he is attacked by a snake but manages to kill it. Then another snake enters the crypt with three leaves in its mouth. It uses the leaves to bring the dead snake back to life. The young man sees this and uses the leaves to bring the princess back to life. They escape the crypt and get on a ship heading for his father's village. During the voyage, she falls in love with the captain of the ship. They ambush the knight, throw him overboard, and he drowns. The young man's servant steals a boat, recovers his body and then brings him back to life with the leaves. Finally, the princess and the sea captain are found guilty and set adrift in a boat with holes in it.

When Beam finished, I thought for a while but couldn't see the connection he'd promised. "I don't get it," I said.

"You will," he said, and the way his words sounded gave me a slight chill.

I didn't return to the courtyard for a few days after, but concentrated on the tale of the three snake leaves. For all the time I spent thinking about it, it left me totally blank. The day I decided to return to Grimm Beam, it snowed. On the way across the vast lot to the rocket works, I saw, through a wind-blown white veil, the Kirst Brothers hauling door-sized sheets of thin metal toward the dump. When AJ spotted me he ran over. "Where you going, Ceil?" he asked.

"Just taking a walk in the snow," I said. He made me nervous.

"Why don't you come with me and Mope. We're going to the Trash Mountains to do some sliding down."

There was something genuine in his look. His smile made that pudding face handsome. I thought if I didn't go with them, they might follow me and find Grimm Beam. I knew how that would end. So, I went with them. The Trash Mountains weren't really mountains, just debris piles that reached up pretty far. They were covered in snow, and that decoration, like something out of an old tale from the north, drew me. We climbed halfway up, slipping and sliding on the skeletons of old technology, the boulders that were once buildings. Rats darted in and out of the snow. We stopped on a ledge, all of us out of breath. "Good enough," said AJ. "You ready?" He looked at me.

I peered down and didn't like the angle. "Kind of steep," I said.

"If it's not, you can't get no speed up," said his brother.

AJ laid his metal sheet on the ledge and sat down upon it. One end of it was bent upward, and he pushed himself along the metal until his heels were firmly against the bend. "Come on," he said and motioned for me to take a seat between his legs. I did. He wrapped his arms around my stomach, and yelled, "Give us a push, Mope!"

We flew down the incline of harsh jolts, picking up speed. The world was a blur but I heard AJ laughing. I was startled to find myself also breathless with laughter. We hit the bottom of the mountain and the metal sheet glided out across the factory lot and didn't stop for a long way. "What a ride," he said in my ear. I got up and helped him to stand. We turned back to see Mope make his run. When he reached the bottom of the hill, his sled hit something hidden by a snow drift and became airborne. Mope flew off backwards and twirled in the air like a doll. We laughed even harder.

We made at least a dozen trips up to that ledge. In late afternoon, we rested up there, our backs against the snowy junk, staring out in one direction at the factories, and in the other toward my neighborhood and beyond it the crumble. The snow had stopped and the day was disappearing. Mope smoked a cig, snot running from his nose. He had a big purple bruise across his forehead, having been thrown on nearly every run. AJ reached into the pocket of his coat and brought out a grimy looking handkerchief. He carefully opened its corners like the petals of a flower. Waiting inside were four shiny chunks of glass. "Star candy," he said and held it out for me to see. Mope reached over and snatched two of the pieces out of his brother's hand.

"We bought this with some of the money we got for Ms. Proof. Most of it we gave to our mom, but this was for us. We each got 6 pieces and this is all that's left."

"What is it," I asked.

Mope put one in his mouth. "Sweetest thing you ever tasted."

"Some astronaut brought them back from Neptune ages ago. Shadfella, the crumble's head salesman, found them in a refrigerator, which was still working, in an office building out by the launch pads. Nothing else tastes like them and they make you warm inside. No worry for hours."

He reached into his palm, plucked one up with his thumb and forefinger and handed it toward me.

"You're gonna give me this?" I said while taking it.

He smiled. "I've got one for myself." He put his in his mouth. "Don't chew it or it'll make you puke. Just let it melt."

There was a sweetness to it that never became too much. It stunned me at first. I felt the tension draining from my shoulders and neck.

"One more ride," said AJ. "If me and Mope don't get back through the crumble before night, we'll never make it home alive. Let's go."

That ride down the mountain felt like it took a week, like we were syrup slowly flowing, and the landscape of our life, the rocket works, the lot, the field, even the crumble, seemed beautiful. When we reached the bottom, AJ helped me up. I thanked him for the candy, and for some weird reason shook his hand. He held onto mine, and then he suddenly fled, Mope following. I floated back home through the dusk, images of Grimm Beam's stories parading through my thoughts. I made a promise to myself to go and see him in the morning.

The star candy wouldn't allow me to feel anything when I arrived home to find my mother on the kitchen floor all used up. I lifted her and propped her at the table in her chair. Her mouth was agape, her eyeballs gone black, burn marks on her temples, half her hair vanished. She wasn't breathing and wouldn't again. I sat with her calmly until the sweetness of the candy wore off, and then her death hit me like a punch in the side of the head. I collapsed to the floor and cried myself to sleep. She and Uncle Stu had abandoned me. My loneliness was as bitter as the candy was sweet.

I had her stiffened corpse removed as soon as possible the next day. Two men came in a horse drawn wagon and took her away to the mulcher. An hour hadn't passed before a representative of the sapping mills arrived, having noticed my mother wasn't at work. He offered his condolences, and then told me that I had a day to grieve before I was required to punch in and take her place. As soon as I could get away, I ran to the courtyard. Grimm Beam greeted me, and I blurted out my dilemma, tears in my eyes. He shook his head and sighed as I carried on. When, finally, I dried my eyes, he launched into the tale of "Stick Man Wincellard." He had no answers for me but it relaxed me to hear his voice. When he was finished, and I was about to go, he said, "You say you have no one, but we will always be friends." He put out his hand to shake. I took it in mine. It was colder than the snow.

When I got home, I found AJ Kirst sitting in my mother's seat at the kitchen table.

"What do you want?" I said.

"I heard your mother burned out at the mill. I came to say I'm sorry."

My anger at his intrusion passed, and I sat down across from him. "I have to take her place tomorrow."

"You would have money then," he said. "People in the crumble would kill for a job, but, you know, they think we got no good day-dreams."

"I'm gonna run away," I told him. "I'm not going over to the mill to be sucked out by a machine. I don't care if I die alone in the waste."

"Where you going?"

"Do you remember, before you and Mope busted up Ms. Proof, she told us about a forest and a town far to the West?"

"I never listened to her jabbering."

"She said it's due West."

"How far?"

I shrugged.

"I'll go with you, but we'll need money. Do you have any? It might come in handy when we get there."

"No, but I think I know where we can get some," I said.

Instead of showing up at the mill the next morning, I led AJ and Mope through the hallways and buildings of the rocket works. They pulled a wagon that carried their metal pipes and hacksaws. When we reached the door to the courtyard, I stayed outside. The brothers entered, leaving it open. I heard Grimm Beam say, "Come in, have a seat, and I'll tell you a story." Mope laughed with delight. "I'm Grimm Beam," said the robot, "and I'm going to tell you 'The Tale of…'" Then I heard the pipes resound off his metal head. In his smooth storytelling voice he repeated, "Treachery, treachery, treachery…" until there came the crackling of sparks. A few seconds later it was just the incessant banging of metal against metal. I cried through the rasp of the hacksaws.

By the time we crossed into the crumble, pulling along the remains of Grimm Beam, the mill agents were no doubt at the house looking for me. When I left there that morning, I took Uncle Stu's gun, some extra bullets, whatever food I could find and a small backpack of clothes. I knew I'd never return. They could seal that tomb without me in it. In the crumble, which was nearly civilized during daylight, I kept my hand on the gun in my pocket, finger on the trigger. AJ led us to a shop in a broken down building, only half a roof, on a block of broken-down buildings. The crumble was a land of grimy, weed grown streets, broken glass, rotted bricks. No one showed themselves on the main street, but darted and skulked in alleys and on those few intact rooftops.

In that shop we sold the remains of Grimm Beam to an old woman who chewed tobacco and carried a sawed off particle weapon. AJ haggled with her but the best he could do was fifty bills. We took it. Fifty for all the folk and fairy tales in the world. The thought of it made me laugh the way my mother did each month when the money was gone. As soon as we were outside on the street, Mope demanded his cut. "Star candy," he said, and held his hand out. AJ motioned for him to come closer. As Mope stepped up, AJ swung the metal pipe and caught his younger brother on the left temple with it, sending him unconscious into a snow pile on the broken sidewalk.

"What are you doing?" I yelled.

"You think I'm dragging that snot nosed, pecker across the waste? Don't worry, he'll pop up after a while and be good as new," said AJ. "Besides, we need his money."

I looked down at Mope, who lay perfectly still, his head at an odd angle, the blood from his mouth, staining the snow.

"Move fast," said AJ, taking my hand. "They know we have money."

We ran into an alley, and traveled through the crumble without going out on a main street. The path took us to Shadfella's Den, an enormous old warehouse. I was beginning to think that following AJ's plan was like being set adrift in a boat with holes in it. "What are we doing here?" I whispered as we entered through the huge wooden doors. All he said was, "Get ready to fight." Shafts of light shone down through the decrepit roof like spotlights among the shadows. We were surrounded by rows of shelves holding old machines, tools, clothes. Ahead of us there was an office sitting on stilts at the top of a rickety flight of stairs. I could see, through a large window, someone in there behind a desk set with candles.

AJ led me directly up the steps and opened the office door. The man in the chair spun around, and yelled, "Stay," an order to a glistening blue metallic wolf with a thick coat of needles, diamond tipped fangs, and electric eyes that lunged forth, snarling, from the dark behind his chair. I should have pulled the gun but the sight of it made me numb with fear.

"What brings you?" said Shadfella, waving us toward him. "Something to sell?"

"I want something," said AJ as we moved closer to the desk. The wolf sat, at ease, and became still as a piece of furniture.

Shadfella was ancient, as if carved from bone, straggly white hair and fingernails nearly as long as Uncle Stu's toenails. He maneuvered his chair to face us.

"What's the metal pipe for?" he asked, shifting his glance toward the wolf as a warning to us.

"I want the keys to your lift," said AJ.

"Just a whistle and Nero, here, will tear you to shreds."

"Not before I kill you first, though," said AJ. "Just give me the keys."

As the old man drew in breath to whistle, I heard the metal creature begin to power up for a leap. I took the gun from my pocket, and at point blank range, shot three times into the wolf's head. It stood with a shudder, said, "Emergency," in a distant electronic voice, and then keeled over like a statue, the three gaping holes still smoking. Shadfella couldn't get any spit to whistle after that. He reached into his desk drawer and brought out the key to the only lift in the crumble. AJ took it from him with one hand and with the other brought down the metal pipe and cracked his skull like an eggshell.

We fled through the dark warehouse, through the beams of sunlight, encountering workers who stared at us dully, an army of grown up Mopes. AJ held my hand and pulled me along, weaving our way around them. "Shadfella is dead," he yelled, and we left the building through a gaping hole in the back wall. There ahead of us in the field was a lift, blue with chrome trim, hovering four feet above the ground. We ran through the snow and hopped in.

"You know how to drive this?" I asked.

"I watched Shadfella drive it a lot when he'd take me on retrieval runs out by the launch pads." He put a flat rectangle of plastic in a slot in the dashboard, and the lights went on.

"Why'd you kill him?" I asked.

"Once Mope dropped something in the warehouse that was worth a lot of money. It broke and the old man had him beat so bad I thought he would die."

I winced, recalling the image of Mope, head twisted weirdly, bleeding into the snow, but thinking about it became impossible as the lift rose up and we were gliding eight feet off the ground. AJ hit the pedal, and we moved down alleyways like a boat on a swiftly flowing river. When we hit open ground west of the crumble, we flew along, my hair streaming back, AJ laughing like he was sliding down Trash Mountain. After we'd gone a few miles past where you could no longer see the rocket works in the distance, he hit a button and a glass roof bubble came up around us, protecting us from the wind and cold.

We flew on across a vast flatness covered with snow. I dozed off and woke to find AJ with the same expression of determination on his face, staring ahead into the late afternoon sun. I had to go to the bathroom and asked him to stop. He brought the lift down a few inches off the ground and hovered there. The bubble retracted, and I leaned over the side and jumped down. The wind was fierce and it was freezing. There was a large snowdrift to my right that I thought would give me some privacy. I ran around behind it and went. Teeth chattering, shivering all over, I pulled up my pants, and sprinted for the warmth of the lift. When I came around that snowdrift, though, the lift was gone and my backpack was laying in the snow. In the wind, I heard Grimm Beam saying, "Treachery, treachery, treachery…" And I finally saw the promised connection to his 100th story. I never saw AJ, the lift or the money again.

I sit in my garden now, at my home in the town of the forest, jotting down my own tale. It was a long time ago, but I remember, after I was alone for a few minutes in the waste, and I'd overcome my anger that AJ had stranded me. I felt a great sense of relief slowly building, like the effects of some truer confection than star candy. He was another tomb I luckily avoided. I zipped up my coat, tied my hood, lifted my backpack and headed west through the white nothing. Living off snow and the few morsels of food I'd brought, sleeping when I could, curled up at the base of a large drift, out of the wind, I survived, and after four days reached a way station manned by soldiers from the forest town. They fed me and brought me here in an ancient gasoline auto. When asked by the mayor and the council what skill I had to offer that might be useful to the town, I told them all "The Tale of the Ylak of the Oak Wood," and when I was finished, they welcomed me home.

The End

Jeffrey Ford is the author of the novels, *Vanitas, The Physiognomy, Memoranda, The Beyond, The Portrait of Mrs. Charbuque, The Girl in the Glass, The Cosmology of the Wider World*, and *The Shadow Year*. His story collections are *The Fantasy Writer's Assistant, The Empire of Ice Cream, The Drowned Life*, and *Crackpot Palace*. A new collection, *A Natural History of Hell*, will be out in 2016 from Small Beer Press. He lives in Ohio and currently teaches part time at Ohio Wesleyan University.

THE THREE SNAKE-LEAVES

by The Brothers Grimm, Tale #16, Alt Title: *The Three Snake Leaves*

There was once on a time a poor man, who could no longer support his only son. Then said the son, "Dear father, things go so badly with us that I am a burden to you. I would rather go away and see how I can earn my bread." So the father gave him his blessing, and with great sorrow took leave of him.

At this time the King of a mighty empire was at war, and the youth took service with him, and with him went out to fight. And when he came before the enemy, there was a battle, and great danger, and it rained shot until his comrades fell on all sides, and when the leader also was killed, those left were about to take flight, but the youth stepped forth, spoke boldly to them, and cried, "We will not let our fatherland be ruined!" Then the others followed him, and he pressed on and conquered the enemy. When the King heard that he owed the victory to him alone, he raised him above all the others, gave him great treasures, and made him the first in the kingdom.

The King had a daughter who was very beautiful, but she was also very strange. She had made a vow to take no one as her lord and husband who did not promise to let himself be buried alive with her if she died first. "If he loves me with all his heart," said she, "of what use will life be to him afterwards?" On her side she would do the same, and if he died first, would go down to the grave with him. This strange oath had up to this time frightened away all wooers, but the youth became so charmed with her beauty that he cared for nothing, but asked her father for her.

"But dost thou know what thou must promise?" said the King.

"I must be buried with her," he replied, "if I outlive her, but my love is so great that I do not mind the danger." Then the King consented, and the wedding was solemnized with great splendor.

They lived now for a while happy and contented with each other, and then it befell that the young Queen was attacked by a severe illness, and no physician could save her. And as she lay there dead, the young King remembered what he had been obliged to promise, and was horrified at having to lie down alive in the grave, but there was no escape. The King had placed sentries at all the gates, and it was not possible to avoid his fate. When the day came when the corpse was to be buried, he was taken down into the royal vault with it and then the door was shut and bolted.

Near the coffin stood a table on which were four candles, four loaves of bread, and four bottles of wine, and when this provision came to an end, he would have to die of hunger. And now he sat there full of pain and grief, ate every day only a little piece of bread, drank only a mouthful of wine, and nevertheless saw death daily drawing nearer.

Whilst he thus gazed before him, he saw a snake creep out of a corner of the vault and approach the dead body. And as he thought it came to gnaw at it, he drew his sword and said, "As long as I live, thou shalt not touch her," and hewed the snake in three pieces. After a time a second snake crept out of the hole, and when it saw the other lying dead and cut in pieces, it went back, but soon came again with three green leaves in its mouth. Then it took the three pieces of the snake, laid them together, as they ought to go, and placed one of the leaves on each wound. Immediately the severed parts joined themselves together, the snake moved, and became alive again, and both of them hastened away together.

The leaves were left lying on the ground, and a desire came into the mind of the unhappy man who had been watching all this, to know if the wondrous power of the leaves which had brought the snake to life again, could not likewise be of service to a human being. So he picked up the leaves and laid one of them on the mouth of his dead wife, and the two others on her eyes. And hardly had he done this than the blood stirred in her veins, rose into her pale face, and colored it again.

Then she drew breath, opened her eyes, and said, "Ah, God, where am I?"

"Thou art with me, dear wife," he answered, and told her how everything had happened, and how he had brought her back again to life. Then he gave her some wine and bread, and when she had regained her strength, he raised her up and they went to the door and knocked, and called so loudly that the sentries heard it, and told the King.

The King came down himself and opened the door, and there he found both strong and well, and rejoiced with them that now all sorrow was over. The young King, however, took the three snake-leaves with him, gave them to a servant and said, "Keep them for me carefully, and carry them constantly about thee; who knows in what trouble they may yet be of service to us!"

A change had, however, taken place in his wife; after she had been restored to life, it seemed as if all love for her husband had gone out of her heart. After some time, when he wanted to make a voyage over the sea, to visit his old father, and they had gone on board a ship, she forgot the great love and fidelity which he had shown her, and which had been the means of rescuing her from death, and conceived a wicked inclination for the skipper. And once when the young King lay there asleep, she called in the skipper and seized the sleeper by the head, and the skipper took him by the feet, and thus they threw him down into the sea.

When the shameful deed was done, she said, "Now let us return home, and say that he died on the way. I will extol and praise thee so to my father that he will marry me to thee, and make thee the heir to his crown." But the faithful servant who had seen all that they did, unseen by them, unfastened a little boat from the ship, got into it, sailed after his master, and let the traitors go on their way. He fished up the dead body, and by the help of the three snake-leaves which he carried about with him, and laid on the eyes and mouth, he fortunately brought the young King back to life.

They both rowed with all their strength day and night, and their little boat flew so swiftly that they reached the old King before the others did. He was astonished when he saw them come alone, and asked what had happened to them. When he learnt the wickedness of his daughter he said, "I cannot believe that she has behaved so ill, but the truth will soon come to light," and bade both go into a secret chamber and keep themselves hidden from every one.

Soon afterwards the great ship came sailing in, and the godless woman appeared before her father with a troubled countenance. He said, "Why dost thou come back alone? Where is thy husband?"

"Ah, dear father," she replied, "I come home again in great grief; during the voyage, my husband became suddenly ill and died, and if the good skipper had not given me his help, it would have gone ill with me. He was present at his death, and can tell you all."

The King said, "I will make the dead alive again," and opened the chamber, and bade the two come out. When the woman saw her husband, she was thunderstruck, and fell on her knees and begged for mercy.

The King said, "There is no mercy. He was ready to die with thee and restored thee to life again, but thou hast murdered him in his sleep, and shalt receive the reward that thou deservest." Then she was placed with her accomplice in a ship which had been pierced with holes, and sent out to sea, where they soon sank amid the waves.

The End

THE MADMAN'S UNGRATEFUL CHILD

by Peadar Ó Guilín

based upon *The Bremen Town-Musicians*

1. The Shelter

In that land, after the Apocalypse, inside a place called Bremen's Hill there lived the happiest of madmen. Radiation mottled his skin and brown stains by the thousand had stiffened his uniform into a wilderness that even fleas disdained. But his wide, wobbly smile rarely failed him, and his gleeful, booming voice ruined the girl's sleep, no matter how hard she clung to it.

"Wake up, Miranda! What'll you have for breakfast, dearest child?"

Her real name was Allison, but what was that to a madman? Some mornings she replied with a groan, for the cold came even into the shelter. Other times, she would answer, "I'm not your child! You look nothing like me!"

This line would fluster him and his eyes would lose focus for 3…4…5…seconds. Then he would laugh. "Of course, my dear girl! Waffles it is!"

He'd open a random can of beans or peaches or whatever he first laid his trembling hands on and cry, "Oh, that smell!" He'd slop out two portions and dig in, his eyes half-closed in ecstasy. *That's* how much the madman enjoyed "waffles."

Afterwards, he'd go straight back to his bunk with the words, "I think I'll work from home today." Then, he'd just stare into space, smiling or frowning or wiggling his fingers in the air, as though typing.

It wasn't much of a life, but it's all Allison had to look forward to, until, that is, Mr. Donkey came along.

Breakfast was no different that morning than any other. After clearing the plates, Allison picked out one of the shelter's thousands of old books intending to read it outside.

"Where are you going?" cried the madman. "I hope you're not running away. *Terrible* things can happen to children who leave their parents. Especially girls."

"Yes," Allison growled. "I could be kidnapped by a madman, for example, and held captive for four years."

He covered his mouth in horror. "Oh, my Lord! That's even worse than what I was thinking!"

In spite of these words, he never noticed if she spent one hour above ground or ten. He never checked to see if she was getting irradiated or infected or swarmed by rats. Yet his madman's intuition alerted him if she wandered past the base of the hill. He would arrive all flustered at the hatch with rifle in hand to urge her back to "safety."

On that special day, Allison climbed outside into sunlight. From the hilltop, she could see for miles in all directions. For the first time in years, long dormant seeds had become flowers. "The world hasn't ended," she told herself, as much a fool sometimes as her captor. "Momma's alive and waiting for me back home. There's Ben and Jerry's in the icebox…"

But over yonder, mount Spindle still sported a crater where the city had been, and the wreckage of not one, but two passenger airplanes lay scattered about the valley below her like confetti.

The madman was wrong to fear her running away, for where could she go?

Allison set her book on a rock and washed her face in the freezing water of the well. She could have had it from a tap down below, but it felt so much better to scoop it over her head with her bare hands, shivering and laughing.

But today something smelled…*wrong*.

Below the hill, lay a series of boulders that may have been rolled off the summit when the madman built his refuge. From behind these now rose a series of bizarre and terrifying creatures. They were made of fur and blood and flapping skin, with great misshapen heads. At the same moment, a change in the wind swept a cloying stench up the slope towards her, lodging in the back of her throat like a film of oil.

Before she could flee, a voice cried, "Don't be alarmed! We're friends."

"You're…you're human?" said Allison.

"Oh, indeed." He straightened up: a tall man made even taller by the head of a donkey that he wore for a hat, while the rest of the pelt hung around him like a rotting cloak.

Others stood now too: a woman wearing a dog; a man with a lion's skin that must have come from the zoo; a filthy child of indeterminate sex, plastered with chicken feathers.

"We're entertainers," said Mr. Donkey. "Actors, if you will. Musicians even! The new world needs them too, am I right? And, in exchange for a song, all we ask is five minutes to fill our flasks at your well."

"She's just a girl," said the dog woman. Were it not for the dirt, she might have been a model from an old magazine. Her hungry grin made Allison shiver. "She's on her own. And that hatch is open." The woman clambered onto the boulders, but then, as though summoned, the madman appeared. He looked every bit as frightening as the beast people with his burned skin, his ridiculous looking glasses, and his rifle.

"Zombies!" he cried. "I *love* this game!"

Mr. Donkey pulled the dog woman down from the rocks to stand in front of him. "My good sir, how lovely to see you! What my colleague was saying just now, is that she wishes to sleep with a man just like you. A man who had the foresight to prepare for this little mess we're all in. Isn't that right, dear?"

"That's right," she muttered. "He looks real fine."

"Exactly!" said Mr. Donkey. "The woman you have appears… inexperienced. Amateur. Am I right? All we ask, is to use your well, and maybe a few cans of food. It's not too much, is it? Or if you're lonely—and who wouldn't be, out here?—you could come back to the airport with us, you could—"

Allison almost jumped out of her skin. "The airport?" she cried.

"Oh sure, little miss. It's the only reason the rebels nuked our happy backwater. To take out the airport. They hit everything else, but missed that completely."

The madman, meanwhile, hadn't moved an inch. Apart from his hands, that is. They shook so badly, it was a miracle he hadn't dropped the rifle already. Seeing this helplessness, the dog-woman grinned.

"Let's just rush the bastard, already." She wrenched herself free of Donkey's grip and ran up the slope. This turned out to be a mistake. Her head exploded, followed, a heartbeat later, by Donkey's and then Lion's. The chicken died too, and when five more men, previously hidden, suddenly appeared from behind the ridge, all of them met their end in less time than it took to blink.

"Head-shots for zombies," the Madman said, happily. His hands still shook as his erratic gaze wandered the valley. "No more waves, Miranda?" he asked.

"N-n-no," said Allison.

And that was the end of that. Game over.

Except for two things. The first, was that Allison saw Mr. Donkey crawling away. The madman's incredible aim had shattered the animal's skull, but not that of the man beneath.

The other thing, was that she had learned something vital. The airport still stood. Nothing else that had happened today mattered as much as that. Not the corpses, not the new flowers. Nothing.

That night, Allison mashed up a few sleeping pills from the supplies and dissolved them in water. "Look, poppa," she said, "I've brought you a glass of wine to help you sleep."

The madman studied the liquid for a moment too long and shook his head. "That's not wine!" Allison's heart was hammering. What would she do if he didn't drink it? But then, he grinned. "That's champagne!" he cried. "For your birthday. Happy birthday, my girl!"

He clinked glasses—hers was empty—and took a delicate sip. "Oh, that *is* good."

The next morning, passing the boulders, Allison turned to look up to the top of the hill, but the pills had worked and the madman's uncanny ability to sense her wanderings had failed to wake him.

He wouldn't recognize her anyway, she thought. She had hacked off her own hair and strapped down her breasts in order to pass for a boy. Bad things happened to those who ran away. Isn't that what he'd said? Especially to girls. And hadn't Momma always told her the exact same thing?

The "entertainers" lay where they'd fallen. And there were older bodies too. Each skull bore a hole in the exact center of the forehead and Allison realized that the madman must have faced other attacks in the past, maybe while she slept soundly in her bunk.

She ought to have been curious of his impossible abilities, but all she wanted now, was the airport.

This was not the first time she had tried to find the place.

She remembered her twelfth birthday. The TV showed nothing but panic, while frightened people clogged every stream on her tablet. Momma never came home from her job at air traffic control. She wouldn't, or couldn't answer her cell. Men shouted in the street. Somewhere nearby, glass shattered.

Allison told the house to call her if Momma came home, and off she went. Momma would have been horrified. "Never, never go out there by yourself!" It was the one thing she and the madman had in common. On that day, the day the world changed, a bus lay burning at the stop, so Allison walked down onto the freeway, her pace double that of honking cars full of weeping children.

Then, everybody was screaming and clawing at their eyes as the sky behind Allison lit up. A giant fist smashed the road hard enough to send vehicles tumbling. She ran, she ran, but somewhere along the way, momma's warning about the awful things that could happen to a girl alone proved to be correct, because an ogre found her and carried her off.

"Let me go!" she cried. "I need to get to the airport. Momma's in trouble!"

She might as well have been punching concrete. He never paused, leaning into a sudden storm, sheltering her with his body from flying dust and stones until they came to the bunker in the hills.

He let her go once the hatch was closed. His skin glistened with burns and he wept like a child for Haley and Miranda, whoever the hell they were. "The car…ohmygodohmygod, the car. Oh Lord!" It seemed the ogre had been expecting the Apocalypse. Looking forward to it, even! But for all his years of preparation, he'd failed to save his own family. With shaking fingers he fished out a strange pair of glasses and pushed them on. What a strange contraption they were! Black and shiny. Far too large for his head, yet the arms fastened on to him like those of an octopus clinging to its prey. Then, while Allison cowered in the corner, he spent a few minutes talking to himself.

"Y-yes," he said. "Activate. Yes."

He'd been mad ever since.

Now, as an older girl, with darkness falling, she crouched at the airport's chain link fence. She had expected planes, but the lone runway boasted nothing larger than an overturned ambulance.

In the distance, tiny people wandered around campfires. The sight of them quickened her breath. She had expected to die with nobody for company but a filthy lunatic, and the urge to approach them, no matter who they were, no matter how dangerous, came close to overwhelming her. However, something even more important lay at the edge of the runway: the control tower.

Allison worked her way over and snuck inside. It wasn't her first visit. Momma had taken her in one time, up in the elevator, every surface bright and clean.

This time, she climbed the stairs in the pitch dark, saving the batteries of a flashlight borrowed from the shelter. Momma would have left a message for her child. Surely she would. And Allison would need the light to find it under all the dust. So, she mastered her impatience and didn't flick the switch until great big windows told her she'd made it into the control room.

And there before her, were the new swivel chairs Momma had boasted about. Each supported a uniformed skeleton with a gaping hole in its chest.

It mightn't be her, Allison thought, looking at the central figure, the only woman. But hope crumbled when her flashlight played over a tattered hummingbird scarf that she would have recognized anywhere.

"No!" she cried. "No!"

Then there were footsteps on the stairs, and a stench of rotting fur. Now, the girl realized how foolish she'd been, but it was too late.

2. The Duke

In the small arrivals hall, they chained Allison behind a cage of luggage trolleys. It gave her a front row view of the feast. And what a feast it was! A great fire of old books roared in the center of the floor, where men and women wearing the corpses of animals danced around it for the amusement of a giant in a high chair.

They were every bit as crazy as her supposed "poppa", except that she'd been safe with him, and here, they would likely eat her.

Allison recognized the giant as a wrestler from TV. The Duke, they'd called him, and now, he lived up to that name. Beneath his throne, lay a thousand rusting food containers and bottles of every description. Women sat at his feet, half-clothed and so miserable, they made Allison glad she had dressed as a boy.

Every now and again, the women would present their leader with meat from a platter. He would fling it away with a cry. "I want peaches! I want the madman's peaches!"

Further offers of food only increased his fury, until at last he shouted, "Bring me the prisoner!"

Allison thought her time had come, but it was Mr. Donkey they dragged forth and not her.

"You promised to get me the madman's peaches, but you failed!"

"It's impossible!" Mr. Donkey replied, his head hanging low, his knees knocking in fear. "We couldn't even get close. He's like a demon. You know that, Duke. You gotta know that by now."

The Duke didn't know it. "String him up," he commanded, and other men, also wrestlers by the look of them, hanged Mr. Donkey then and there while the court cheered. Then, with the corpse still warm, the Duke stood and everybody fell silent—even the fire seemed to burn lower in anticipation.

"Listen, now!" he called. "Listen! That madman, has cans of fruit in his lair. Fruit! You hear me? Any man here gets it for me, can have my women and be leader when I die." And that wouldn't be long, for a red growth the size of a fist clung to his neck.

"Who will step forward?"

Nobody volunteered. The men, so rowdy only moments before, all smiles and shouts, now shuffled away from the light.

He made the offer a second time, producing a gleaming machine gun. "Do I have to shoot somebody to get my peaches? Do I?" Holes in the wall proved he had done so before. "One last time, this is my third and final—"

"I'll do it," Allison shouted.

The purple growth stopped the Duke from turning his head properly, so he had to move his whole massive body around to face her. "A boy?" he sneered. "A little boy? Oh, I don't think so. You just don't wanna to be dinner. Earl? Put a bullet in his face."

Allison should have been terrified, but she kept her voice perfectly calm. "The madman lives on a hill fifteen miles to the North."

Earl, nearly as big as his master and wearing the rotting skin of a cow, had passed the fire by now, and had drawn a pistol.

"There is a fresh spring and 14,000 cans of beans. 17,000 of tuna." Earl removed the safety and aimed it right at her face. "He has stored up tinned pears, strawberries, peaches and grapefruit. He grows his own tomatoes and—"

"Earl! Stop!"

The Duke stepped down from his throne and ran over to her, knocking dancers from his path. He pulled Allison out of her cage of trolleys, and so strong was he, that one massive hand around her neck was enough to hold their weight aloft along with hers. He was choking her, but she knew that to give in to terror or tears would be the end of her.

"I know how to get past him," she said. "The madman. I know everything about him."

The Duke kept her dangling for a moment. Then, he grinned. "Everybody, meet my new heir!"

They applauded, and later, when the Duke said he would lead the expedition himself, cheers rang around the hall, but some, such as Earl, seemed angry.

3. The Trick

The next day, Allison led a party of fifteen ex-wrestlers and the Duke himself cross-country towards the shelter.

"Great!" said Allison brightly when it came into view. She had spent the whole night in a terror the giants would kill her or discover she was a girl, but she knew a display of courage was the only thing that might keep her alive. "There's the hill." She turned to the Duke. "Now, I'll get you your peaches. Did you really mean it when you said I would be your heir?"

"I sure did," he said. Allison nodded, pretending to believe him, but knowing he didn't really care what happened after he was gone.

She made herself smile. "None of your men can stop me anyway, because I'll have the madman's miraculous rifle. The one that never misses. I'll get it right now. You won't believe how easy it is to trick him."

She made as if to leave, but Earl stopped her, grinning slyly. "So, how are you gonna trick him, boy."

"Oh, it's simple. See those boulders at the bottom of the hill? When we get close to them, the madman will appear out of the hatch. Then, he'll call us zombies, but he won't shoot until somebody gets a bit closer. All I'll do is clap my hands three times once I've passed the rocks. He thinks it's a password, see? Now, off I go to get my reward."

But before she could advance a single step, Earl threw her to the ground and ran forward in her place.

Just as she had predicted, her "poppa" jumped out of the hatch before the wrestler had reached the boulders.

"Zombies!" he cried.

Earl clapped his hands three times. "You're supposed to do it *after* the rocks!" shouted Allison, as though in despair. It was too late. Earl made it to the bottom of the slope, but his brains did not.

"I can't believe it," said Allison. "It's so easy, let me—"

A second wrestler—this one wearing the remains of a horse—pushed her aside. The man waited until he had passed the boulders before smacking his palms together, but before he could manage the feat a second time, his ears hit the ground moving in opposite directions. It was an incredible shot by the madman. He hadn't even been looking when he pulled the trigger.

"I love this game!" he cried.

A third hero, with arms like tree trunks, had to die before the Duke, tiring of the wait, gave Allison her chance.

She swaggered off as she imagined a young man would, aware of the Duke's narrowed eyes on her back and the itchy trigger fingers of the twelve surviving wrestlers. But the greatest threat by far stood waiting for her on the top of the hill. What if the madman failed to recognize her with hacked off hair and her clothing all torn?

She clapped three times in the appropriate place, but only to convince the men at her back—it meant nothing to the madman. But step by step, her confidence grew, until halfway up the slope, he shouted, "Miranda! I knew it was you! Thank you! Thank you for bringing zombies!" He ran down to meet her.

The Duke must have realized he'd been fooled, and the madman, coming down the slope, had put himself in range of the wrestlers' inferior guns. They opened fire.

Allison threw herself to the ground as bullets whizzed everywhere, but the madman...the happy madman danced. He knew exactly where to step to avoid enemy fire, when to lean back, when to duck. His rifle spat too, ridiculously fast, every shot finding the exact center of a wrestler's forehead, until silence reigned once again.

"Here, Miranda," he said gently. "Let poppa help you up."

For the first time ever, when he hugged her, Allison hugged him back. "I'm sorry," she said. "You've been so good, but I had to...I had to find Momma, I—"

"There, there, my poor girl." He had both arms around her, and probably, that's why he failed to get his rifle up in time. For the evil Duke had hidden behind a boulder when the rest of his men had stood up to fire.

The madman must have seen him rise to his feet. He threw Allison to one side, aimed, shot...but even as he hit his mark, blood bloomed over his heart and he struck the ground hard enough that a stone knocked the glasses from his face.

"Poppa!" cried Allison. "Oh, Poppa!" She had brought this about with her ingratitude and she realized now that he had never kidnapped her all those years ago. That had been a rescue, pure and simple, and for all his strange ways, the man had kept her alive ever since.

Blood dribbled from his mouth. He squinted up at her. "Who…," he said. "Who the hell are you?"

"I'm Miranda. Your daughter."

"W-what? You…you look nothing like me."

She dragged him inside, but already his eyes were turning cloudy.

Her heart felt empty. She'd lost everything, even the madman. Now, his ridiculous glasses lay on the floor, looking as lonely and out of place as she felt. Allison wasn't sure what made her try them on. Was it loneliness, curiosity, or something else? Perhaps it was the slight warm glow they emitted, like they were trying to attract attention. They fit her smaller head far more snugly than they should have. Had they shrunk? Was such a thing even possible? Then, her scalp prickled all along the length of the frame, as though needles had grown from it and had burrowed straight into her skull. But she felt no fear, only an odd sense of comfort.

She opened her eyes, and the madman surprised her by sitting up and stretching.

"Wow!" he said. "That was close. I thought I was a gonner for sure."

Allison cried out in delight, for she too had thought him dead. She moved as if to hug him. "No, Miranda, or, Allison, as I should call you. It's all right. My madness is cured now and I know you're not my daughter. Poor Miranda is out there somewhere and I must go and find her."

"Don't go," Allison said. "I went looking for my Momma too… and…and—"

The madman smiled. "It's all right, Allison. Your mother's not dead either. That was a stranger's skeleton you saw in her chair. Look! Here she comes now!"

It didn't occur to Allison to ask how he had known what she'd seen in the traffic control tower. Instead, the girl cried out in delight as her mother, smiling and weeping with joy, climbed down the stairs to hug her.

All the while she wore the madman's glasses, and for the next few days everything was wonderful. They had glorious feasts together. Ice cream and waffles and anything they desired. They watched their favorite TV shows and went shopping for the perfumes Momma loved so much.

Yet, Allison was stronger in spirit than the madman had ever been, so, when she had recovered a little from the awful things she had seen, she made herself remove the glasses. Despite the needle-like tendrils that had grown into her skull, they came away easily.

The madman's corpse had begun to smell, she saw, and needed burying. The glasses couldn't help with that, but they knew where to find a shovel amongst all the supplies and where on the hill the soil could be most easily shifted.

They also knew how to read the sensors hidden under the boulders for the detection of intruders, and they could work, she learned, with the targeting system in the madman's rifle.

Allison wept again for her momma. "Don't bring her back," she told the glasses. "I don't want her if she's not real."

But nor did she wish to live alone.

So, the next day, she put the glasses back on and secured the rifle to her shoulder, and off she went back towards the airport.

Perhaps terrible things would happen to her, a girl going into the world alone like that. Or perhaps she was the terrible thing and it was the world that needed to watch out. But Allison was determined to be happy, and even in that land, after the apocalypse, such a thing might still be possible.

The End

Peadar Ó Guilín grew up in beautiful Donegal in the far North West of Ireland. These days, he lives in Dublin where he toils day and night for a giant corporation. His next book, *The Call*, a very Irish YA horror, will be released in 2016.

THE BREMEN TOWN-MUSICIANS

by The Brothers Grimm, Tale #27, Alt Title: *The Musicians of Bremen*

A certain man had a donkey, which had carried the corn-sacks to the mill indefatigably for many a long year; but his strength was going, and he was growing more and more unfit for work. Then his master began to consider how he might best save his keep; but the donkey, seeing that no good wind was blowing, ran away and set out on the road to Bremen. "There," he thought, "I can surely be town-musician." When he had walked some distance, he found a hound lying on the road, gasping like one who had run till he was tired. "What are you gasping so for, you big fellow?" asked the donkey.

"Ah," replied the hound, "as I am old, and daily grow weaker, and no longer can hunt, my master wanted to kill me, so I took to flight; but now how am I to earn my bread?"

"I tell you what," said the donkey, "I am going to Bremen, and shall be town-musician there; go with me and engage yourself also as a musician. I will play the lute, and you shall beat the kettledrum."

The hound agreed, and on they went.

Before long they came to a cat, sitting on the path, with a face like three rainy days! "Now then, old shaver, what has gone askew with you?" asked the donkey.

"Who can be merry when his neck is in danger?" answered the cat. "Because I am now getting old, and my teeth are worn to stumps, and I prefer to sit by the fire and spin, rather than hunt about after mice. My mistress wanted to drown me, so I ran away. But now good advice is scarce. Where am I to go?"

"Go with us to Bremen. You understand night-music, you can be a town-musician."

The cat thought well of it, and went with them. After this the three fugitives came to a farmyard, where the cock was sitting upon the gate, crowing with all his might. "Your crow goes through and through one," said the donkey. "What is the matter?"

"I have been foretelling fine weather, because it is the day on which Our Lady washes the Christ-child's little shirts, and wants to dry them," said the cock; "but guests are coming for Sunday, so the housewife has no pity, and has told the cook that she intends to eat me in the soup tomorrow, and this evening I am to have my head cut off. Now I am crowing at full pitch while I can."

"Ah, but red-comb," said the donkey, "you had better come away with us. We are going to Bremen; you can find something better than death everywhere. You have a good voice, and if we make music together it must have some quality!"

The cock agreed to this plan, and all four went on together. They could not, however, reach the city of Bremen in one day, and in the evening they came to a forest where they meant to pass the night. The donkey and the hound laid themselves down under a large tree, the cat and the cock settled themselves in the branches; but the cock flew right to the top, where he was most safe. Before he went to sleep he looked round on all four sides, and thought he saw in the distance a little spark burning; so he called out to his companions that there must be a house not far off, for he saw a light. The donkey said, "If so, we had better get up and go on, for the shelter here is bad." The hound thought that a few bones with some meat on would do him good too!

So they made their way to the place where the light was, and soon saw it shine brighter and grow larger, until they came to a well-lighted robber's house. The donkey, as the biggest, went to the window and looked in.

"What do you see, my grey-horse?" asked the cock.

"What do I see?" answered the donkey; "a table covered with good things to eat and drink, and robbers sitting at it enjoying themselves."

"That would be the sort of thing for us," said the cock.

"Yes, yes; ah, how I wish we were there!" said the donkey.

Then the animals took counsel together how they should manage to drive away the robbers, and at last they thought of a plan. The donkey was to place himself with his forefeet upon the window-ledge, the hound was to jump on the donkey's back, the cat was to climb upon the dog, and lastly the cock was to fly up and perch upon the head of the cat.

When this was done, at a given signal, they began to perform their music together: the donkey brayed, the hound barked, the cat mewed, and the cock crowed; then they burst through the window into the room, so that the glass clattered! At this horrible din, the robbers sprang up, thinking no otherwise than that a ghost had come in, and fled in a great fright out into the forest. The four companions now sat down at the table, well content with what was left, and ate as if they were going to fast for a month.

As soon as the four minstrels had done, they put out the light, and each sought for himself a sleeping-place according to his nature and to what suited him. The donkey laid himself down upon some straw in the yard, the hound behind the door, the cat upon the hearth near the warm ashes, and the cock perched himself upon a beam of the roof; and being tired from their long walk, they soon went to sleep.

When it was past midnight, and the robbers saw from afar that the light was no longer burning in their house, and all appeared quiet, the captain said, "We ought not to have let ourselves be frightened out of our wits;" and ordered one of them to go and examine the house.

The messenger finding all still, went into the kitchen to light a candle, and, taking the glistening fiery eyes of the cat for live coals, he held a lucifer-match to them to light it. But the cat did not understand the joke, and flew in his face, spitting and scratching. He was dreadfully frightened, and ran to the back-door, but the dog, who lay there sprang up and bit his leg; and as he ran across the yard by the straw-heap, the donkey gave him a smart kick with its hind foot. The cock, too, who had been awakened by the noise, and had become lively, cried down from the beam, "Cock-a-doodle-doo!"

Then the robber ran back as fast as he could to his captain, and said, "Ah, there is a horrible witch sitting in the house, who spat on me and scratched my face with her long claws; and by the door stands a man with a knife, who stabbed me in the leg; and in the yard there lies a black monster, who beat me with a wooden club; and above, upon the roof, sits the judge, who called out, 'Bring the rogue here to me!' so I got away as well as I could."

After this the robbers did not trust themselves in the house again; but it suited the four musicians of Bremen so well that they did not care to leave it any more. And the mouth of him who last told this story is still warm.

The End

STORIES OF THE TREES, STORIES OF THE BIRDS, STORIES OF THE BONES

by Kat Howard

based upon *The Juniper-Tree*

Genevra stopped in front of the apple tree, slid the interface into the bark, and listened as it told her its story. In a voice like rising sap, it spoke of seasons and time, long cold winters and the melting warmth of spring. Of wind in its leaves and bees in its flowers. Of branches grown full and heavy with ripening apples, and of the release of the harvest. Of the strength of storms, and the pleasure of sunlight. It was a story not very different from that of the other trees surrounding it, but Genevra still made a point to listen to each one. Once the story started to repeat, she moved on to the next tree, and repeated her actions.

She hadn't thought she would like the stories when she first took the job. The whole thing seemed too weird, being surrounded by a forest of voices when she didn't even particularly like to hear her own.

Trees, as it turned out, even ones that told stories, were easier to be around than people, and listening to the trees was a way to be quiet, without her own head trying to fill the quiet with thoughts. Standing in a forest of talking trees was relaxing, peaceful.

Genevra moved on to the next apple tree, spinning the sharp end of the interface between her fingers as she did. Technologically speaking, the interfaces had been a failure. They were supposed to read the trees' genetic memory, extract the information stored in the cells set in layers of rings. The process was meant to provide useful data to help strengthen heirloom species and create new hybrids, help increase longevity and crop yields.

It hadn't worked like that at all. The trees had given information, but it had come in the form of stories—about winters survived and birds nesting in their branches, not about preferred planting depth and nutrient combinations in the soil.

The woman, Marlina, who had hired Genevra to install the interfaces in the trees, didn't care about mixing the most useful fertilizer to increase fruit size or anything like that. She wasn't a farmer. She was, well, Genevra wasn't sure exactly what she was. A wealthy eccentric, a nature lover. Something like that. Someone who was interested in the stories of the trees and could afford not only to buy the remaindered interfaces but also to hire Genevra to install them. "I think if things want to speak to us," she had said, "we ought to try and listen." Genevra wasn't sure how much choice the trees had—she'd never installed an interface and had silence result—but she supposed there was something to be said for listening to stories you wouldn't normally get to hear.

Besides, Genevra liked the work. Even when it rained, being out in the trees was better than scrubbing toilets or wiping kids' snotty noses, or any of the other crap jobs she had done, and she liked the trees' stories. They were similar to each other, true, but it was a comforting kind of similar. They'd all endured the vagaries of time and weather; they'd all survived. Being surrounded by the whisper of their voices made her think that she could put her feet on the ground and stretch her arms to the sky and root herself here among them. She stood like that, sometimes, arms raised, listening to the trees.

And the birds. From the moment she'd arrived, it had been impossible not to hear the birds. They didn't have interfaces or any sort of AI that Genevra could see, but they spoke anyway. Tiny sentences: "What a beautiful bird am I!" "It was not you, it was not you." Always twice, that last one. Sometimes when a whole flock of them set to chattering, it seemed like they were disagreeing—"What a beautiful bird! Not you, not you!" Genevra laughed, and the birds broke out in short, harsh chirps that sounded like they were laughing with her.

Marlina lived in an area that had been replanted about one hundred years ago, after one of the great summer fires, and so her two-bedroom house was in the middle of an actual forest. There were more trees together than Genevra had ever seen. Best of all, Marlina had apple orchards on her property. Antique apples. She'd told Genevra to help herself to as many as she wanted. It had taken her a few days to feel comfortable picking the apples after she had started hearing the trees, but none of them talked about the harvest hurting, so she decided it was fine. Her favorites were the Snow Apples—brilliant red skin and fairy tale white flesh. Her teeth crunched through the red and the white and the sweet-tart juice ran down the back of her wrist as she walked.

It wasn't just the apple trees Marlina wanted interfaced. It was every tree on her property. She had been very specific. She had, she said, a great desire to hear a forest of stories, and she wanted to be sure she didn't miss any. As she walked through the property, Genevra had pressed the interfaces into maple trees that told her of sugaring season and birches that whispered like the wind, slow-speaking white pines, and one great willow that had told her of the fish that passed through the river beside its roots.

And this one, whatever it was. Needle-leaved and twisted branches. Sharp-smelling, with blue-purple berries. She pressed the interface into its rough bark, and waited to hear the voice of the tree.

"My mother she killed me, my father he ate me, my sister she buried my bones."

Genevra yanked her hands away from the tree in horror. She had learned what the voices of the trees sounded like. They sounded like sun-warmed greenings and lines of time written in rings. They were different in tone, in quality to human speech—once you had heard a tree, you would never mistake it for something else.

This voice sounded human. Like a child. It repeated: "My mother she killed me, my father he ate me, my sister she buried my bones."

Genevra turned and ran.

❖   ❖   ❖

Marlina had turned pale when Genevra told her what the tree's interface had said. "Say it again. Exactly."

Voice shaking, Genevra did.

She pressed her hands to her head, clutching at her thoughts. "What did the tree look like?"

Genevra described it.

"The juniper tree," Marlina said. "Of course the juniper tree."

"It…it sounded like a person. Speaking."

"I think it probably is," Marlina said, her voice hollow, as if she was talking to herself, and Genevra was only incidentally there to hear her.

"Can I get you something?" Genevra asked. "Call someone for you?"

"That's just it. There's no one left to call." Marlina scrubbed her hand across her eyes. "I want you to take me to the tree."

❖   ❖   ❖

The idea for the interfaces had come from Ever After technology. Ever After had been designed to be a kind of AI that could preserve the replica of someone's consciousness. It scanned brains, analyzed thoughts, speech, and behavior patterns, and then put all of that together to be an interactive model of a person.

It was rumored that the inventor had lost a member of her family in tragic circumstances when he was very young, that the AI was her way of trying to make sure no one else had to suffer in the same way she did, that gone wouldn't have to mean all the way gone. But the inventor had disappeared before Ever After was completed, and maybe it had only been a story made up by someone in marketing.

As it turned out, marketing should have made up a good story. Ever After had been advertised as a way to have a happily ever after, even if real life hadn't let you. The tastelessness of the tag line hadn't stopped the devices from being hugely popular.

Until they weren't. Turns out, talking to an unchanging almost-facsimile of someone you knew after they've died is one step too far into the uncanny valley. The interactions were never quite right, and that crack of wrongness eventually turned into a chasm. The Ever Afters were nothing but reminders of what was already lost.

❖   ❖   ❖

When Genevra and Marlina got back to the juniper tree, it was speaking with a different voice.

"My child was buried, here with me, alone and forgotten, beneath the juniper tree." It was older sounding, a woman's voice, not a child's.

"I swear to you, that wasn't what it said," Genevra said. "I would never make something like that up."

"Do the stories change, once the interface is in?" Marlina asked.

"They can. But, like, small changes. The changes that have happened in the life of the tree since the interface was installed. Not like"—Genevra batted her hand next to her ear as if she could push the sound away. "Not like this. Not like a completely new voice telling a completely different story."

The voice switched back: "My mother she killed me, my father he ate me, my sister she buried my bones."

"Maddox?" Marlina asked. She flattened both of her palms against the rough bark of the tree, leaned her forehead between them as if trying to get closer to the voice. "Mad?"

"Do you know who that is?" Genevra asked.

"Yes. Maybe. I used to." Marlina sighed, so deep her entire body sank with it. "I had an issue, with my memory. So much is gone. I've never heard that woman's voice. But this one—I think it's my brother. My dead brother.

"We need shovels."

❖ ❖ ❖

The two women dug into the ground, and they hadn't gone very deep before they found the first bones. White and horrible, and tangled in the juniper tree's roots.

Marlina sighed, so deep her whole body moved with it. "I was hoping that I remembered wrong, that maybe he wouldn't be here."

"Do you want to stop, maybe call the police or someone who deals with dead people?" Genevra asked. She was kind of creeped out by the idea that they were digging up actual skeletons, but it was better than leaving them there. Maybe.

Marlina delicately untangled the bone and placed it to the side. "No. This isn't something for the police. This something I need to do. But if you feel weird about it, you can go. I won't make you help."

Genevra thought of the way the other woman's face had collapsed when she heard her brother's voice. "I'll stay. I'd like to help."

The birds chattered cheerfully about how beautiful they were, and the apple trees around them quietly told the stories of their seasons past and the loveliness of those voices seemed almost an obscene soundtrack to digging up bone after bone.

The juniper tree's interface alternated between the two voices as they dug, but then it started to glitch, to skip words. The glitching got worse, the more bones they removed. "My…killed…father… bones." At one point, Genevra had reached up, to take the interface out of the tree and stop the horrible broken voice from coming out of it, but Marlina had reached up her hand to stop her. "He's been gone for almost my whole life. If he's talking, I want to hear him."

Genevra didn't know how Marlina could stand to listen to those words over and over, making less sense each time, but it wasn't her decision. It wasn't her brother they were unburying. She kept digging. "Do you remember any more of what happened here?"

"I feel like I almost do, like I'm right on the edge of it, at least about Maddox. Now that I'm here, I remember that's where he was, I remember that I'm the one who buried him. But I don't remember why all that was left was bones. I know what the tree said, but I don't remember that happening." She set the second skull gently next to the first. "As awful as it is, I wish I did."

Genevra opened her mouth. Closed it. Brushed dirt away from roots and saw bones, a small hand of them, in the ground. Holding on to the roots of the juniper tree. Holding on, as if the tree made that poor, unfleshed hand less lonely. She picked it up, set it with the other bones.

"I don't know if this would work. I mean, the technology failed. But considering where it came from. The interface? I could try?" She couldn't spit the words past her teeth, the half-formed idea that the interface could somehow accomplish what its technological inspiration had tried and failed to do, could read back into someone who was dead and let them tell their story.

"We should use the skulls then. To make sure they each have a chance to speak." Marlina closed her eyes, tipped her head back, away from the dark roots of the juniper tree and the piles of bones beside it. "I'll do it."

Genevra winced at the sound it made—a cracking pop—as Marlina set the interface into the first skull.

"How long does it usually take before it speaks? With the trees, I mean."

"Not long," Genevra said.

"This all truly happened. Quite a long time ago."

Genevra scrabbled back in the dirt, tripping over her feet and landing hard on her ass, because it is one thing to think about a talking skull telling you its story in the abstract and quite another when it actually starts speaking.

"Very long ago, now. In the early days of my marriage, I used to stand here, underneath this juniper tree that I had planted with my own hands, and weep. All I wanted was the one thing I did not have. A child. A son.

"Even in the winter, I would come here and speak to the juniper tree, and I would water her roots with my tears as I told her of my unhappiness.

"One such day, I had brought an apple with me, and when I was cutting the skin from the apple, I cut the skin from my hand. Blood fell on the snow, and it was so beautiful that I wished with all my heart that I could bear a son, as red and white as blood on snow.

"By the time the grass grew green two months later, I knew that I had conceived a child. All through my pregnancy, I returned here, to the juniper tree. Four months in, I shared the joy, that first summer morning when I felt my child move inside of me. In the seventh month, I shared my sadness, when I felt myself grow weaker. The juniper tree kept me alive, that long eighth month when I could eat nothing but its berries.

"And when, in the course of giving birth to my beautiful red and white son, I knew that I would die of it, I begged my husband to bury me here. He did, and now my son is buried here with me and how that happened is not my story to tell. But if I could still weep, my tears would again water the roots of the juniper tree."

The interface went silent.

"I think that was my father's first wife. Maddox's biological mom. I never knew how she died. For a while, I think I was afraid that… Well…" Marlina shook her head. "I still can't quite remember."

The crack as the interface pierced the skull was just as horrid the second time.

"All I wanted was an apple."

Marlina barked out a sob.

"An apple, red and white. But it was the death of me. My mother, she killed me."

Marlina tore the interface from the skull. "I remember now. I remember all of it."

Her words came fast and harsh from her throat. "It was my mother, his stepmother, who killed him. He was joking, trying to steal an apple, and she hit him so hard, it broke his neck. After it happened, she set up his body in my room, so that it would fall over when I opened the door and make me think that I had done it. Anything to make herself less of a monster.

"But my brother had this bird. He had trained it to speak. And when I found Maddox's body, it sang, 'It was not you, it was not you, her evil heart should crack in two.' So I believed it, not her."

"They still sing that. The birds in this forest. The first part of it, anyway," Genevra said.

Marlina nodded. "I've heard them. One of those things that felt familiar, but I didn't know why it should, and every time I tried to think about why I recognized the words, it was like my thoughts got too loud to listen to."

Genevra nodded.

"After she killed Maddox, she made a stew of him, and fed him to our father." Marlina's voice was so flat it took Genevra almost a full minute to process what she had said.

Marlina continued. "He ate and ate. Bowl after bowl. I'd never seen anyone eat so much at one sitting as my father did that night. My mother smiled as she watched, because she knew that now she wasn't the only monster in the house.

"My father never even asked where Maddox had gone.

"When he finished eating, I gathered Maddox's bones, and I brought them here, and I buried them. I had to do something for him, and this was the only thing I could think of.

"He always loved this tree."

"Is that when you forgot everything?" It made sense to Genevra. How could you bear to live through something like that, if you remembered it?

"Not then. For a few years after, I remembered everything that had happened. I hated it, but a part of me was grateful, too, because when I made sure my mother was gone, I used everything she had taught me. No one will ever find any bit of her, and there is nothing in this world that will speak with her voice."

Genevra was pretty sure she understood what Marlina had just confessed to her. But she didn't ask. There are some stories that are safer unspoken, no matter what voice tells them.

Marlina gripped a handful of dirt, let it fall through her fingers. "But still, I missed my brother so much. I would have done anything to bring him back, and I started to wonder if there was some way I could. Some way to make it so that he wasn't all the way gone.

"It was his bird that gave me the idea. The talking one. Even though it hadn't been Maddox talking to me, it was enough of a reminder that I wondered if there was a way that someone could talk after they were dead."

"Wait. You're the one who invented Ever After?"

Marlina nodded. "I did a lot of the early work. But before the first prototypes were ready to be tested, I had my breakdown."

"What happened?"

"It was right after my father died. His death brought all the emotions I had been trying to ignore back to me, all at once. I lost myself, and when I came back, I couldn't even remember my name until I found my ID in a bag."

"How did you wind up back here, then?"

"The house and the land were still mine. And my more recent memories mostly came back within the first year after I'd lost them. The doctors said I'd have a better chance at getting the rest back if I lived in a place that had been familiar to me when I was a child. The talking birds were still here, and the more I heard them, the more I wondered what else might talk. Hence the interfaces, and the trees.

"I do like the stories of the trees," Marlina said. "Most of the time."

"Now that you remember what happened, what will you do?" Genevra asked.

Marlina passed her hand over her brother's skull, not quite touching, but love in the gesture all the same. "I don't know."

It was growing dark by then, the sounds of night calling out from the surrounding trees. "Should we do something for them?" Genevra asked, gesturing at the two piles of bones.

"The night air won't hurt them," Marlina said.

❖   ❖   ❖

When they returned the next morning, Maddox's skeleton was gone. Every last bone of it. His mother's skeleton was still there, precisely as they had left her the night before.

"I don't understand," Marlina said. Tears cut tracks down her face, falling into the dirt at the juniper tree's roots. "We were the only ones who knew he was here."

Genevra looked around. They had smoothed the dirt back over the juniper tree's roots last night, not wanting to leave the tree uncovered. The shovels still stuck out of the ground where they had left them, and the only footprints were the treads of her hiking boots and the whirled pattern of Marlina's sneakers.

She walked farther out. Still no footprints beyond theirs. It was as if the thief had flown away. She looked up. For the first time since she had started working on Marlina's land, there were no birds in the trees. Their lack made her realize what she had been missing all morning: the birds. While the trees around them still whispered histories, no birds sang. Neither their regular calls, nor the strange repeated human phrases.

It would be impossible, of course. Birds could maybe carry off some of the smaller bones, though Genevra couldn't imagine why. But the long bones of the legs? The pelvis? The skull? They had to be much too heavy.

A rustle in the apple trees as one of the birds returned. "My mother she killed me."

A second. "My father he ate me."

Two birds landing near Marlina, thought and memory, speaking together. "My sister, she buried my bones. My sister, my dear sister, you were the only one who showed me any kindness. Even though you didn't know, you returned me to the arms of my loving mother."

One bird on its own flew through the air. In its beak, a golden chain. It landed next to Marlina, and dropped the chain into her lap. "I have never forgotten you," it said.

On the necklace was a charm, a tiny golden phoenix, rising up out of flames. Marlina's hand shook as she held it. "Maddox gave this to me for my birthday. I'd thought it was lost forever."

A shadow flew across the sun. In the air, a flock of birds, carrying a square of fabric. On the fabric, Maddox's skeleton, a bird holding on to each piece, so that the flock might tell his story.

"Bury me with my mother," he said, the birds his voice. "Beneath the juniper tree."

❖   ❖   ❖

"When I die," Marlina said to her as they laid Maddox and his mother to rest, "I want you to bury me under the juniper tree with them. If you do that, this house, the land, everything is yours."

And so when word came, years later, of Marlina's death, Genevra returned. She smiled to hear the stories of the trees—it was like catching up with old friends as she walked through the orchards she had worked in. No longer drowning out her story, they were part of it. There were still birds, of course, chattering from tree to three, but these flocks didn't speak in human words, or if they did, they kept that speech secret.

Someone else had already done the difficult work, and so all that remained of Marlina was her bones. Her bones, and a gold phoenix on a charm. Genevra wrapped them in silk, and buried them beneath the juniper tree.

When she was finished, she smoothed the dirt, and took one of the old interfaces out of her pocket. She slid it into the juniper tree's bark. She knew the story already. But that didn't mean it shouldn't still be told.

The End

Kat Howard is an award-nominated short fiction writer who lives and writes in New Hampshire. Her novella, *The End of the Sentence*, co-written with Maria Dahvana Headley, was named one of the Best Books of 2014 by NPR. Her debut novel, *Roses and Rot*, will be published in the summer of 2016 by Saga Press.

THE JUNIPER-TREE

by The Brothers Grimm, Tale #47, Alt Title: *The Juniper Tree*

It is now long ago, quite two thousand years, since there was a rich man who had a beautiful and pious wife, and they loved each other dearly. They had, however, no children, though they wished for them very much, and the woman prayed for them day and night, but still they had none. Now there was a courtyard in front of their house in which was a juniper-tree, and one day in winter the woman was standing beneath it, paring herself an apple, and while she was paring herself the apple she cut her finger, and the blood fell on the snow. "Ah," said the woman, and sighed right heavily, and looked at the blood before her, and was most unhappy, "ah, if I had but a child as red as blood and as white as snow!"

And while she thus spake, she became quite happy in her mind, and felt just as if that were going to happen. Then she went into the house and a month went by and the snow was gone, and two months, and then everything was green, and three months, and then all the flowers came out of the earth, and four months, and then all the trees in the wood grew thicker, and the green branches were all closely entwined, and the birds sang until the wood resounded and the blossoms fell from the trees, then the fifth month passed away and she stood under the juniper-tree, which smelt so sweetly that her heart leapt, and she fell on her knees and was beside herself with joy, and when the sixth month was over the fruit was large and fine, and then she was quite still, and the seventh month she snatched at the juniper-berries and ate them greedily, then she grew sick and sorrowful, then the eighth month passed, and she called her husband to her, and wept and said, "If I die then bury me beneath the juniper-tree."

Then she was quite comforted and happy until the next month was over, and then she had a child as white as snow and as red as blood, and when she beheld it she was so delighted that she died.

Then her husband buried her beneath the juniper-tree, and he began to weep sore; after some time he was more at ease, and though he still wept he could bear it, and after some time longer he took another wife.

By the second wife he had a daughter, but the first wife's child was a little son, and he was as red as blood and as white as snow. When the woman looked at her daughter she loved her very much, but then she looked at the little boy and it seemed to cut her to the heart, for the thought came into her mind that he would always stand in her way, and she was for ever thinking how she could get all the fortune for her daughter, and the Evil One filled her mind with this till she was quite wroth with the little boy, and slapped him here and cuffed him there, until the unhappy child was in continual terror, for when he came out of school he had no peace in any place.

One day the woman had gone upstairs to her room, and her little daughter went up too, and said, "Mother, give me an apple."

"Yes, my child," said the woman, and gave her a fine apple out of the chest, but the chest had a great heavy lid with a great sharp iron lock.

"Mother," said the little daughter, "is brother not to have one too?"

This made the woman angry, but she said, "Yes, when he comes out of school."

And when she saw from the window that he was coming, it was just as if the Devil entered into her, and she snatched at the apple and took it away again from her daughter, and said, "Thou shalt not have one before thy brother." Then she threw the apple into the chest, and shut it. Then the little boy came in at the door, and the Devil made her say to him kindly, "My son, wilt thou have an apple?" and she looked wickedly at him.

"Mother," said the little boy, "how dreadful you look! Yes, give me an apple."

Then it seemed to her as if she were forced to say to him, "Come with me," and she opened the lid of the chest and said, "Take out an apple for thyself," and while the little boy was stooping inside, the Devil prompted her, and crash! she shut the lid down, and his head flew off and fell among the red apples. Then she was overwhelmed with terror, and thought, "If I could but make them think that it was not done by me!" So she went upstairs to her room to her chest of drawers, and took a white handkerchief out of the top drawer, and set the head on the neck again, and folded the handkerchief so that nothing could be seen, and she set him on a chair in front of the door, and put the apple in his hand.

After this Marlinchen came into the kitchen to her mother, who was standing by the fire with a pan of hot water before her which she was constantly stirring round. "Mother," said Marlinchen, "brother is sitting at the door, and he looks quite white and has an apple in his hand. I asked him to give me the apple, but he did not answer me, and I was quite frightened."

"Go back to him," said her mother, "and if he will not answer thee, give him a box on the ear."

So Marlinchen went to him and said, "Brother, give me the apple." But he was silent, and she gave him a box on the ear, on which his head fell down. Marlinchen was terrified, and began crying and screaming, and ran to her mother, and said, "Alas, mother, I have knocked my brother's head off!" and she wept and wept and could not be comforted.

"Marlinchen," said the mother, "what hast thou done? but be quiet and let no one know it; it cannot be helped now, we will make him into black-puddings." Then the mother took the little boy and chopped him in pieces, put him into the pan and made him into black puddings; but Marlinchen stood by weeping and weeping, and all her tears fell into the pan and there was no need of any salt.

Then the father came home, and sat down to dinner and said, "But where is my son?" And the mother served up a great dish of black-puddings, and Marlinchen wept and could not leave off. Then the father again said, "But where is my son?"

"Ah," said the mother, "he has gone across the country to his mother's great uncle; he will stay there awhile."

"And what is he going to do there? He did not even say goodbye to me."

"Oh, he wanted to go, and asked me if he might stay six weeks, he is well taken care of there."

"Ah," said the man, "I feel so unhappy lest all should not be right. He ought to have said goodbye to me." With that he began to eat and said, "Marlinchen, why art thou crying? Thy brother will certainly come back." Then he said, "Ah, wife, how delicious this food is, give me some more." And the more he ate the more he wanted to have, and he said, "Give me some more, you shall have none of it. It seems to me as if it were all mine." And he ate and ate and threw all the bones under the table, until he had finished the whole.

But Marlinchen went away to her chest of drawers, and took her best silk handkerchief out of the bottom drawer, and got all the bones from beneath the table, and tied them up in her silk handkerchief, and carried them outside the door, weeping tears of blood. Then the juniper-tree began to stir itself, and the branches parted asunder, and moved together again, just as if some one was rejoicing and clapping his hands. At the same time a mist seemed to arise from the tree, and in the center of this mist it burned like a fire, and a beautiful bird flew out of the fire singing magnificently, and he flew high up in the air, and when he was gone, the juniper-tree was just as it had been before, and the handkerchief with the bones was no longer there. Marlinchen, however, was as gay and happy as if her brother were still alive. And she went merrily into the house, and sat down to dinner and ate.

But the bird flew away and lighted on a goldsmith's house, and began to sing,

> "My mother she killed me,
> My father he ate me,
> My sister, little Marlinchen,
> Gathered together all my bones,
> Tied them in a silken handkerchief,
> Laid them beneath the juniper-tree,
> Kywitt, kywitt, what a beautiful bird am I!"

The goldsmith was sitting in his workshop making a gold chain, when he heard the bird which was sitting singing on his roof, and very beautiful the song seemed to him. He stood up, but as he crossed the threshold he lost one of his slippers. But he went away right up the middle of the street with one shoe on and one sock; he had his apron on, and in one hand he had the gold chain and in the other the pincers, and the sun was shining brightly on the street. Then he went right on and stood still, and said to the bird, "Bird," said he then, "how beautifully thou canst sing! Sing me that piece again."

"No," said the bird, "I'll not sing it twice for nothing! Give me the golden chain, and then I will sing it again for thee."

"There," said the goldsmith, "there is the golden chain for thee, now sing me that song again." Then the bird came and took the golden chain in his right claw, and went and sat in front of the gold-smith, and sang,

> "My mother she killed me,
> My father he ate me,
> My sister, little Marlinchen,
> Gathered together all my bones,
> Tied them in a silken handkerchief,
> Laid them beneath the juniper-tree,
> Kywitt, kywitt, what a beautiful bird am I!"

Then the bird flew away to a shoemaker, and lighted on his roof and sang again the same song.

The shoemaker heard that and ran out of doors in his shirt sleeves, and looked up at his roof, and was forced to hold his hand before his eyes lest the sun should blind him. "Bird," said he, "how beautifully thou canst sing!" Then he called in at his door, "Wife, just come outside, there is a bird, look at that bird, he just can sing well." Then he called his daughter and children, and apprentices, boys and girls, and they all came up the street and looked at the bird and saw how beautiful he was, and what fine red and green feathers he had, and how like real gold his neck was, and how the eyes in his head shone like stars. "Bird," said the shoemaker, "now sing me that song again."

"Nay," said the bird, "I do not sing twice for nothing; thou must give me something."

"Wife," said the man, "go to the garret, upon the top shelf there stands a pair of red shoes, bring them down." Then the wife went and brought the shoes. "There, bird," said the man, "now sing me that piece again." Then the bird came and took the shoes in his left claw, and flew back on the roof, and sang,

> "My mother she killed me,
> My father he ate me,
> My sister, little Marlinchen,
> Gathered together all my bones,
> Tied them in a silken handkerchief,
> Laid them beneath the juniper-tree,
> Kywitt, kywitt, what a beautiful bird am I!"

And when he had sung the whole he flew away. In his right claw he had the chain and the shoes in his left, and he flew far away to a mill,

and the mill went, "klipp klapp, klipp klapp, klipp klapp," and in the
mill sat twenty miller's men hewing a stone, and cutting, hick hack,
hick hack, hick hack, and the mill went klipp klapp, klipp klapp,
klipp klapp. Then the bird went and sat on a lime-tree which stood
in front of the mill, and sang,

> "My mother she killed me,"

Then one of them stopped working,

> "My father he ate me."

Then two more stopped working and listened to that,

> "My sister, little Marlinchen,"

Then four more stopped,

> "Gathered together all my bones,
> Tied them in a silken handkerchief,"

Now eight only were hewing,

> "Laid them beneath"

Now only five,

> "The juniper-tree,"

And now only one,

> "Kywitt, kywitt, what a beautiful bird am I!"

Then the last stopped also, and heard the last words. "Bird," said he,
"how beautifully thou singest! Let me, too, hear that. Sing that once
more for me."

"Nay," said the bird, "I will not sing twice for nothing. Give me
the millstone, and then I will sing it again."

"Yes," said he, "if it belonged to me only, thou shouldst have it."

"Yes," said the others, "if he sings again he shall have it." Then the
bird came down, and the twenty millers all set to work with a beam
and raised the stone up. And the bird stuck his neck through the
hole, and put the stone on as if it were a collar, and flew on to the
tree again, and sang,

> "My mother she killed me,
> My father he ate me,
> My sister, little Marlinchen,
> Gathered together all my bones,

> Tied them in a silken handkerchief,
> Laid them beneath the juniper-tree,
> Kywitt, kywitt, what a beautiful bird am I!"

And when he had done singing, he spread his wings, and in his right claw he had the chain, and in his left the shoes, and round his neck the millstone, and he flew far away to his father's house.

In the room sat the father, the mother, and Marlinchen at dinner, and the father said, "How light-hearted I feel, how happy I am!"

"Nay," said the mother, "I feel so uneasy, just as if a heavy storm were coming."

Marlinchen, however, sat weeping and weeping, and then came the bird flying, and as it seated itself on the roof the father said, "Ah, I feel so truly happy, and the sun is shining so beautifully outside, I feel just as if I were about to see some old friend again." "Nay," said the woman, "I feel so anxious, my teeth chatter, and I seem to have fire in my veins." And she tore her stays open, but Marlinchen sat in a corner crying, and held her plate before her eyes and cried till it was quite wet. Then the bird sat on the juniper tree, and sang,

> "My mother she killed me,"

Then the mother stopped her ears, and shut her eyes, and would not see or hear, but there was a roaring in her ears like the most violent storm, and her eyes burnt and flashed like lightning,

> "My father he ate me,"

"Ah, mother," says the man, "that is a beautiful bird! He sings so splendidly, and the sun shines so warm, and there is a smell just like cinnamon."

> "My sister, little Marlinchen,"

Then Marlinchen laid her head on her knees and wept without ceasing, but the man said, "I am going out, I must see the bird quite close."

"Oh, don't go," said the woman, "I feel as if the whole house were shaking and on fire." But the man went out and looked at the bird:

> "Gathered together all my bones,
> Tied them in a silken handkerchief,
> Laid them beneath the juniper tree,
> Kywitt, kywitt, what a beautiful bird am I!"

On this the bird let the golden chain fall, and it fell exactly round the man's neck, and so exactly round it that it fitted beautifully. Then he went in and said, "Just look what a fine bird that is, and what a handsome gold chain he has given me, and how pretty he is!" But the woman was terrified, and fell down on the floor in the room, and her cap fell off her head. Then sang the bird once more,

"My mother she killed me."

"Would that I were a thousand feet beneath the earth so as not to hear that!"

"My father he ate me,"

Then the woman fell down again as if dead.

"My sister, little Marlinchen,"

"Ah," said Marlinchen, "I too will go out and see if the bird will give me anything," and she went out.

"Gathered together all my bones,
Tied them in a silken handkerchief,"

Then he threw down the shoes to her.

"Laid them beneath the juniper-tree,
Kywitt, kywitt, what a beautiful bird am I!"

Then she was light-hearted and joyous, and she put on the new red shoes, and danced and leaped into the house. "Ah," said she, "I was so sad when I went out and now I am so light-hearted; that is a splendid bird, he has given me a pair of red shoes!"

"Well," said the woman, and sprang to her feet and her hair stood up like flames of fire, "I feel as if the world were coming to an end! I, too, will go out and see if my heart feels lighter." And as she went out at the door, crash! the bird threw down the millstone on her head, and she was entirely crushed by it.

The father and Marlinchen heard what had happened and went out, and smoke, flames, and fire were rising from the place, and when that was over, there stood the little brother, and he took his father and Marlinchen by the hand, and all three were right glad, and they went into the house to dinner, and ate.

The End

BE STILL, AND LISTEN

by Seanan McGuire

based upon *Little Briar-Rose*

Be still, my darling girl, my trinket, my treasure; be still, be still now, and listen.

Our bed is made from a cacophony of shadows, blankets snarled and strewn as careless as pine needles over new-fallen snow. There are old bones beneath the coverlets and duvets, cushioned in the depths where light never warms them; there are secrets there as well, trapped under layers of wedding quilts and tangled in strata of down-filled silk. Our bed is our true castle, unringed by roses, untouched by the hands of greedy, grasping princes.

This is the bed where I have slept and dreamt uncounted thousands of fever dreams. Someday I intend to die there, leaving my bones to join the ones already slumbering beneath us. I will sleep here forever if the world allows it, nestled in my cave of cloth and silence, and my skeleton arms will rock you gently when you waken, weeping, from unquiet dreams. My skull will tell you stories, until your eyes can close again, until you can be still. Until you can listen.

My parents never thought to have a faerie child nor sought to birth a princess; they never feasted on stolen rampion or challenged strangers to riddle-games by moonlight; they did not dredge the bottoms of enchanted lakes to find princes turned into frogs, nor quest for unicorns in shadowed forests. They never asked for me but they received me all the same, a gift of Mother's hidden, hated heritage. Parents never truly choose their children. Their blood does it for them.

Mother was soft and quiet, with thick ankles and graying hair and eyes that were only eyes, not doors to some unseen land or fairy story; only a mother's eyes, that saw the truth of me and would not let her look away. I was small and dark, and my eyes were strange, and my voice was harsh and sudden as a raven's cry; there could hardly have been less to mark us as sharing blood, even had she wished to deny me, name me changeling-child and cast me away. There was never any bond between us deeper than a shared heritage and the secrets that burned like stars between our unwillingly joined fingers—but in the end, that was enough.

Enough to stir her to walk into the forest, to find the ruins of the old castle, with me curled in her arms, dazed and dreaming and not yet fifteen years old. Enough to spur her steps up the curving stair to the highest tower, where she lay me down in the beginnings of this our bed, poppet, this our place of safety and of secrets. Still she comes, year on year, her arms laden with blankets and with bunting, to wrap us deeper still in dreaming.

She wept when first she saw you. You were asleep; you did not see her tears.

I will see my mother, your grandmother, buried, for I am young yet, even though my dreams have always been old. When the day comes for them to ring her funeral bells I will rise from our bed, tugging you by the hand to keep your sleepy, stumbling feet in motion. We will walk behind the funeral train, scattering black feathers like shadows or secrets on her grave, and she will go to dust with nothing but fading memories to bind her to me. I can let her go because she was my mother, whether she meant to be or not, and because I love her, even though I never wanted to. Family binds us all, in the end.

She told me once that she wept when she heard that her firstborn child was a girl. She remembered the old curses, and that her grandmother's grandmother was royalty, and that the Kindly Ones never forget. She remembered it all too well, and she remembered the warnings her own mother once whispered to her, and she mourned me as soon as I was born. I laughed to see your face for the same reason. You were mine as I could never have been hers; you were always meant to slumber by my side. But I? Ah, I was the hammer which broke the fragile glass of our family. My mother, your grandmother, never recovered from the birth of me.

I remember my own grandmother, sitting by the fire, back in the days when my mother still held hope and light in the fragile glass of her eyes, when they thought that I might grow up quick and burning bright, not as I am, not as I was always meant to be. "Never be still," was what she used to say, old woman trembling with the effort of repressing her own stillness. How it must have eaten her alive, to see me sitting so, to know that I was already lost. Still, she tried. "Run and run and never look back. Do not think to seek for secrets, or murmur mysteries, or tell tales. Marry young and do as you are told; bear sons instead of daughters, let our bloodline die. Do not walk in forests or dance by streams; do not sit by the sea or listen to the things the wind may try to tell you. Grow old, grow tired, and let the world steal what little you believe in before it turns poisonous and destroys you. Run until you fade away, and never question the roses that bloom in winter, or invite the wolf into your home, or listen to the songs of the ravens. If you are never still, you may die with a soul that you can call your own."

My grandmother had run for so long that she no longer understood her own longing to be still. She wore the marks of the curse that taints our family on her face, in her gestures, in the power draped acid-sweet over every word she spoke in the ninety years of her life. She was human and inhuman at once, and she hated the world for creating her. She used the power of her words to write a litany of motion across her only daughter, scribing a text that no one else would ever see…no one but me, the future granddaughter, who would someday know her words for the lies they were. She used the denial of a heritage she never wanted to keep the dark she feared to face at bay, and never wondered whether this might invite a deeper darkness to come and find her. She was never still, and some things chase only when you run.

Grandmother had eyes like snow resting on the peaks of ancient mountains and hair that was paler still, like captive clouds. Those eyes peered into my cradle when I was newly born and still dreaming of the womb, looking at and over and through me with disapproval so profound it burned. She could see everything she'd worked so hard to cut out of my mother waiting in me; my eyes echoed her own, but they were filled with the longing to listen to what was hidden, not what was said, and the yearning to be still. She saw my future in the subtle inhumanities I shared with her—the shape of my eyes, the half-slant of my ears—and she named me as no child of hers, giving me her disdain for a Christening gift.

You would carry that disdain as well, my darling, my dear one, had she but lived long enough to see you. Be grateful that the witch is dead, and her own bed is roots and stones, and never a pillow at all.

When I grew up and old enough to understand who and what my grandmother was to me—what she had been to my mother, who might have been an ally had she not learned her own mother's lessons so early and so well—I returned the gift of her disdain tenfold. We circled each other at a distance, never meeting one another's eyes, never trusting the other enough to turn away. My hatred of her kept me moving, and for a time, she won.

Ravens flocked from miles around on the day my grandmother died, covering the roof in a veil of clashing wings and coal-black feathers. They gathered in numbers beyond counting, shoving one another aside as they fought for anchor on the rain-damp shingles and filled the wind with their raucous cries. They delighted my ears, stuffing me to the brim with the stories they threatened to cast, bare and bloody, into the open air. The ravens knew the things I had been ordered not to hear, and though I did not understand them then, I greedily drank in every croak and scream, saving their cries for the day when I would know the language they had spoken. For them, I would be still, and I would listen.

Grandmother concealed her heritage behind words of motion and control, but even that would not keep her soul from its destination; not all her threats could change the power hidden in her blood. My mother wept when she saw the ravens coming, for she knew what they meant even before the doctors came to tell her it was over, and I raced to gather fistfuls of feathers, running as my grandmother had bid one final time before I took my treasures to the comfort of my bed. I held them close to my face and burrowed into the covers, breathing the musty scent of an ancient sky until I slept at last.

The family roused me from my bed with cries harsher than the songs of the ravens, thrusting me into a black cotton gown and binding my sleep-snarled hair in childish braids. They left my stolen feathers scattered on the pillows like brands of shattered shadow, deserted while I was carried away to my grandmother's funeral march and to humanity. I wept, reaching for the blankets and the secrets that I feared to lose, and my family that had grown so used to running mistook my tears for sorrow, and tried to comfort me. They could not see that I was reaching, instinctively, for the sweet release of sleep.

"Come," they said to me, one after the other. "Come, and move with us, and do not listen." I wouldn't listen, I promised I wouldn't listen, but what didn't they want me to hear? The crying of the ravens that fanned their wings atop our tattered battlements, demanding a murder forbidden to them by natural death? The rain that drummed against the eaves and the bodies of the birds, begging me to turn away from the formality, cajoling me to flee into the wood just beyond the cemetery gate, where mosses would be my pillow and the leaves of the forest my blankets? Or should I fail to hear the voices of my blood-family, made high and shrill with their fear of death? They would not tell me, and I finally saw that they did not know.

For them, the refusal to listen was enough. They needed no more answer than that, and so they had nothing more to give me. I was left to make my own choices, and I made the one they feared the most.

Listen.

Grandmother's power was in her voice; she never saw anything but the world around her. My mother bore no outward signs of what she was or what the family had once been; there was nothing in her voice to command or cajole, save what life grants to all mortal women, and there was nothing in her face to mark her as Grandmother's kin, or mine, save for the pinched fear Grandmother had planted there and the bruised-rose shape of her mouth when she lay sleeping. I could see the blood between us when she slept. In those rare moments of forbidden stillness, I could look into her face and see my own.

I was too young when my grandmother died to understand why my mother fought so hard against sleep, why she ran so fast and tried to keep me from my bed, and when I was old enough to wonder and ask she turned away from me, hiding the visions she held captive in her eyes behind a shield of well-worn denial and half-fractured truth. She never learned to listen, and so she could not answer me; Grandmother did her work too well, leaving her poor shattered goose-girl with a princess of a daughter and a crumbling house for her ivory tower.

There are twenty-six dark feathers scattered in the shadows of our bed, black warring against black in lasting, bloodless combat. I have counted and recounted them to soothe myself to sleep during the endless nights when I huddled in the comforting arms of the blankets and dreamed of flying. I twine them with dried roses stolen from funeral wreaths and tiny braids woven from my grandmother's hair, snipped from her corpse as she lay in state, finally still, waiting for the earth to spread its own blankets above her. The roses were stolen but the hair was not; it was my right to take it from her, granted by blood and bone and birth.

She never gave me anything else.

"Mother," I said once, when I was small and you were an unspoken dream and the contents of our bed were still being assembled from the great swirl of motion in the world outside, "Mother, why do you always tell me to run? I want to sleep. I am tired of running."

She turned from her cooking pot to look at me, my younger brother clinging to her leg as if he could work his way back into her body and away from the strangeness of the world through the contact of flesh on flesh. His eyes were my mother's eyes, and like hers, they were filled with fear for anything less than normal, brimming with simple, bovine terror. I hated him from the day they brought him home, when my father spread his arms and declared "There's my boy!" in a bright benediction of this child that he could look on as the fruit of his flesh.

I never held our father's blessing. I was the spirit-child, the girl that spoke with ravens and huddled in her bed until she was forcefully cast out into the sun, dreaming things he had no way to understand. He had no need of me and I had no need of him—he was never a part of my story—but I could still hate him for rejecting me. I never claimed I was rational; I only claim to be as I am.

Be still now. Be still, be still, and listen.

"Mother, why?" I said again, and shoved my hated brother aside, trying to force her attention on me, the eldest, the one who walked through the rain behind Grandmother's coffin, the one that knew what the ravens whispered to us both, long into the night. The one she should have been a mother to, if she was to be a mother to anyone. "Tell me, Mother, tell me!"

She closed her eyes, and for a moment I knew in waking what I had always known in slumber; she was my kin, and however much we denied one another, we were the same, I with my bedclothes laden with treasures and she that had done as she was told and married young and faded away, still running. We were the same. "Do you really want to ask me that?" she said, and the sorrow in her words made me draw away, yearning for the comfort of my bed.

I would have run from her, breaking my stillness—possibly forever—had it not been for the good child, the human brat, who watched me with satisfaction in his eyes. He saw my fear, and his joy was written on his face, as the terror must have still lingered on mine. In my moment of weakness he'd seen that mortality would one day win, however long I was still and quiet in my self-inflicted darkness. His joy was bitter to my eyes and it gave me the strength to ask again, placing iron along the length of my spine, burning cold, like a wound rubbed with salt.

"Yes, Mother," I said, "I want to ask. Tell me."

"You must run because stillness will leave you vulnerable," she said, turning back to her cooking. "You must run because if you do not, the world will come knocking at your door."

"But I want the world to come to my door, Mother! I want to see the world!"

"Are you sure?" she said, and her eyes were sad, like they were on the day I declared the fire to be my finest friend, or the day I swore I wouldn't marry unless the man had come from beyond the glass mountains to seek my hand. She loved me, for all that she knew she would never understand me, and I think she grieved for my loss, even though she never asked to bear me. We were of two different worlds, even then.

"Yes," I said, and my heart whispered, "No." How could I be sure? I had barely run out of fingers to count my years on, barely learned the reasons for hearth and heartache and home. What could I be sure of? That the sun would rise and the rain would fall? Nothing more… and perhaps not even that. Yet I could give no other answer, not with the favored son watching me, for I knew pride, even then.

"Then you will have your wish," she said, and no more. She asked no more of me after that, but she no longer roused me from my bed or cajoled me into running. I was lost to her, and because she loved me in her own way, she was able to let me go. My bed grew darker as the years passed; the tunnels beneath the blankets ran deeper and deeper still, filling with ever-stranger treasures. Spiders spun webs over my face as I slept, mistaking even those brief plunges into stillness for the quiet that waits in death…and indeed, for me, there was little difference.

Finally freed from running, I was still; still as stone in my own private world, cradled in the arms of my self-made nest. I found the truth in my dreams, unraveling the knots of the story no one would tell me, until I knew the reason that my family ran, and understood why I found my peace only in slumber.

Hundreds on hundreds of years ago, when once upon a time was tomorrow, an ancestor of my family line tricked a faerie into his bed. She went willingly but stayed against her will, and when he used his own blood to bind her, she fought back in the only way she knew, calling down her family from the trees, stone and sky, begging them to set her free. It was too late and she knew it, even if she dared not give that knowledge voice; it was too late from the moment he entered her, pressing his body to hers and crying psalms of passion to his gods. Time passed, and her chains were given flesh in the form of a girl-child with golden hair and pale ice eyes, dreaming eyes.

My grandmother's eyes.

Your eyes.

Her kin answered, even though they could not save her, coming in ones and twos to the palace of the prince who held their fairest cousin and giving the newborn child every trinket their kingdom could spare. Beauty, yes, beauty so terrible that it would inspire fear long before it brought forth love; wisdom to force the realization that the world was dying and everyone in it was dying with it; truth, to make the girl see that she could be spared, if only she would be still, if only she would listen. That promised stillness was the crowning gift, offering freedom in the form of dreams that would last until there were no more castles, or kingdoms, or wicked princes. She could be free as her mother had once been and was no longer, if only she could learn to be still.

Those were the gifts my family feared: the gifts of truth and stillness. They saw the truth for lies, and they marked the stillness as a curse, not as what it was meant to be; a blessing, a way to regain the freedom our long-ago grandmother lost in the arms of her prince. They rejected the very things that could have saved them, believing they were right, never realizing that they ran only from their own salvation.

It is an old story now, told to children huddled in bedclothes that do not hide bones, or feathers, or secrets. The spindle; the Christening; the sleeping castle and the thicket of roses. They do not say that the girl was the daughter of a fae mother and a cruel prince, or that she touched the spindle willingly, or that she struck the man who woke her so fiercely that he feared for his life. They do not say she spent the days before her marriage weeping, or that she spent the time after she was wed sitting silently, willing herself to fall into a sleep that never came.

They do not say that she hanged herself the day she looked into her daughter's eyes and saw her own childhood waiting there, a childhood that had become a womanhood against her will when the world forbade her stillness. They do not say the child grew into a woman and had children of her own, or that the line continues even now, too inhuman to stop dreaming, too human to be truly still. They do not say it, but all of it is true.

I told my mother I would see the world, and I have, for I am still, and so the world comes to me, even as ravens will come to the hand that is held out long enough and with enough patience. They flock to me now, slipping through my open bedroom window to nestle beside me as I sleep, like courtiers dressed in fine and flawless black. They sing to me, and sleep comes ever easier.

Your father did not come from beyond the glass mountain; he was no prince, no questing hero, no adventuring knight. He was a stable boy, and I roused myself to meet him, waiting long enough for him to know that he was wanted. That he had been invited. He came to me three times. Once for blood, once for bone, and once for the bonny babe we got us in-between. You were born here, my beautiful girl, and no one will ever tell you to run. You, of all of us, will sleep without regret.

Be still, I tell you now. Be still, be still, and listen.

Our bed is a welter of objects: bones and feathers, braids and cobwebs, tangled in a tapestry of promised slumber. I spend my days there, watching the roses that bloom outside my window even through the frosts of winter. I watch the roses and listen to the songs of the ravens and the breathing of the child at my breast, and I wait. I will be still, for we have run too long, and it is time this story ended. Each day we sleep a little longer, and one day we will not wake at all. Then the world will sleep with us, and at the end of a hundred years, when the prince comes to cut down our roses and wake the last of the sleeping princesses, he will find our ravens waiting for him, dressed in necklaces of braided hair and bones, with feathers black as dreaming.

"Go back," they will say. "Go back and find yourself a girl with thick ankles and human eyes. Go back, and leave the Sleeping Beauties sleeping. Go back."

And he will go, and the ravens will return to the castle. They will shed their necklaces and their feathers alike into the tangle of our blankets, free at last, for their gifts will finally be fulfilled, and their debts to the cousin they could not save finally paid. The roses will grow higher and higher still, tying themselves in lover's knots against the sky, until no one remembers the story at all.

And we will sleep, my darling girl; we will sleep until the end of the world.

Be still, I tell you now.

Be still, be still, and listen.

The End

Seanan McGuire was born and raised in Northern California, where she learned a healthy respect for venomous animals and a slightly unhealthy fear of weather. She has studied fairy tales and folklore from a very young age, and never met a fable that she wouldn't pick to death for fun. Seanan is the author of more than twenty books, under both her name and the name "Mira Grant." Keep up with her at www.seananmcguire.com.

LITTLE BRIAR-ROSE

by The Brothers Grimm, Tale #50, Alt Title(s): *Briar Rose; The Sleeping Beauty*

A long time ago there were a King and Queen who said every day, "Ah, if only we had a child!" but they never had one. But it happened that once when the Queen was bathing, a frog crept out of the water on to the land, and said to her, "Your wish shall be fulfilled; before a year has gone by, you shall have a daughter."

What the frog had said came true, and the Queen had a little girl who was so pretty that the King could not contain himself for joy, and ordered a great feast. He invited not only his kindred, friends and acquaintance, but also the Wise Women, in order that they might be kind and well-disposed towards the child. There were thirteen of them in his kingdom, but, as he had only twelve golden plates for them to eat out of, one of them had to be left at home.

The feast was held with all manner of splendor and when it came to an end the Wise Women bestowed their magic gifts upon the baby: one gave virtue, another beauty, a third riches, and so on with everything in the world that one can wish for.

When eleven of them had made their promises, suddenly the thirteenth came in. She wished to avenge herself for not having been invited, and without greeting, or even looking at any one, she cried with a loud voice, "The King's daughter shall in her fifteenth year prick herself with a spindle, and fall down dead." And, without saying a word more, she turned round and left the room.

They were all shocked; but the twelfth, whose good wish still remained unspoken, came forward, and as she could not undo the evil sentence, but only soften it, she said, "It shall not be death, but a deep sleep of a hundred years, into which the princess shall fall."

The King, who would fain keep his dear child from the misfortune, gave orders that every spindle in the whole kingdom should be burnt. Meanwhile the gifts of the Wise Women were plenteously fulfilled on the young girl, for she was so beautiful, modest, good-natured, and wise, that everyone who saw her was bound to love her.

It happened that on the very day when she was fifteen years old, the King and Queen were not at home, and the maiden was left in the palace quite alone. So she went round into all sorts of places, looked into rooms and bed-chambers just as she liked, and at last came to an old tower. She climbed up the narrow winding-staircase, and reached a little door. A rusty key was in the lock, and when she turned it the door sprang open, and there in a little room sat an old woman with a spindle, busily spinning her flax.

"Good day, old dame," said the King's daughter; "what are you doing there?"

"I am spinning," said the old woman, and nodded her head.

"What sort of thing is that, that rattles round so merrily?" said the girl, and she took the spindle and wanted to spin too. But scarcely had she touched the spindle when the magic decree was fulfilled, and she pricked her finger with it.

And, in the very moment when she felt the prick, she fell down upon the bed that stood there, and lay in a deep sleep. And this sleep extended over the whole palace; the King and Queen who had just come home, and had entered the great hall, began to go to sleep, and the whole of the court with them. The horses, too, went to sleep in the stable, the dogs in the yard, the pigeons upon the roof, the flies on the wall; even the fire that was flaming on the hearth became quiet and slept, the roast meat left off frizzling, and the cook, who was just going to pull the hair of the scullery boy, because he had forgotten something, let him go, and went to sleep. And the wind fell, and on the trees before the castle not a leaf moved again.

But round about the castle there began to grow a hedge of thorns, which every year became higher, and at last grew close up round the castle and all over it, so that there was nothing of it to be seen, not even the flag upon the roof. But the story of the beautiful sleeping "Briar-rose," for so the princess was named, went about the country, so that from time to time kings' sons came and tried to get through the thorny hedge into the castle.

But they found it impossible, for the thorns held fast together, as if they had hands, and the youths were caught in them, could not get loose again, and died a miserable death.

After long, long years a King's son came again to that country, and heard an old man talking about the thorn-hedge, and that a castle was said to stand behind it in which a wonderfully beautiful princess, named Briar-rose, had been asleep for a hundred years; and that the King and Queen and the whole court were asleep likewise. He had heard, too, from his grandfather, that many kings' sons had already come, and had tried to get through the thorny hedge, but they had remained sticking fast in it, and had died a pitiful death.

Then the youth said, "I am not afraid, I will go and see the beautiful Briar-rose." The good old man might dissuade him as he would, he did not listen to his words.

But by this time the hundred years had just passed, and the day had come when Briar-rose was to awake again. When the King's son came near to the thorn-hedge, it was nothing but large and beautiful flowers, which parted from each other of their own accord, and let him pass unhurt, then they closed again behind him like a hedge. In the castle-yard he saw the horses and the spotted hounds lying asleep; on the roof sat the pigeons with their heads under their wings. And when he entered the house, the flies were asleep upon the wall, the cook in the kitchen was still holding out his hand to seize the boy, and the maid was sitting by the black hen which she was going to pluck.

He went on farther, and in the great hall he saw the whole of the court lying asleep, and up by the throne lay the King and Queen.

Then he went on still farther, and all was so quiet that a breath could be heard, and at last he came to the tower, and opened the door into the little room where Briar-rose was sleeping. There she lay, so beautiful that he could not turn his eyes away; and he stooped down and gave her a kiss. But as soon as he kissed her, Briar-rose opened her eyes and awoke, and looked at him quite sweetly.

Then they went down together, and the King awoke, and the Queen, and the whole court, and looked at each other in great astonishment. And the horses in the courtyard stood up and shook themselves; the hounds jumped up and wagged their tails; the pigeons upon the roof pulled out their heads from under their wings, looked round, and flew into the open country; the flies on the wall crept again; the fire in the kitchen burned up and flickered and cooked the meat; the joint began to turn and frizzle again, and the cook gave the boy such a box on the ear that he screamed, and the maid plucked the fowl ready for the spit.

And then the marriage of the King's son with Briar-rose was celebrated with all splendor, and they lived contented to the end of their days.

The End

ACKNOWLEDGMENTS

Putting together an anthology is never truly a solitary project, even when your name is the only name listed as "editor" on the book. This is especially true with the members of NESFA Press who come together to make each book possible. I would like to thank everyone at NESFA Press for all of their hard work and dedication with special thanks going out to David G. Grubbs, Rick Katze, Tim Szczesuil, Tony Lewis, Steven Lee, Lis Carey, Priscilla Olson, Bob Kuhn, Sharon Sbarsky, and Alice N. S. Lewis for going the extra mile. I would also like to thank our authors since this book would not exist without their imagination and talent.

And, then there are the two gentlemen who started it all, Jacob Grimm (1785–1863) and Wilhelm Grimm (1786–1859). Special thanks to them for taking the time to collect and publish the original version of these stories.

Erin Underwood
November, 2015

TECHNICAL NOTES

This book is set in Adobe Garamond Pro, except for the titles and drop caps (which are set in Yellow Magician by Érico Lebedenco), using Adobe InDesign CS6. The book was printed and bound by Sheridan Books of Ann Arbor, Michigan, on acid-free paper.

The New England
Science Fiction Association

www.nesfa.org

NESFA is an all-volunteer, non-profit organization of science fiction and fantasy fans. Besides publishing, our activities include running Boskone (New England's oldest SF convention) in February each year, producing a monthly newsletter, holding discussion groups on topics related to the field, and hosting a variety of social events.

If you are interested in learning more about us, we'd like to hear from you. Contact us at info@nesfa.org.